Unleashed

Emmanuel Ben Bekoe a.k.a. Pops

-

You hold the strength and honour of infinite soldiers.

Everything I am, everything I hope to be, you are.

We shall overcome.

Madison, Michael

-

Endless love and loyalty.

Family would be an understatement.

Chapter One: Dig Deeper

I held back my tears. Crying was for the weak, at least that's what I was told. My dad used to tell me that if I cried, I couldn't be strong. He told me that those who got knocked down and got back up were stronger than the ones who never got knocked down. He always said fighting wasn't good, but sometimes I would have to fight, that I wouldn't have any other option. That's what he used to tell me. But how wise could he be when he was where he *is*. I shook my head. I couldn't believe where I *was*. Over and over in my head I replayed Jace's last words to me. "If you don't want me to go out, then stop me." *Stop me. I should have stopped him. How could I be so stupid?* Now it's on my conscience. Forever.

I bent down to pick up some dirt. My hands felt cold but I ignored the feeling. With a fist full of earth in my right hand, I walked over to the hole. It was six feet deep and the winter sun shone bright making the gold casket gleam. I stood at the end of the hole, the width of it. Everyone else who attended the funeral stood on the sides. For some reason, I felt like I was there alone. I took a deep breath in. When I exhaled I could see the casket shining through the fog my breath created. I sprinkled the dirt over the casket. I looked straight ahead at the headstone: "In Loving Memory of Jace Ayew." I couldn't believe I was burying my brother. Someone I used to strive to be like. Beside the headstone on each side were flowers, it was kind of ironic to me. Bright flowers, red and white, so full of life. I reached into the back pocket of my dress pants, pulling out a picture of my brother and me I studied it. I stood beside my brother, I was wearing one of his hats, his Chicago White Sox hat, and held my skateboard in my hands. He had a funny look on his face. He was confused as to why I was wearing his hat. I remembered Jace wearing the hat the night he left the house. It was his lucky hat, *but how lucky was he really?* Shaking my head, I dropped the picture into the grave. I watched it fall slowly, like it was a feather, like everything that was happening in this moment was in slow motion. The picture flipped a few times before it fell into the grave, face up. Other people dropped dirt into the grave, covering the picture I dropped. I didn't understand. One after the other. First, my father leaves me, now my brother. It seemed to be struggle after struggle and person after person, gone but never forgotten. There was no getting used to the hood, but it was my home. Uptown New York City, better known as The Bronx.

I closed my eyes every time I thought about my brother, those thoughts were too deep for me to process. My brother laid dead at the age of 24 and the only thought going through my brain was *whose next?* Everyone I've ever loved just seemed to have a time limit. I only ever remember talking to my father through a glass window, only ever saw him in a jumpsuit and I don't even remember what he looks like. I can't picture my father's face in my mind. I couldn't count all the years that have gone by without me seeing him. I was raised with no choice but to be used to his absence. My brother was the only one who gave me motivation. He helped me get past my struggles, at one point in time, he was my role model. I looked up to him. But now I was looking down at him. I didn't cry for my brother, nor did I cry for my father. Nobody cries for the bad guys.

The groundskeepers were finishing up burying my brother. The more they filled his grave, the emptier my heart became. Every bit of dirt that helped conceal my brother in that permanent underground prison was like a shot to the heart.

"Calvin, let's go." My mom lightly tugged my arm. I continued to stare at the headstone. *This was your Christmas gift to mom? The happiest of holidays,* I thought. We were supposed to go back to my Uncle's apartment to have a celebration for the life my brother lived. I didn't see what there was to celebrate. He wasn't even halfway through life. I was too upset. Not that my face was filled with tears. Upset to the point where I was angry. I wanted revenge.

I turned my head slowly to look at my mother. "I can't." I looked my mom in the eyes. "That's my brother in there." Tears flowed down her face.

"Calvin, please," She begged me. She didn't want to lose me too. She struggled to get her words out, "I'm going with Uncle Kofi, please find someone to come with." I nodded my head.

Behind me, I heard my brother's best friend.
Xavier. I didn't like him, I blamed him for Jace's death. He
was the guy Jace was always getting into trouble with. I
could picture him without even looking at him. The tattoos
were peeking out of his white collared shirt. He had light
brown skin and always looked like he fit the description.
"Mom, I'm sorry about your son. He was a good man." He
said he saw my mom as a second mother, so he always
called her mom. Although, his voice did not sound sincere
enough to me.

"Thank you, Xavier. Take care of yourself," my
mother responded.

A few seconds later I felt a hand on my shoulder.
"Not now, G." Thinking it was Giovanni, I turned my head,
only to be disappointed by Xavier. "Get your hand off me."
My words cut like knives. The disrespect from me forced
him to frown.

"Ay bro, you got the wrong guy," he said as he removed his hand.

I looked back at the dirt-filled grave. "Don't tempt me." I was not in the mood, my vibe around Xavier had always been off. He was too sketchy for me. He was always looking over his shoulder.

"I'm sorry about all of this. Believe me when I say, if I could have taken the bullet for him, I would have. But I wasn't there at the time to put my words into actions." He was trying to win me over.

I chuckled a bit. "Shoulda, coulda, woulda, but you didn't." I paused to think. My face went back to frowning. "And bullet?" I looked back at him, and I raised my voice. "Uh ... try bullets! Plural, my guy! Ain't no gunshot wound ... it was gunshot wounds! You lucky you got the invite to this bullshit. It's over now, so you can leave!"

"I wasn't there and I've regretted that every second since it all went down." He was shaking his head. "Calvin, I'm sorry. If you need anything, any help, money, please just ask. You know where I'm at, G." He started to walk away. I looked back at my brother.

As everyone began to leave, I sat in front of my brother. There wasn't any snow on the ground but it was cold. But at this moment in time, I ignored the cold. With my knees in front of my chest and my arms wrapped around my knees, I began to talk to him. "You know what mom has been through, how could you do this to her?" I put my head down. "She only had us. You're so selfish. I told you, she told you!" I got upset. "Was all that gang shit worth it? Look where it got you?" My brother was gang affiliated. He was killed in a shootout with a rival gang, at least that's what his friends told us. At this point I was raising my voice, "You thought you were so tough. Gang banging, shooting guns and robbing people. But look at you now, you're dead. Look at you!" Everyone had left, except

me. I sat in the graveyard for an hour. Waiting for my

brother to wake up.

Chapter Two: Dig Deeper II

I got up. The cemetery was empty. My brother was buried and I stood in front of him. "I'll see you later." I left the cemetery, it was now around 5:00 p.m. Flurries of snow began to fall from the sky. The sky turned orange and pink as the sun was finishing setting. It was a great day to bury a soldier

I walked home from the cemetery, it took me about an hour. My mom had called my phone three times but I never picked up. I didn't want to talk to her. I had to speak to my homeboy, Giovanni. He was at the funeral, but he left with everyone else. I didn't give him the chance to talk to me. I didn't give anyone the chance. I didn't want to hear the same words over and over, *I'm sorry for your loss.* Those words couldn't do much for me. But Gio, he was a brother to me. I needed to talk to him.

I changed my clothes. I put on a black hoodie, light blue jeans and black high top shoes. I then grabbed my skateboard and headed for the door. I walked past my brother's room. His door was open. I took two steps back and entered his room. I looked around. His bed wasn't made. His closet door was open and he had around ten pairs of shoes in there, mostly Jordans. I walked up to his dresser. I went through it. I didn't know what I was looking for, but I wanted to know what he had left behind. The first drawer had some clothes in it, a lot of red, along with some smoking paper. I shook my head as I continued to the next drawer. In this one I just found more clothes. "Come on." I mutter under my breath. A little piece of metal let out a small reflection of light. I moved some clothes out of the way to find a belt buckle. *Wait,* I thought. I picked up the metal. It wasn't just any piece of metal. It wasn't a belt buckle either. In the second drawer, my brother left brass knuckles. I was shocked. Not that my brother owned these, but that I was the one to find them–that the police didn't care enough to investigate this far into my brother's case. They didn't take a look into his room, and neither did my mother. I tried the brass knuckles on. It was uncomfortable at first but I thought I'd get used to it. *Get used to it.* I stopped the thought before it went any further. I put the metal into my pocket. I walked out my brother's room and closed his door behind me.

I walked down the stairs of the apartment. I looked down the road, 173rd Street. With the skateboard in my two hands I looked at it. Holding it like a baseball bat, I was getting upset. I thought about the picture I put into my brother's grave. Nothing in that picture would ever be the same again. I held the skateboard above my head and hammered it against the stairs of the apartment. I continued to bash the board five more times. Every time the board smashed against the stairs I was pushed further away from Jace. The deck of the skateboard began to crack. Pieces of the wood were sticking out and some broke off. I put the skateboard on the ground and started to stomp on it. This was my way of forgetting the past. The skateboard finally cracked in half. I grabbed each piece of the skateboard in two different hands. I started walking and threw the pieces in the alleyway beside the apartment. I was breathing heavily. My body was so alive but my spirit was so dead.

One of the guys my brother used to hang out with on the street corners saw me. As I got closer to him, he looked me in the eye and spoke. "Ay blood, sorry about your big bro. I heard about that shit."

I looked around before I looked at him to respond. I hated when people called me blood, young buck, or young blood. I wanted nothing to do with it. "Yeah, I mean it's whatever. It happens. Thanks for the love though." I shook his hand with my right hand, and continued to walk. I decided to stop to talk to Paulo. I opened the door of his convenience store. "What's good, Paulo?"

"The usual my friend," He said with a smile on his face.

"And what's the usual, my man?" I questioned him while I walking over to buy a bottle of juice.

"Stressed," He said shaking his head.

I nodded my head as I walked back over to him. "I hear you Paulo! Eat your veggies, keep your blood pressure down! I need you to stick around."

"Well with this murderer on the streets, everyone is scared." He had a worried look on his face. His eyes were glazed and his eyebrows were raised.

"They haven't got him yet?" I said in shock.

"No! The count is at seven now."

"Seven, Paulo? Seven?" No way ... four girls little girls in two weeks? That's bullshit Paulo!" I frowned really hard.

He looked at me as if my face was lifeless. "Stay safe out there, my friend. Please stay out of trouble. You're a good kid."

I nodded my head, "I'll do my best Paulo." I grabbed a chocolate bar from the one of the candy stands. He smiled. I thought I did too, but my face stayed straight. Chills spread through my body. I gave Paulo a dollar and began to walk out the door. "I'm worried about you Paulo, eat those veggies!"

"Why don't you worry about bringing the correct amount of money next time?" He raised his voice when he noticed me leaving, "You're a dollar short!"

I never paid Paulo the correct amount but one day I would give him everything I owed him.

I was already trying to forget about the fact that I'd never see my brother again. The frown on my face would allow people to read my mood and what was on my mind. I was never one to hide what was on my mind, I was devastated and upset. But this was nothing I wasn't used to.

Chapter Three: Borderlines

Two Weeks Earlier

I was walking back from the subway station. I was on my way back from Highbridge. I began to walk to the Deli shop that was down the block from my house. I was familiar with the store owner. He was a nice guy, he always let me go whenever I didn't have enough change on me. Those were the best kind of people. He was an original gangster. He was Latino or Puerto Rican, one of the many that lived uptown. Whenever my parents asked me to get alcohol for them, he would let me buy it, knowing I was underage. He trusted me, I never gave him a reason not to. I lived here my whole life and I'd never stolen from him, and sometimes when he needed help carrying boxes into the store I'd help him out. I didn't ask questions and did it all free of charge. I wanted him to know that I was grateful for his kindness. When I opened the door to the store, the owner was to the left behind the desk, closing a cash register. I walked up to him and gave him a handshake. "What's up, Paulo?" He had curly and thick black hair, thick eyebrows and eyes that were very detailed but tired. He had a permanent five o'clock shadow, along with an oil-stained shirt on. He was a typical bodega owner.

A gold tooth shone as he smiled at me. With a thick Puerto Rican accent, he responded. "Stressed like always!" He always told me he was stressed, although he said it with a smile on his face. I didn't know if I was supposed to believe him.

I walked over to the fridges to look for some juice. "Tell me, Paulo, why are you stressed?"

He chuckled a bit, "Oh, my friend! Have you seen the news lately?" I never watched the news. The first reason was that I am never home to watch TV. Second, the news caused too much stress with everything going on these days. Third, we didn't have cable. Paulo seemed worried. "This guy is killing everybody."

"Woah. What are you talking about?" I stopped looking for my drink and walked back over to the counter. "Who's killing everybody?"

"There's a serial killer, or rapist, or whatever!" Paulo shook his head. "He is raping girls and killing them. It's so sad. Three girls from Harlem have been found dead." He pointed to the TV screen behind him. It was a news channel, yellow police tape caught my eye as a reporter stood in front of it talking about the bodies that were discovered. The headline read, 'Third Harlem female found raped and killed" I was shocked. I never heard anything like this. Although New York was grimy at times, it didn't get like this.

"That's bullshit, Paulo! Isn't that bullshit? Why is everybody killing everybody? Y'all can't just chill, live in peace, humbly get money?" I shook my head over and over. I walked back over to the fridges and grabbed a large bottle of Sprite. I looked at the TV screen again. I put down two one dollar bills on the counter top. "Keep the change, Paulo!"

"What change? You're short 50 cents, Pappi!" I continued to walk out the door.

I looked down the street, towards my spot, a taxi pulled up beside my apartment. I wasn't sure who it was but when everyone got out of the cab I was able to make some guesses. Four people got out of the cab. There were three men and one lady. As I got closer, I knew exactly who they were. I laughed before I yelled over at them. "Ah! Okay, I see y'all! Welcome back!" The family turned around. *Jerem was about 5'5" and 12 years old,* I thought. *K.C. was closer to my age, he was 16, and he stood at about 5'9" or 5'10".* He got so much taller since the last time I saw him. It's been a few years. I walked over to the woman and gave her a hug. "Hey, Auntie Ellen, long time, no see!" I said while laughing.

She smiled. "What! You grew so quickly in the last year!" She joined in on the laughter. "What pills did you take to get those muscles? I will give it to Kwesi." She could see the shape of my arms through my grey skin-tight hoodie. Now everyone was laughing, except for Jeremiah. Jeremiah was Kwesi, Kwesi was his middle name, or first, I couldn't remember. Jerem had always been a sore loser.

My Uncle pulled the last bag out of the taxi. I looked at him and smiled. "Oh Uncle Mike, let me get that for you." I handed my bottle of Sprite to Jerem. I grabbed the bag from him and started walking towards the apartment with everyone.

"So, you think you're so strong now, eh?" my Uncle asked.

"I have to keep in shape. Uncle, how else am I going to impress these Ghanaian ladies?" My Auntie continued to laugh, I've always been able to make people laugh. I love to laugh. If I wasn't joking around, there was probably something wrong with me. "So, my mom is inside but I'm not sure where Jace is. I think he went to hang out with some friends," I explained as I opened the door of the apartment.

"It's okay, we're here for about two days, so we'll see him soon," Auntie responded.

I wasn't planning on staying home with adults all day. It'd be more fun messing around with my cousins. "Alright! Now that you're all settled in," I paused and looked around for a moment.

"We're not…" protested Jeremiah.

I ignored him. I thought about where we could go. "Let's go!" I pointed towards the door with my thumbs. I was talking to Jeremiah and K.C.

"Where are you going, Mr. Ayew?" My mom came out of her room. She began hugging everyone while smiling and laughing. "Wow, long time, no see!"

"Yeah, I know! Next time you all have to come to Toronto. We have to take turns visiting," Said Jerem. Everyone was laughing but Jerem was serious. He always had to say some smart ass response to people.

"Mom, we're going to walk around and maybe see Gio. We might even go downtown," I told my mother.

"Okay, but you boys be careful! Stay out of Harlem, Calvin you know they are not from here!" My mother spoke these words with a serious tone in her voice. We walked down the apartment stairs. My cousins seemed a bit nervous, scared about the whole Harlem thing. Harlem wasn't that bad, you just got to watch your step, and keep your eyes to yourself. It was an area where if you saw something you weren't supposed to see, someone would try and make you un-see it. In other words, they don't like witnesses.

"This way my friends," I was talking to them as if they were on a tour bus, sightseeing The Big Apple. "If you look to the left there is a park, it just re-opened."

"Why was it closed?" Asked Jerem.

"Hey, keep your concerns and questions until the end of the tour…But if you must know, someone was shot two weeks ago." I continued walking but K.C. stopped. I turned around to look at him.

"For real?" K.C. asked. I could see the concerned look on his face.

"Yeah man, I don't joke about those things." It went silent for a bit, I continued walking and they followed. I didn't want to scare them, but that was the reality of The Bronx. People can and will hurt you. That's why I tried my best to stay out of the violence. I looked at my cousins again, they now seemed fascinated, looking at the detailed and high-rise apartments. I loved New York but I was used to it. I wish I could have the feeling they have right now every time I left my house. "We're gonna go to Gio's spot, I need to pick up my board."

"Still? You *still* board?" Jerem sounded shocked, or confused.

"Yes! What's wrong with that?" I looked at Jerem. Jerem stayed silent.

"Alright Calv, then what?" K.C. questioned.

"Then we'll take the subway downtown." We all agreed.

When we arrived at Gio's apartment he was already outside. "Yo! The whole gang! He yelled. "What's really good? I haven't seen y'all in a hot minute." Gio was excited.

"Yo, pipe down! Go get my board," I responded.

"Why are you gonna skate when they're walking? Does that make sense? Nah, come get it later." Gio spoke with so much attitude. But it was how he was. He was a joker, you'd have to have thick skin to be friends with him, or even hang out with him. "You're going downtown? Like downtown, downtown?"

I rolled my eyes. Gio always did this. "Boy, why do you always say that. Alright, hurry up and come. We're tryna catch the D-Train." Gio walked inside and came out about two minutes later. Gio and I were kind of the same person, we always joked and like to get into trouble together.

We all began to walk towards the subway station, "Y'all got money right? Cause' I don't do handouts," Gio explained. We all began to laugh.

"Yeah, come on, man. You know I'm balling," K.C. replied.

"I don't know nothing," Responded Gio.

"Yeah, I could tell," Said Jerem. We all continued to laugh. I was laughing to the point where I couldn't really breathe, just to annoy Gio even more.

"Bruh that came out wrong," Gio tried to explain, but no one would listen. When we got to the station I went to the booth to add money onto my MetroCard. I had to pay for K.C. and Jerem to get around the city.

"Where do you work?" Asked Jerem.

I laughed before I even gave him an answer. "On these streets! Don't get curious, boy!" I answered, it kind of made me sound like some type of thug, like I was dealing drugs on the low. Although, I did have a job, a *real* job. It was easy for a teenager to get a job in New York, especially if you just wanted to be paid in cash. We were now waiting in the subway tunnel. I could tell Jerem and K.C. were grossed out by the rats running on the train tracks. I couldn't really picture a world outside of New York. I never really left the city. I've only gone to Mississauga to visit K.C. and Jerem twice when I was really young. They mostly came to New York. It was the place to be – the best city in the world. The train arrived, the air behind it forced our clothes to wave as it came to a stop. We got onto a cart and Gio and K.C. sat in the middle of the cart, while I sat across from them with Jerem. We were lucky to get a place to sit. A Saturday in New York City, especially around Christmas, was a busy time of year.

As soon as the train began to move, two boys stood up, one holding a big speaker. I rolled my eyes and looked at Gio. I knew exactly what these boys were about to do. Krumping music and terrible dancing was about to take place.

The dancing wasn't actually bad, it just got annoying when the same people did the same moves almost every time I got into a subway cart. The two boys took turns dancing, they used the poles for standing passengers to help them do flips and twists. They stomped and did bone-breaking moves. When their performance came to an end, the boys began to walk around asking for donations, one boy stuck his bag in front of Gio. Gio gave the dirtiest look I've ever seen in my life, "Yo … beat it kid!" The boy gave Gio a dirty look back and we all started to laugh. Everyone in New York had an attitude, it was what the city did to you.

We all got off of the subway at 42nd Street, walking the rest of the way to Times Square. I wanted my cousins to see some stuff on the way. Jerem was staring at some of the people dressed up in superhero costumes. Those were the immigrants that couldn't find a job or need more money on the side, so they charge people to take pictures with them. K.C and Jerem were fascinated, they continued to look around from homeless people to the famous people, the small vendors to the million-dollar shops, the crooks to the heavily armed police officers. I could see K.C. and Jerem's eyes light up. There was so much to take in.

We walked around Times Square for a bit, there were ladies walking around with nothing but panties on. Their breasts were out and painted red, white and blue just like the American flag. It was warmer downtown but it was still pretty cold. They asked us if we wanted a picture with them. Gio covered Jerem's eyes. "Please Lady! We have a child with us," Gio spoke with a sarcastic tone.

"Come on! I'm missing the good part!" Jerem pleaded with Gio. I started to laugh. Gio joked too much. K.C. was staring at a souvenir shop that had all the "I Love NYC" items. He began to walk over there so we all followed behind him. When we got into the store we all separated, we were looking at different things. I wanted a New York bottle opener. I looked up to see one of the employees breathing down K.C.'s back. The employee was an Indian woman, who clearly didn't understand personal space.

When K.C. looked back at her, she spoke. "Is there anything I can help you find?"

K.C. tilted his head, he seemed confused. "Yeah, actually I was just looking for some personal space, could you get off my back?" K.C. spoke from the back of his throat with his fist balled-up. The K.C. I knew got upset easily. He had a temper, but he had only good reasons to be upset. He was an overprotective friend. The woman frowned and walked away, she groaned at K.C. then walked away in a hurry. I saw K.C. rapidly turn his head to the right towards the entrance. I looked to see what caught his attention. Two police officers walked in, one a Latino, the other was a white officer. The white officer had red hair. He was a ginger with a moustache. Out of all my encounters with white male police officers, the most corrupt ones had moustaches. They were just assholes. I've never been a fan of the police and I don't see my perspective on them changing.

Jerem yelled, "Y'all are racist!" I looked over to see him throwing down a stand filled with glass mugs. The glass shattered making a huge crashing sound. Everyone in the store looked over at Jerem. It was time to leave.

"Let's go!" I yelled as I quickly headed for the exit.

"Stop right there!" One of the police officers yelled back.

"Run!" Gio howled! I looked back to see if everyone would get out alright. The white police officer was right behind K.C. I watched K.C. grab a stand filled with keychains and pushed it over so it would block the officer from getting to him. As soon as I saw that K.C. was fine, I sprinted out the door. Jerem followed then Gio. K.C. was last to get out. I was in front of the group, constantly looking back to see if K.C. was okay. I continued running while inevitably bumping into tourists. "What the fuck!" I heard a lady yell at me. I continued running. While running I thought to myself, *why is this happening*? This easily could have been avoided.

I led the group to the nearest subway station, where I jumped the stairs to get into the subway tunnels. I landed awkwardly stumbling but catching myself. When we got to the turnstile I took a stutter step then hopped over it. Gio hurdled over it next, followed by Jerem. The three of us got onto the train to see K.C. ready to jump over the turnstile. The police officers were hot on his trail, commanding us to stop. Just when we thought K.C. was in the clear, his back foot was clipped by the turnstile, forcing him to fall to the ground. He grunted in pain and struggled to get up, that's when Gio and I ran out of the train to pull him up. Jerem held the door of the train open as Gio and I held K.C. by each arm, pulling him into the subway cart. As K.C. got up we all stood looking out of the glass window of the closed door on the subway cart. The police officer running over, but the cart was already moving. He was banging on the glass as the train began to move. He looked into my eyes. He knew we'd gotten away as we left him behind. For once there were no consequences. We all huffed and puffed trying to catch our breath. K.C. looked at Jerem. His face clenched together.

"I thought you we're gonna get shot!" said Jerem.

Gio immediately responded, "They can't shoot, there are thousands of people at Times Square, they could hit other people."

I began to laugh thinking about what just happened. "Why did you tip over the stand?" We all looked at Jerem for an explanation.

"They were racist." Standing up in the crowded subway, we shook our heads continuing to catch our breath. The people in the cart looked at us like we were some criminals.

"Y'all gotta chill! I can't be running like that every time we go out. You're lucky I wore my running shoes. I don't know what type of anger problems they be promoting in Canada, but in the U.S. we channel our anger through our words. You need to calm down. Let's go to my house and chill," Gio said. We all started to laugh. I didn't expect my cousins to be like this, but after this situation I knew it was going to be a fun two days.

Chapter Four: Borderlines, Part II

When we reached Gio's apartment, we hung out in his living room. We were going to play on his PlayStation. I looked around his living room. I hadn't been in Gio's house for a very long time, I would usually just hang downtown with him, or just chill on the block. K.C. was staring at the baby pictures of Gio. One of the pictures was a family picture. It had Gio, his older sister and his mother. His father wasn't in the picture, figuratively and literally. I have never seen Gio's father. It had me thinking, I haven't seen my father in over a decade. My father was –   My thought was interrupted, "K.C., you got a PlayStation?" asked Gio.

"Yeah, we got a PlayStation," K.C. responded.

"You got FIFA?" Jerem asked eagerly.

"Do I got FIFA?" Gio responded with a real sarcastic tone in his voice. It was obvious that he had FIFA.

Jerem laughed, "You wanna get crushed?" Gio and Jerem began their game of FIFA. We all continued to talk while they played the game.

"Jerem, do you get girls?" I asked, just out of curiosity.

"Um, duh. Is that even a question?" replied Jerem. A confused look came across my face as I turned to look at K.C. for confirmation. K.C. shook his head no. I held in my laughter, I knew Jeremiah was lying. He was a kid, that was just all talk.

"What about you K.C., do you have a girlfriend?" I asked K.C. His face lit up. He was not prepared for this question.

He began to stutter, "Uh, well, it's complicated...I'mma leave it at that." That relationship seemed like a headache.

Jerem chuckled, "Complicated? You're basically married to Nasri. Stop playing games."

"What do you know?" K.C. was getting defensive, which means Jeremiah must be telling the truth.

"I know that you're both in love with each other," Jerem replied to K.C.'s rhetorical question, continuing to laugh.

K.C. shook his head, he got frustrated easily. "We're talking, but I guess it's just not official yet."

I nodded my head, his explanation was good enough for me. "I get it. Women, you will never understand them."

"Women don't even understand women. Yet they expect us to. That's some bullshit if you ask me." Gio added his two cents. Although, from my experience he was right. I've heard girls say things like 'I'll eat wherever, it doesn't matter to me,' then I would respond saying, 'okay how about Chinese?' then they would say 'no let's go for Italian.' I just don't get it. You said you'd eat whatever. You can't win. Sometimes you'll find yourself apologizing for things you didn't even do.

"Calvin, do you have a PlayStation?" asked Jerem.

I haven't had a game console in so long. I wanted one. "No, I don't."

"XBOX?" Jerem continued asking.

"No, but I think I'm gonna get a console soon," I explained. I was sure of it.

"Really? When?" asked K.C. "You have that type of money saved up?"

"Tomorrow. I get them for free." I sounded dark, or scary.

"What? How?" K.C. was confused.

"Don't get curious," I told him.

"If you get free PlayStations, I want seven," Jerem said. I gave Jerem a dirty look. "No! What a fluke!" Jerem was losing in FIFA, we all knew he was going to lose.

After playing a few games, we went back to my apartment for dinner. When we got home, the table was filled with food. Chicken, beef, fish, rice, noodles, salad, and more. I was in heaven. My mom never cooked this much, only when people came over. I thought to myself, *K.C. and Jerem should come more often.*

"Jace! What's good man?" I looked over to see K.C. shaking Jace's hand. They were all just staring at him, all of them, K.C., Jerem, my Aunt and Uncle. I think it was because Jace had changed a lot since the last time they saw him. He had neck tattoos, they symbolized which gang he was in. I looked at Jace's face. I realized he was high out of his mind. His eyes were red, so red that they matched his clothing. Red shirt, red shoes, black jeans, and his favourite black White Sox hat. We all sat down for dinner and Jace was spaced out. I was so mad at what he was doing. He was making us look bad. He never used to be like this. Ever since he started hanging out with that Xavier guy, his so-called best friend, he made a turn for the worst. Xavier was gang affiliated, just like Jace, he was the one who got Jace involved in all of that. I hated him for that. After the hype about Jace went down, we all prayed over the food and began to eat. I looked up to see Jace across from me, he was eating like he hadn't eaten in weeks. I tried to shake it off, but he was embarrassing me. I knew Jerem, and K.C. knew Jace was high but they kept silent about it.

When we finished our dinner and helped clean up, K.C., Jerem and I went back to my room. K.C. and Jerem were going to be sleeping on the floor. I wasn't the type to share a bed. I liked my space.

"Alright, so tell us exactly how you're gonna get a free PlayStation," Jerem demanded to know.

"Truth be told, you can get anything for free." I realized I sounded a bit dark there. "If you want something, just take it. But the real question here is whether or not you *can* take it," I explained.

"Stealing? Is that what you mean? Or am I missing something?" K.C. asked.

"Are you two 'bout that life?" I asked.

Jerem looked at K.C. He was confused. "Yeah, um, you got it, fam," Jerem spoke with a crack in his voice, "Just don't get caught."

"How do you expect to run into a store to steal a whole console without getting caught?" K.C. said while chuckling at me. "If you can come up with a foolproof plan, I'm in." He then rolled over to his side, facing away from me.

"Not a store! I'm not a psychopath." There was a pause. "We're gonna break into an apartment." I could see the fear in Jerem's eyes, I could only imagine it was the same in K.C.'s eyes.

The next evening, the three of us hopped off a train and walked up the stairs to the street level. We were on our way to Giovanni's house. My cousins were leaving the next morning, it would be the last time they saw Gio for a while.

"Yo, Gio! Hurry up! We're going downtown," I yelled from the street.

Gio stuck his head out the window from the top floor of the apartment. "Like downtown, downtown?" he said while laughing, he knew we were sick of this catchphrase.

"Yeah, that doesn't get old," Jerem yelled back sarcastically.

When Gio finally came down he spoke, "So what's the motive?" He wanted to know what the plan was for the night.

"I'm about to get a PlayStation," I clarified.

"From where?" Giovanni gave me a dirty look.

"Brooklyn," I responded. I knew Gio would react to this answer.

"Like Brooklyn, Brooklyn?" Gio actually sounded confused. "We got beef in Brooklyn."

"Seriously, you gotta stop doing that!" Jerem was over Gio's catch phrase.

"That's why we're going at night," I explained.

Gio gave a pitiful laugh. "Yeah, they're just gonna forget that they don't like us because it's past 9:00 p.m."

"No, I meant they won't be able to see us," I said.

"Let's just hope my skin is dark enough," Gio laughed. The four of us walked back to the subway station.

"We're all brothers, so watch your brother's back." K.C. was giving us a motivational speech.

When we got to Brooklyn there were more people on the streets than in the Bronx. We continued to walk deeper into Brooklyn, past the downtown area. I was taking them to Bed-Stuy. We arrived around 10:00 p.m. and we waited in an alleyway between two apartments.

"How do we even know there's a PlayStation in there?" Jerem questioned me. But I didn't have the answer to his question, but I had an answer for every other question.

I looked down both ends of the alleyway. "Let's just hope we get lucky."

I walked up the stairs of one of the apartments with K.C. Looking through the front window of the house, all of the lights were off. I wanted to make sure there was no one home before we went inside. *Bang! Bang! Bang!* There was no answer. We waited a few more seconds then I knocked again. Again, there was no answer. I tried to open the door, but it was locked. I attempted to pull the window up that was beside the front door of the house. It wouldn't budge. I was most likely locked from the inside. I walked down the stairs frustrated, and K.C. followed behind me. Jerem and Gio were still waiting for us to find a way in. Shaking my head, I pulled out a large stone from the dirt beside the apartment.

"Bro, I don't think that's a good idea." There wasn't fear in Gio's voice but you could tell he was concerned. I continued to do what I was doing, I was too determined to listen to anyone. I walked up the stairs with K.C. again.

"That's gonna make so much noise," K.C. said to me. I still hadn't said a word.

I threw the stone at the window. The sound of shattered glass crashing to the ground motivated Gio and Jerem to come up the stairs of the apartment. When the window was glass-free, K.C. climbed through first to see if the room was empty. We saw a light turn on. The three of us looked at each other.

"Guys, get in," K.C. hollered.

We all began to crawl through the open window. Right away, I began looking for a game console. Looking around, I saw family portraits. It was either a white, or Hispanic family that lived here, I didn't focus enough to determine their ethnicity.

"Look around and tell me if you find anything valuable." After speaking these words I realized how determined I was. Gio went up the stairs and K.C. followed behind him. I was still in the living room with Jerem. We were going through cabinets and drawers in the TV stand, looking for anything. I looked at Jerem, he was walking over to a sofa. I watched him take a seat. I squinted my eyes in disbelief and anger. "For real? Are you for real right now? Boy, you better get up! This ain't the time to relax." I was upset with Jerem. He acted so childish at the worst times.

"Oh, come on. It's been a long day," he argued.

I walked over to him, my palm was open ready to slap the hell out of him. "Please tell me what you did today!" I was calm.

Before Jerem could respond we heard Gio yell, "Bingo!"

After those words were yelled, we heard heavy footsteps on the ceiling and a door creak open from upstairs. Whispers were shared upstairs, Jerem stood up, and we walked towards the staircase.

"Get the fuck outta my house!" A voice yelled from upstairs. I knew it wasn't Gio or K.C.

"Run!" I heard K.C. say.

I heard heavy steps on the staircase. "Let's get the fuck outta here," Gio yelled. When the two got to the bottom of the stairs, I saw the front door begin to open, someone was just getting home. K.C. tackled it shut, as the door was beside the bottom of the staircase. The tackle was followed by a grunt that came from the other side of the door.

"To the back! Go to the back!" K.C. yelled at us. Gio ran past him, towards the kitchen. I followed Gio and so did Jerem. There was a window above a countertop in the kitchen. Gio hopped through it, I followed. Jerem was next. While Jerem was climbing through the window Gio ran down the steps of the patio. K.C. was still inside the apartment. The man that chased him down the stairs had a big belly, he was in plaid boxer shorts, and a blue robe. He carried what looked like a broom stick.

He was wildly swinging it at K.C., hitting him in the ribcage. I was about to hop through the window again. When the man went to swing the stick again, K.C. blocked it with his left forearm. K.C. began to throw fist back, I don't know if he was really trying to hit the man, but he was definitely scaring him. When the man backed up a bit, K.C. turned around and ran for the kitchen window. I backed up and I jumped the ledge of the patio and landed on the grass in the backyard. Jerem was still on the patio. I was running up to the fence to hop that too. Gio stayed on that side of the fence. When I got on the other side of the fence I saw K.C with no hesitation, jumped head first through the open window. He made it through, but he fell onto the patio that Jerem was on, crashing through the wooden railing, landing on the grass below. I knew that he had to be hurt. Jerem got down and helped him up. Gio tossed the PlayStation over the fence for me to catch. The wires attached made it difficult to catch. He hopped the fence right after. K.C. gave Jerem a boost over the fence and hopped over after. We all began jogging away from the apartments, there was a school and a playground on this side of the fence. K.C. was limping but he was as strong as soldier. When we got closer to the school we all started laughing.

"I've never been so scared to see a white guy," K.C. said catching his breath.

"That dude was crazy, swinging his shit like that," responded Gio.

"Y'all are just lucky he didn't have a gun," said Jerem.

"I told y'all I'd get a PlayStation today," I said with a gloating tone in my voice and a smirk on my face.

"My guy...Gio and I did all the work," explained K.C.

We all laughed and continued to walk, searching for a subway station. I was a bit scared for my cousins, I didn't think they had done anything like this before. I was a bad influence and I knew that. I wasn't going to change though. I've always been this way.

"Merry Christmas, punk," K.C. said to me. "If I didn't hold that door closed, we'd all be in handcuffs right now."

"Truth be told, you're probably right," said Gio.

As we returned to Gio's house, he gave us a bag to put the PlayStation in. My cousins were leaving the next morning, so Jerem and K.C. said their goodbyes to Gio.

"When Calvin comes to Sauga, you gotta come with him," said Jerem.

"I'm seriously thinking about it," responded Gio.

"If you come, we'll shut down the city," K.C. said.

"You already know," he laughed.

After we all said our goodbyes, we went back to the subway station. It was a dangerous night and I knew it was risky to pull off a stunt like this the night before my cousins' flight.

"I thought New York was the city that never sleeps," K.C. said confused.

"Yeah, well this is the Bronx, and we need our sleep," I clarified.

We got back to my apartment around 1:00 a.m. As we got ready for bed, Jace got ready to go out.

"Bro, where you going?" I asked my brother. I was furious.

"Don't worry about it," Jace replied.

"Don't be dumb. You always got mom worried sick. Can you chill for one night, fam?" I got more upset with every word I spoke.

"Yo! Don't question the shit I do. If you don't want me to go out, then stop me." He walked out the door, and I stood there, frozen. I couldn't move. The apartment door slammed shut and I shook my head. I felt chills through my body. I walked back into my room. That night, I couldn't sleep. I could sense something wasn't right. I laid awake with my eyes open. But then I thought to myself, it would be easier to pretend that I don't care, than admit it's killing me. I closed my eyes but stayed awake.

Chapter Five: Jungle

The Present

My name is Calvin Ayew. I'm 17 years old, which makes me just another African-American teenager raised under a single parent roof. With a broken family, and poverty knocking at our door, I preferred to stay on the streets. The street lights stayed on at night. I never knew when the lights at my mom's spot would go out. My mom struggled to pay the light bill. Or any bill for that matter. I didn't think anything of it. Everyone had battles, that's just life. I didn't feel sorry for myself, I had to keep moving. I wasn't sure if I was moving forward. I just couldn't stay in one place for a long period of time. I'm adventurous, a bit fearless and hot-headed. My appearance wasn't useful to these personality traits because of the stigma and stereotypes facing my people. I'm about 6 feet or a little bit over. I'm quite slim but with toned muscles. I wear somewhat baggy clothes. It makes me feel bigger and comfortable.

At the moment I was walking further uptown. I was going to Highbridge, another area in the Bronx. I was going see Giovanni. He was a brother to me. My whole family knew him. We went to the same school, at least whenever we were in the attendance. People called us skaters but I mainly used my skateboard to get around. I've injured myself several times on it. I've been sent to the hospital with a broken arm. I apologized so many times to my mother. She had to pay the hospital bill, I realized that my mom couldn't be spending that type of money on me. But for some reason, I continued to use it. The skateboard kept me occupied. I knew how to do a lot of tricks. I used to get in so much trouble practicing kick flips in the apartment. When my mom worked the graveyard shift I would stay up practicing. I was so happy when I landed it for the first time, I went to show Giovanni. He was fascinated to the point where he wanted a skateboard too. He wanted to do whatever I could do.

I thought back to how Giovanni got his board. Coming from broke families, we didn't have money to buy a skateboard. At the age of twelve, we took the subway downtown to Brooklyn. We walked down the Fulton strip looking for Mother's Day flowers. Before we got to Fulton mall, a white boy rolled past us on a skateboard. The street was busy, downtown Brooklyn was always busy. It was a Friday night and summer break was fast approaching. I looked at Giovanni, we both had the same thought going through our heads. I told Giovanni to follow my lead. We ran to catch up with the boy. He was around the age of 15 or 16. He had several piercings, in his lip, eyebrow, and ears. He had huge headphones around his neck. He flicked his hair to the side every few seconds. He was a typical skater. He had chains all over his blue jeans. I asked the kid if I could have a test ride. The kid had one foot on the skateboard and another on the ground, thinking about whether or not he should let me. Giovanni begged the kid. Uncomfortably, the boy slid the board over to me with his foot. I acted like I've never rode a skateboard before. I slowly rolled down the sidewalk, trying to avoid pedestrians. I was about 50 yards away from them. I heard Giovanni yell – he was telling me to be careful. He chased after me with a worried look on his face. The white kid stayed where he was. I stopped the skateboard and waited for Giovanni to catch up to me. We looked back at the kid, he was slowly walking over to us while waving at us, signalling us to come back. He was originally going in the opposite direction before we stopped him. I picked up the board and began walking backwards. Giovanni noticed. He turned around, now facing the white boy, he began to walk backwards with me. Continuing to walk backwards, I saw the white boy begin to chase after us. I turned around and yelled, "Run!" We were running through all the pedestrian traffic as fast as we could. I was bumping into so many people.

We turned a corner, looking for any subway pole. I looked down the street to see the pole with the letter 'C' on it. It was about 30 yards away. I dashed with Giovanni alongside me. When we got to the pole we had to skip down the stairs to get into the subway tunnel. As we got to the gates, we didn't have time to pull out our metro cards, but someone was exiting through the gated doors to get back to street level. I ran to hold the door open. When Giovanni got through, it I shut it. The white boy would have to use his card to get through. A subway zoomed by, beginning to slow down for travellers to get aboard. I heard the boy yell, "That's my board!" He had an angry tone in his voice. The subway train's door opened and we got inside the 'C' train. The white boy finally got through the turnstile. He began to sprint over to the door of the subway. I was scared, I knew we were about to get into a fight. With the board in my hand I tried to act natural. The bell sounded and an automated voice spoke. "Stand clear of the closing doors please!" The doors began to close, just as they were about to shut on the white boy's face, he held them open with his hands. Whenever someone interferes with the door, it re-opens. When the door opened back up, I swung the board at the white boy, forcing him to back up and block the blows. When he backed up, the subway doors closed on him. I sighed in relief, Giovanni was smiling and he was relieved too. We turned around when the train started moving. All the passengers were staring at us. That was the day we became takers. We didn't love to steal, but we had sticky fingers. If you had it and we wanted it, then consider it ours. Our only rule was; do not take from a hardworking man. This was because we've seen it all. We knew how many people were out there struggling to provide for their families and loved ones. Although, if we really needed something, Giovanni would always say, "You gotta do, what you gotta do, to get where you're going." It made sense to me and that's just how we were living.

After my brother was found dead, I lost interest in my skateboard. I felt like everything I used to do reminded me of better times. Although a lot of things weren't great, I'd rather live a struggle with my brother alive. I was into skateboarding when my brother was still here and well. But I feel like all my interests have died.

When I got to Giovanni's spot in Highbridge, I walked up the few steps to knock on his apartment door. It was nearly 7:00 p.m. He didn't go to the celebration at my Uncle's house after the funeral. It didn't bother me. It was more of a private, family-only thing, besides I didn't go either. My mom didn't want my brother's so-called "friends" to show up, she thought they were the reason my brother was six feet under. Giovanni opened the door and stepped out. He had a taper fade, with a mini afro and a black muscle shirt on. Although, he didn't have much muscle. He also wore black sweatpants, he wasn't wearing shoes. He was fully black but he had pretty light skin. "What's good bruh?" He smiled and dapped me up. Dap was just slang for a handshake.

"I'm blessed, G. But this whole thing is messed up," I said to him.

"Not much we can do at this point. But damn Calv, our people just leaving us day after day. He's lookin' out for us now … so we're good." He was giving me motivating words.

"I don't understand why he had to go out like that. But I gotta stay focused. I can't let this hold me down," I shook my head as I spoke those words.

"We got each other. No one's gonna look out for us like we do for each other." He was right, he was a brother to me.

"Gio, you tryna reach downtown?" I had to get my mind off of today's events.

"Like downtown, downtown?" He was confused.

"Yeah G, like Manhattan."

"Hold up, let me change." He walked back into his house.

I walked down the stairs from the apartment. I looked down the street from where I was. To my left were a few Latinos walking my way, and to my right was a mixed group of kids. Latinos and blacks. They were stomping in the water on the street, which was being blasted out of the fire hydrant. It was kind of cold for them to be playing in the water but busted open fire hydrants were common in New York City, at least in The Bronx. Giovanni's door slammed shut behind him as he began to walk down the steps. He had on a plain white hoodie and black jogging pants. His shoes were also black. "We best be taking the subway. These are my good shoes."

I laughed a bit, "You're crazy." We began walking to the subway. I could feel my phone vibrate in my pocket. I didn't want to pick it up. I knew it was my mom. She was just going to ask where I was. I didn't want to talk to anyone. I just finished burying my brother and I didn't want to think about it. My eyes started watering, but I looked up hoping the tears would go back into my eyes. I didn't want to shed a tear. Not for my brother. He made his own decisions. He left the battle early, he shot himself in the foot. I'm still fighting this war. *Life,* I thought. We walked down the steps to enter the subway station. I swiped my metro card and walked through the turnstile. Giovanni followed behind me. We took the D-train going downtown. We had to run into the train because the doors were closing.

Giovanni entered the train late, blocking the door from closing, forcing it to re-open. We looked around the somewhat packed train for a place to sit. The subway cart was always dirty, but you had to expect these things in New York. I found two seats at the end of the cart. As we sat down, I looked around, noticing a lot of Latinos were on this train. The Bronx and Harlem had the majority of the Latinos in New York City. I didn't mind them, they were cool. They just did their own thing. Working hard to make some money. Whether it was legal or illegal, I respected any grind. I always had respect for hardworking people, plus it's New York, you can do anything here.

The two of us sat down waiting for our stop. Gio sat to my left. To our left was the door to enter the cart in front of us, and to our right was the rest of the cart.

The subway stopped and about ten people got off. Three boys got onto our cart. Everyone was sitting except for the boys. Looking to my right, one held a bucket hat, another held a speaker. The third didn't even have a shirt on, although he was dressed up in tattoos. They seemed to be Latino. The boy with the speaker flipped a switch and music started blasting on the cart. It was krumping music. I looked at Giovanni with a "here we go again" look on my face. The boy with no shirt started to pop his chest in and out in an exaggerated way. He started hopping around the poles. Almost like a stripper, but a stripper with a lot of upper body strength. He was now upside down with his feet hooked on the pole that traced the middle of the ceiling of the subway cart. He was now dancing upside down. The other boys started to do a rehearsed dance behind the guy hanging upside down. The two boys were jumping and flipping on poles. Backwards and forwards. This was annoying, we've seen it all before, this was only cool to the tourists. There were no tourists in the cart. I could tell when someone wasn't from the city. They didn't have the same accent, like they were foreigners. They were always looking around, like they were lost. They walked without purpose, like they didn't know where they were going. After the three boys finished their dance, they walked around asking for donations. The boy with the bucket hat walked over to Giovanni and I with his hat out. "Ay bruh, y'all got any donations for me and my brothers?"

I gave him a dirty look. With a calm tone of voice I responded, "What do I look like? Move from me."

The kid frowned. He seemed to be around the same age group as us. Just another teenager. "Come on bruh, this is how I make an honest living."

Giovanni giggled. "Yeah, yeah, yeah, heard it all before! You're honestly making money, but do you live honestly? We all broke."

The boy had a confused look on his face, he didn't know what Gio was asking…I didn't even think Gio knew what he was asking. "Whatever, puta!" The cart stopped and he walked out of the cart with his two dance partners.

I turned to Gio, "How long is he going to be dancing in carts? Once you hit 30 you're going to throw your back out." We both started to laugh and the subway began to move again.

Chapter Six: Outlook

We got off the subway and began walking around lower Manhattan. Manhattan during Christmas time was the best place to be. The streets were packed, and it was loud, yet I felt like I was alone. I was broken down, but I refused to say it out loud. I refused to grieve – not for my brother.

"School's about to start back up," Gio said.

"It's not like we really go anyways," I responded. I was known for skipping school. I was in senior year and I didn't know if I'd be graduating.

Gio laughed, "You right."

As we continued to walk around, we got to Battery Park. Walking down a pathway in the park, the water was to our right. I think it was the Hudson River, it connected to some other body of water.

I looked down as I walked and talked. "Honestly, I think I'm done skateboarding. I can't do it anymore," I explained to Gio.

"Why not? You love it, you're known as the skater." Gio was confused. "Why you wanna quit?"

"I don't know, we're growing up man. I feel like we gotta do something new."

"I'm all for something new, but don't give up something you like because of recent events." He was trying to persuade me not to let my brother's passing effect my decisions.

"Just like grieving, you finish that at some point in time. I'm tryna move onto a new chapter…a fresh start."

"A fresh start?" Gio asked, then paused.

"Yeah," I said emotionless.

"I'm in," Gio said, he then stuck his hand out for a handshake. I gave him the handshake he desired.

"I just don't know what my fresh start is," I said.

"Well, mentally, you're a fighter. I couldn't imagine going through what you're going through. It takes ridiculous mental strength. Emotionally, you're strong, I haven't seen you shed one tear my whole life. And physically, y'already know we hold it down!" He spoke in a crescendo. Gio began to laugh, I joined in a bit too. "What I'm saying is, ain't nobody ever shown you how to fight. You've been fighting your whole life, why not make something of it?" He said, rhetorically, turning his head to look at me, putting his hand in front of my chest forcing me to stop. We were now facing each other.

I looked Giovanni in the eyes. "I feel that. You're my brother for real, G. This is blood right here." I looked forward again. "So what are you saying, what are you proposin' we do?" I questioned.

He lightly tapped my chest a few times. "I'm saying you can channel your struggle, your mental struggle, that emotional strength, and physicality into something bigger, my brother. Let's start boxing!" He was smiling, waiting for me to join in on his energy.

I smiled a bit, "Let's do it." Legally fighting, with no chance of getting in trouble for it. I felt like I couldn't refuse that proposal.

"Just hope you don't ever gotta fight me. They callin' me Giovanni. Float like a butterfly, sting like a bee. You'll lose a few teeth boxin' with me," He laughed.

"You really had to make it all rhyme?" I asked rhetorically as he laughed. Gio and I continued to walk again.

To our left were benches. On the benches, I saw a homeless man. I pulled ten dollars out of my wallet to give to the man. He had very long grey dreadlocks that came together in a ponytail. He was light-skinned and had a medium built. Beside him was a shopping cart, he carried all his belongings in it. By the way he was shivering, I could tell he was freezing. It was the end of December and it wasn't snowing much, it wasn't too cold, but he must have been out here for awhile. The man was not prepared for the cold. I looked at his face he had freckles, wrinkled skin and watery eyes. I usually didn't feel bad for these type of people, it was because I saw this stuff all the time. I felt like a majority of the time, the homeless brought this on themselves. But I didn't know his situation. I didn't have the right to judge. He held out a cup, and I placed the ten dollar bill in there. That was a little much but I didn't care about money right now.

"Thank you," he spoke while smiling.

I nodded my head, "No worries." I stopped walking to look into his cart. He watched me, as if he thought I was going to take something. I looked back over at him. "Bro, you got a blanket in there. Ain't you cold?" I pulled the blanket out to give it to him. I helped him wrap it around his body. Gio and I were now standing in front of the man. He stared at us while we stared back. I decided to take a seat beside the man. Gio joined me. Looking straight at us, Gio was on my right, and the homeless man was on my left. All of us were looking straight at the water in the distance. It was basically night time, we couldn't see much out there but we could see one another, the park was well lit with lamp posts.

"What's your name?" I asked the man while I was still looking in the distance.

I could see him turn his head to look at me from the corner of my eye. "Cornelius." He sighed. "What about you two?"

"Calvin," I responded.

"Gio…and I've gotta go," Gio spoke looking at his cellphone. He stood up, "My mom needs me, Calv."

"Yeah, it's all good. I'll catch you later, G." I shook his hand and he walked out of the park.

My mother always told me that grey hair symbolized wisdom. I'm pretty sure this was just a way to make me respect my elders but it was worth a shot at this point. "Cornelius, how do you do it? Man, I bet you out here every day, fighting through this struggle." I paused. "What do you tell yourself to get through every day? I need hope. I need to find a way to forget."

He took a deep breath. "Now, you know that tomorrow promises nothing." As soon as he spoke these words in his overly raspy New Yorker accent, I knew he had some type of wisdom locked up. "Not every day can be lived to the fullest but it's about trying. Calvin, a great woman once told me, it gets better. Three words that have

got me through my toughest battles in life. I've lost a lot in

my life…I mean look at me, look at where I am sitting.

But, I refuse to focus on the negatives. I've realized that

things have to blow up before they can blow over. You

have to wait for the smoke to clear. Bad things are going to

happen and all those experiences will shape you into a man

you will soon be grateful to be. If you think about it, there

would be no joy if the bad things didn't exist. And in the

long run, the things you have no control over shouldn't

ever effect the way you feel. There's always going to

unfortunate events, people get sick, people die – but they'll

always be with you. Use their spiritual presence to keep

moving in life. We do not control what happens on this

planet. I am a child of God, and the Bible tells us, we are *in*

the world not *of* the world. And when people wanna tell

you things to bring you down, you got to remember, it is

better to take refuge in the Lord, than to trust in man. The people closest to you possess all your trust, meaning they can do the most damage to you if they wanted. Be careful with who and where you invest your energy."

I looked at Cornelius. I had a semi-frown, semi-shocked look on my face. When I first saw him I didn't expect this and I knew he could read that from the expression on my face. "Woah," I replied.

"Next time don't come here to judge a book by its cover," He laughed while he said that, following it with a few coughs.

"Nah, it's just…that was deep," I smirked. "You sound like you've lost some people in your life."

"I lost my whole world about ten years ago." Looking at him, I saw his eyes were watery. "My wife, my daughter," I could hear his voice crack. I put my head down in disbelief. "Both killed in the same day. We used to live in Long Island. There was a drunk driver driving on the opposite side of the road, swerving back and forth. I slowed down and tried to maneuver away from his vehicle. Every direction I turned, he matched. It was like he was trying to hit us. I tried to make a quick U-turn to get onto the opposite side of the road but he sped up, hitting the passenger side of my vehicle." I shook my head. "My four-year-old daughter died in the crash. My wife, who was also expecting a second child, died later that night in the hospital. I've never been so torn in my life like I was the day after that crash. I felt like it all happened in slow motion. The shattered glass that flew through the air, the screeching sound from tires, the lights of the cars passing by. Sirens blasting in my ears, the flashing red and blue lights from the police cars." He closed his eyes. "Not being stable enough in the workplace, I got laid off. Soon, I wasn't able to afford the mortgage. I was evicted, the bank took my house. That's when I moved to the city. I wish I died with them." His head was down.

I didn't think he'd give me all that info within the first few minutes of meeting me but I felt like he hadn't been seen or heard in years. People need to vent. In disbelief, I took a deep breath. "I'm sorry about your loss, Mr. Cornelius. Looking at you I would have never guessed what you've been through. I guess we all have our secret battles."

"Those battles shaped us into the people we are today. Don't be like me, Calvin. I never brought these words outside of my head. I felt like if I said the words out loud, it would make them true. But they are...no matter what I do. I need help."

I thought about telling him about my brother but I didn't need to. I was already inspired and he's been through enough. "My mom always told me, God gives the toughest battles to the strongest soldiers." I looked at Cornelius. "I'm sure he wouldn't throw anything your way that you couldn't handle."

He smiled at me. He seemed to be contemplating something. I looked back at the water. "You know Calvin, my wife use to ask me the same question every time I left for work. I'd be wearing a suit, clean shave, low top fade. I was handsome, you know!" He laughed, "She would ask me, *where you going?* Where am I going? *Yes, where are you going?* I gotta go see my girlfriend, it's been a while. We'd both laugh. I miss her, man." Cornelius began laughing and shaking his head thinking about his conversations with his deceased wife. He was laughing to the point where he began to cough. I joined in on the laughter.

I stood up, "You're a good man, Mr. Cornelius. I'll be back soon," I told him.

"I'll be here," he responded.

"Take care of yourself, my man."

"You know I will," he smiled.

I shook his hand and began to walk away, "Don't go spending my money on drugs, eh!" I ordered him.

"Don't tell me how to spend my money, kid!" He responded in a joking tone.

Laughing and confused, I turned back to look at him, "Boy, if you don't get your old ass out of here!"

Cornelius was laughing too. From his personality and attitude, I could tell he was a good man, he probably used to be really playful and outgoing. It's sad what life can throw at a good person.

I urged myself to go back home, I was hoping my mom was home by now. I wanted to talk to her. I wanted her to know I was going to be there for her. She had gone through too much for me to just abandon her like this. I was the only person she had left.

When I got home, I knew my mom was there already. My mom and I took this loss differently. I was the type of person who never cried. I was obviously sad losing my brother but I couldn't shed a tear for him because he wouldn't have wanted me to. He had no one to blame but himself for going out like that. I walked up the stairs inside the apartment, we hadn't painted our walls in years and you could tell. The paint was peeling, and the stairs would make a creaking noise after every step. The hallway was packed with things. Things that we didn't need but for some reason my mom thought was necessary enough to keep. When I walked into my mom's room, she was sitting on her bed, looking at pictures of my brother. My heart felt for her. There was no way for me to make her feel better. She knew I was in the room but she never broke eye contact with the picture she was looking at. I was never really close with my mother but my brother was. Towards the end of his life they began to drift apart. I walked up to her and sat down beside her. I put my arm around her. She had tears in her eyes. My mother, the strong independent woman I had always looked up to, was in tears.

She rested her head on my shoulder. "Calvin, promise me you'll never leave me." Those words were spoken with a soft voice, a voice that had given up.

I couldn't make that promise. "The Lord gives his toughest battles to his strongest soldiers. God will help you through this. It's hard and unfair but if you couldn't get through this battle…you would have never received it." I looked at my mom's head which was still on my shoulder. Tears were falling onto my hoodie from her eyes. I was so mad and so disappointed in my brother. He strain he put on my family, the stress he put on my mother, and the pressure he put on me. *A dysfunctional family,* I thought. But even then, you'd have to have present family members to receive that title. With Jace gone and Pops locked up, this was no longer a family.

Chapter Seven: Schoolyard

Three weeks after my brother's funeral, I decided I needed to do right for my mother. I didn't want to cause any trouble. The struggle she's been through was enough for two lifetimes. It had been several days since the Christmas break had ended. It was the morning and I was getting ready to go to school. I hadn't been since my brother died. I rarely attended school anyway. We'd been in school for about five months, it was January. It was unusually warm for January, we were hitting the high forties and low fifties. I only went to school this year for maybe 20 days. I hated school. I'd normally be on the street corners. Or at Gio's house. I was already late. I was trying to make it on time for second period. I told Gio I'd be in school today. I didn't want to go to school because I felt bad for leaving my mother alone. But she made me promise I'd start going. She was given days off from work to grieve.

But I thought sitting around would only make things worse. I grabbed my bag and headed to my mom's room to give her a hug goodbye. As I walked down the stairs to leave the apartment, I heard a knock on the door. I looked through the peephole to see a police hat. I open the door to see two officers staring at me. "Wassup?" I asked.

"How're you doing today, Son? Is your mother home?" the officers both held poker face expressions.

I nodded my head with a bit of a frown on my face. "I'm alright." I turned around to yell, "Ma!" My mother came down the stairs to where I was standing.

"Come inside, officers." After my mom spoke these words the officers walked through the frame of the door. I walked up three steps on the stairs and sat down on the fourth. I was now looking at the faces of the officers and the back of my mother's head.

Both of the officers took off their hats and began to converse with my mother. They both were white with brown hair. They weren't taller than six feet. I focused on the officer on the right as he began to speak. "Ma'am there is no easy way to explain this to you. With the lack of evidence, no leads, and no witnesses…There is no way to find your son's murderer. Unfortunately, we've been given orders by the chief of the department to close this case. We will no longer be looking into this case unless a witness comes forward or a great deal of evidence is introduced to us. We're shaken and deeply sorry for your loss."

My mom stood silent. I couldn't see her face but I knew there were tears flowing down from her eyes. I couldn't believe this. "So that's it? You're barely three weeks into the case." This is when I stood up. "This is what you guys are paid to do? Run down our door to deliver bad news? This is what you receive benefits for? Serve and protect, right? Well y'all didn't protect my brother, and y'all ain't serving us now … so what do y'all do? It seems like every time y'all come around you make my mama cry. Don't come around here no more." I had inexpressible anger. I took it out on the cops because I've never been a fan of them.

The second officer began to speak to me. "We understand you're very upset about this, but we've done all we could for this case, and we're –"

"All you could? You're telling me within three weeks, you did all you could? Y'all better leave my house right now." Through all the back and forth between the officers and me, my mother stayed silent. "Please leave," I said with a firm voice.

The officers turned around and left the apartment. I closed the door behind them. I turned around to hug my mother. She wouldn't be able to rest knowing the person who took her son from her was roaming the streets. I walked back up the stairs with my arm around my mom comforting her. We walked back to her room. She sat on the bed. I stood in the frame of her door.

"Calvin, I want you to go to school now." She looked at me with tear-filled eyes.

With a straight face, I slightly nodded my head up and down. "Yes, mom." Walking up to her, I bent over to give her a hug. I rubbed her back "I'm sorry, mom." I released from the hug to go upstairs and collect my things. I ran into my room, I went into one of my drawers, I grabbed the brass knuckles from it. *The police didn't protect Jace...They definitely aren't going to protect me.* I put the brass knuckles into my bag as I headed out of the apartment. I didn't want to miss any more classes than I already did. I got to the subway station and waited for a train to school.

As I got to school, I tried to enter through a back door but it was locked. I started walking around the school. All the windows had metal bars guarding them. The school looked like a prison. It had about six floors. It seemed odd to a lot of people, but it's a city. You're always going to have high-rise buildings. Every door I checked was locked. I arrived at the main entrance of the school. There was a security guard at the front of the door. But I knew him, it was Giovanni's cousin.

I nodded my head when we made eye contact. "You out here like a bouncer, G." He was standing with his arms crossed. He was in a light blue collared shirt and black dress pants. He had a utility belt that didn't have much. I dapped him up.

"Yeah, my shift is almost over, but you know…Just tryna make an honest dollar, Calv. It's a warzone out here," he smiled.

"I respect that. Do your thing, G." He nodded his head. "You think you could let me in? I'm already late, I promised my ma I'd start going to school again."

"Yeah, I just gotta pat you down, no homo," he laughed. After patting me down he spoke again. "I gotta look into the bag, Calv."

"Look bruh, you know I ain't got nothing in there." I was worried he would find the brass knuckles.

"I know but there's cameras on us. They'll check me if I don't check you." He looked uneased.

"Alright, G." I was nervous but I put on a poker face.

He looked up at me and smile. "Damn, Calv."

"What?" I said worried.

He started to laugh again, "You ain't got no school books or nothin'?" All I could do was attempt a smile but my face stayed straight.

After he finished investigating, he opened the door for me to walk through. Just before I walked into the school, he put his hand in front of my chest, stopping me from entering. I looked up as he spoke. "Sorry about your brother, I heard about that. He was a good kid."

"I mean, it is what it is. Thanks though, I 'preciate it," I said with no expression on my face.

He pulled his hand from my chest, allowing me to enter. "Keep your head up, G." He said in an attempt to keep me motivated. I continued walking. It seemed like everyone knew about my brother. I didn't like the attention. It just got me fuming and I didn't want to be upset about my brother. He's affected enough people.

When I finally got inside, the second period classes had already started, I was the only one in the hallway. I took all my stuff with me to my class. It took me a while to figure out which room I was supposed to be in. As I walked into the class, everyone's attention was drawn to me. The class was mainly filled with Latinos and African-Americans. "Glad you could make it, Calvin!" said the teacher. I couldn't even remember her name. It was English class and I had no idea what was going on.

"Wassup?" I sat down in the center of the class and looked up at the blackboard, written on it was: Poetry.

The teacher walked up to my desk and put a lined piece of paper on my desk. The colour of the white paper wasn't far off from her skin tone. She had blue nail polish on. She would probably say it was Tiffany Blue, or some other type of shade, but it was all the same to me. "Calvin, I'd love it if you wrote a poem about a past experience."

"A past experience? I ain't got nothing to write about," I responded with a frown on my face.

"Calvin, you're in the twelfth grade. With the 17 years you've lived, you're telling me you have nothing to write about?"

"Nothing that y'all would care about, or could even relate to," I crossed my arms.

The teacher walked to her desk and returned to mine seconds later. She dropped a pencil on the desk and spoke, "Calvin, I'll never be able to understand you. But if I could … what would I need to hear?"

I had to admit, she was smooth with her words and well-spoken. She didn't have a New Yorker's accent. "Miss, where you from?"

"I'm from Montréal," she smiled.

"Like Canada?" I asked.

She smiled and nodded. "Yes. Québec, Canada."

"What's your name?" I asked. I had no shame.

"Ms. Laurent." She was disturbed that I didn't know her name. It's almost been a whole semester.

"Nah, like first name…" I asked.

"Calvin, why are you interviewing me?" Her eyebrows lowered and her eyes squinted.

"It makes me more comfortable to know who I'm learning from. You're living in the X?" I asked.

"The X?" She questioned with a confused look on her face.

"The Bronx," I clarified.

"Yes, Calvin. I am," she smiled.

"Ms. Laurent, from Montréal?" She nodded her head to confirm. "Welcome to the jungle."

The confused look came back. "Thank you, Calvin. Now write what's on your mind."

"You're brave, miss." I said with a little giggle. I thought to myself. *Young white lady from Montréal living in The Bronx.*

"Start your poem, Calvin." She said as she walked back to her desk. I'm not going to lie, I checked her out as she walked back to her desk. She must have been in her late twenties. She was fit with long brown hair. She was wearing a white dress shirt that was tucked into a slim grey skirt. With her black heels on she was probably around 5'10". She was a sweetheart. I picked up the pencil she dropped off at my desk. It was sharpened perfectly. I looked down at the lined paper. I wrote my name at the top. Graffiti style. I thought of some lines to incorporate into my poem. I knew these poems where supposed to be rated E for everyone. But I changed the E word to Explicit. Only because my life was explicit. I wasn't writing for the kids, I was writing how I lived. I started writing the poem. At first I was just trying to rhyme, but then it started to get deep. In cursive, the words I wrote may have been too much for the ears of Ms. Laurent. The words flowed so easily for me, maybe I just had a lot on my mind. The conversation I had with Ms. Laurent was the longest conversation I've had with a teacher this year. I normally sat at the back of the class silently. No one really cared what I had to say. So why speak? *Maybe it'll be different if I put it on paper.*

I finished my poem with more than 20 minutes left in the class. I wasn't sure if everyone else had finished but I noticed Ms. Laurent's brown eyes staring at me. "Calvin, are you finished?"

"Yeah," I responded looking at my paper.

"Would you like to read it for the class?" she said smiling again.

"Not at all," I said frowning again.

"Oh, come on. I'm sure it's great, Calvin," she
seemed to be begging.

I stood up and put my bag on. I grabbed the paper
and pencil in each hand. I put the pencil on the teacher's
desk which was at the front of the class. The teacher looked
at me confused. I turned around to face the class. I cleared
my throat and lifted the paper to my face to begin reading
it.

*"Ms. Laurent, Ladies, Gentlemen. We all in The
Bronx, that's kinda tight.*

*Miss, since you're new to the city here's some
advice ... don't go out at night.*

I paused as a few students started giggling. I looked at Ms. Laurent who smiled with her eyes squinted. There was nothing to be confused about. I continued reading.

They say two wrongs don't make a right... gang violence, and gunshots.

Why's my mother stress-free without my brother's burden in sight?

You may have been raised where I was, but we do not fight the same fight.

A loud knock on the door. Who's that? Uh, Ma ... it's the feds.

Sorry ma'am, but we regret to inform you, your son is dead.

They came back three weeks later, closed case they
said.

Yeah? Well, who did it? They need to be locked up I
said.

They killed my brother for wearing the colour red.

Ridiculous how a colour earns you a bullet to the
head.

He lays six feet deep with his mind filled with lead.

His casket is gold but that's cold metal for a bed.

Look, I ain't looking for sympathy I'm not tryna
make a scene cause that ain't me.

My pops in jail for a crime he didn't commit so I'm
just wondering why he's not free.

But that's just life, no opportunities in the land of
the free. So, you gotta slang for a G.

They ask me why I'm not outgoing or why I don't smile, but would you if you were seeing what I see.

I got a lot on my mind, who's gonna put food on the table? Who's gonna help my mom?

If you got your eyes on me right now you're looking at a ticking time bomb.

I don't care if you like me or not, I don't care if I got a few fans.

I have to do this, I have to do that, would I be a tough guy if I ran?

My mom is suffering, I'm suffering, so right now I have no choice but to be a man.

All I know is if you want something done right, you gotta put matters into your own hands."

I looked up at the class who stared at me in silence. I dropped the paper on the teacher's desk. I looked at the teacher's face; eyes filled with tears, her mouth was partly open and I could see the shock in her watery eyes. "I'm not saying you needed to hear that. But it seems to me like you're starting to understand me." I nodded my head. "I'll see you tomorrow." The class wasn't over but I've never let the bell decide when the class was dismissed. I left the class and started walking down the hall. Then I heard my name get yelled from behind me. I turned around to see Ms. Laurent. She was about ten yards away from me. I could see the streams of tears on her face, and the mascara running down her cheeks. She began to walk towards me. I shook my head.

"Calvin, I'm sorry about your loss." She was wiping her tears as she spoke to me. "You're so strong."

"Miss, stop. I told you, I don't want no special treatment, I don't want sympathy. You told me, write a poem ... so that's what I did." I had no expression on my face.

"You have so much potential. Don't let it go to waste. Please be here tomorrow." She was staring into my eyes, talking to me like she already knew me.

I wasn't going to let this get to me. "Miss, I'm not vulnerable. I can't change the past. So I've learned to live with it. It's an experience for a reason."

"I want to help you get past this," tears began to stream down her face again.

"Miss, it's in the past. So I'm already past it. And besides, it's not your fight to fight." I turned my neck to look behind me and down the hall I saw Gio. I turned back to say goodbye. "Alright, Ms. Laurent. I promise… you can catch me here tomorrow." I turned around to head down the hall when I bumped into a guy just my size. "My bad, G." I continued walking towards Gio.

"Yeah, it is," said the boy I had just brushed.

I turned around to look at the boy. "Come again?" I didn't think I heard him correctly.

"You don't know me, cuh." After he said those words I studied his appearance. He was wearing a blue shirt and had a blue bandana hanging out of his back pocket.

"Cool it!" I dragged the words out as I smiled. "You think I'm scared? On my motha, son. I ain't scared." I laughed a bit. "I've had guns pointed to my head, the colour of your shirt ain't gonna make me shake."

"You should be. I could hook you up with a first-class ticket to see your brother," he stared at me and smiled.

"What?" I asked in an angry tone. At this point, there was only one way this dispute could go. I took off my bag which was hanging off of my body with one strap. I quickly pulled back my fist, I threw a right hook which landed on his cheekbone. I didn't even know who this guy was. *How did he know about me, or my brother?*

"Calvin, stop!" Yelling at the top of her lungs, Ms. Laurent was still standing behind me. I didn't look back.

After watching the boy stumble backwards, I tackled him into the lockers. At this point I was draping him against the lockers with my left hand, while throwing fists with my right hand. His nose began to bleed, but I wasn't going to stop. I'd never been this angry before. A second boy pulled me off of the kid I was manhandling. Then, a third came and sucker punched me from the left side of my face. I fell to the ground in a daze. I could hear screaming in the background. As I gained my sight back, I saw Gio throw a punch to knock out the kid who sucker punched me. I got back onto my feet to see Gio's victim on the ground having a seizure. I wasn't surprised that Gio started swinging with no questions asked. He was my brother. Ride or die was our lifestyle. Ms. Laurent yelled at another teacher to call the school security. There was a circle of students around this brawl. It was two against two but it seemed as if there were so many more people involved. But all these boys were homeboys, I could tell by their colour-coordinated outfits. They were all wearing blue. *Uptown Crips?* I thought. Gio put his hands up to his face, as if he was a boxer. I did the same thing. "So what's good? Make a move, G." Gio taunted the kid I was originally dealing with.

"If it ain't the pretty boy." The boy came at Gio in a malicious manner. But before he could do any damage, a police officer tackled him to the floor. Another officer bear-hugged Gio and began pulling him towards the office. Security guards started grabbing me and the other standing kid. The boy who was on the ground was surrounded by teachers. The high school was more like a warzone, but this was what it was known for. It was one of the most violent

schools in the country.

Chapter Eight: Distribution

Gio, myself, and all of the students involved were physically pulled into the office. We were all yelling at each other while being tugged. The boy I was originally fighting yelled out, "You're dead! I'mma kill you!"

"You're the one leaking blood!" Gio yelled back.

I joined in on the trash talk. "You ain't bleeding blue."

Gio and I were pulled into a separate office from the other two kids. In the office was a police officer, a security guard, and a black lady in a skirt. I assumed she was a principal or some type of person with authority. I didn't come to school enough to know who she was. Both Giovanni and I were breathing heavily. We were fuming because of the dispute. They forced us to sit down in attempt to get us to relax. Gio looked at me. I was on his right and he was on my left. The desk in this office was directly in front of us, probably about six feet ahead of us. The three authority figures were in between us and the desk. The chairs we were sitting in were against a white brick wall. Gio stuck out his right hand, pressing the outside of it against my chest. He wanted a handshake. I gave him one. "You're my fucking brother! You got my back! You're a real one!"

"Of course! No questions asked, G. That's how we do it!" Gio responded.

"Yup, straight up!" I confirmed. The police officer was staring at me, then started looking at Gio. I recognized him. I've been seeing police officers a lot lately. Although, this officer wasn't from my brother's case.

"Fuck," I dragged that word out muttering it under my breath. I looked over at Gio, he was staring at the officer too. I knew Gio remembered him. I thought back to when K.C. came to visit New York. Jerem tipped over a stand in a Manhattan gift shop. This police officer chased us all the way to the subway station. I didn't know what would happen next.

"You could be charged with assault!" The police officer said to Gio and me.

"Nah. That was self-defence." I replied with a relaxed tone in my voice.

That only made the officer more upset. "For an act to be self-defence you have to be using the same force as your oppressor."

"And that's what we did!" I replied again. Straight-faced.

Gio began to laugh, "We from The Bronx. We don't get even, we get ahead."

"It is what it was," I said.

"Yeah, and unless you change, that lifestyle will either get you arrested or killed." The officer spoke as if that was going to scare us.

"You don't think we know that? My question is: do you think we have a choice? We were born into this. You never had to wake up and question if today would be your last day. I got homeboys who know how to cook dope but can't read. Drugs are some people's only source of income. Without it, they starve. We fight because that's all we know. We been fighting our whole lives. Fighting to get a meal, fighting to pay rent, fighting to survive. That's a life you have no part of – a life you ain't ever gonna understand." After I spoke these words, the conversation was no longer about the previous dispute.

"Y'all put us in the system knowing we supposed to fail. So why would we wanna stay in the system? We just gonna create our own. Y'all don't think we sick. You kill our brothers and sisters. We see it on the news. It's all over the country. All over the media. No filter, we seeing all that. Blood spilling out. Mamas crying. Y'all don't care about us. We look like we up to no good so y'all wanna lock us up…or put us in a grave. So no we ain't gonna change. Not for you. Like my boy Calvin said." Gio looked over at me, I could see it from the corner of my eye. He then looked back to the officer. "We was born into this. Y'all wanna change this? Then fix the hood. Don't kill it." Gio's words were like daggers.

"You in the Bronx, you're not gonna change lives. Y'all did this to us, so the way I see it, if you really need something then you gotta go get it, even if that mean blood and death. That's what they did to my brother, those are the grounds I was raised on, and that's how I'm gonna live my life. Y'all are licenced killers, justified murders. That's you! Your people!" I said looking directly into the cop's eyes. "You got blood on your hands, so if we're determining who's guilty by looking at the red-handed folks… you in trouble." I gave my final thoughts and following those words was silence.

There was a knock on the door and Ms. Laurent entered. She dropped off my bag. "Thank you, Miss." I said looking over at her. She smiled at me, without teeth. She then left closing the door behind her. The room stayed silent for about 30 seconds. You could hear the clock in the office ticking.

"You two think you know it all. You think you got it all figured out! You better change that lifestyle. I wish you two would just smarten up! Stay in school and knock some sense into your brains." The lady in the skirt seemed shocked after the police officer spoke these words. He was brave, I had to give him that. Two ghetto kids who had little to no respect for any type of authority stood in front of him and he was about to figure that out.

"Are you mad?" Gio stood up.

I got up as well. "So take off your badge...come outside and knock some sense into my brain." I was fed up with everything. I hated the police, more than anything.

"No, Stop!" The lady in the skirt yelled.

"Sit back down!" said the security guard as he pushed Gio back into his seat, he then stood in between the officer and me. He was looking into my eyes. We were the same height but he was carrying more pounds than me. "Take a seat," he said.

I continued to stand. Starring back at him. "Nah."

"Please Calvin, sit down," said the lady in the skirt. I had respect for black women, I looked back at my seat to sit down. I looked at the lady. She looked nervous.

"I remember you two," said the officer. Gio and I didn't speak. "You boys trashed that store in Manhattan."

"Ain't nobody trashed nothin'," I said in a quick manner.

Gio shrugged his shoulders and spoke in the most sarcastic voice I've heard. "Who's Manhattan?" he laughed.

"Where are the other two?" The officer demanded.

"I don't recall." Gio shook his head, he wasn't breaking character.

"Y'all were just chasing us for no reason. We never stole nothing," I explained.

"What are you gonna charge us with?" asked Gio. At this point, we were just targeting the police officer. We were just waiting for him to react.

"You were disturbing the peace, so, a cause of disturbance, destruction of property. Misdemeanor criminal offence. You could face jail time for that."

"What kind of nonsense is that? There's nothing peaceful about New York. You're overdosing on stupidity for that one," I replied.

Gio laughed. "They were disturbing us."

The lady in the skirt finally began to talk. "Let's stay on topic. Boys, I don't want this to happen again. Please, keep your hands to yourself. I don't know how the fight started but I don't want it to happen again."

"Ask Ms. Laurent how it all started, you'll know it's not our faults," I explained to the lady.

"It doesn't matter who started the problem. What matters is how you're going to prevent this situation from happening again."

"Alright … can we leave now?" I asked.

Gio and I were both escorted by security out of the school. They suspended us for the next four days. I didn't care and I don't think it phased Gio either. We walked home together. I was confused about what happened during the fight. "We got the whole school out watching our fight!" I shook my head

Gio looked at me, "Yeah, everyone and they mamas was watching us. That boy and his crew was grimy."

I laughed. "He look like the type to sharpen both sides of his pencil when he was in elementary school." We were both laughing now.

He spoke while laughing. "Why you so damn creative?"

"One side break, that boy just flips the pencil and he's ready to go." I laughed harder.

Gio stopped. "Nah, Calv. You're doing too much!" He looked at me and started laughing again because I was laughing. "You're too much."

"Wait hold up. Gio, why'd homie call you pretty boy?"

"Oh..." He laughed. "I was tryna get at his girl in the morning. I had her laughing. He wasn't having none of that." Gio continued to laugh at himself. "She's so sweet though."

I could tell Gio liked her. "You're a dog," I said while laughing.

"She's got a cute name too." Gio paused to look at me. "Bea," He was smiling. "It's short for Beatrice."

"That name sounds immaculate! Don't tell me you're in love, son." We both started laughing.

"I can't be held down by one girl," He explained.

"We'll see about that, you're looking like a pretty boy right now." We both started laughing.

We got to the outside of the subway station. "Gio, I'll catch you later I gotta go pick something up for my mom. You down to check out that boxin' gym later?" I started walking backwards from Gio.

"Yeah, which one?" he responded.

"Uh, I'm not sure, I'll text you. But be ready for five o'clock. I yelled, running back to a subway station.

"Alright!" He yelled back.

I wasn't picking anything up for my mother. I was about to visit Xavier. My mom wasn't doing well. I knew she would struggle to work so I needed to bring more money into the house. She was in the grieving process and stressing about the lack of money would only prolong her recovery. I thought about if I'd already recovered. Then I stopped thinking about it. Only because my brother didn't deserve my thoughts. He didn't deserve for anyone to feel bad for him. I was running out of options and finding a job in Manhattan or anywhere else around New York wasn't going to pay me much. I wouldn't be able to get decent hours.

I got close to Highbridge, I was a bit further uptown than the Yankee Stadium. I got to an apartment off of 167th. I looked up. The apartment building was a reddish brown. I was pretty sure this was Xavier's spot, but I've only been there once so my memory of it wasn't the greatest. I walked into the building, there was another glass door to enter through. I wasn't able to open the door. It was locked, I needed to know Xavier's buzzer number. I saw a group of Latinos. They stared at me and I stared back. All of them dressed in dark, baggy clothes. Some had bandanas in their pockets, they were red. I didn't know these guys, but they probably knew my brother. They glared with widened eyes and their mouths open. They were in the lobby of the building, I was hoping one of them would open the door for me. I pointed at the door. One of them came to open it.

I nodded my head, "Thanks, G"

He replied in Spanish, "De nada." I raised one eyebrow but continued walking.

I got into the elevator and looked at all the numbers, there were 16 floors. The buttons were worn out. I knew my way to his house from here. I pressed the number four. I wasn't sure if he was home but I needed to talk to him. The elevator opened and there was a Latino lady, she was waiting for me to get out of the elevator so she could enter. I looked at her eyes to see one was blood-stained and had purple bruises all around it.

As I walked out of the elevator I muttered under my breath. "Oh, shit."

She had her thick hair braided back in cornrows, had a grey tank top, black short shorts and pink flip flops on. If I were to guess her age I would say she was in her early 40s. It was obvious she was abusing drugs and someone was abusing her. I examined her within three seconds.

"Fuck off," she replied while scratching her right bicep with her left finger nails.

I didn't think anything of it. I shook it off. I walked up to his door, 403. I knocked on Xavier's door like I was beating a drum. "Yo, Xavier."

"Who is it?" he yelled.

"Son, listen to the sound of my voice. You know who. Open the damn door." After I yelled back I heard the lock click. Xavier opened the door and he stood before me. He was light-skinned, I think he was half black, half Chilean. He wasn't wearing a shirt. But it seemed as if he was. His chest, neck and arms were filled with tattoos. "Put on a damn shirt, what do you think this is?" I said walking into his place. It was dirty in there. Paint was peeling off the walls. He had several cracked tiles and creaking noises coming out of them. I saw a roach on his wall as soon as I entered. It smelled like weed in there. There was nothing I hated more than the smell of weed. I've never done it and I never would. A lot of people say there are several benefits that come from weed but there are also negative effects and that is unquestionable.

He came back with a red shirt on. "What can I do for you, young blood?"

I gave him a dirty look. "Imma need you not to call me that. I need money." I showed him the most disrespect.

He walked over to a cabinet in his kitchen. He pulled out some type of mini safe. He pulled stacks of cash in rubber bands from the safe. "How much you need?"

"What the fuck you think this is?" I shook my head. "I don't want your money, I want in."

He shook his head in confusion. "In what?" he said. I didn't say anything, I just continued to stare at the money. "The dope game?" he chuckled.

"Yeah, I wanna sell white," I said with a serious tone. The only reason I wanted to sell cocaine was because it didn't have a scent that my mom would be able to smell when it's in the apartment. I didn't want her to think I was going down the same path as Jace.

"You wanna sell – boy you're outta your God damn mind?" he raised his voice. I'm supposed to be looking after you. How would your mom react if she knew you came asking for this type of work?"

I shook my head. "How would your mom react if she knew you were selling dope?" he smiled. He knew I had him beat. "Look, I'm doing this for my mom, since my brothers gone, we're gonna need some more income entering the house. I don't want my mother worrying about bills and shit."

"But what is she gonna think when you're bringing in all this cash?" he questioned.

"I don't know, I'll tell her I got a job in Manhattan that tips well. I don't know I'll think of something. Can you help me or not?"

"Fuck," he muttered under his breath.

"You told me, you swore on my brother. If I needed anything…anything, I should just come to you." I paused. I took a deep breath. "I'm here. So…is it what it was?"

"Alright." He walked into his room, I saw a cockroach approach my foot. I stepped on it hearing a crunch sound. I looked back up. Xavier came back and handed me a brown bag. "There are three 8-balls in there. One eighth of an ounce is an 8-ball–"

"Okay, okay, skip the small talk. Where am I taking these?" I demanded.

"Harlem, MLK and Broadway. Two different people. A barbershop and an apartment." He said in a serious tone, "If it goes well, you can keep all the money."

"What do you mean if it goes well?" I asked.

"It could get dangerous," he explained.

"This is Highbridge, say no more." I took off my backpack and put it down, avoiding the crushed cockroach. I pulled out my black spring jacket. I put the brown bag in there. I put on the jacket. "I'll see you soon," I turned around and opened the door.

"Wait!" Xavier blurted out.

"What?" I replied.

He threw something at me, I wasn't sure about what it was until I caught it. "Just in case," he explained. I looked at the item I caught. It was a closed pocket knife.

I shook my head. I tossed the knife back at him. He felt rejected. I started walking backwards. "I don't think I'll need it." I turned around and continued.

I got back in the elevator. When I got back to the lobby, the Latino boys were still there. I began to walk around when one of them yelled out "Young Jace!"

I stopped where I was. "Don't call me that."

"What's the matter, Papi? I'm just showin' love," he said laughing and looking at the other guys hoping they'd laugh with him. He wore red like the other guys.

"I don't care, don't call me that. Y'all ain't got shit going for you in your lives, so you hang around the building lobby, masking your failure in life by hanging out with other failures." I shook my head and continued walking.

"Woah! Relax esé, we just showing love, watch your mouth before theirs a problem," he said widening his eyes.

"I got nothing to lose, son. If there's a problem let me know," I explained looking backwards.

He silenced himself and the other boys in the back made a soft *ouu* sound before I exited the building.

When I got out of the building I began to run, I wasn't nervous. I would say I was more paranoid. Although, I was determined to make money, and by any means necessary. I decided it would be better if I got there earlier rather than late at night. I'd promised Gio I'd meet him at the gym later.

I got onto the subway headed in the downtown direction from Highbridge. It only took me about 20 minutes to get to the streets of Harlem. As soon as I got to street level, a bicycle with a motor on it zoomed passed me. It wasn't a motorcycle. It was an ordinary bike with a motor on it. These were used all the time in New York. Some were delivery drivers, some were just for transportation. Real bikes were in Philadelphia, they loved bikes over there.

I walked by a group of girls, they were Latina's, one of them held boxing gloves. There were about six girls in the group but I was only focused on the one with the gloves. I was looking at the image or design that was put onto the black gloves. On each glove, there was a pink rose. The rose grew out of concrete. It seemed unusual to me, it was a one-in-a-million type of idea. My eyes followed the gloves as the ladies walked by me. I didn't get the chance to see the face of the girl holding the gloves but I saw her long black French-braided hair and blue jeans. She had on a backpack as the group walked down the steps to enter the subway station. When I turned my head to continue the way I was going I was suddenly stopped in my tracks after bumping in to a tall black guy.

"Ay my bad, bruh," I apologized.

"Watch where you going, G," he said in a very deep voice.

I nodded my head and continued walking. I saw the barbershop Xavier was talking about. I read the name of the shop, *Catcha Fade.* I shook my head while I took off my backpack and held it to my chest. As soon as I entered the barbershop, heard a little bell which notified the employees that someone had walked in. Everyone stared at me. I slowly continued to walk to the back of the shop. These were Xavier's exact instructions. Do not talk to anyone, do not give eye contact, and do not be aggressive. I don't know why he gave me these instructions then attempted to arm me with a knife.

The walk to the end of the shop seemed like forever. I looked to the left to see a man staring at me. He must have been in his late thirties. It was some type of cut eye. He then began to stare at my bag. I shook my head. I was not going to let him intimidate me.

"What's in the bag youngin'?" Asked the barber.

I gave a grin, "nothin' for you partna'!" I continued to the back of the barbershop and entered through another door. On the other side of the door were stairs that led to a basement. Every step on those stairs were loud steps. I heard creaking noises after every step. The paint on the walls was white. Although, there were cracks and chips all the way down. When I got to the bottom of the stairs there was another door on the left. I tried to open it, but it was locked. I knocked twice and waited. There was a sliding sound and a black man looked through the rectangular peephole in the door. I could see both his eyes.

I could see his eyebrows sink, "Who's you?"

"Calv," I said

"And…" He continued.

I kissed my teeth. "Man." I looked back up the stairs on my left. I took a deep breath, looking back at the man's eyes. "Xavier sent me," I said, frowning one side of my face.

The sliding noise came back as he closed the peep hole. I heard a few locks get turned before the door swung open. In a dimly lit room, there were about ten men and around six women. They had red solo cups everywhere. It smelled like weed in there. I was disgusted on the inside but this was like every other trap house. Some girls were sitting on sofas, others were standing, and a few men were sitting at a table playing cards or dominos.

"Who you looking for?" said the man who opened the door for me.

"… um Andre?" I clarified. The man pointed to a light-skinned man. I started to walk over to him. As I started walking over, I realized majority of the men in there were holding guns, or had them on the nearest table to them. One female on the couch had a shotgun in her lap. I swallowed my spit.

As I got to Andre he immediately ordered me to pull out the package. "Lemme see the dope." I looked at the table he was sitting at. There was a red lighter, beside the lighter was a scale, and on the scale was a giant bundle of weed.

I looked back at Andre. "Money before the deal." He looked at me as if I was crazy. He had a blunt in between his fingers. He put the blunt between his lips and lit it with the lighter that was on the table. He inhaled, then removed the joint from his lips. He slowly exhaled, blowing all the smoke towards me. The smoke rose into my face. I waved my hand in the air attempting to move the smoke from my face. I quickly got heated, raising my voice at Andre. "Son! Don't be blowing smoke in my face!" I then heard a gun get cocked from behind me. I shook my head.

"You better watch your tone when you talkin' to me," He took another hit from the joint and blew the smoke to the side this time, avoiding my face. "Comin' to my set, disrespectin' me and my people, raisin' your voice and shit." He pulled out a stack of hundred dollar bills from his pocket. I was confused, did he just walk around with that type of money on him? He counted the money, handing me $550. He overpaid. "The fifty is for you. Go catch yourself a fade." He was referring to my hair which hadn't been cut nor combed in a while. I turned around and began to walk back to the door only to hear someone click a gun again. "You forgetting something?" Asked Andre.

My eyes widened. I turned around and walked back to Andre. "My bad." I pulled two 8-balls from out of my backpack. I placed them on the table. I turned around again and exited the room. I got back up to the barbershop to see everyone staring at me again. I left without saying anything. As much as I hated the drug game, I had to respect the charity New York seemed to have. The black community always gave back to their people once they started making it.

I got out of the store and looked both ways in attempt to navigate myself to my next destination. I started walking to my left. I liked the way Harlem looked, the buildings looked really old school, but really detailed. It was hard to explain. My people built these communities against their will, the least we could do was enjoy it.

I was looking up, absent-minded, preoccupied by the buildings. I looked back down to see a badge. An NYPD officer standing in front of me. I tried to stay calm. It was a black officer, very tall and built. I put my head down and continued walking. I didn't look back.

"Hey!" The officer hollered at me.

I stopped and slowly turned around. "Is there a problem, officer?" I said in a monotone voice.

He pointed to my shoes. "Your shoelace is undone." He was smiling. He's probably new here. No one cares if you run a marathon with your shoelace undone.

My heart was beating out of my chest. "Thank you, sir." I knelt down to tie my shoe lace about five yards in front of him.

"What's in the bag?" he asked with a stern voice.

Fuck! I thought to myself. "What are you talking about, officer?" I took my bag off to see that I had left it open. The officer most likely saw the brown paper bag in my backpack. I was now holding the bag in front of me. I stuck my hand in it. He had me on my heels and I was trying to think quickly. "You mean my lunch?" I gave him a dirty look.

"In a brown paper bag?" he wasn't easing up.

"…Yes?" I was pretending to be confused.

"I could have sworn people only used those on TV," he laughed.

"…Ha-ha," I laughed very awkwardly. "Well, moms is old school. You know how that be." I zipped up my bag and put it back on. "Have a nice day, Sir." I turned around and began walking.

"You too, Son," He replied.

I walked quickly. *Close,* thought.

The walk to the next place wasn't far from the barbershop. I got to the apartment and waited in the lobby until someone opened the door for me. I entered the building and went up three flights of stairs. Room 306. I knocked twice.

A man yelled, "Who is it?"

"Calv, for Xavier." I was eager. I was tapping my foot really fast. The door opened and a fat Latino man stood in front of me. He was obese and was wearing a white tank top. It was dirty to the point that it was brown, it had a few holes in it. He was wearing shorts as well, they were black. His chest hairs were curling out over the tank top. I frowned in disgust. He waved his hand telling me to come in. I followed him in, he was kind of twitching. There was barely any furniture in there. He had nothing to show for himself. The paint on the walls were peeling off. He had red stains on his wooden floor. I tried not to think about it. took my bag off. Neither of us had spoken a word yet. I followed him to a table. He had a scale on the table.

"Where is the cocaina?" The man demanded in a thick Spanish accent.

"Money before the deal," I explained.

He pulled out $250 and quickly handed it to me. "Where is it?"

I looked at the man to see his eyes twitching. He had another twitch or tick between his neck and left shoulder. I wasn't sure what to call it but he was shrugging his left shoulder against his neck every ten seconds as if he was itchy. "What's going on with yo' shoulder, my guy?" I knew it was the drugs. But I wanted to know if he knew why he was like this.

"Hurry up?" He said, ignoring everything I had asked.

"Relax, bruh." I was in such disgust. I pulled the 8-ball out from my bag. "Here!" I threw it onto the table, as if he was below me. I began to walk out. When I got close to the door, I heard a loud grunt. I hadn't even put my bag back on yet.

"You tryna chanchullo me?" He yelled angrily.

"What the fuck does that even mean, bruh?" I turned around to see the man charging at me. He slammed the door shut. He quickly swung a fist at me. I ducked and he hit the door. "What the fuck!" I blurted out.

"You left out a quarter of the dope." He yelled again.

"What?" I ran to the other side of the room. I held onto my bag with my left arm, and I reached into my bag with my right. I pulled out the brass knuckles. I tossed my bag to the side. The man came at me again, widely swinging his left fist. I blocked with my right forearm. He widely threw his right fist this time. I struggled to block with my left forearm, it collided with his forearm. I stumbled as he got a piece of my head in that shot. The brass knuckles were on my right fist. I pulled back my fist, throwing a hefty right jab at the fat man. I made contact with his left cheekbone and right away his face began oozing blood. "Oh shit!" I didn't think it would be that bad.

The man fell to the ground and the floor trembled when he hit it. He started screaming in pain. He would need stitches if he decided to go to the hospital though I wasn't going to wait for his decision.

I went to the man's kitchen and found some cloths hanging on the stove. I grabbed them and went to his freezer. I pulled a bag of frozen mixed vegetables from it. I went to the man knelt down and put the cloths to his face. "Your dumbass shouldn't have come at me like that! The fuck is wrong with you…chargin' at me. You from New York, you should know better." I was huffing and puffing, and my heart was beating fast. I put the frozen veggies over his cut. I slid the brass knuckles off of my fingers. I noticed that there was blood on them. I didn't realise how jagged the edges were until now. It was no mystery why the man was bleeding this much. Blood was dripping onto the ground from his face. "Stay off the drugs, man. They're no good." I got up to leave the apartment after attending to the man. He continued to moan in pain as I left.

I was making my way back to Xavier's place. I thought about if the guy would call the police. Then I came to a realization, *he was buying drugs.* He would have to explain why he came at me like that. I was very confused, thinking about why Xavier would try to swindle the man in that apartment. Xavier must have known that a drug addict would get upset when they didn't get the amount of narcotics they paid for.

When I arrived at Xavier's apartment, I was already heated. Infuriated by the conversation I had with myself on the way to the apartment. I banged hard on Xavier's door three times. "It's Calv!" I spoke with an aggravated voice.

When the door swung open, Xavier was frowning. "Whatchu' doin'? Bangin' on my door like you're the feds or something!"

"Nah! What the hell you doing?" My voice was already raised. "You tried to get me set up in Harlem? What the fuck is wrong with you?"

"What are you talking about?" He spoke with confusion in his voice.

"You cut the dope a quarter short! You had a fat dude throwing fist at me!" My voice was stationed at a raised tone.

"For real? What happened?" He seemed entertained.

"I knocked him out. I didn't plan on hurting anyone." I shook my head.

"Really? I'm sorry bro, it was an honest mistake." He didn't sound sincere.

"Shut up. When I left, you told me I could keep the money if it goes well. You tried to set me up. You're dirty, you should have died instead of Jace." I left with no other words.

When I got into a hallway, a black lady was standing in the doorway of an apartment a few doors down the hall. She made eye contact with me. She then went on to make the same noise every African-American woman makes when they're disappointed or displeased with a situation. "Mhm, mhm, mhm. You better stop runnin' 'round with that Xaviah' boy. He's no good." I continued to walk to the elevator. "You gonna end up getting yourself in trouble. A young black male like you should be in school! Learning something useful!" Her voice sounded old and a little raspy.

I left without saying a word to her. I didn't have time. I had to be at the gym with Giovanni.

Chapter Nine: The Gloves

When I arrived at the boxing gym, Gio was already changed into shorts and a tank top. He was talking to a man while he was putting on a padded helmet. I walked over to the two of them. The man Gio was standing with was black, he was probably just over six foot. He was very muscular. He wore a grey tracksuit, had a buzz cut and goatee.

"What's good, my man?" asked Gio. He handed me a helmet and boxing gloves. "I picked these up for you. I knew you'd come here empty-handed."

I shook my head. He knew me so well. "Good looking out, bro."

The man helping Giovanni put on his gloves, looked at me. "Don't just stand there! Go change!" I looked at the man and a gold tooth shined at me from the side of his mouth.

I walked into the change room with my bag and boxing equipment in my hands. I had shorts under my pants and a tank top under my clothes. I was already wearing sneakers. It took me less than a minute to get ready. I walked out holding my gloves and helmet, the man signalled me to come over.

"One thing y'all need to know before we start anything is discipline. Whatever happens outside this gym, stays outside of the gym. The outside world has nothing to do with this gym, they are two separate worlds. After you leave this gym, anything I teach you is to simply protect and defend, not to stir up problems that'll come back to me." Gio and I both nodded our heads. "First things first, my name is Michael. My family has owned this gym for twenty plus years. There are a few rules you need to follow if you're gonna continue training in this gym," he continued with a serious tone in his voice. "When you refer to me, you will either say Sir or Mr. Mike. Nothing else. No cursing, no real trash talk, no fighting unless told or agreed upon. We got little kids in here…coming from torn families. They come here to forget about their problems. It's their safe haven. It could be yours too. You two ready?" He gave Gio a fist bump. He then stuck his hand out for me to give him a hand shake.

I nodded my head, "I'm ready for this…I was born ready," I shook his hand.

"I'm not saying I'll turn you two into superstars. But I'll make you proud to be the man you are." He closed his fist. It was symbolic, a sign of unity and strength. A power to the people type of strength. "Come on, we're gonna start with footwork."

I muttered under my breath, "Aw man." Foot work just sounded like code for cardio. I hated cardio.

There were two boxing rings in the gym and we walked around both of them. There were probably thirty yards between each wall. The ground was concrete and several cracks ran through the floor and walls. On the ground, there were truck tires. I could have sworn I only saw this type of set-up in the movies. Mr. Mike ordered Gio and myself to go back and forth through the tires. After, we began to do suicides and other running drills. I wasn't sure of the names of the drills but I knew I would feel it all in the morning. We continued with the footwork for over two hours. It was past 7pm. It was time for the gym to close. There was a large clock hanging on the main wall of the gym. It seemed to be just one giant room.

"Go get some water and come back," said Mr. Mike. Gio and I walked away dripping sweat, I slipped off one of my gloves to take off my tank top which was now drenched in sweat. I took a drink of water from the fountain. I could feel the joints in my knee ready to give out. I struggled to walk. I didn't have the muscle endurance for this, not yet. After Gio got his water, we walked back to our coach to say goodbye.

"Thank you, Mr. Mike. I appreciate you taken us in like this," I said.

Gio added on, "You're doing a good job here...Same time tomorrow?" Gio and I started to take off our gloves.

"You're not done working out," he said with a confused look on his face. "You two asked me to train you, we're not done training."

"What are you talking about? My guy, my guy, the gym is closing," said Gio.

"I'm talking about the ten suicides you owe me...my guy, my guy!" Mr. Mike was mocking Gio. "Learn the rules before you start talking with that tone."

"Ten suici – are you joking? Bro… I mean, Sir…Mr. Mike, your gym is empty. Count the people in the gym. One, two, three. It's just us! Why are you holding us here?" Gio was frustrated.

"You asked me to train you. I'm not holding you back, I'm trying to hold you up. If you want to leave right now, go ahead. Just don't come back," he spoke with the serious tone again.

Gio shook his head, then kissed his teeth. He tightened up his gloves again and began running.

"Make it fifteen since you love counting so much." He looked back over to me.

I looked back at him nervously. "Mr. Mike –"

He cut me off. "Grab the jump ropes."

I thought to myself, *you gotta be kidding me.* I grabbed the ropes out of a box beside one of the boxing rings.

"I want you to jump until your friend is done the suicides. Every time that rope get tangled in your feet your friend here is going to add an extra suicide to his resume." I took off my other glove. Mr. Mike stared at me until I started. I've never in my life been so focused on jump rope. I was making sure I didn't get caught on the rope, I could tell Gio was beyond exhausted.

After Gio finished the suicides, Mr. Mike ordered us to switch. Gio was horrendous at jump rope, I ended up doing 27 suicides. Running about fifteen to twenty yards for each suicide. I didn't blame Gio for messing up, I expected this from him. It was now half past eight o'clock. I didn't think we'd continue after an extra hour. Mr. Mike smiled. Gio and I continued to drip in sweat. I fell to the ground and laid on my back and Gio was hunched over with his hands on his knees.

"You boys look full of energy," he chuckled. "Alright, at least sit up." I sat up. I looked at Gio who took a knee. "Are you two in school?"

"Yeah. Seniors, sir," I responded.

"Okay, so you got class tomorrow? What time do you start school?" he questioned.

I looked at Gio, he was looking back at me. I think we were thinking the same thing. I didn't know if Mr. Mike would punish us for getting suspended. "We're out of school for the rest of the week. We got suspended for fighting."

"Oh. Why were you two fighting?" he asked.

"Well, it's kind of a long story," I replied.

"Long story? Well you don't have to be in bed anytime soon since you were suspended."

He had me beat. "I don't really want to talk about it," I explained.

"Hm. Alright, get up."

"Me?" I asked.

"Yes, both of you. Put your gloves back on," he demanded.

I thought to myself as I got up, *he's crazy, he's actually crazy.* I look down at my gloves which were at my feet. I wasn't dazed but my eyes wouldn't focus. It just felt like the room was spinning. Even my thoughts. I didn't want to say anything or have any type of facial expression that would make Mr. Mike force me to run suicides or any other intensive workout. I looked up at Mr. Mike who was waiting to see if Gio and I would complain this time.

"Good, you're becoming disciplined," he said, walking towards the other side of the gym. I rolled my eyes. Gio and I walked side by side behind our coach. I looked around the gym as we walked to the other end. There were several banners hanging. Posters of other boxers and other African-American figures. I saw Barack Obama, the day he sworn into office. He was waving to a crowd with several cameras flashing in the background. There was a poster of Malcom X, Martin Luther King Jr., Muhammad Ali, Mike Tyson, and Floyd Mayweather. There were also a few posters of people I didn't know.

"I see you two are tired, beaten up. You look like you've gone through hell and back. I can see it in your eyes," he explained.

"Mr. Mike, you just made us run the New York Marathon. Of course we're tired," I said with an exhausted tone.

He shook his head. "I'm talking about before we started working out. I don't know you two, but I see myself in those eyes. Everyone has their struggle but look where you are. Life is a *war*, we're in a *war*. You're a fighter, you are fighting this *war*." He was putting emphasis on the word war. "In a war, there are several battles. You gotta learn which battles are worth fighting. Not every battle needs to be a knockout." He looked at me and Gio. Gio's head was down. "Hey, head up! In this city, in this society, country, even in this world. I promise you…you will be looked down upon. People will look down on you. Sometimes that's just how it's gonna be… especially being a young black male. You two got in trouble for fighting at school, I don't know why you were fighting but I do know everyone was expecting you to fight. You don't have to fight to be a man. It is very easy to get upset, everyone can get upset. But life isn't about fighting every struggle in your path, you boys got to learn how to pick your battles. Know how to fight these battles. You ain't gotta throw fists to win. If you were to fight someone right now, I bet you any money…you gonna lose. Why? Cause you're tired. But is it possible to win? Yes. How? Use what's up here." He pointed to his head. "Outsmart your opponent. It don't always gotta be fists, my guy! Use the knowledge you got stored up here. Your body is beaten up right now. You will get knocked down." He paused. "This is The Bronx, we're uptown. You get back up if you get knocked down. Kill them with success, baby!"

I gave Mr. Mike a head nod. "Alright!" I replied with a soft tone. "So what are we doing now?" I asked.

"Well, I'm gonna keep you guys for another hour, and then I'll catch y'all tomorrow since y'all don't have school." He smirked as he walked over to the sand bag hanging from the ceiling.

As Gio and I walked over to the sand bag, I heard a door slam shut. My neck rapidly forced me to look over in the direction of the noise. I watched a lady walk out of the women's change room. She was wearing long pink shorts with a black tank top. I looked at her complexion, she was light-skinned, but it wasn't the usual light skin. She couldn't have had any European, or white descent in her. She had two long French braids starting from the top of her head, ending up at the middle of her back. Looking at her body I could tell she was very fit, like she's been doing the boxing thing for awhile. She had those long black shoes that had the laces going above her ankle almost to the middle of her shins. I couldn't take my eyes off her. Dangling from her neck were her black boxing gloves. Each glove had one pink rose. *The pink rose,* I thought. She was the one-in-a-million girl. *The rose that grew from concrete.* She began to walk over to the three of us.

"Hey, Unc!" she said smiling. Her smile was contagious. I began to smile a bit too. "I'm gonna train a bit before I go home."

"Yeah… no problem, baby girl," He smiled back at her.

As I continued to stare at the girl, Giovanni lightly hit me at the back of my head. "You're better than this, Calv," He spoke sarcastically, smiling after he said those words. I shook my head.

"Alright boys. Fist up! Show me how you protect your headquarters." He was referring to our heads. "You hold all the information to success in there." He corrected our stances, making sure our left foot was further forward than our right foot, depending on which hand was dominant. "If you're right-handed the left side of your body should be closer to your opponent." After he corrected our stances and spacing, he told Gio to hold the punching bag while I struck it. "Calvin, we're gonna start off slow and once you get the idea you can start going faster. The faster you move the smarter you gotta be. Hit quick but disciplined!" I nodded at him. "Okay show me your stance. Left jab! Left jab! Right hook! Right jab! Always guard your face! I wanna see your hands come right back up after every shot. Defence is the best offence. Your brain holds the blueprints to success! Keep in mind, all the knowledge you hold is in there! Don't let anyone knock it out!" He was yelling these words. It only made me punch harder.

I began throwing the combination of punches he asked from me. Throwing at an aggressive rate, I could tell Mr. Mike was a bit upset or shocked, I guess it was a mix of both. I could hear him giving me commands, "Breathe, Calvin! Exhale when you throw your fist. Don't forget to protect your face." Although, hitting this bag allowed me to express my anger. And I was angry, I was furious. I felt like all the bad things happening to me weren't karma. I thought bad things were just happening. Like I deserved it. I'd been through too much. I wasn't following the combinations anymore. I was just rapidly swinging. I zoned out thinking about everything that had happened in the last few months. "Don't put one hundred percent into a single hit, Calvin!"

Continuing to punch the bag I began to hear my name, "Calvin! Calvin! Calv – Stop!" I looked up to see Mr. Mike asking me to stop. "Calvin? Did you not hear me?"

I shook my head. "No?" I said softly.

"Go get a drink, I'll meet you over there." He looked over to the girl with the one-in-a-million gloves. "Baby girl! Come spar with this young man over here." The girl came running over as I walked to the water fountains on the other side of the gym.

After I had my water Mr. Mike called me into a separate room, I think it was his office. "Talk to me, Calvin. You got a lot of energy but no control." We were both standing up facing each other. I was looking down at my gloves while he spoke to me. The room was very small.

It barely fit a desk and a few trophy-filled shelves. "Calvin, when I look at you, I only see your mask. You got a tough guy mask on. You tryin' to scare everyone away! Talk to me. Not like a mentor, like a brother."

My eyes quickly focused on Mr. Mike. "I can't." I responded. "If I tell you what's on my mind… It'll make my fight real. Not for me… for you. If I tell people what I'm going through, I contribute to their stress. I've been held responsible for too much," I explained.

He stared at me, I knew he didn't know what to say. "Calvin. I don't think I could be anymore stressed out than I already am. There are things on my conscience that I can never get rid of."

"Like what?" I asked. "You release some stress and I'll follow your lead, Mr. Mike."

He took a deep breath. "Look at this." He unzipped the top of his tracksuit. He pulled down his undershirt from the neck hole. He showed me a scar that ran from his left collar bone, past his neck, almost to the back of his left ear. I never noticed it until now. I felt like it was the only thing I could see now. I looked up at him and kept a straight face as he continued to talk. "Don't drink and drive." He paused again. I could see it was hard for him. "You never think you'd turn into a monster until you're unleashed. Until it's too late to change. Involuntary Manslaughter, I killed three people. One child, and a pregnant woman in Long Island." My eyes widened. There was a connection to make, but Mr. Mike continued to talk. "Eight years, Calvin. Eight… years. For a mistake. I took away lives filled with unknown potential. Every day I wake up, I wish I had died in that crash along with them. But I didn't. So here I am… boxing. I'm trying to shape the young ones in this building into someone special. Make them show their potential. Someone that other young bulls can look up to. So every time I fight in that ring, I feel like I'm fighting for a change." I looked down at my gloves in disbelief. "I was the guy who bottled up all his emotions... then drank it. I scared everyone off, there was help, and I just ignored it. So now I have to live with that. Don't be like me, Calvin."

I'd been hearing those words a lot. Don't be like me. There were so many people not to be like, not a lot to look up to around here. "Sir, I... I just got done burying my brother almost a month ago." I shook my head and smiled in disbelief. "My Father been locked up my whole life, I don't remember what he looks like. I got suspended from school because I was fighting... a guy told me he'd make me end up like my brother. I didn't like that... there was only one thing to do." I got a bit upset thinking about what that boy said to me. "People say stuff that get me upset, I had to shut him up. Then a few of his boys jumped in, I was out numbered. That's when Gio came to help me, cause y'know... that's just what brothers do. He's my brother."

"Calvin, people say what they want. Let them talk, but why should you have to change your emotions to deal with them. You control your body. Don't give them the opportunity to control your thoughts, your actions, your emotions... you control your body. Nothing you don't have control over should be allowed to have a negative effect on you."

I nodded my head. "Facts, I understand." He grabbed the back of my head and lightly bumped my head against his.

"Life's got you against the ropes. Being in The Bronx, the system put you in the trenches. But you're gonna climb your way out!" He pushed me out of the office, "Come on, baby boy! Let's get this work in!"

I felt my eyes watering. I looked up as I walked out. I still didn't want to express any type of emotion. I was hoping the tears would fall back into my eyes. I came out to see Gio on the ground and the girl with the one-in-a-million gloves laughing over him. "You're tired already?"

"Come on, G! You're embarrassing us," I said while laughing a bit.

"Calv, you don't understand. She's a beast," he pleaded.

She looked up at me then smiled with teeth. "You wanna go one round in the ring?"

"I didn't come here to hurt anyone," I replied with a smirk on my face.

"Hurt anyone? You think you can take me? Alright…let's go! Helmet off, only body shots." She smiled and began to walk over to the ring.

"Where you going, I didn't agree to nothin'." I looked down at Gio after I spoke those words.

"My brother...You don't know what you got yourself into," Gio spoke looking up at me.

"Alright! Let's see it!" Mr. Mike yelled from the office doors.

"Sir! No, I didn't agree to nothin'!" I yelled back, I was going to listen to Gio after seeing him on the floor. I coughed twice. "I think I'm coming down with something, it's been a great day, but I think I'm going to head out now! Come on Gio!" I attempted to pull him up.

"You from The Bronx or something? Everyone in Harlem be saying that The Bronx is filled with children!" she said laughing.

I felt my facial expression change. I was sickened by her words. "Aw, hell naw!" Gio and I both stood up. "You ain't about to disrespect my set like that!" I walked over to ring and pulled myself up with the ropes. When I got in the ring, right away I knew I was in trouble. Her stance was intimidating. I slammed my fist together. "You got something to say about The Bronx?"

"I'm gonna let my fist talk for me," She said while smiling.

We tapped each other's gloves before we started sparring. She threw two quick jabs with her right hand. I jerked back in order to dodge the two shots. I could hear her exhale as she threw the punches. She smiled at me with teeth. Her smiled forced me to smile again. I examined her as we hopped around in the ring. She had light skin, a fair and clear tone. She had to be mixed with another background, she wasn't just African-American. I threw a right jab aiming for her right arm, she weaved out of the hit with ease, then gave me a left hook to my lower right ribs.

"Alright, Harlem! That's it," I spoke out of frustration.

"First to three, wins!" yelled Mr. Mike.

"Too easy, man! Are you afraid to hit a girl?" She said smiling.

I looked into her eyes, they were a greyish brown, I'd never seen such an attractive girl before and it was odd I was fighting her. I threw another right jab. I hit her on her left arm.

"Good hit!" she said. She was teasing me, I didn't appreciate that.

I laughed, putting my fist to my face, I tried to stay focused. I could hear Gio cheering me on in the back while Mr. Mike was mutual. She put her fist down to taunt me, shuffling side to side. I shook my head. I threw a left jab at her right shoulder, I put all my force into that shot. She dodged the jab, forcing me to stumble a bit after following through on that punch. She quickly gave me a right hook to the gut. I gasped for air, I was winded. I took a deep breath.

I didn't hesitate to start again. I was determined to win. I looked at her, she was still smiling. We tapped gloves again. This time she swung at me with her left fist. She went for my head with that shot. I bobbed my head avoiding a knockout. "Be careful, Harlem!" I said.

She laughed at me. I kept my hands close to my face. I was playing defense. She faked a shot to my right arm with her left fist. When I attempted to move out of the way for a blow that never came, she used her right fist to give me two jabs to my left shoulder. I was knocked backwards by the power in her fist. After she gave me another shot to the left side of my ribs.

"Ay! Chill, lady!"

"Ding! Ding! Ding!" yelled, Mr. Mike. "It was a good round! You did well Calvin, I didn't think you'd get her once," he said laughing.

I shook my head. "She got lucky! She made an illegal shot to my head! And she was hitting after the bell," I pleaded for my case.

Gio was laughing. "You were talking a lot of trash before the fight. What happened?" I laughed with him. I didn't have anything to say back to him. I took off my gloves with the help of Gio. I made my walk of shame with Gio, back to the change room to grab the rest of our stuff and leave.

There were benches on each wall. We sat across from each other trying to gain the strength to get changed. "I saw Xavier today. I needed quick money." I didn't exactly know how to explain to Gio that I had been selling drugs. We both had never been the type to use or sell drugs. "I moved some dope for him…"

Giovanni looked at me puzzled. "For Xavier? Are you serious?" He laughed a bit, like I was joking about the matter.

"Yeah… it's quick money." I reached into my bag. "Look." I pulled out the money I got from selling the narcotics. "I don't think I'll do this forever but right now I really need the money."

"Everyone needs the money, Calvin," He shook his head and gave me a dirty look.

"Yes, but you know my situation, man. It's hard right now and –" Gio cut me off before I could finish.

"Ain't this what your brother was doing?" he asked. I stayed silent and looked away. "This is how it starts, man," He chuckled. "You gave him advice, you gave him demands, you begged him…begged him to stop! Now look…you're doing the same thing."

"Gio…Look at the money… almost one grand in less than three hours. Besides, I'm not in a gang or anything."

"Okay, but this is where it starts… What's three hours to thirty years in prison?" he questioned me.

"You don't understand," I replied.

He raised his voice at me. "No, you don't understand, Calvin! You told Jace, not to sell drugs, not to be a thug and all that. You're so quick to give advice but slow to take your own! All that tells me is that you don't even take yourself seriously." He walked past me, brushing my shoulder on his way out. "You're a joke."

Gio left the change room before I could say anything else.

Chapter Ten: Spanish Harlem

When I got outside of the change room, Gio, Harlem, and Mr. Mike were standing beside Mr. Mike's office. "Do you need a ride home, baby girl?" Mr. Mike was asking his niece.

"Um...no, Uncle. It's all good, I'm gonna take the subway," she explained.

He nodded his head, "Gio?" Gio shook his head no. "Calvin?" he asked.

"Uh...I think I'm good," I responded.

"Okay, be here tomorrow at noon. Don't be late. Suicides." He left it at that as he walked into his office. Gio left the gym right after this.

Harlem and I walked out of the building together. "So am I gonna have to call you Harlem forever? Or do I get to call you by your real name?"

"I guess you deserve a reward after being able to throw down with me," she smiled again.

"Being able? Oh…you thought I was trying back there?" I said sarcastically. "No, ha-ha… I wanted to give you a chance," I continued.

"Oh… I see. I guess I got the wrong idea when you pounded your fists together and said 'that's it, Harlem!'" She nodded her head after speaking with a sarcastic tone.

"I don't appreciate that sarcastic tone. I think I put up a good fight," I smiled.

"Yeah, you did… for a beginner," Her smile never left.

I shook my head. "How far do you live from here?" I asked.

"I live about four or five blocks from here. Why?" she replied.

"Can I walk you home?" I asked, nervously.

"Why? You don't think I can protect myself?" She seemed offended.

"No it's not that." I was trying to think of something to say.

"Are you worried…do you think something might happen to me?"

With all the news about the serial killer and rapist, the number of females killed, I didn't want her to walk alone. Although, I did want to get to know her as well. "I'm not worried about what'll happen to you. I'm worried about the person who tries to hurt you," I explained. She laughed at my words. "They don't know what they're getting themselves into," I finished explaining.

"Alright, that's a good reason." We began walking. "My name is Aaliyah."

"Aaliyah, I like that. It's cute."

"Cute?" She punched my left shoulder. It was still sore from our spar.

"You're not good with words, huh? Keep your hands to yourself!" I started laughing.

She half-frowned and half-smiled. "Watch it, I was going easy on you."

"Yeah, yeah! How long have you been boxing?" I asked

"Like ten years, I would say." She shrugged her shoulders. "A long time… I'm not sure."

"That's a long time. I'm gonna call you if I ever get into a fight."

"Alright, I gotchu." She was looking at me. I looked down at her. She was about 5'7" or 5'8". "How old are you?"

"I'm seventeen, turning eighteen in the spring. And you?"

"I just turned nineteen."

"Oh, so you're done school?"

"Yeah, I'm still figuring out what I wanna do." She pointed her finger to the subway station. "I think your legs are a bit tired, your boy Gio told me all about the suicides y'all ran." She laughed. "My uncle can be a bit harsh."

We began walking in the direction of the subway station. "A bit harsh? I think he just wanted to see us suffer!" I said.

"He just wants to see people working hard and to the best of their ability." She spoke seriously.

"Fair enough," I replied.

We walked down the steps of the subway station to hear some screaming. The scream had to be coming from a man. It was deep-toned and sounded very aggressive. When we got to the bottom of the stairs, we stopped there. The man yelling was wearing all black. Though his clothing was ripped or torn in many places. The way he was walking and swinging his arms around I could tell he was either intoxicated or under the influence of some type of drug. I looked at Aaliyah, I could tell from her facial expression that she no longer wanted to take the subway.

He pointed at the wall. "Hey you! Where's my money, boy!" The drugged-out man had a hoodie on. His hood was up, I could only tell he was a black man when he turned around while throwing his arms through the air. Looking back down at Aaliyah, I could tell she was scared. I knew if it came down to it, she could protect herself, but she only would if she absolutely had to.

"Calvin, let's go." She whispered to me, after the druggy began asking for money. The man's behaviour was very unusual compared to other crackheads in New York City.

I didn't reply to what Aaliyah had said. I continued to watch the man pace around.

"Somebody better give me some answers!" His voice was raspy, like he had been yelling for a while.

Aaliyah grabbed my left forearm with her right hand. "Calvin…" her grip was tight.

"Ay, chill…don't worry…he won't do nothin'." I hoped I was right. Aaliyah seemed like a person who avoided all problems.

Drug-influenced people were nothing new in New York but this guy had a lot more energy. There were a few people in the subway station, about three others. We were in The Bronx, the side of the station we were on was going downtown towards Manhattan. We could see the other side of the station going uptown. There were over ten people on that side. They were staring at the wild man. The three people on our side consisted of an old man and two ladies. The old man walked closer to the train tracks avoiding the crazy man in black.

The druggy was yelling several curse words, he turned around to look at Aaliyah and me. From a good five yard distance he began to taunt us, "Pay up, bitch!" he demanded.

"I ain't owe you nothin'," I replied with a normal tone.

The crazy man started laughing uncontrollably. He was psychotic and that was obvious. His teeth were yellow and black like the song. And he was missing a few of them. He then started walking rapidly towards Aaliyah and me. At this moment, Aaliyah gripped my forearm tight, attempting to pull me. She was tugging me in the direction of the stairs so we could leave. I didn't let her move me.

I stepped in front of Aaliyah. The man came to my face, he was now very serious. So was I. "Where's the cash?" He asked. His breath was terrible. His skin was very dirty and dry. Looking at his hair under the hood, I could see it hadn't been combed or cut in some time.

Aaliyah's grip was still tight on my arm. Her nails were digging into my skin through my sweater. "I'm not giving you a dime," I finalized with a straight face.

The sound of a train in the background was coming to my ears as the man turned around and ran towards the train tracks. "I need my fucking money!" He screamed, as he ran with his arms swinging again. He shoved the old man who tried to avoid him onto the train tracks.

"No!" yelled Aaliyah.

"Shit!" I said while breaking free from Aaliyah's grip to run over.

As I ran towards the tracks, the crazy man ran past me and up the stairs. The old man was moaning in pain. Aaliyah was beside me now, both of us were kneeling down putting our hands out, begging the man to grab one of our hands. He was trying to stand up but he couldn't. I didn't know if he was falling in and out of consciousness, whether he had bumped his head, or if any other part of his body was injured. The people on the other side of the subway station going uptown began looking over. They were all in a panic, the other two ladies were crying aloud as well. "O'mah gawd!" A lot was going on but I had to focus. Adrenaline was running through my sore body and I wasn't taking in much besides what I was focused on.

"Sir! Come on! Please, grab my hand!" His eyes kind of rolled to the back of his head. "Sir! Sir! My man, come on! Please!" I was pleading with him.

"Mister! Please! You need to get up!" Aaliyah was yelling. The train was getting louder. I thought the man was about to die.

I stood up while Aaliyah tried to persuade him to get up. "I think I'm stuck," explained the old man.

As soon as I heard him say that I threw my backpack off to the side. I jumped off the ledge and onto the tracks.

"Wait! Calvin! What are you doing? There's a train coming!" I could hear the panic in Aaliyah's voice.

"Don't worry, just focus and we'll all be okay." I tried to keep my composure so I could remain focused. I attempted to pull the man up from the tracks but his body wouldn't let me. I noticed that his pants were caught on a screw on the tracks. The lights on the train were now pointed at me, I could see the train in the distance. I began tugging on the man's pants. "Come on!" I yelled. I looked over at the train to see it creating sparks against the tracks. I could see the conductor, I couldn't hear her but I knew she was screaming. She was waving her arms telling us to move out of the way. I was freaking out to the point where I couldn't keep my composure to slowly remove the man's pants from the screw. I pulled the pants as hard as I could, creating a large tear in the man's pants. I pulled him up to his feet. I was carrying all his weight as he was still a bit unconscious. When the old man was upright, Aaliyah was pulling the man from each bicep with each of her hands. I began pushing him up by bending down to wrap my arms around is legs and pushing upwards. I could feel the sweat dripping down my face. When the man was on the ledge the two other ladies came to help pull him away from the tracks.

Tears were flowing from Aaliyah's eyes. "Calvin, give me your hand!" Aaliyah cried out. I reached out with my right hand, and put my left hand onto the ledge. Aaliyah pulled me up with two hands and the subway sped past us only to slow down for the stop. Aaliyah pulled me in to hug her. The subway created a strong breeze that forced Aaliyah's braids to blow is the same direction the subway was traveling. "You crazy as hell!" her voice was muffled by my sweater, as she had her face buried in it during our hug. When we released from the hug, she had streams of tears going down her face. She hammered her fist into my chest about three times. "estúpido!" she repeated that word with every hit.

"I'm sorry, Harlem…don't cry." I could see how frightened she was, I was scared too. I was confused about why the conductor didn't slow the train down as soon as she saw what was happening.

"My heart is beating like crazy!" She slapped my left shoulder. "Calvin, I swear you gave me a heart attack!"

I wiped her tears, "I'm sorry. But you really gotta stop hitting me," I explained, as I could still feel the pain on my chest and shoulder.

We went over to check on the guy who was pushed onto the train tracks. Soon, the subway transit officials came to check on the situation along with two police officers.

Later, paramedics attended to the old man. The police officer asked us a lot of questions, mainly about the drugged-out man. Aaliyah, the two other ladies, and me summarized the story for the officer.

"You two are really brave and courageous. Believe it or not, some police officers wouldn't even do that."

"Oh, I believe it," I replied. He wasn't asking a question, but he needed to hear that.

His eyebrows dropped in discomfort. "Well, you two are heroes."

"Thank you, officer," said Aaliyah, she was looking at me as if I had been rude.

"Would you be able to give a description of what the man looked like?" asked the officer.

"No." I was the first to respond. I think I laughed a bit. "If I give you that man's description, you're just gonna go out and arrest the next brother you see. We're all the same to you peop—" Aaliyah cut me off before I finished getting my point across.

"Calvin! Can you just…walk away for a second?" She begged.

I looked over at the old man who was being put onto a stretcher. I spoke without giving eye contact. "I bet I fit the description. Huh, officer?" I walked over to him, he was fully conscious now. He stuck his hand out for a handshake. While we were shaking hands, he looked me in my eyes. "Thank you," he struggled to smile.

I nodded my head. "It was nothin'," I replied. He let go of my hand as the paramedics wheeled him into an elevator to take him to the street level.

After we finished answering what we could for the officer, Aaliyah and I decided to walk the rest of the way.

"I think this is the last time I'm gonna walk you home," I said sarcastically while smiling.

She didn't think it was funny. "Calvin, you could have died. You're crazy!"

"I'm okay, you're okay, and the man is gonna be okay...what's the problem, Harlem?"

"I'm still shaking! That's the problem!" She explained.

"I think I'm a lifesaver. I deserve the key to the city."

"Who you foolin'? I did most of the work!" She laughed saying this.

I looked at her surprised. "Wow...I can't believe you just said that. You're real cute, but lying ain't. You're just lying through your teeth," I smiled.

"Oh! That's how you're feeling? Watch your mouth before I knock out some teeth!"

"Try me!" I replied, while she laughed. "Are you gonna go to the gym tomorrow morning?"

"I'm not sure, actually. What's your number? How about I let you know tomorrow morning?" After she said this, I smiled in shock, staring at her. "Calvin..."

"Oh, uh here, put your number in my phone," I handed her my phone.

When we arrived to Aaliyah's apartment she gave me a hug. "Thank you for walking me home, crazy." She smiled, "You better stay off them tracks." She said in her thick Harlem accent.

"I'll be careful," I replied.

"You better, crazy boy. Don't forget to text me." She walked up the stairs to the apartment and I watched her walk up the whole way. When she got inside I began walking to the nearest subway station. I shook my head smiling as I walked away. I was catching feelings for that girl.

When I arrived home, my mom was in her bed. I entered her room to let her know I was home. "Hey ma, I'm home," I said while waving.

"Calvin..." As soon as she said my name I knew something wasn't right. "Sit down."

"S'wrong?" I spoke with a serious tone.

"Have you heard from K.C. or Jerem?"

"No," I replied.

"Ghana is in a civil war..." I could hear her voice crack in between her words. "K.C., Jerem, Uncle, and Auntie still haven't come back from Ghana yet. Uncle's brother said that some rebels stopped Auntie and they took her. They haven't heard from her since, and K.C., Jerem, and Uncle are nowhere to be found." I could see tears forming in her eyes.

It seemed like life was just tragedy after tragedy and the awkward moment between them. It was awkward because just when you thought things were getting better and you were starting to forget about the recent tragedy, another one exposed itself. I was tired of all the mourning. *Whatever happens, happens,* I thought.

"Have faith and leave it to God. He will see our prayers through." I spoke those words humbly as I really believed them. I knew my mom would too, having such confidence in her faith. I gave her a hug. "It's time for us to stop stressing, we've been through too much. God will handle this for us." I helped her wipe the tears from her eyes. I got up and I reached into my bag.

I pulled out $200 of the drug money. "I found a job where I help pack boxes and prepare them for shipping in Manhattan. The more boxes I pack, the more I get paid. This is what I got from working today." I put the money in her hands. "I promise I'll start helping with money."

"Hm. Calvin. Tell me, why were you fighting at school?" She waited for my explanation.

"It wasn't me who started it…A boy was talking bad about me…He put his hands on me. So I hit him back. I'm sorry mom, it won't happen again," I explained.

"Let this be the last time you fight at school. Hm, you want to be like your brother?" she said.

I closed my eyes and took a deep breath. *That's why I'm fighting.* I looked at my mom again. I shook my head, "No." I got up to leave her room. I hated being compared to my brother, especially now that he was dead. I'm nothing like him. I entered my room and dropped all my stuff. I hid the rest of the money. I got in my bed, only to stay sleepless through the night. I thought about Aaliyah, I wanted her to want me. I thought about if she would like me, if she really knew me. She didn't, I didn't want her to think of me as some drug dealer. I was selling drugs, but for some reason I didn't feel like that was my title when I looked at the man in the mirror. I closed my eyes.

"Calvin, come on. You really think I'd do that? Look, there's more to it." A man was talking to me, he had a deep, raspy voice. I couldn't make out his face, it had blood all over it. The voice was familiar.

"Jace?" I asked.

"It's time to give back to the people, Calv. Look at the bigger picture." I felt like the person was moving away from me. I stayed silent trying to figure out who the person was. "People aren't always gonna be what you make them out to be." He spoke with a New Yorker's accent. I tried to follow the person but the harder I tried, the further they got.

They were shining, "What happened to you?" There was no response, "Jace...Jace, please! Talk to me." I begged. "Talk to me!" I demanded in a scream.

I gasped, waking up from my sleep. I sat upright. The tank top I went to bed in was soaked with sweat. I could feel it dripping down my face. I took it off and threw it on the floor. I thought about the dream I just had. I wanted to believe it was Jace talking to me. I got up to sit on the side of my bed. I knew my mom always had these types of dreams where she'd see something and it would later come to pass. But this wasn't something that was going to happen. *It was advice.* I thought. The rest of my night was sleepless.

Chapter Eleven: Amerikkka's Most Wanted

After I left boxing practice, Gio still hadn't spoke to me. I stood outside the gym with Aaliyah. "You're walking me home again," she said.

"Wait…Are you asking me, or are you telling me?" I questioned.

"Okay, good! I'm glad you agree."

"How are you just gonna volunteer me like that? I gotta be in Highbridge soon!" She smiled and pulled me to walk with her. This time we didn't attempt to take the train, she told me that I didn't mix well with trains. I've only known her for two days but it didn't seem to bother her. She would link arms with me as we walked, or hold my hand.

"Have you ever talked to a girl from Harlem before?"

"No…just from The Bronx. Harlem girls are psycho, I hear."

"Rude! Y'all guys from The Bronx think you're all that!"

"Well I am…Are you psychotic?" I looked at her.

"No…" she was confused.

"Are you sure?"

"Sometimes Calvin, just sometimes…People aren't always what you make them out to be." When she finished her sentence, I froze, then I frowned. Those words reminded me of my dream the night before. She stopped too.

"Why'd you say that?" I asked. My voice got deeper when I was confused or upset.

"What's wrong?" She was concerned, I've never seen Aaliyah with so much distress in her eyes. I could tell she was worried. I continued walking.

"No," I put my head down. She stopped walking and stopped me from walking as well. I looked away from her. She grabbed my chin – this girl was really aggressive.

She pulled my chin to force me to look at her. "What'd I do?"

"Nothin'," I responded, emotionless.

"Then what's wrong?"

"Nothing!" I raised my voice this time.

"Calvin, tell me." *She's scared,* I thought to myself.

"Alright, how about I'll tell you the next time I see you." I was trying to avoid telling her.

"Okay. Close your eyes," I listened. "Take a very deep breath," she continued.

I sighed, "What is all this?" I said annoyed.

"Open your eyes," I saw her smiling in front of me.

"What?" I asked. I didn't know what I was waiting for.

"It's next time!" She continued to smile, which forced me to smile as well. "Tell me what's wrong?"

"Aaliyah. Give me time…please," I pleaded.

"Alright, fine! Tomorrow." She was persistent.

"What? How? Neither of us are going to the gym tomorrow," I explained.

"Doesn't mean we can't see each other. You know where I live," she clarified. I could tell she was into me. I didn't want her to think I was like any other guy.

When we reached Aaliyah's apartment in Harlem, I hugged her goodbye. When we broke from the hug, she looked at me, still holding onto me. "You better text me tomorrow. I don't wanna hear no excuses, talkin' bout, I can't I got work, I can't I'm busy." She smiled, then walked up her steps.

I sighed. "Aaliyah, I can't," I said softly.

She ignored what I said. "I'll see you tomorrow, crazy." I stood outside the apartment waiting until she was in. I then started towards the subway to go back to Highbridge. I was going to do some drop-offs for Xavier before I went home. I was going to make more than 500 from the drop-offs. As long as nothing goes wrong. I thought about what Xavier said the first time I made a run for him. *If everything goes well.* I was still convinced he set me up. However, my fear for a jail sentence or death wasn't as strong as my urge to provide for my mom.

When I got onto the train, I waited for the doors to close. I closed my eyes.

I tend to only see the wrong. Some may say I've lost a lot, but now I'm ready to make a sacrifice. A change is necessary in my life. Show me how.

I didn't know if I was praying or just spilling thoughts. I just needed to be heard. An announcer came on the speakers and spoke, "please stand clear of the closing doors." A bell went off and the doors on the subway cart closed.

A loud and powerful voice began to speak, "Hello, ladies and gentlemen!" *Oh boy,* I thought to myself. Not another dancer. "I am N.Y., The Social Poet! I am not looking for any donations, I am not begging for money, but if you would like to support me, donations are welcome. All I ask for is a thumbs up if you enjoy it, or a smile if you hear something you like. This poem…this poem is titled, 'Slaves.'" He took a deep breath and started his poem. He spoke about the past and how our present actions in the black community resemble what we were afraid of years ago. "Interesting how during slavery we were beaten with whips and bound by chains, but now we're driving whips and rockin' chains. You gotta know the past to change the future." I appreciated his poem. It was probably one of the only subway acts that I had truly respected. He was talented, I hope one day people will travel to hear him speak.

When I left Xavier's apartment, the black lady was standing in the hallway. She was staring at me. She was the one who told me to stop running around with Xavier. Before I started walking towards the elevator I stopped to stare at her too. "I got eyes too," I said.

"You just wait and see!" I didn't say anything. I had no idea what she was talking about. "Don't worry, they're coming. Mm, soon baby, soon! Serve and protect, I tell you!" I continued to walk, I assumed she was crazy, I didn't understand what she was trying to get at. I walked into the elevator, then left the building with the packages on me.

After I picked up the narcotics from Xavier, I had already made two drop-offs. I was on my way to the third and final drop off point. I was dealing to a few teens from Harlem, however, I was on my way to the West Bronx area. I had already made 400 dollars from the drugs I had sold, even with Xavier's cut. I looked around the city. I could smell sewer water, the gum on the sidewalk that had gone bad over the years looked like black connect-the-dots. There were a lot of people walking around. It was about three in the afternoon. *Broad daylight*, I thought. This couldn't be any worse.

I stood in an alleyway waiting for the clients to arrive. They took about twenty minutes to get to my location. They got to the middle of the alleyway where I was. The rest of the alley was to my left and the street was to my right. There were three boys standing in front of me.

"Let me see that gas," said the boy in the middle. He had dreaded hair with bleached tips, the length of his dreadlocks did not pass his chin. He was dark-skinned with a tattoo on his face. It was small writing in cursive. "Gas" was another way of saying weed. In my opinion, there were too many ways of referring to one drug. No matter what you call it, it does the same thing to your body. The boy on the right was looking at the boy in the middle, like he was their leader. He was also dark-skinned with short, curly, black hair. The boy on the left had light skin and he was wearing a black White Sox hat. The main colour the boys were wearing was blue.

"It's one ounce, my guy. You ain't needa see nothing. Money before the deal." He gave me a dirty look after I spoke these words.

"Let me see the gas or I ain't buying shit," he tried to scare me.

"I don't really like repeating myself, but you seem like a nice guy…Money before the deal," I finalized.

The guy in the middle walked up to get in my face. "Oh what, you think you bad?"

"I think…I want the money before the deal," I clarified, again.

The two other boys got up close to me as well.

"Oh…was I supposed to be scared? Y'all niggas don't scare me," I spoke with my chest up.

"You gonna end up a homicide talking like that." The boy on my right spoke these words.

I started to nod my head. This got my emotions to rise up in frustration. I was now speaking at the top of my lungs. "You scary right? You scary right? Show me! Show…me! Please! Make a move, make my day!" I could see someone at the beginning of the alleyway from the corner of my eyes, but I was too focused on the three boys to care about who it was. I needed to keep my guard up.

The boy in the middle took two steps back and reached into his pocket to pull out a knife. It was about five inches long. The boy on the right took a look at the boy holding the knife. I took one step back in attempt to gain power to punch him. I punched him directly on his left cheekbone. He stumbled back attempting to catch himself but his knees were not stable. He then fell to the concrete. "You scary right? I'm waiting, boy! I'm here! Show me!" I was beyond livid. The boy with the knife came at me. He wasn't trying to stab me in my body. He wasn't jabbing at me with the weapon. Instead he was hacking the knife at me, at my face. I knew what he was trying to do. He was

trying to slash my face. He wanted to leave his mark on my

body. To let people know he did that. I wasn't going to let

that happen. I wasn't going to wake up with a constant

reminder that a druggy from Harlem had his way with my

face. The other boy was now approaching me as I

continued to back up to avoid the slashing of the leader's

blade. His dreads swung around as he swung his blade

around. The light-skinned boy on the left tried to kick my

legs so I would fall to the ground. I dodged his first kick,

but the second time around I was seeing my way to the

ground. They began to kick me and I was blocking most of

them. I looked up to see the dreaded boy coming down at

me with the knife. I rolled to the side avoiding it. At this

point we we're at the back of the alleyway.

I was able to get onto my knees. I saw the guy who

was standing at the entrance of the alleyway, he was

already a few yards away from us. Already swinging his fists, Giovanni sucker punched the boy with the knife. The dreaded boy fell to the ground, I could hear the knife clanging against the cement as it tumbled away. It was now two against one. The boy began to run to the entrance of the alleyway. We chased him, I hacked at his legs with my right foot. He fell to the ground and we began to stomp on him. He began to yell in pain.

"Run your money!" yelled Gio. We were going to steal from these kids. We didn't change one bit.

I ran over to the boy with the dreads who was still passed out on the ground. I went through his pockets and I took out around 200 dollars. Gio had already got done taking the money from the other two boys.

We began walking to the front of the alleyway. "How'd you know I'd be here?" I asked. I didn't need to thank him. I would have done the same for him, whether we were mad at each other or not.

"I didn't, I was for real just walking by. You a lucky boy!" He looked at me and stuck his hand out for a handshake, I gave him one. He deserved it. We weren't the type to say apologies, the apologetic words were voiced through the handshakes. "I was coming from Bea's spot. She told me she wants me to be hers, my guy. She ended things with that guy we fought at school." He was smiling.

I could tell he was happy, "Okay! Say no more! You're in love – wait, you were at her spot?" I asked.

He nodded his head. "Yeah, why?"

"Did you and her…you know?"

He laughed, "My guy! Why you always askin' these kinda questions?"

I laughed too, "Nah, I'm just sayin' you, The Giovanni, don't just go over to a girl's house and not do nothing!" I explained.

"I do if we're just chillin'." He set the record straight.

"Well, I know you ain't goin' there to just chill. You out here gettin' girls left right and–" Before I could finish my statement I heard some police sirens go off. As we got to the front of the alleyway, a police car's screeching tires stopped beside us with its lights on. "Run!" I yelled.

Gio and I sprinted down the street as two police officers got out of the car to chase us. We turned right onto another street. We we're headed closer to my house. There was another police cruiser that cut us off. We turned into a different alleyway. I looked back to see four police officers following Gio and me. The adrenaline going through my body was unbearable. The only thing I was thinking was: *I'm not going to let my mother lose me.* There was a fence at the end of the alley. I gave Gio a boost to get over. I threw my bag over the fence for him to catch. I then began climbing it. The fence had barbed wire on the top of it. I had no choice but to get injured climbing the fence. Both of my hands gripped onto sharp pieces of metal at the top of the fence and I pulled myself over. I could hear myself breathing heavily, my heart was beating out of my chest. I landed on a puddle and water splashed everywhere as I made contact with the ground. Gio helped me up, and we started running again. We were getting to 173rd street. Near Paulo's shop. I cut the street corner to see the sign of the Deli.

"In here!" I ordered Gio. I opened the door to Paulo's shop and the chimes on the door began to play a rapid melody. We got into Paulo's shop and he was staring at us. "Paulo, please!" I yelled, while gasping for air. "The police are after us!" He continued to look at us. "Paulo, please...please help us." I tried to say this calmly. I stared at him directly in his eyes.

"Okay, okay!" He spoke with his thick accent. He bent down and opened up a part of his floor behind the cash register counter. "Hop over the counter!" He said, slapping his palm on the countertop. "In here!" Gio hopped over first and I followed. It was like a small bunker. You had to walk down a few steps to get in there. It was about ten by ten feet long. When he shut the door, it was completely dark in there. I was still huffing and puffing along with Gio. I heard the chimes go off.

"Good morning, police!" said Paulo. "Anything, half price! Policia discount!

"It's the evening," clarified the officer in a deep voice. "We're looking for two African-American boys who are running through the area, have you seen anything?"

"My English, no good! No hablo ingles!" explained Paulo. He was covering for us the best way he could. Pretending he couldn't speak English, which he barely could.

"I see nobody! Two hours, nobody here." He continued to speak.

"Okay, thank you," said the officer. "Call 9-1-1 if you see anything!" The door chimed again. Gio and I stayed put, and stayed silent for another 20 minutes. *Thank you, Paulo,* I thanked him in my mind.

"Calv, you gotta stop playin' with the drug game. It ain't gonna get you nowhere but situations like these. Man, we've been through too much to be locked up for nothing."

"You ain't gotta say nothin' else. I hear you, G."

"I don't gotta say this, but you needa hear this. You talk 'bout how you wanna do better for ya'mom. You know better why you ain't doing better." My eyes were focused in the dark now. I could see Gio looking at me. "Calv man, I could never understand the pain your mom went through, but think about how much more it would be if you were to lose your life today or get locked up. She's trying to get over the pain. Why do you wanna prolong it?" He shook his head. "We said we wouldn't go down this road. We were gonna correct the mistakes of the people before us. Rewrite history, not repeat it. If you continue down this path…you ain't nothing but a sellout."

"I ain't no sellout, I'mma do better. I give you my word, G. No more words, all actions. From here on out."

We got out of Paulo's mini bunker. I climbed out first, grabbing onto a hand Paulo held out. I then did the same for Gio. I could see on his face that he was still in his feelings about me selling drugs. He didn't believe in me. I reached into my bag as I looked over to Paulo, he was upset too. He started speaking in Portuguese, they weren't nice words, I could tell that much.

"Paulo…Paulo, listen!" He stopped talking so I could get some words in. "I'm sorry about that, I made a few mistakes, I thank you for protecting us." I spoke slowly so he could understand perfectly. "I've been causing a lot of trouble to a lot of people lately, I didn't mean to bring any trouble to you. I know you're a good man because you showed me that today, you mean a lot to me, and I don't think I could ever repay you. But I'm going to start trying today." I took off my bag to reach into it, I pulled out two hundred in cash to hand to Paulo. I felt like I owed him that. At the least.

Paulo pointed to the newspaper on his countertop as he counted the cash. "It's eight now, Calvin."

"Eight girls, Paulo? I can't even think about that right now." I shook my head.

"Someone needs to stop him. He won't stop on his own!" Paulo was clearly upset. His face was red and his voice was raised.

"I'm going to talk to you later, Paulo. You gotta pray, my guy." I turned to the door to walk out with Gio. The chimes played a jingle one more time as Giovanni and I left the store. "I gotta go to Xavier's house one last time, just to drop off the stuff. Then I'm done…for good."

"Alright, I'm coming with you," Gio explained.

I knew Gio was a ride or die type of person. There was no way I could have convinced him not to come. I sighed. "Okay, let's get this over with."

As we walked, he spoke to me about Bea, I could tell he wanted a future with her. She wasn't an ordinary type of girl to him. "I know it sounds wild coming from me, but bro, I ain't ever thought I'd settle down…actually not even that. I just never thought I'd meet a girl who'd make me want to settle down. What I'm about to say to you Calv…it's madness." He smiled a bit, while shaking his head.

"Lemme hear this," I responded curiously.

"She's the one," he spoke with a serious tone. I refused to question it, I believed him.

"I'll start the speech," I replied.

"What speech?"

"I'mma be the best man, right?"

He nodded and smiled, "It's only a matter of time." He looked at me, I could see it from the corner of my eye as we walked. "What about you and Aaliyah?"

I wasn't sure about what he was referring to, I hadn't told him anything about her. I started talking to her when Gio stopped talking to me. "What about her?"

"Stop playing, y'all are talking. I could tell…I saw it in her eyes when I left the gym the other day," he explained.

"My guy, I for real just met this girl a minute ago. I know she wants me, but I –"

"So do I." Gio cut me off.

"What?"

"I know she wants you too," Gio clarified.

"You said that already…" I spoke with a confused tone.

"No I didn't…She did," he clarified once again.

"Word?" I needed confirmation.

"I swear. And… so what you just met her, you can't get to know her?" he questioned.

I paused for a second. "I never seen you talk to her."

"I never knew you were a drug dealer," he said in a quick manner.

He had a point. I shook my head. "Well I'm done now, and so is that thing with Aaliyah."

"Didn't I say stop playing? Calv, why is it so hard for you to appreciate the good things in your life?"

Everyone always felt like they had to give me advice, like they knew exactly what I was going through. I raised my voice a bit. "You know why! Gio! My guy! All the good things leave." I settled down again. "Always. They always leave. I'd rather not have the good things."

Gio stopped me, stretching his arm out and putting his palm against my chest. "This time you got the choice to let the good thing stay. Could you really push away a force stronger than you?" He spoke these words looking at me but I never looked back at him. I began to walk again, I looked back to give Gio a shocked but impressed face. I didn't want to answer the question.

"It's here." We entered the building after someone walked out of the doors. We walked through the lobby to the elevator. I pressed the number four. We stayed quiet in the elevator, it dinged when it got to our requested floor. We walked out. I knocked on Xavier's door. There was no answer. "Fuck," I muttered under my breath. I knocked a second time, this time harder than the first.

"You don't have a key?" Gio asked.

"If I had a key, we wouldn't be standing here right now," I explained. I heard a door in the hallway creep open. I knelt down to look for a key under the doormat.

"Calv, ain't nothing gonna be there. What dumbass drug dealer leaves a key under his mat?"

I heard someone kiss their teeth in the background. I looked down the hall to see the old black lady again. "Mhm, mhm, mhm!"

"Shut up!" I said, just loud enough for the woman to hear. I was tired of her. I stood up and reached above the doorframe to see if there was a spare key up there.

"Calv, chill… do you know when he's coming back? Cause… we ain't gonna find no key out here." A door slammed shut.

I felt cold metal. "Got it!" I smiled, picking up the key with my thumb and index finger.

"What? Oh my God. He's an idiot." Gio said as I began opening the door.

When the door swung open we both walked in, keeping our shoes on. I dropped the rest of the drugs on the table. I started looking around. "Calv, look at this man's sneaker collection." He had about fifteen pairs of shoes on a rack beside the entrance. I wasn't entertained by that. I took a left into a small hallway were there were four more doors. One on the left side, two on the right and one straight ahead. I looked into one on my right, there was nothing but a couch in there. Straight ahead was a washroom. I walked a bit further where there was Xavier's room, the second door on the right. I slowly turned the doorknob, I wasn't sure what I was about to see. I swung the door open quickly. The room had no one in it. It smelled like weed in there, it was still a bit smoky. There was a bed, TV, dresser and a large window. I walked into the room. I was about to walk out, then I saw his closet. I walked over to it. I slid open the door. He had a lot of hoodies and jackets, along with more shoes. I looked at a pair of red Nike shoes. There was a blue face sticking out of them. I knelt down. He kept his money in shoes. I started pulling the cash out. All of the notes were one hundred dollar bills. I started pocketing the money. I wasn't thinking about the repercussions of my actions, I was planning on making my means be justified by the end goal. I stashed away about ten grand. Xavier was going to notice but I wasn't scared. Gio entered the room, he saw me pocketing the money.

"Say no more." Gio took a few bills too. We got up to leave the apartment. Gio left the room, but I walked over to Xavier's bed. I felt in between Xavier's mattresses. People always kept stuff between their mattresses. I felt nothing on the side facing the closet. I went to feel the other side of the mattress. I felt cold metal again. But it was heavy, I pulled out a gun from in between the mattresses. I looked at it. I shook my head. I thought to myself. *One of these killed my brother.* The metal was so cold. I shook my head and threw the gun into my bag. I was still high on adrenaline. I walked out of Xavier's room closing the door behind me. We'd been there for about 20 minutes. I put my bag on properly and I walked towards the apartment entrance with Gio to leave. I reached for the door knob to hear loud knocks. I paused before I said anything. I pulled my hand back from the door.

A yell came from the other side of the door. "New York Police Department! Open up!" My eyes widened, I sharply and viciously looked at Gio. I was scared, the thought *don't let mom lose you*, came rushing back into my head. Gio and I slowly walked backwards towards the living room area. The officer repeated his words. "Police! Open up!" I knew there wasn't just one of them. It was a raid. I was looking around trying to think. Gio was pacing, he placed his hands on his head. He was in a panic, and so was I. The look on his face was more anger then worry, he was mad that I put him in this situation. There was so much to lose in that moment. I couldn't think straight. I knew this apartment was infested with drugs and we were automatically the ones to blame. I felt the adrenaline burst into my body. I looked behind me to see the balcony of Xavier's apartment. I signaled Gio with my hand, waving him to come. I slowly slid open the door to enter the balcony. We both got onto the balcony, the wind was blowing and we were four stories high. It was cold, but I could see sweat forming on Gio's forehead. As I closed the door behind us, I heard the police counting down from five.

He was speaking with a whispering yell, "Fuck, Calvin! This is why we don't fuck around with drugs! Why the fuck am I here right now! Why the fuck are we here?" Gio was panicking. "What the fuck! Come on think! How we getting out?"

I started climbing over the railing of the balcony, there was only a small gap between the apartments' balconies. "Come on! We don't have a fucking choice! You know what…actually, by all means stay here for the cops.

Mr. Freeze." We weren't in trouble until we got caught. And neither of us planned on getting caught.

Gio looked over the edge of the balcony, I knew he was beyond nervous. "Fuck you, Calvin!" He began climbing over the railing. He followed me onto Xavier's neighbour's balcony.

We hopped about six balconies. I was breathing heavy, my heart was beating out of my chest. We reached the last balcony on the fourth floor. "We need to go down."

"Okay, hold up! I never signed up for this shit!" Gio begged.

"Gio, come on! I'm not gonna let them get you…or me! Don't I always have your back?"

Gio sighed. "God look out for me." Gio hopped onto the outside of the balcony's rail. His back was towards a small park while he was facing the building.

I held his hand as he went down. He was now hanging from just my hand. I was leaning over the edge. "Put your feet on the next balcony." He was swaying and it only put more pressure on my arm. My ribs were being dug into by the railing of the balcony. I groaned in pain. "Gio! Put your feet on the next railing!" I yelled at him.

"I can't reach it! Lean a little lower," he pleaded.

"I can't! Bro you're palms are too damn sweaty." He was slipping from my hand, I didn't want to worry him. "Giovanni, reach for the railing with your fucking feet!" I was losing grip on his hand.

"Calv, I can't! Bro hold tighter! I'm fucking slipping," Gio was screaming at me. "Calvin! Pull me up." I looked into Giovanni's eyes. He feared for his life in this moment. I didn't want his blood on my hands, just like how I felt like my brother's blood was already on them.

"Gio, put your feet on the fucking railing!" I demanded in a scream.

"For the millionth time! I can't fucking reach – pull me the fuck up!" Gio was terrified.

"Gio, I'm sorry." I swayed Gio away from the building, his body began swinging. As he swayed back to the building, I tried to let go of him. His upper body collided into the balcony I was still on.

"What the fuck! Why the fuck you tryna let go? Calvin, you're my boy! Don't do this!" I could hear the fear in his voice.

I swayed him away from the building again, this time he got more speed. "Trust me, Gio!" I yelled.

"No!" Gio held that word in a scream as he swung back to the balcony below me. He let go of my hand, falling onto the balcony. I heard a thud but I couldn't see him. There was a silent pause.

"Gio?" I asked as I watched the sweat from my nose drip and fall to the park below.

"Fuck you, Calvin! You fucking crazy ass nigga. I hate you! You tried to fucking kill me." I could hear Gio hyperventilating. "This is why I don't mess with drugs! That shit ain't no good! Fuck you! Fuck them drugs! Fuck Xavier! Fuck all that!"

"Save it for later!" I hopped over the railing of the balcony, holding onto the rail. The wind was blowing and sweat was rolling down my face. "I'm gonna jump. Make sure you got my back." I was scared, but I feared getting caught more. I took a deep breath. "Giovanni. Make sure you got my back." I heard the door from Xavier's balcony slide open. I looked to my right. I saw a police officer step out. I let go, falling one floor my biceps slammed onto the railing of the balcony on the third floor. I struggled to hold on but Gio helped pulled me over. I was struggling to breathe. "Oh fuck! Thank you."

We banged on the glass door of the apartment. A female, shocked but worried, opened the door for us. "Thank you, thank you! We're leaving don't worry, and please don't tell nobody either." I pulled a one hundred dollar bill from my pocket and handed it to her as I walked through her apartment. There was a baby on the floor. He had a pacifier in his mouth. We got to her front door in a hurry. I opened it to leave with Gio. We got into the hall and ran to the stairs of the building, skipping steps on the way down, we quickly got to the main floor. We began walking to act calm, there weren't police officers in the lobby but we saw cop cars at the front of the building. Gio and I walked towards a side door. Exiting the building we walked down a side street, both of us were out of breath but we continued running for about four blocks. I know Gio was beyond mad at me. We stopped running when we got into a subway tunnel.

"You're a real one." I stuck my hand out for a handshake. He quickly gave me one.

"Calvin." He said still catching his breath, "you know I'm afraid of heights!"

"When you get home, tell your mom about this. You'll be grounded," I responded.

Gio gave me a dirty look and we continued walking. "Who do you think called the police?"

That was a good question. "It was definitely the old black lady in the hallway. She's been there every time I went to Xavier's."

"Madness. It be your own people," Gio explained.

"Trust me," I replied. Then I thought to myself, *why wasn't Xavier home? Why did the police show up?* I shook away the negative thoughts. "We shouldn't go home yet. The block is hot."

"Mad hot," he repeated what I said to put emphasis on it. "Go see Aaliyah," he told me. "You need to talk to her."

"Nah, I'll see her tomorrow. I'm gonna go somewhere else. Maybe downtown," I explained.

"Alright, then I'mma go see Bea. Let me know when you're going home. Stay outta trouble, brother. We got too much to live for," Gio said to me. He gave me another handshake and walked away.

"I feel that. I gotchu," I responded.

"Avoid them uniforms," Gio said from a distance.

He was right, in this moment I felt like we were the most wanted men in America. As if I was a person of interest. I knew people wanted to see me. It was just for all the wrong reasons.

Chapter Twelve: Evidence

I got off the subway, I began my walk. I was close to the water, it was colder over here. I could see the lamp posts start turning on, the sun was almost done setting. It wasn't that late but the sunset was earlier in the winter. I saw a sign: "Battery Park", I read. I saw a shopping cart squeaking as it rolled through the park in the distance. "Cornelius," I called the man. He looked over at me. He didn't seem to know who I was.

I walked closer to him, we were not four yards apart and he started smiling. I saw a picture frame in the grocery cart he had. I thought to myself, *it's time to give back to the people, Calv. Look at the bigger picture.* "How you been, my guy?"

Cornelius looked at me. He spoke with his raspy voice, "I've been trying." He seemed to be losing hope.

"What happened to all the prophetically words, Corny? Can I call you that? Corny?"

"First of all…you didn't use the word correctly. And no," he explained.

"Cornelius. I need your wisdom right now! Don't lose hope! I lose when you lose." He stayed silent. "You know…when I first met you, you knew I was going through something. I just didn't want to tell you what it was. I'm struggling Cornelius." I shook my head, "The day I met you, I just got done burying my brother. Your words saved me, Cornelius. I'm here now, I wanna save someone too. But I don't have the words. I don't have the ability. But I have the intentions."

His eyes focused on me. "I'm sorry…about your brother. That will always be a hard thing to go through," he sighed.

"It's fine." I expected more from him. Everyone has said that to me already.

"You know what a teeter totter is?" Cornelius asked.

"Yes."

"When you were down, I was up. I gave you some of my stored away wisdom to lift you back up." We stood looking at each other. His jacket had holes in it and his cart was filled with random stuff but I couldn't help looking at the picture frame. It had a picture of him with a woman. I couldn't help but think it was his wife. Cornelius looked really young in the picture. His hair was short, brushed and well-maintained. I looked at him now, he was stressed. It showed. His hair was now long and dreaded. It'd been several years since that photo was taken. "According to our mindsets, I was high up, on a pedestal. You were down, below ground level. I stepped off my pedestal to help you.

Now this isn't about me, but that's what you gotta be willing to do. You're a good kid. But sometimes, you gotta put yourself down to pick others up. You're not down right now. I know you're not. I can see determination in your eyes. I can see intent. You're just being held back. Now, you're strong, but that force is stronger." This was the Cornelius I knew.

"Cornelius, it was fate. You lifted me back up, you made the playing fields even. I know I've been held back, and so have you. It's my turn to do the same…I'm trying to make the playing field even. " I pulled out cash, I counted about three thousand dollars. "Now I know you're gonna say, 'I can't take this money, Calvin', I know you're gonna ask me how I got it. I'm telling you now I earned this money and you will take this money. Please find yourself a place. I'm not asking you, I'm telling you. You deserve more." I put the money into his hand.

He looked at me with a shocked face. "Calvin," tears formed in his eyes. "Wow, I don't even know what to say. This must be a dream." He broke down into tears, I grabbed him and pulled him in for a hug. He was about my height, just a little shorter. He smelled, so did his hair. But I ignored the stench. I broke from the hug.

"Come on, my guy. Get yourself a haircut, take a shower, and buy some clothes. Actually you know what..." I reached into my pocket and pulled out three more hundred dollar bills. "Use the three grand for first and last rent. You got a month to find a new job, or go ask for your old job back. This three hundred is for your fresh fade, that's what's in style right now. Groceries, transportation and whatever you need. I know it's not much, but I believe you'll get back on your feet, Cornelius. Don't prove me wrong. I don't wanna see you back here next week. I want to see you back on that pedestal."

"Calvin, you're a hero. Thank you. I really am sorry about your brother. I know he had a good brother while he was here," he smiled and chuckled a bit, it was cold enough for me to see his breath.

I nodded my head, "Take care of yourself, Corny." I turned around and went down the walkway again. Christmas had pass but I was still giving gifts.

I was back on the train, I heard the screeching sound of the cart against the tracks. I was thinking about seeing Aaliyah tomorrow. I was thinking about what to say to her. How I needed to tell her everything. I didn't want to hide anything from her, I had a connection with her. I never thought anyone in my life would take time to actually look into my life. I have the opportunity to hold on to someone special, I should. I thought about what Gio said, whether I was capable of pushing a force stronger than me. He told me he spoke to Aaliyah. I wanted to know what he said, and what she said to him. Cornelius said the exact same thing as Gio, talking about holding me back. I pulled my phone out to text Gio. I told him I was going home. I wanted to rest. I put my head down, I was waiting to get back uptown.

I walked up the stairs to my apartment, I walked into the kitchen to see my mom was getting ready to go out. "Ma, where you headed?"

She gave me a dirty look. "You're asking me? Where have you been? You don't tell no one nothing!" She grabbed her keys off the kitchen table. "I got called into work, I'll probably be there overnight, maybe a little longer." I didn't look at her when she spoke. I followed her hands, with my eyes, to her keys on the table. I noticed my brother's hat beside her keys.

I looked back up at my mom. "How'd that get here?" I demanded.

"Xavier brought it! I don't understand why that boy still comes over here. He's brought nothing but trouble." My mom continued to say a couple of insults in Twi.

"Mom, this doesn't make sense. How did he get it?" I was confused.

"Ah, I'm late! I can't be here for your interview!" she walked past me.

"Hold up," I said.

"Hold up, who?" She cussed again in Twi. "You don't want to respect, eh?"

I pulled out about one thousand dollars from my pocket. "This is from work," I looked at her.

"Work? This much for how many days?" She looked confused. I knew she didn't believe the work thing.

"I told you, I work off commission, it's a man's job. The more boxes I pack the more money I get. You raised a strong boy, these muscles aren't here for nothing." I tried to smile.

"Kwasia, give me the money."

"You calling me foolish after I give you money?" I said these words to her back as she walked towards the stairs. Sometimes I feel like she forgets that I speak Twi too. She wanted to raise me as Ghanaian as possible. I felt like all Ghanaian mothers are gold diggers.

She laughed a bit. "Thank you, I'm going. See you soon."

"Be careful out there, madam," I said as she walked down the stairs of the apartment. I heard the door shut and I snatched my brother's hat. Xavier lied to my face. How could he have Jace's hat? At the funeral he told me he wasn't there when Jace was killed and how he didn't see him that day. It's bullshit. I saw my brother walk out of the apartment for the last time. He had the hat on. Hundreds of thoughts ran through my mind as I walked to my room. I sat on my bed. I felt like I hadn't been here for so long. I replayed that night over and over. I got angry. I don't know if it was because of myself, Jace for even hanging out with Xavier, or just furious with Xavier. I took a deep breath. I was angry.

I heard a loud knock on the door. I ran down the stairs to look through the peephole. It was police officers. I didn't know why they were here. I hoped it wasn't for me. "Who is it?" I asked.

"NYPD."

"What do y'all want?" I asked again.

"We are dropping something off. Please open the door." I unlocked the door and opened it slowly. I was nervous, I knew they could tell. "How are you today? Calvin, right?" It was the same officers that came to close the case on Jace's murder earlier this month.

"Yeah, I'm good," I explained.

"Is your mother home?" They asked.

"Nah, she just left to work."

"What's that?" I pointed at a large clear plastic bag. It had a bit of writing on it but I couldn't make it out.

"Evidence bag. Here." I grabbed the bag from the officer. "Once again, I'm sorry for your loss." They began to turn around.

"Officers, wait. I need your help." I looked at the bag in my hand. "You know everything about the case right? Except for who did it?" The officers looked at each other. "I wanna know…I deserve to know. What type of gun was used to take my brother's life? That's all I wanna know."

"We can't reveal that type of infor–" I cut the one officer off.

"I need to know," I said with a serious tone.

The same officer inhaled then exhaled. "It's just confidential. I could lose my job. Calvin, I'm sorry."

"You know…I've been hearing those words a lot, along with 'If there's anything I can do for you, and I mean anything, please do not hesitate.' Well this is me calling in my favour. What weapon killed my brother? You mean anything right?" I said with a mocking tone.

The second officer sighed. He put the back of his hand against the chest of his partner. "Okay, the weapon used to kill Jace was a CZ 85 Combat. It's not really heavy-duty, it's a common gun. We shouldn't really be telling you this but you said you needed to know."

"Not really heavy duty? It managed to kill my brother, officer. Please use your words wisely. Thanks for the bag." I lifted up the bag to show them. "I'll cherish what's left of him. Thanks…for nothing." I closed the door. I walked up the stairs already ripping the bag open. I threw a pair of jeans, his shirt, and bandana onto the kitchen table. I was looking for his hat, another hat. It didn't add up. Why did he not have his hat when the police found him? Why did it end up with Xavier?

I grabbed my brother's hat to study it. There was no blood, dirt, or creases in it. I put it on my dresser. I looked at it with disbelief, "Fuck!" I yelled.

Chapter Thirteen: Show Me

I woke up in the afternoon, sweating. I looked at my phone, Aaliyah had texted me. "Are we still chillin' today?"

I responded, 'yeah, I'mma be there in like an hour or two.'

I didn't really sleep much or well, ever since my brother died. I fell asleep around 5 a.m. It was now 12 p.m. I woke up several times throughout the night. I got out of bed and walked to the washroom to get into the shower. I let the water run for a bit, waiting for it to get warm. It never did. It was going to be a cold shower. As often as this has happened to me, to my family, I could never get used to it. I shivered as I scrubbed my body as fast as I could to get out of the cold shower. *I gave mom over a grand, how could she not pay the hydro?* I questioned. I went to my room again and got dressed. I was ready to leave but I started staring at my brother's hat again. I questioned whether I should wear it. *No, not today,* I thought. I left the apartment.

As I arrived to Aaliyah's place I texted her to come out, to my understanding she had a strict mother. She hopped down the stairs of the apartment, she was really giddy. I couldn't help but smile. It was snowing a bit, it was the calm type of flurries that floated to the ground gently.

"How you doing?" I asked her.

She jumped into my arms, "You crazy boy, I'm good! How you doing?"

"I'm fine," I said, it wasn't convincing at all. I knew she was going to question that.

We released from the hug, "It's next time now! Like actually! What's bothering you?" She smiled. She wanted to know everything about me, so soon.

"Aaliyah, I don't kn–"

She didn't let me finish my sentence. "You never call me Aaliyah...For real talk to me, don't bottle your problems up. I'm a boxer, I'll knock them outta you." She put her fist up.

"You're way too aggressive, even when you're not trying to be." I shook my head while I laughed. "What did you and Gio talk about?" I looked at her as we started to walk.

"He told me he knows you and he knows you bottle stuff up. He knows when you like something or someone." She stopped herself.

"That's it? Nah, there's more to it. What did you say?"

"I said you were crazy."

"Very funny," I said. We walked by a deli, it had a patio but it was closed. She sat there anyways. I went in to buy us hot chocolates. I came back out and put one on the table for her.

"Thank you," she said while smiling. "Okay tell me, why are you holding back so much on me. You know I care about you."

I sat across from her. "I know, I know. I just don't want my problems to be yours." I looked away from her, towards the street. She pulled my chin back to face her again. I looked her in her eyes. "I don't want you stressing over my problems."

"But I don't think that's your decision to make, I wanna decide whether I wanna help you get past your problems. And I wanna. So please let me."

I looked away again, "Aaliyah…" I started people watching, I was absent-minded. She grabbed my chin once again, pulling it in line with hers. "Aaliyah," I grabbed her hand. "You gotta stop doing that!"

"I'm sorry, I just want your attention. Look at me. Tell me what is on your mind right now," She spoke with a concerned voice.

"My brother is dead," I said, looking into her eyes with a serious look on my face.

Her eyes widened, and her mouth opened in shock. "Calvin, I'm really, really, sorry to hear that."

"I know," I said because I've heard that every time I break the news.

"I don't know what that feels like." She shook her head. "I'm sorry, I'm here for you."

"But what does *that* mean? Cause a lot of people say they're here for me, but them being there won't change the fact that I'm going through it." I chuckled. "Aaliyah, I thank you for being here now, I really do appreciate that. I really don't want you to feel like I'm targeting you, but that doesn't mean nothing. Imagine, being woken up by a call from your mom. You pick up the phone to hear your mom yelling and crying. You know she's crying because you've heard her cry on many other occasions. You know how her voice gets when she's in tears." I was still looking into Aaliyah's eyes. Her greyish brown eyes shone they were filled with tears. I saw one tear slide down her face. I hesitated, but I continued. "'Calvin, she continues to cry, she's a mess. I need you to go to the morgue.' The what? 'The morgue.' I thought I was dreaming. 'They think it's Jace', she says. 'I need you to go and identify the body.' The only reason your mom isn't going is because she's in Philly on a work trip, taking care of people with intellectual disabilities, she couldn't come back, not right away. I didn't even shower. I put my clothes on, a jacket and put my shoes on. I didn't take the subway. I ran." I choked on my words. Aaliyah stood up to sit in the chair beside me. She grabbed one of my hands as I continued. "I ran. Four miles. Every step of the way I told myself it's not him. But why wouldn't it be? We hadn't seen him in about a week, especially with his history, I felt like I already knew it was him. I opened the door of the morgue. Three officers walked with me down a hallway to the body. They pulled back the sheet covering the face of the body. I looked at my brother. He was hurt. He had a bullet in his head. It was still in his head. I looked at my brother. He had dirt all over him. His clothes were wet. A ditch. A snow filled…muddy ditch is where they found my brother." I could feel the tears begin to form in my eyes. I chocked on my words, over and over. I never spoke these words out loud. "I don't wanna cry. I can't cry. Not for him. Everyone wants to say he's at peace, but how Aaliyah, he was shot in the head. Cold blood. How is he resting?" I shook my head and looked down. "I am crazy. I'm insane. He told me the night he left the house for the last time, 'If you don't want me to go out, then stop me.' I'll never forget those words...never, Aaliyah. Aaliyah, it's my fault. I promise you I could have stopped him. But I didn't, I stayed still. I could have stopped him...stop him. Jace... Jace." I sighed in disbelief. "I'm not sad, I'm mad, furious. All the evidence was dropped off at my house last night. My brother is gone and no one, not one single person is being held responsible. This is crazy. I'm losing it, I'm crazy." She grabbed me and pulled me in for a hug. Her arms were wrapped around my neck and head.

I closed my eyes as she hugged me, it was an attempt to force the tears back into my eyes. "Calvin, this isn't your fault. It could have happened any other way. It's not fair for you to take all the blame." She pulled back to look at me, wiping my tears before they came down.

"I'm trying to be better, Aaliyah. I'm just…I'm just crazy, like these Harlem girls." We both laughed a little bit. Her laugh was more of a pity laugh.

She looked me in the eyes. "I don't want you to think you're alone, all of that bottling your problems up, enough of that. It was different back then, I wasn't there then. But I'm here now. I don't plan on leaving," she said.

That was something I needed to hear, I felt like nothing in my life was permanent. "Thank you, Aaliyah."

"If it makes you feel any better, I told Gio I was crazy too…" She paused to focus on my eyes. I looked back into hers. Snow fell onto her long hair. She smiled at me. I looked down at her lips.

"I could have told you that." I explained, looking back up at her eyes.

"For you," she finished her sentence.

I leaned in to kiss her. Her lips were really soft, I never connected with anyone for a long time. This wasn't normal to me. We began to make out without focusing on who was walking by. I felt her hands on my face, she was really into it. For some reason I could feel so much, my senses were heightened. I felt like I could feel the indents of her fingerprint against my skin. Her fingers slowly drifted down to my chin to end the kiss. After we stopped kissing, our foreheads were still touching, we were holding hands and looking into each other's eyes. "I'm here for you," she said softly. I nodded my head.

We continued to talk about our lives, what we were into and more. She told me everything from her past relationships, how she never had anything serious before. She told me about her half-siblings. She hasn't met all of them but they were all older than her. She used to live in Brooklyn, but her mom didn't like it, she said there weren't enough Spanish people. I felt like I knew her now, I didn't think I needed to hold anything back from her or sugar coat anything for her.

"I gotta go." She stood up in a hurry. "I gotta do some stuff for my mom."

Already? I thought. "Okay, I'll walk you." I didn't want her to go. I didn't even finish my hot chocolate.

"Thank you, Calvin." She smiled at me. I got up and began walking with her. As we walked, she smoothly interlocked our fingers and we started to hold hands. It felt right. "You never told me about your dad." I looked at her, she was already looking at me. "You told me stories about your family, a lot of them included your mother…nothing about your pops." I don't think it would be a shock to her. A lot of fathers in New York were absent. Those that had the option to be around and stuck around, were the real ones. The one-in-a-millions, they were good people.

"My father is locked up. My moms tells me it's for a crime he ain't commit. But I haven't seen or spoken to him in almost a decade so...can't really be the judge," I explained.

"Oh. Same." She was still looking at me, I was looking straight ahead. "My dad is locked up too. I'm sure he committed the crime though."

"I'm sorry about that," I said.

"It's fine, it's not your fault." As we got to her house she gave me a hug, along with a kiss goodbye. I felt like I was re-learning how to express emotions. I watched her walk up the stairs to her apartment. She waved goodbye as she closed the door.

I stood there for another ten seconds collecting my thoughts. *Did that just happen? Aaliyah... how did you make me care?* I didn't want to care. I felt like caring led to losing. I turned around and grinned. I exhaled, then began my journey to Gio's house.

When I arrived outside his apartment, he yelled from his bedroom window. "What are you saying?"

"I just got done talking to Aaliyah," I said.

I could see him smiling from where I was. "Okay, playa! What're you tryna do now?" I shrugged my shoulders. "Downtown, Downtown?"

"My guy, can you just come down here?" I waited for Gio to leave his house. When he got down he dapped me up, we never needed to plan our appearances to each other's houses. Most of the time our visits were unannounced. "Aaliyah and I might be official…or at least getting there." Gio and I began walking to Paulo's.

"Okay so now we're both married men, huh?" He asked, rhetorically.

"I never had anyone look at me like that before, it was crazy, G. I really like her. I don't even know how to explain why, or how much." I smiled a bit thinking about it.

Gio patted my back. "Welcome, Calvin. We've been expecting you."

"Man, shut up!" I blurted out.

"Welcome to love, the everlasting emotion," he tried to say those words in a smooth jazzy voice.

"You need to not, it ain't even like that," I laughed.

"The more you deny, the more I say facts." He laughed too. "You don't even gotta know what's happening for it to happen, you just gotta let it happen." I didn't know what Gio was trying to say. When we got to Paulo's we both bought some snacks. "Paulo, you know I've been meaning to ask you something." I knew Gio was about to ask a stupid question.

"Talk to me…But no more favours! I don't want no more trouble from you two."

"You got some type of bomb shelter, bunker-type kidnaping shed down there…Why do you got that?" He laughed a bit.

Paulo laughed too. "Well you gotta be prepared for when immigration comes knocking!"

"You're crazy, Paulo!" Gio responded.

"We'll catch you later, Paulo." We left the store with our hands filled.

I closed the store door and we began walking down the block back to Gio's house when we heard tires screech. My head turned to pair the noise with an image. "Ay, there goes that nigga Calvin right there!" Gio and I watched three boys stick their heads out of car windows. The car was stopped in the middle of a one-way street, driving to my right. They all held firearms while the driver was focused on the getaway. Two of the boys were on our side and the third boy with a gun was behind the driver's seat, his arms were on the roof of the car. The boys began to open fire at Gio and me.

"Oh shit! Run!" I yelled. We began sprinting in the opposite direction than the car was facing. I was just ahead of Gio but the snow on the sidewalk caused me to slip and fall. Gio tripped over me, "Get down!" I yelled, again. Gio and I ducked, taking cover behind parallel parked cars on the side street, dropping all the stuff we had just purchased. I tightly shut my eyes as I put my back against the parked car. People started screaming, running in all directions trying to avoid being involved in the one-way crossfire. The street population consisted of panicking fathers and mothers trying to shield their children from bullets, and other young adults and children avoiding bullet holes in their bodies. I felt like I was going insane waiting for the bullets to stop being sprayed. In these ends, gangbangers didn't shoot guns to injure people, they shot guns to kill people. Just like they did to my brother who I wasn't planning on ending up like. The glass from the shattering windows fell onto Gio and me. The pops from the guns attacked my ears.

"Fuck! Fuck! Fuck!" Gio screamed. The bullets continued to leave the handguns. I covered my head and balled my body up. Car alarms were going off. I just couldn't believe they were firing in broad daylight. The amount of witnesses that wouldn't say a word to police was probably everyone on the street.

The guns finished shooting and we heard the guns click, meaning they were empty. The car tires screeched again and the boys in the car zoomed down the street. "Oh fuck!" Gio was patting all over his body, checking for bullet holes. "I'm good, you good Calv?"

I checked my body, if I did get shot I didn't feel it, especially with the boost of adrenaline. "Nah! I'm good, G!" We were both gasping for air trying to catch our breath. I was hyperventilating. "I know who those guys were," I yelled.

"Fuck those guys! They ain't shit!" Gio was still catching his breath. "Who was they?"

"One dude called you pretty boy and the other guy we robbed when he tried to stab me." I looked up into the sky, taking a deep breath, exhaling when I stood up. I helped Gio up. "This life ain't for me, man…Only got one to live. I'm lucky."

"We're lucky! My mom would kill me if I died." I don't think he was thinking straight. I wasn't. I was traumatized.

"Reach my house, we need to cool it for a bit." I suggested. The streets were empty now. Everyone had scattered in different directions.

"Yeah, I'm down." We took a detour to my house just in case those boys were following us.

Walking up the stairs to get to my apartment I yelled out to see if my mom was home, there was no response.

"She ain't here." I walked into my room and Gio followed. "Look at this bullshit!" I picked up my brother's hat and threw it at Gio.

"What's the problem? This is from the police's evidence?" Gio sounded confused.

"No. It's from Xavier. The same nigga who said that he ain't seen my brother the day he died," I explained.

"Yeah, but Calvin, they found your brother a week after he left your house, you don't know he could have seen Xavier any of the days before they foun–"

I cut him off. "No, G! The autopsy said that he was killed about a week before they found him! Something don't add up!"

"This is a crazy accusation, Calv." Gio seemed worried.

"Something ain't right," I finalized.

"You just gotta come with backup if you're gonna say this stuff out loud, my guy. I think this ain't for you to handle. If you got a problem, take it to the police. I know it's probably crazy for me to say that, but my guy, you're going through too much right now. You got a price on your head, you ain't officially outta the drug game yet, and feds are on you too! You got a girl to think about now. This just not something you should do…at least not on your own, feel me?"

"No…not really. My guy, the police gave up after three weeks. They was the ones who were supposed to be looking into this! They don't care about my feelings, they don't care that another brother died! How many times have we seen this? They kill our people, they don't care. They don't care my brother is gone. I ain't ever gonna see him again. No one is paying for that! Ain't no justice!" I had a serious tone in my voice.

"Calvin, you know I'm all for you, forever by your side, but this ain't the one man, this ain't the battle to fight. The system is broken, wait till it's fixed."

"The system isn't broken, it was built like this. They want us to lose. They could care less and I don't care that they don't care. If you want a job done well you gotta do it yourself right? Cause every time I see Xavier, I see

Jace but with a bullet in his head. Every time I hear Xavier's name, I see my brother's casket. Every time I think of them drugs, I think of my brother's headstone. There is no escaping it. It follows me everywhere." I paused, the apartment was silent. I took a deep breath. "Closure, G. That's what I'm looking for." I walked over to my bag to pull out the gun I stole from Xavier's apartment. I put it on my desk. It seemed like Gio's eyes were bulging out of his head.

Shaking his head he yelled at me. "You're packing now?"

"Yeah, I got to," I replied.

"You're out of the drug game, who you protecting yourself from? Where did you even get that?" Gio was clearly upset.

"I got it from Xavier's house. Yesterday. I am out of the drug game but you saw what happened today! I can't be out here sitting like a duck." I spoke with my voice raised a little bit.

"Calvin, this isn't the way, that's the gun that took your brother's life. Think of it that way," he spoke with anger in his voice.

"If it can take my brother's life, it can take the life of the man that took my brother's life. I'm not ending up like my brother," I spoke while frowning, "And if I do...I'm not going out alone." I explained.

"Calvin, I know you're hurting. I've been through this type of thing. You know I have, when my cousin died last year I didn't get off track. You're my boy so I gotta tell you when you're fucking up. Calvin, you're fucking up. If you give all your problems to God, I promise you'll never have to think about it again." I stayed silent. I could tell Gio was mad, but more disappointed than anything.

"God helps those who help themselves," I explained. My phone rang. I looked at it, then back at Gio.

"Calv, I'mma get outta here."

"Alright, lemme know when you get home." I looked back at my phone, it was Xavier. I answered. "What?"

"Where you at?" He demanded.

"America." I heard the door shut after Gio left.

"Stop being stupid." He seemed frustrated.

"Uptown...Highbridge, whatchu want?" I was sick of this guy.

"You need to come to AJ's spot. For real, be there in thirty." The demands continued. I had a short temper for these things.

"Who the fuck is AJ? Send me an address. I'm coming through." I was going to go, not because he demanded but because I had a few words for him. He was

going to answer them.

Chapter Fourteen: Favours

I hammered on AJ's door with my fist. I looked around, I was paranoid from the earlier drive-by shooting. The door swung open and Xavier grabbed me and pulled me into the apartment. "You need to stop banging on doors like you the mother fucking feds."

"Get your dirty hands off me, I ain't gonna tell you again," I said, while raising my voice. I looked around the spot to see AJ, I assumed, he was some Latino boy. Chubby, well…fat.

"You been to my house recently?" Xavier asked.

I didn't hesitate to lie. "Nah, why?"

"Cause I can't go back! One of my boys told me the feds ran through it, raided my spot, probably took my money, drugs and whatever they thought was evidence." He was stressed.

"Evidence for what?" I asked. He didn't know that I robbed him.

"I don't know, drug charges." He frowned. "Do you have my money? You're lucky I didn't ask earlier." He continued to demand things.

.

"Money?" I replied.

"Yeah, where's the money?" Asked AJ.

I looked at AJ. "Shut up, AJ. Who asked you to speak?" I looked back over to Xavier. "Nah…How'd you get Jace's hat?" I asked emotionless. It was my turn to get answers.

"What? He left it at my spot. I thought your mom would want it." He spoke quickly. "When did he leave it their cause you told me you weren't there when he died, you ain't seen him that day," I clarified.

He paused. "What are you accusing me of right now?"

"What are you hiding right now? Cause y'all a real gang right, doing a whole lotta gang shit, right? You ain't revenge no blood. My brother was killed, why y'all didn't get revenge. You just let my bro go out like that? Y'all don't care. This ain't no gang!" I yelled.

"We we're working on that, I got your brother's back," he tried to be sincere.

"You don't have his back. You didn't have his back. He's dead."

"I told you, I regret not being there every day. I'd do anything to keep your family happy. I said if you need anything, to let me know. Good or bad! I've been there, you can't deny that!"

He didn't sound guilty, he sounded sincere and he sounded like he wanted payback. So did I, "I need one more favour," I explained.

"Okay, anything. Tell me."

"Take me to my brother's killer," I spoke with a mindset that was irreversible.

He looked at me for a solid twenty seconds. "Calvin…You know I can't do that."

"You said anything. This is what I want, nothing else. I won't forgive you until this happens." He put his hand on his forehead, dragging it down his face. "Let me know when you find him…And fuck your money, you're in debt," I clarified.

"What?" He felt disrespected, he was confused as well.

"I'm waiting for the payback," I replied. I shook my unzipped jacket. "If you want a job done well you gotta do it yourself." I turned around to leave.

"Be ready. Death moves fast. Once it happens…there is no turning back, there is no taking it back. It's a hard sight to see."

I opened the door. "That's why they call it eye for an eye." I walked out closing the door behind me. I walked home, I had a murder to plan.

Chapter Fifteen: Payback

It was Thursday night and the three of us finished in the gym. Gio and Aaliyah waited outside of the doors for me. Before I left I walked into Mr. Mike's office. He just hung up the phone before I walked in. "Hey sir...I mean Mr. Mike."

"Calvin! What's up, brother?" He was smiling.

"Nothing really, just going through a lot," I explained. "I'm gonna say a few things, please don't try and stop me. I've already made the decision." He nodded his head and let me continue speaking. "I gotta quit boxing. Today was my last practice. At least for a while. I got to be there for my mother, I found a job and I work every day after school now. I don't want my mom stressing over money. You taught me a lot, Mr. Mike. You're a man I look up to, you're a father figure, and a leader. You taught me to fight for what matters, and defend the defenceless. That's what I plan to do, I hold those teachings close to me." I shook my head. "I apologize for any problems I've caused and you have my word that I am going to do better. I will be in school this Monday after my suspension is over. I'm going to make a change, Mr. Mike." I finished my speech.

He stared at me. "Obviously I can't force you to stay here, you're a good man for providing for your mother and being so selfless at such a young age. I'm glad you've learned a bit from me, I've also learned from you too. Calvin, you hold a lot of potential…so I need you to know that these gym doors are always open for you. I've never seen someone progress this fast this soon. You could be great. If you ever need a job change you could work here…training the kids. They'll look up to you. The offer is on the table, always. I will be here. Don't ever stop trying to improve. Be better than the person you were yesterday."

He nodded his head after he spoke those words, sticking his hand out for a handshake.

While we shook hands I thanked him again. "I really appreciate you, Mr. Mike, I'll be back soon enough. I just need some time." I looked away from him, the clock on his wall read 8:05 p.m., or so. I looked back at him.

"Take care, Calvin. We'll see you soon." He released from the handshake.

"For sure." I turned around to leave his office.

I stepped outside of the building where Gio and Aaliyah were. They were facing me with their boxing gloves hanging from their necks. I had mine on my shoulder. "What'd you talk to my uncle about?" Aaliyah asked.

"Nothing really…he asked me about my suspension from school," I said.

"Oh, when does that end?"

"Monday. I'm back in school on Monday. Gio too."
I looked at Gio. He was still a bit upset with me. He didn't
show it in front of Aaliyah, I guess he felt like he was
wing-manning for me.

"Are you walking me home tonight?" She asked.

"Oh...you decided to ask this time?" I laughed.

Gio gave me a handshake while he looked at my
backpack. "I'll catch y'all later. You kids stay safe. And
always, WWGD...what would Gio do?" He smiled.

"Forever and always, boss man," Aaliyah said.

I was sure Gio looked at my backpack wondering if
I had the gun with me. I did. I had plans tonight. I was
trying not to focus on them yet. "Later, G." He took a few
steps backwards then turned around to continue walking in
that direction.

Aaliyah and I found ourselves outside her apartment. I stared at her gloves. "Calvin?"

"Why those gloves? What do they mean?" I asked.

"The rose?" She questioned.

"Yeah, it's coming out of concrete right? What's the meaning behind that?"

"Have you ever seen a rose grow from concrete? This literally never happens." She smiled. "It means...I'm one-in-a-million." It was exactly what I thought it meant.

"You are," I said. She continued to smile, looking into my eyes. It was hard for me to give her eye contact at this moment. "I saw you before I met you. Walking somewhere with your girls into a subway station. I don't know. It may be fate or something, you just happened to go to the same gym I decided to check out with Gio."

"Or you followed me," she said laughing. I heard a car make a fast turn forcing its tires to screech. My head turned sharply to look for the car. I started to breathe quicker and heavier. The sound made me flinch. I pulled Aaliyah behind me. I was focused on protecting her. My fist clenched. "Calvin! Look at me! What's happening?" She was worried.

I began looking around. "Nothing." She pulled my chin, forcing me to look at her. I had to talk to her, I didn't know how to go about it since it was nothing positive. "Aaliyah, I need to say something."

"What's wrong?" She looked me in the eyes. At that moment I didn't want to lie to her. But I wanted to protect her.

"I don't really know how to explain this, I've never really done this before," I said.

"Calvin, do you want to come in and talk? My mom isn't gonna be home for a bit." She smiled.

I knew this wasn't the best idea given what I was trying to do but I couldn't resist her. I walked up the stairs to her apartment for the first time, I watched her unlock the door. She grabbed my hand and pulled me into her house. She turned on the lights and right away I began to look around. There wasn't much space but they made it work, it was a very clean house. A lot of pictures hung from the walls. "Give me your bag and jacket." I unzipped my jacket and handed it to her. I held my bag in my hand, I hesitated to hand it to her. The situation would be way worse if she knew what I was packing.

"Aaliyah, I need to talk to you," I spoke calmly.

"Oh yeah, you were saying something. I'm sorry, here come to my room. We can talk there." She grabbed my hand and pulled me again. When I got into the room she closed the door behind me. The room was lit by a very dim lamp. *Damn,* I thought. I turned to look at her and she pulled my face to hers to kiss me, I kissed her back.

I pulled away, "Wait Aaliyah, stop." She looked confused. I spoke fast and scrambled to find the words. "I'm sorry, I feel real bad but…I'm not the one. I'm not the right guy for you. I feel like I'm not good enough, I can't keep you safe. Especially with everything going on around me. I'm supposed to take your problems away, not bring more. I really like you, but I don't want to do that to you."

"You don't think you're good enough?" How did she only get that out of everything I said? She pushed me onto her bed. I looked up to see her taking off her shirt. She was now in her bra. I suddenly forgot everything that I was supposed to say to her. She pulled a hair tie off of her wrist and tied her hair into a ponytail. She walked over and climbed on top of me. She began kissing me again, stopping mid-kiss to speak. "Calvin, your problems are my problems." She pulled my hoodie off and my undershirt came off with it. Her fingers traced the muscle indents on my chest. We continued to kiss as she sat on top of me.

"You're perfect." I thought that ever since I met her. This was the first time I told her.

She smiled while she kissed me, I could tell by the feeling and shape of her lips against mine. "I want you," She replied. I turned her over, I was now on top of her. I pulled the covers over us.

We laid beside each other, sweating. "Was that your first time?" I asked her. We laid in bed together, her head was on top of my chest. Our legs were tangled with one another's.

"Having sex? No. Making love?" she moved her head enough to look at me, "Yes."

"What's the difference?" I was confused. It was my first time.

"I never had these type of feelings before," she clarified.

"Aaliyah, I don't want your mom to find us like this…I should go." I adjusted my position.

"Don't worry. She won't be home for another hour at least." She didn't want me to leave. "Don't go yet."

"Aaliyah, I got to go." I moved her off my chest to get myself off the bed. "I'm sorry."

"What's wrong, Calvin?" She was really worried. She wrapped herself in her bed covers.

I spoke as I put my clothes back on, "I'm a threat to you. I really can't be with you. I'm risking your safety every time I'm out with you. I can't do that no more. I've been selfish."

"What are you talking about?" She got upset really quickly. "Calvin, you're being crazy. I feel safe when I'm with you. I trust you."

"That's the problem, Aaliyah. You don't know you're in trouble when you're with me. That's why I can't be with you."

I could see tears form in her eyes. "What do you mean? Why are you doing this?"

I shook my head. I tried to avoid showing sympathy. "My brother was killed, someone needs to pay for it. And when they do…I might pay for it. I don't want you to be involved. I know this sounds crazy to you and I am crazy. But right now, finding who killed my brother is the most important thing to me. I don't want you in the crossfire. I can't have you getting hurt. I don't want that on my conscience."

She held her mouth in her palm. Tears flew from her eyes. It broke my heart. She struggled to get her words out. "Calvin, don't do this. You don't have to get revenge. Let your brother be at peace."

I yelled at her. "You don't understand!" I opened her room door and walked out. When I got to the living room I tried to collect my things. Aaliyah followed me. She was in a bra and shorts.

Aaliyah grabbed my arm before I picked my stuff up. I turned around to look at her. She was now a mess. "What about when we're at the gym, Calvin? What are you gonna do then? You just not gonna talk to me?"

"I spoke to your uncle before I left. I told him I had to quit. I'm sorry." I struggled to look at her. I broke her heart.

She walked up closely to me, yelling. "Calvin, this isn't you." She yelled and pounded on my chest with her fist. Her eyes continued to fill with tears.

I grabbed her hands and looked her in the eyes. "You don't know me," I said calmly. I lightly pushed her back.

She continued to yell. "Yes I do. You know I do. You don't wanna do this." She was right, I didn't want to leave her. I just wanted my brother's killer gone. I stayed silent. I was at her front door. I put my jacket on and I grabbed my bag. I put it on. She slowed her words down, she tried to speak calmly as she choked on most of her words. "You know what? Fine! You win, Calvin! But listen to me. If you leave now, don't you dare come back."

I looked at her as I opened the door. "Goodbye, Aaliyah." I closed the door behind me and walked to the bottom of the steps.

I pulled out my phone to call Xavier. "Yeah, how far away are you?"

"Like two minutes," he responded.

"Didn't I say 9:30? Hurry up!" I was taking my emotions out on him.

When Xavier pulled up, I got into the car. I saw Aaliyah come out of the apartment. I looked at Xavier and nodded my head. He looked past me to Aaliyah. "That's your girl?" He asked. I looked back over to Aaliyah. I tried not to show her any emotions.

"Used to be," I clarified.

"She's fine…real fit!" He sounded excited. I didn't say anything. We drove off and I stayed silent. "I gotta make one drop-off, alright?" Xavier explained.

"Right now? Okay, whatever." I looked straight ahead, questioning my decision. *I lost my brother, did I have to lose her too?* I clenched my left fist. I held it like that for some time.

When the car pulled up to a building in Harlem, Xavier got out immediately. I watched him walk over to the side of it. I could still see him. He was talking, I didn't know what he was saying and I couldn't see who he was talking to either. I unclenched my fist and looked down to my palm. I saw it bleeding. I clenched my fist so hard my nails dug into the skin on my palm. I wiped the small amount of blood onto my joggers. I looked back up to Xavier. He was still talking. All I could hear was the ticking of the four-way hazard lights on the car. My foot was tapping the floor of the car. I wouldn't say I was nervous. I was more eager than anything. I looked in Xavier's glove department. I found a wallet. I looked through it. There wasn't any cash. There were IDs, a driver's license. The picture looked nothing like Xavier. "BACHELOR, Chase" I read the name on one of the IDs out loud. I looked back over to Xavier, this wasn't even his car. He was walking back over to the car, and I saw the woman he dealt the cocaine to. She turned to her side to enter the apartment again. *Pregnant.* I damn near went blind. Xavier opened the door to the car and sat down. "Are you mental? You're selling crack to a pregnant lady?" I spoke with a tone that was serious, but not loud.

"Life," he responded.

"Nah...that ain't right man." I shook my head. "You can't be ruining futures like that! That baby don't even know his life is about to be ruined. That's on you. Your conscience."

"Conscience...I don't have one of those. Supply and demand. I got it, who wants it? That's how it goes, that's just the way it is." He put the car in drive and continued down the street. This was so wrong, I couldn't believe my brother was hanging out with this guy, idolizing this guy, putting him on a pedestal. He was the devil, I felt sick to my stomach. I wasn't sure if it was because I was planning on taking a life, or because Xavier had just ruined one. There used to be a code, a distribution code that dealers lived by. Although they wanted money by any means necessary, they still thought about the community. If a kid was destined to make it to the big leagues they wouldn't sell to him, nor would they let him sell to others. They didn't want him to risk his future. They knew if that boy made it out of the hood he would come back and give back to his people. Dealers never dealt to pregnant women, these women held the future in them. Future leaders, life-changing leaders, ones that would build a better future for the people. The dealers also never dealt to children. But times have changed. My brother told me that. He had a heart. Xavier didn't. It didn't make sense that they were friends.

We were on our way to Brooklyn. I felt like it didn't make sense for Jace's killer to be in Brooklyn. Why would they travel to the Bronx to take a life? I felt like it was an on-site type of dispute, where there was only a problem if you were on my turf. Now we were on their turf.

We got to an apartment in a part of Brooklyn I had never been to. It was filled with house apartments that all looked the same. There were stairs leading up to the house entrance, kind of like Aaliyah's apartment in Harlem. I sat down in the stolen car. My palms were sweaty, my mouth was very dry, and my mind was everywhere. I could feel my heart beating out of my chest. "How do you know it's this place?" I asked.

"Niggas speak when you threaten them." Xavier spoke as if this was nothing new to him. "People would give up a friend if you threaten family. That's what I did." I took his word for it.

"What's his name? The guy who killed my brother." I wanted to know.

"They say he goes by Cee-lo."

"Cee-lo. Today's your last day," I spoke under my breath.

"You ready?" Xavier looked at me.

"Yeah." I reached into my bag and pulled out the gun I stole from Xavier. "Let's go." I wasn't scared. I was focused and looking for revenge.

"Woah, where'd you get that?" Xavier was confused but a bit upset. "Ain't that my gun?"

"So you own every gun in NY now?" I challenged him. "You might have the same gun but this one is mine." Xavier handed me a black ski mask from the back seat, I grabbed it and put it on. We got out of the car. It was probably around 10:30 p.m. by now. I put the gun at the back of my waistband. Xavier had a gun too, he put his at the front of his waistband. We parked down the block. We walked up the stairs to the front door of the apartment, I knocked on the door three times. Not too hard. My heart was pounding. The vapour from my breath blurred my sight a bit. A light came on in the window beside the door. I held my breath. Xavier stood in front of me, when the door opened I pulled my gun out immediately pointing it at the man's head. "Move back!" I yelled.

His eyes lit up. "Aye what the fuck is this?" He quickly came to a panic stumbling backwards. He was forced further into his house. Xavier and I entered closing the door behind us.

I walked over to his kitchen to grab a chair and I put it against a wall in his living room. "Sit your ass down." I said.

The man sat down on the chair. Moving his head and eyes back and forth, switching his focus between Xavier and me. "Take whatever you want, please, I don't have much but take everything! Please, I don't know what you want." He really feared for his life at this moment, that's what I wanted.

Xavier began knocking all the stuff in his house over. He threw the flat screen TV on the TV stand to the ground. Picture frames on the wall were thrown off the wall. Xavier kicked over a coffee table. "Fuck your stuff!" Xavier yelled.

"I don't want your shit! I don't care about what you got." I took my mask off. "I care about what you took."

"I don't understand. I didn't do anything!" The man pleaded. "Please, man! I got a kid! I gotta be there to provide."

"That's bullshit, what's your name?" I yelled. I pointed my gun at his head.

"Andrew," he said, raising his hands to his face in fear.

"What?" I went silent. I put my gun down. "What do they be calling you on the streets?" I asked.

"Cee-lo! They call me Cee-lo," he spoke fast and with fear.

"Why the hell do they call you Cee-lo if your name is Andrew?"

"The game! I gamble a lot, I'm good at dice!" He explained. His hands were still over his head and he was shaking as he spoke to me.

"You gambled with your life today," I said.

"I don't know what you're talking about! I don't know what I did...but I'm sorry! Please."

"You killed my brother," I said angrily.

"I never killed no one! I just gamble a lot!"

"Shut up! I know you did!" I screamed.

"Look, my guy! I be gambling, robbing people, but I ain't no killer. I ain't killed nobody," he said.

I raised my gun to his head again. "Jace. My brother's name was Jace. You killed him! I know you did. You don't know how much pain you caused my mother. You put a void in my family that will never be filled again. I want your family to experience the same thing. I want them to wake up knowing they ain't ever gonna see you again. You're dying today."

"Please!" He begged me. "I got a kid to take care of." He wasn't crying but I could see the distress in his eyes. Almost like he was being sincere. I thought back to a rule Gio and I had. *Never take from a hardworking man.* I was about to take his life.

"Shut up! Did you think about my family when you killed Jace? I buried my brother! Buried him! He's gone! Your kid will go through what I went through!" I still had the gun pointed at his head. I could hear Xavier's footsteps behind me, he was pacing back and forth. "You think this is a joke. You can take lives and not face the consequences? Life has repercussions. You will pay for this," I said fearlessly. I could hear the anger in my voice.

"I swear on my kid's life! I swear to God! I don't know a Jace and I never killed no one. Please don't do this. I have to provide for my kid." I could see sweat on his forehead. His eyes trembled. They were dark enough to the point where his eye looked like it was all one colour. I studied him. He had short hair and was wearing a blue shirt. His skin was really dark. He was an African American. He had a patchy beard and a moustache. His hairline was receding.

I gripped the gun real tight. "Look at me…eye for an eye." I said, pulling the hammer on the gun back. The gun clicked and the man continued to shake. He was staring at me in the eyes. I could see the fear. The weakness in him, the sight of him being powerless, and the inability for him to defend himself made me feel like he was incapable of causing anyone real harm. "I hope you're happy. I hope it was worth it. I'm the beast you just unleashed." The gun was pointed at his head. The gun was shaking. My hand was causing the shuddering. I could feel my face frowning to the fullest. My whole body was hot. I could feel the adrenaline going through my body with a great force. I screamed. I lowered my hand with the gun. It wasn't him. I didn't believe this man killed Jace. It couldn't be, I could see it in his eyes. He was innocent. "It's not him," I said.

The man sighed.

Xavier grunted. "What?" He pushed me to the side. He aimed his gun at the man without hesitating to shoot him. Bang. He shot the man in the head. His blood splattered onto the white wall behind him. "You're weak," he said to me.

"No!" I yelled. "What's wrong with you? He was innocent." I really believed my words. The man's body slumped over and fell to the ground. I began to hyperventilate. I couldn't catch my breath. "You're crazy! Why would you do that?" I was the one panicking now. I looked to the door. Xavier bent down to pick up a shell casing. He began walking towards the door. He turned off the lights and opened the door to leave. I put the gun in my waistband. "We gotta run!" I yelled.

Xavier grabbed me, "Nah, nah! We don't run. Real gangsters don't run. No rush. We walk." I kept looking around as we walked to the car. I was paranoid. I got into the car with Xavier.

I was still out of breath. I couldn't feel my hands. I felt like my body was going numb. My heart was beating out of my chest. "You're crazy! You're fucking crazy! I said he didn't do it! I know he didn't do it!" I continued to yell. I couldn't get a hold of myself.

"How could you be convinced so easily? You're weak! I know he did it. I could see it in his eyes." His eyes were the exact reason why I didn't do it. "People will say anything so they don't get in trouble for the things they know they did." He looked at me while he started the car. "The person causing your nightmares is gone now. Dead. You should sleep well tonight."

"You're insane. You're a monster." It had only been a few minutes but I had already played the murder in my head over hundreds of times. I thought about how easy it was for Xavier to pull the trigger, how he didn't even hesitate. He was a murderer. He walked away like it was nothing new to him. Why did he want this over so badly? I was still trying to catch my breath as the car drove off.

"I'm not a monster. Jace was my best friend. He deserves justice." He looked at me. "He just got it." I focused back on the road as he drove across the Brooklyn Bridge. He tried to ask me several questions in attempt to change the subject, he wanted me to get my mind off of it. I stayed silent throughout the rest of the ride. I thought only about the murder. How killing was like second nature to Xavier. I thought about how the kid the man was raising was going to have no choice but learn how to live without his father. At this moment, I was regretting everything I had done. Everything I had asked for. I didn't feel like Jace was resting in peace. I didn't feel like Jace's killer was dead.

Chapter Sixteen: I'm Trying

Jace's assumed killer was dead. I didn't feel any better about the situation. The more days that went by the worse I felt about it. Time did nothing to heal me. I walked down the steps of the fifth floor. I was headed to the third floor. I continued down the hallway. I knocked on the door of the English office. It wasn't a formal office, it was just a large room with a lot of teacher's desks in there. It was filled with bookshelves and papers. "Hi," I spoke as if I was asking a question.

"Calvin!" Ms. Laurent was excited to see me. "How are you?" She was smiling. She was sitting at her desk and I joined and sat on a chair on the other side of the desk. A student was sitting in a second chair on my side of the desk. "I'm good but school sucks. How aren't I in any of your classes? I hate my teachers. The one with the bald head and big belly is talking up. I almost had to put him in his place this morning. It's a Thursday morning, Miss. You think I wanna deal with a teacher on a Thursday morning. He talking real sweet with his shiny head." I spoke really fast. Ms. Laurent tried not to laugh as I made fun of her coworkers. "You're done, my guy!" I said to the guy sitting in the seat next to me. He nodded his head and got up to leave. I don't think he was really done, I think he was just scared. He was probably a freshman.

"Calvin! Be nice...I'll talk to you soon, Samuel!" said Ms. Laurent as the freshman walked out of the office. "And the bald man's name is Mr. Zapata. Calvin, you can't be disrespecting teachers like that. It's not right. I don't want you getting suspended no more," she said with a bit of sass in her voice.

"Miss, I've been good! I been coming to class every day! My attendance is perfect this semester. But these idiots are playing with my patience."

"Calvin! Language! You're going to get yourself in trouble." She looked to her right. There were other teachers in the office. "You should go back to class," she explained.

"Let them report me! I'll know who did it!" I laughed a little. "I'm a thug. Let 'em bad boy principals try me." I got up. "Miss, please try and get the counsellors to switch me into one of your classes! I can't stand the ones I'm in." I put my hands together as if I was praying to salute and thank her.

"Calvin, you failed every class but mine…and I was just being nice. You showed up to less than a quarter of the semester." She tried not to laugh at me. "You have no one to blame. You have to retake those courses."

I rolled my eyes. "Yeah, yeah, yeah." I began to walk backwards. "I'm innocent! I promise I'll work hard, just get me in one of your classes."

She laughed before she even spoke. "Tell it to the judge."

"Very funny, Ms. Laurent." I said in a sarcastic tone. I turned around to leave the office. "I'll be back after the period ends!" I yelled.

"No you won't!" She yelled back.

I walked out of the office, and I noticed Giovanni's girlfriend, Bea. She smiled at me, she didn't really know me. But I'd heard a lot about her. "Bea, right?" I nodded my head at her.

"Hey, Calvin." She quickly stopped smiling. "Have you seen Gio? I need to talk to him."

I looked down the hallway, then focused on Bea again. "I haven't seen him for a while, but I think he's got PE. Why what's wrong?" I asked.

"No, nothing…I just wanted to talk to him," she simplified.

But it wasn't that simple. I could tell she wasn't being genuine. But I wasn't going to force it out of her. I began walking beside her, we were headed to the same staircase. "Let me know if you find him." I smiled.

"I will, but if you see him tell him to come find me!" She seemed eager. She then stopped walking abruptly. She put her hands on her stomach.

"You good?" I asked. She didn't say anything. "Bea?" She put her hands on her mouth. Bea began to look around. She started running in the direction of the washroom. I ran over with her, stopping at the door while she went in. I heard puking sounds. I gagged myself. "Are you good?" There was no answer. I ran back over to Ms. Laurent's desk in the English office. "Miss! I need your help! Come!" The panic in my voice forced her to get up from her seat to follow me. I didn't look back because I could hear her heels clicking against the ground in the hallway. "My friend Bea is in here and I can't go in! I think she's puking! Please help her!" Ms. Laurent went into the washroom with no hesitation. I could hear them speak but their voices were a bit muffled from the door. They both came out seconds later.

Ms. Laurent had her arm around Bea's shoulder. "Calvin, you can go back to class. I'll take care of her."

I nodded my head. "Bea, I'll find Gio for you." I turned around to go to the gym. I ran down the hall. I turned to the staircase. I skipped down the stairs to the first floor. I pushed open the doors to the gym. The class in the gym was playing basketball. I walked through the gymnasium looking for Giovanni. I saw him on the bench, by the time I got to him I was huffing and puffing. "Fam, you gotta come right quick!"

Gio began jogging out of the gym with me. "What happened?"

"Bea, she's puking." I opened the door for Gio to enter the hallway. "She's really sick, I think. She's been looking for you for a hot minute she said. She's with Ms. Laurent."

"Word?" He was shocked.

"Yeah, they're probably in the office now." I let Gio go to the office on his own. I had to get back to class. It would count as a skip if I was gone for over fifteen minutes. Any small incident would result in a suspension and I'd be put under consideration for an expulsion. I got back up to the fifth floor where I saw three police officers escorting one boy down the hall. That normally only happened when you were being kicked out of school or suspended. As they got closer to me I recognized the boy as the one that fought Gio and I when we got back from the

Christmas break. The same boy who tried to kill us with a drive-by shooting, along with those boys from Harlem who tried to buy drugs off me. I stared at him.

"Whatchu looking at?" he blurted at me.

It didn't scare me. "Nothing special," I responded.

He stepped away from his path and towards me. "You gonna get a bullet in your head like your brother." he claimed.

I forgot about my current probation status with the school. I did the same thing he did, stepping away from my path and towards his. The hallway wasn't more than 10 yards wide. "You gonna do it? 'Cause I'm here now," I spoke in a crescendo.

"I'll take your head off your shoulders!" We had just got in each other's faces when the police noticed us taking detours, they quickly came to break it up.

I threw a fist destined for his face but my arm was stopped. The police pulled me away from the guy I continued to yell. "You a punk! You couldn't even pull up to my face! You had to drive by. I'm still living!" I wasn't afraid of him. I didn't even know his name. My mind was just flooded with angry emotions every time I saw his face. He used his fingers to symbolize him shooting at me. I continued to stare at him until the police shoved my face-first into a locker. They began to pat me down. They proceeded to put me into handcuffs. One officer walked with me down the hallway, while the two other police officers went the other way with the drive-by shooter. They made the two of us go down separate staircases to get to the office.

As I was going down the staircase, Ms. Laurent was going up. "Calvin! What did you do?" She was shocked as she followed the officer and me to the office. They sat me

in the same room they did for the fight that took place
earlier that year.

When I sat down in one of the chairs I could hear
Ms. Laurent speaking to the officer, "Please let me in. I
want to speak to him." The doorknob turned and she
entered the room. I looked down at my feet, taking deep
breaths. I was furious. I didn't want to talk to her. I didn't
think she would understand. Teachers always thought that I
had anger problems. They forgot about the things that
drove me to that point. I don't just get mad for no reason.
"What happened, Calvin?" she said in a serious tone. I
looked at her, then looked back down to my feet. "Calvin!
I'm here to help."

I didn't want to believe those words but I felt like
she wasn't like the other teachers. "I threw my fist and then

got put into handcuffs." I spoke without giving her any eye contact.

"Calvin, you're lying." She knelt down to my level. She moved her face to give me eye contact.

I looked up at her. "He said he was gonna put a bullet in my head. Like Jace." I continued to give her eye contact.

"Who is Jace?" She asked.

"My brother." I said, still giving her eye contact. "Was my brother." She stayed silent. "It's okay...I'll find another school." I smiled at her. I knew being in this room meant I was about to be expelled. I was just thinking about how to break it to my mom.

"I'll talk to the principal for you." she said. I nodded my head and she left the room.

My hands were still bind behind my back as I collected my thoughts. I looked at the blank walls, they were white bricks. That was the street name for the cocaine and crack I sold. I looked out the window, I saw a lot of cars driving by. Horns went off, I looked at my shoes. I was wearing Timberlands, the orange ones. It was a New York thing. I looked at the desk in front of me. It had all sorts of school supplies I didn't have, along with some paperwork. I sat there and closed my eyes. I kept them closed for about twenty minutes. I didn't sleep but I daydreamed about Aaliyah. I didn't think things would ever be the same, whether she forgave me or not. The way I ended it was wrong. She wouldn't understand, I barely understood. Seeing Aaliyah in tears was the hardest thing for me, I was the person who was supposed to protect her. But I ended up being the one to hurt her. I really didn't think I would be forgiven. I heard the doorknob shake. I looked over to the door to watch a police offer walk in. I looked back down to my shoes.

"Get up," said the officer. I was slow to get up, only because I didn't want to respect him, but I had to. I never gave him eye contact. "Turn around," said the officer. He grabbed my left wrist and unlocked the handcuffs. I started to rub my wrists. The handcuffs were on too tight. "Get back to class," he ordered me.

I turned around to look at his face. We met eye to eye. "Yeah," I said with no emotion on my face. I walked out of the room I was in, I was now in the secretaries' space in the main office.

I saw Ms. Laurent standing by the exit where I was headed. I met up with her. "I got you out of the trouble, Mr. Collins understands that it wasn't your fault." She smiled.

She handed me a green note. I didn't look at it, I just knew it was a get back to class free card. Mine were usually red. "Thank you. I honestly don't know how to repay you." I smiled back at her without teeth. I was relieved, I didn't know how I'd break an expulsion to my mom.

"No worries, Calvin." We walked through the doors into the hallway. "Make sure you're in room 409 last period…on time, Calvin."

She continued to walk past the doors to the staircase. "Wait, I can't I have class," I said confused.

"Yeah. 409. With me," she confirmed.

"You lying. Stop playing, I can't be late to my classes," I said.

"And you can't be late to mine," she said from a distance. "You owe me one." I didn't say anything. I let her continue to walk away as I went through the doors to the staircase. I didn't think of her as a teacher anymore. It was more like a friend. She had my back. When I got back to my class, the students were packing their things up.

"Calvin, where have you been?" Asked the teacher.

"Here." I handed him the green note. I could see the light in the class room shine off his head. I stood with a disgusted look on my face.

"Lucky you, you're off the hook," he said trying to make me smile.

"Alright." I walked to the back of the class to grab my bag. I walked past the teacher to exit the class room. I kissed my teeth as I left.

Chapter Seventeen: St. Laurent, Part I

In Ms. Laurent's class, I was still livid and I wasn't sure why. Everything just felt off. She was telling the students to copy something off of the whiteboard. I couldn't see much because a girl in front of me had her hair all done up. She was blocking my view. I threw a whole eraser at the back of her head. "Yo. Could you move your head-top to the side? I can't see."

She looked back to give me a dirty look. "You're rude as hell! Shut your mouth." She gave me attitude.

"Don't tell me what to do! Move your big head!" I got mad at her for getting mad at me. "My momma pays taxes for this education! I deserve to see what's on that board!" I explained.

"If you want me to move you're gonna have to move me," she said aggressively

"Brianna, stop!" Ms. Laurent stopped the fight right away. "Calvin! Go out in the hall," she said with a disappointed tone in her voice.

As I got up I looked at Brianna. "My bad." I didn't want her to get in trouble.

"Save it," she said. I gave her a dirty look as I walked by her.

When I got to the hallway it was empty. The windows let in a lot of natural light. I gave Ms. Laurent the eye contact she deserved. I didn't ever break eye contact. Her eyes shined, she faced the windows behind me and I faced the outside wall of the classroom which was behind her. "What's wrong, Calvin? I've been watching you. You're not doing any of the work. You're just acting up! I promised Mr. Collins that I'd get you caught up within a week. We're three weeks into the semester. You weren't even supposed to switch classes this late." The concerned look on her face made me feel bad. I had promised a lot of people that I'd do better, I just had a hard time getting around to it.

"How'd you get Mr. Collins to let me back in class? I know they've been wanting to expel my ass for a long time now." I frowned at her. "I wanna know why you have faith in me. I don't think I deserve this much sympathy, or to even cross someone's mind. I haven't put a smile on many people's faces for a very long time," I explained. I continued to look at her as she was silent.

When she finally began to speak I felt like she really cared for me. It wasn't like she just felt bad for me. I knew that because everyone did. No one wants to see their brother die. No one wants to bury their brother. She wanted to see me do better. "Calvin, I'm not here to be sympathetic, it is sad. It is tough, I haven't experienced anything like what you're going through. But that's not why I'm trying to help you. I want you to succeed. I see something special in you, that you refuse to see in yourself. I feel like anything you do, you can do it well. But that's only if you want to do well." I looked away from her. She sighed. "Calvin, look at me." I looked at her. "You don't want to do well in school. That's why you're not here. But to this day I still remember that poem you wrote, I still tear up thinking about it. You wrote that in a few minutes, Calvin. In a few minutes. Why can't you see that you're special?" She took a deep breath, then exhaled right away.

I felt like she'd never disciplined a student before. She sounded disappointed in me, although I didn't get that vibe. I felt something else. "I want to do better…but I need help." I looked at her, I think I was frowning a bit.

"Calvin. I will only offer my help in school if you're willing to help yourself as well," she explained.

"Okay. When do we start?"

"Today, three o'clock. In this classroom," she clarified with a stern voice.

"Lady, I don't think you understand that's like fifteen minutes after school, I already have plans with Gio." I fought back.

"You don't seem like you want to help yourself," she said again with a firm voice.

I kissed my teeth. "Okay. Three. When do we end?"

"We end when we end," she said. She walked back into the class and the bell rang as I continued to stand outside. Soon, the hallway was filled. I walked back into the class to grab my stuff. I left the class to walk to my locker, my locker was beside Gio's.

I stood at the locker waiting for about five minutes. When Gio finally showed, he looked tired, but a bit nervous. "You good?"

"Calvin, bro. I can't even wrap my head around this." Gio gave me a handshake. It was different this time because he came in for a half-hug, when he released he began to panic. "I'm not ready. I never planned for this. Niggas ain't making that much money right now. I ain't know what to tell my moms. She might just whoop my ass. Nah, nah, she will just whoop my ass." He looked to the sky.

I laughed a bit, "What'd you do, boss man?" I asked for a second time.

"Calvin, she's not sick. Bea is not sick." I was confused. "Calv, she is fine. More than fine. They seem fine. For so long, she's known for so long," he was muttering under his breath. It was hard for me to understand him. It was like he was talking to himself, like I wasn't even there.

I grabbed both of his shoulders and shook him. "You're scaring me, G. What's happening?" I yelled.

"Bruh, I mean shit…I be scared too! But it ain't like I don't ever want a child," he said a little clearer.

"Child? Whatchu mean?"

"She's not sick. Calv." He took a deep breath. Then released the air. "She was puking 'cause she's pregnant. I'm 'bout to be a father."

I let go of his shoulders. "Shit…Is she sure?"

"She found out about it four weeks ago. She already seen a doctor."

"Damn. She wasn't tryna abort it?" I said shamelessly.

He gave me a dirty look. "You're joking right? I don't want her to abort it, and she doesn't want to either. I'm gonna be a great father. Better than my father was." He looked at me. He didn't even go into his locker. He just walked away. I took my jacket out of my locker and walked back to Ms. Laurent's classroom.

I walked into the room at 3:03 p.m. It was just Ms. Laurent and I in the room. "Miss, how you supposed to catch me up in every class? You're an English teacher?" I asked.

"I also teach math and I can teach any math class in this school, Calvin. For any social science class, I can help you with essays, structure and whatever." She explained with a smile on her face.

"Good to know."

"You're stuck with me." She laughed. I forced a smile. "Pull out your books." I stared at her with a blank expression. "Your math textbook?" She was confused. My eyes looked away from her then focused on her again, all within a split second. "Mr. Zapata." I was still staring at her. "Calvin, the class where you said your teacher had a big head."

"It's bald not big, miss. That's rude. He's your coworker." I smiled.

She rolled her eyes. "Oh, be quiet."

Ms. Laurent helped me with a lot of my work. We started with history. "After Christopher Columbus discovered the New World –"

"He didn't." I laughed a bit.

"What?" she said puzzled. Her eyebrows squeezed together and her eyes squinted.

"Africans had been traveling back and forth from Africa to America for decades before this Chris man came and claimed he found it."

She sighed. "Calvin… just listen…please."

"How can I learn fake news?" I laughed again, "It's like me breaking into your house and saying 'I live here now!'"

"Okay, let's work on something else." She shook her head.

She created algebra questions for me to answer. I went through them answering what I could. I looked up to see Ms. Laurent blowing the hair from her bangs out of her eyes.

I smiled at her with teeth, "You're like a grown-up baby."

"That's mean! I like to have fun – I can be fun, okay?"

"I never said you weren't fun!" I never stopped smiling.

Ms. Laurent raised her face towards the ceiling. She tried to balance a pen on her nose. "Ah, ah? Fun! See?" she pointed at the pen on her nose as she got it to balance.

"Now that's just childish," I laughed out loud.

"You're no fun! Get back to work!" she demanded in a playful tone.

I couldn't help but procrastinate. It was about five o'clock now. "Can I ask you something?"

"Don't ask if you can ask a question, just ask the question," she said.

"Why'd you leave Canada? Montréal, right?"

"I lived in a small town outside of Montréal." Avoiding my question, she smiled.

"That's not what I asked." I confronted.

She stopped me. "Let's keep the questions school related."

"How can I learn anything from someone I don't really know?" I said

"Really, Calvin? You don't think you know me?" She laughed.

"Well, I only really started regularly attending school a few weeks ago," I replied, seriously.

"You have a point. But, you'll have to save that question for next time," she said.

"Close your eyes, Miss."

"What?"

"Trust me, just close your eyes," I said. She listened.

"I don't see the point in this," she smiled while she spoke.

"Okay, open them." She listened. She looked around confused. "It's next time," I said.

"Very funny, Calvin. Where'd you get that one?" She smiled really hard looking back down at the math textbook. *Aaliyah,* I thought to myself. I was flirting with the teacher, I think. "Let's get back to work. I got to leave in twenty minutes," she said eagerly.

"Damn miss, where do you gotta be? What happened to we end when we end?" I mocked her.

"I have plans."

I didn't believe her. I laughed a bit. "Plans, with who? You just came from the North Pole. Who you gotta see? Don't be out too late. Your curfew is seven o'clock."

She looked at me lost, "Are you kidding? Yes, I have plans! I have a date," she clarified.

I gave a confused smile. "Date? Stop playing. Be home by seven."

"Excuse me, Calvin? I have a date! I'm going on a date. That's that." She stood up to pack her things. "Get home safely." She didn't find what I said funny. It wasn't meant to be funny. I was serious.

"I'm sorry, you're new to this city. You still gotta grow your New Yorker skin. I get it, you're fragile. My bad." I stood up too.

"I think my personal life should stay personal," she claimed.

"You're the one who brought it up." I replied. "Let me put it like this... You're new here. I'm worried about your street intelligence."

"I know my way around," she said.

"So do I, but I know who's around. You don't." I looked at her with a very serious face. "It be dangerous out here, miss. Stay safe."

"It's in Brooklyn, don't worry." She said with a know-it-all type of tone in her voice.

"Oh my God! Even worse," I blurted out. "Who are you going to see?"

"Calvin! It's none of your business! Go home," she raised her voice. It was clear that she was uncomfortable.

"Now we're done? Alright. Same time tomorrow." I finished packing my things in my bag. "Seven o'clock…I'm serious." I left after she shook her head at me.

Chapter Eighteen: Calm Down

I was outside when the sun was beginning to set. I went straight to Gio's house. I could tell the days were getting longer, it was about 5:30. I know the time I asked Ms. Laurent to be home was unrealistic. But I had to let her know it really wasn't safe these days. Especially when the weather is warm in The Bronx, people stay outside later. *It doesn't have to be cold outside for the streets to be.*

I knocked on his door, waiting for him to answer. He opened the door and gave me a quick handshake. "How was study hall?" He asked as we walked into the apartment.

I took my shoes off and continued walking with him into his living room. "I don't even think I could call that study hall. Pretty little white girl like Ms. Laurent tryna go on dates at night! My guy, it's dangerous out here."

"I don't even know who that teacher is...But if she's been living in N.Y. you got nothing to worry about," he explained.

"The one that broke our fight up the first day back. She moved here in the middle of the first term," I said as I sat down on one of his couches.

Gio continued standing up as he spoke. "Oh, long brown hair? How do you know? You weren't even going to class." He laughed.

"I remember, I had a different teacher the first few weeks in September. She's new to the city," I explained.

"True, she's wild for that. She the type that needs to be home before the street lights turn on." He shrugged his shoulders.

"Whatever. Leave it to the jungle," I said. "You down to play FIFA?" He nodded his head at me. We played for a two hours or so. We spoke while we played.

"You hear from Jerem and K.C. yet?" Gio asked.

"Nah, my mom is worried sick. They been in Ghana for over two months. They left from LaGuardia bottom of December and it's now the top of March."

"That's messed up. Leave it in God's hands man. This ain't a battle that we can take care of," he reassured.

I nodded my head. I stopped playing and focused on Gio. "You worried about the baby?"

He paused the game. "I'm worried about what my moms is gonna say. I already know what I'm gonna do." He seemed to have it all figured out.

I put the controller down. "Say no more. You know I got your back no matter what goes down. I know what I said was messed up. But I swear, I gotchu. I'll even buy all the diapers for you," I reassured.

He nodded his head at me. "Calvin, lemme ask you something," he sounded concerned.

"Wassup?"

"Why don't you talk to Aaliyah anymore, man?" He shook his head.

"I'm not about to talk about that, G. I just need things to cool down before I start talking to anyone."

"What needs to cool down? She's a ride or die. We be at the gym and all she talks about is you. She been asking what's going on with you. I never know what to say. Cause if you ain't right, she will get you right. She's a good girl. Don't let that go, my guy," he lectured me. "For real, Calv. Whatever needs to be calmed down…she's all for it. She'd be right by your side. I'm your boy, but I mean damn…there's only so much I can do to calm you down." He smiled. "But truth be told, what I feel for Beatrice… I see in Aaliyah's eyes when she speaks your name." He finished.

"In time," I said. "Things will change, in time." I picked up a PlayStation controller. "Let's play again."

"Calvin."

"G, I can't talk to her man. I broke her heart. I know she's hurting. If I go see her it'll only make everything worse."

"No it won't. She wants to see you. And I know you wanna see her too. Why you fighting it."

There was more to it. I just couldn't tell Gio about the guy Xavier killed in Brooklyn. "I'mma put it like this. I got love for that girl. But everything I've been doing recently has been putting everyone down. When I think of her, I think of someone who's so happy. I can't change that. I don't want to change that. And I know I will if I see her." I wanted to forget about this conversation about Aaliyah. She still had my heart. I knew that, she didn't. I hadn't seen her in several weeks. I never stopped thinking about her. I missed how aggressive she was, how she always wanted my attention.

"You changed her smile." He shot those words at me, I felt them.

"I only knew her for a week."

"Shut up, Calv. You know time ain't mean a thing. If you can honestly say it doesn't feel like you've known her your whole life, then I'll believe you." I didn't reply. I stayed silent. "Why you being stubborn? Alright man, if I beat you in this next game, then you gotta go see her." I nodded my head.

My phone began to ring, it was my mom. "Hello?"

"Calvin! Where are you? I need you to get home now," she said in a bit of a panic.

"I'm at Gio's house. What happened?" I asked. She yelled back at me in Twi telling me to hurry up. "I'm on my way." I dropped the controller in my left hand and used the same hand to grab my backpack. "I gotta go, G!" I said in a hurry.

"Alright, lemme know if y'all need anything." He pounded my fist and I ran to the door to put my shoes on. I jumped down the stairs and began running home. It was going to take my about ten minutes to run the whole thing. I was worried there was trouble at the house. I didn't have the gun on me, it was at the house. I wouldn't be able to get the weapon past security at school. I continued running in my heavy-duty Timberlands, I was stepping on puddles and the water was splashing onto my pants. I didn't care about that. I was beyond worried.

I was out of breath by the time I got back to the apartment. I ran up the steps and pulled out my keys, struggling to unlock the door. I swung the door open, running up the rest of the apartment stairs. My heart was pounding, beating out of my chest. "Ma!" I yelled. I ran into my room to pull the gun from one of my drawers. I put it at the back of my waistband. I started hearing gospel music, right away I knew the panicking voice wasn't as serious as my brain made it out to be.

"Calvin!" I could hear the cracking sound in the floor as she walked over to my room. She was singing along with the music. I pulled the gun out of my pants to put it back in the drawer right before she came into my room. "They are back!" My mom said, she was smiling but I could also see that she had been crying.

"Who's back?" I asked. My heart was still pounding.

"Auntie Ellen! God is so wonderful!" She said. Smiling with her arms raised to the ceiling and her face doing the same.

"Thank God," I said. "What about Jerem, K.C. and Uncle?" Are they all okay?" I asked.

"K.C. and Jerem are back." she said. "But Uncle was killed."

I put my head down. I walked over to hug my mom.

"Don't be sad! He is with Jace now! They are okay. At peace," she said. When we broke from the hug she was smiling. She was trying to be strong for me.

I didn't feel the same way as her.

I hung out with my mom for about an hour. I attempted to get her mind off of the death of her brother-in-law. We were on the couch in the living room. She checked the news – still in tears. I made her change the program. The news only caused more stress. She started to watch a Ghanaian film. I wasn't too interested. "Ma, did you eat already?"

"Yes. Are you hungry?" I nodded my head. "Go to Paul's and get your American Hamburger." She always called hamburgers American. She liked her Ghanaian food and only her Ghanaian food.

"It's Paulo," I corrected her.

"Oh, shut up! Same thing." She never stopped looking at the TV.

I smiled and shook my head. "Alright." I went to my room to put my stuff on. I took the gun with me. I tucked it into the back of my waistband again. I grabbed a stack of one dollar bills I had in the drawer beside the gun. There was probably about forty dollars in the stack. I came out of my room. "I'll be back soon." I said as I walked down the stairs to get to the door of the apartment.

Chapter Nineteen: St. Laurent, Part II

I swung open the door to Paulo's. "Paulo!" I spoke in a crescendo. "What it do, OG?" Paulo was the original gangster.

"I'm doing well. I hope you're staying outta trouble," he spoke with his thick accent.

"I am! I am." I walked to grab a Sprite. "Lemme get a Cali burger. Make that deluxe though. I need them fries, my guy."

"Cali Deluxe!" Paulo yelled to the guy in the back.

"Cali Deluxe, coming up!" The man yelled back.

Paulo looked at me, "What have you been up to?"

"I swear I've been staying out of trouble. I'm back in school. Studying." I nodded my head at him. "I just heard that my cousins got back from Ghana, so I'm in a good mood."

"That's the country in the civil war, right?" He asked.

"Yeah, my uncle died in it. Majority of the people I know are okay now."

"I'm happy to hear they're okay! And sorry about your uncle," he said. "I hear American Government was selling the guns and explosives to them! Funding wars but they won't feed their people or aid the sick." He raised his voice.

"For real? I'm not even surprised. This country is fucked up! Our president is on social media talking about blowing everything up! It's crazy! People like you and I, we're out here working, and tryna build something. That boy Donald wanna come and just blow shit up!"

"Yeah! Crazy Americans!" Paulo laughed. When my food came out, I sat on a chair and ate. I continued my conversation with Paulo while I ate. There was no table so my drink was on the floor, the fries were on my lap and my burger stayed in my hands the whole time. I could feel myself sitting on top of the gun. My thoughts were quickly interrupted. "You know my wife and I have been to Ghana. What's the name of the Capital? We went there before we had kids. Beautiful city! On the coast, very peaceful, very nice people," he explained.

"Accra! Yeah, that's the place to be! If it ain't Ghana, it ain't G! You know what I mean?" I smiled with food still in my mouth.

"No?" He said confused.

"Well...Ghana isn't what the media portrays it as. Its more, great food, land, people. You want it, we got it," I explained.

"When was the last time you visited Ghana?" He questioned.

"Two years ago. I try to go every two years with my mom."

"That's good. You should always keep in touch with your culture."

"Yeah, always." I took the last bite out of my burger. "This been lovely, but I'mma head home, Paulo."

"We're supposed to have a thunderstorm! Where's your umbrella! And stay out of trouble!" he said with a serious look.

I smiled without teeth. "You too, Paulo."

I began walking towards the door, "Tell your brother to come by. I haven't seen him in a long time." He sounded genuine.

He probably didn't hear. If I didn't tell him about it, no one would. I didn't plan on telling him anytime soon. "For sure. I'll let him know." I nodded my head and my smile quickly left my face. I opened the door hearing the wind chimes. The thought of Jace ruined my mood. I still hadn't come to terms with it. I still refused to believe it. I just felt like justice still hadn't been served.

I didn't feel like going home yet. I decided it go for a walk further uptown. I heard high heels clicking a few yards ahead of me and across the street. I looked over to see a woman walking in a hurry. She was wearing a white skirt that passed her knees. She had on a black leather jacket and her heels were black. It was really dark outside so I couldn't really see her face. But her skin tone was white. I could tell she had a handbag on her shoulder. She was walking in my direction. It was starting to rain. I could hear thunder in the sky.

As I approached an intersection, she was at the same one but on the other corner. She made a left turn to go down a street that was to my right. When she made that turn I noticed a man make the turn as well. He was in all black. He had the hood on his hoodie over his head. The rain started to come down harder. I took a turn to the street on my left. I thought to myself, *is she being followed? Nah.* I continued walking down the street just to stop after a few steps. *Better safe than sorry.* I turned around and began jogging down the street to catch up to the two of them. I pulled my gun out from my waistband, it was beginning to slip down my pants. I crossed the street diagonally to the left. I could now see the two of them, the man was keeping his distance from her. The woman turned left down another street, the man followed her. *He's following her,* I thought. When I got to the street they turned on, the woman was now speed walking, clutching onto her handbag. The man copied her pace to keep the same distance between them, I decided to do the same. The lady turned again, not onto a street, but into an alleyway. I caught up to the alleyway but didn't enter. I stayed behind the building and poked my head out to see what the man was going to try and do before I intervened. He stood with his hood still up, he had black cargo pants on and black Timberlands. His hands stayed by his sides.

The woman turned around to face the man. She had her hand in her bag, raised close to her upper body. "Why are you following me?" She yelled. "I have pepper spray and I am not afraid to use it!" She continued to speak with her voice raised. I shook my head. The man was slowly walking towards her. I looked at the woman whose makeup was running down her face. I studied her from a distance. I was sure it was Ms. Laurent. *Out past curfew,* I thought to myself. "Back up!" She yelled again with a firm voice. I wondered what was going through her head at this moment.

Especially when she didn't know I was there to save her. Me of all people. "Who are you and what do you want?" I wasn't even surprised that she was asking stupid questions. Through all these questions, the man stayed silent. I was confused as to why she was still talking and not putting her words into actions.

The man pulled a gun from the front of his waistband, holding it at his side. He slowly raised it, pointing it at Ms. Laurent. "Strip," he said. I could barely hear him over the rain hitting the concrete and puddles.

As soon as I saw the gun, I came out from behind the building and began walking towards the two of them.

"Not a chance!" Ms. Laurent yelled. The man faced Ms. Laurent and couldn't see me coming. Ms. Laurent looked at me, I don't think she recognized me. It was dark and the rain didn't assist her sight.

"Get naked." The man said, Pulling back the hammer on his gun in attempt to intimidate Ms. Laurent.

As I got right behind the man, I put the gun I was holding to the back of his head. "Give me one good reason why I shouldn't blow your brains out," I said. The man lowered his gun right away. "Lady, grab the gun from him." She quickly walked up to the man and grabbed the gun. She then looked me in the eyes. Shocked that it was me. I shook my head at her. "What'd I say about 7:00 p.m.?" I questioned.

I didn't know what to do from here. My palms were sweating, it could have been the rain. My hand was shaking. "Miss, come to my side." When Ms. Laurent was standing beside me I kicked the man in his lower back forcing him to step forward. "Turn around, chump." I ordered him. He didn't listen. "I ain't gonna say it again." I knew I just caught the man Paulo had been complaining to me about. "You're the rapist, huh?" The man didn't move. He was still facing the same way as me. "You killed all those little girls? That shit ain't cute. Turn around before I kill you with your mouth open…with your thirsty self. You out here tryna steal pussy. That's real fucked up, man," I lectured. I stopped pointing the gun at him and I pulled Ms. Laurent's hand up so she would point the gun she stole from him towards him. She seemed confident with it, but I was sure she wouldn't be shooting it. I didn't think she had the willpower.

I walked over to the man to search him. "Move and you die today," I said to him. I still couldn't see his face, at this moment I didn't care who he was. Learning who he was would only make it harder to kill him. I held the gun in my hand as I reached into his back pocket to find a wallet or something. When I moved on to his second pocket, I saw his body turning. He swung his arm over my head and around my neck, putting me into a head lock. "What the fuck!" I yelled. He spun us around and I looked at Ms. Laurent. She was holding the gun in both her hands. She was unable to shoot in fear of hitting me. I didn't trust her to pull that trigger.

He squeezed harder every time I moved. He cut off my air circulation. With my hand holding the gun, I pointed it at his head and shot it. I was going to kill him without hesitating but he was fast enough to push my hand up forcing the bullet to be shot into the sky. It was like a sound grenade went off in my ear. The popping sound the gun made pierced through my eardrum. I grunted with the little air I had in my lungs. I started losing vision, I was about to faint. I tried elbowing him in his gut as hard as I could with my other free hand. He loosened the grip and threw a punch to the side of my head. I couldn't see the punch coming since he was behind me. He let go of me and I stumbled dropping to the ground. I was coughing trying to regain oxygen in my body. I swung my fist backwards with the back of my hand being the main force. My attempt missed and he tackled me back onto the ground. The gun I was holding fell out of my hands, skidding towards Ms. Laurent. I didn't really see his face but I could tell he was light-skinned. I was lightheaded from his chokehold and punch.

He got off of me and ran towards Ms. Laurent, "Shoot him!" I yelled at her. She didn't pull the trigger. I could see Ms. Laurent, she didn't want to shoot and the facial expression on her face was plain fear. The man ripped his gun back from Ms. Laurent, shoving her against one of the building walls. I got up and started running towards him. He ran past Ms. Laurent to the entrance of the alleyway. I ran in front of Ms. Laurent, picking up the gun on the ground. I aimed the gun and began shooting. I shot two bullets. The man ran forward while his gun pointed

backwards at us. I missed him. He opened fire shooting

about three times at us. I saw a bit of fire leave from the

barrel of his gun. It was a flash of light that pierced through

the rain. Small black clouds of smoke came into the air. I

shielded Ms. Laurent from the bullets, I screamed in pain as

a bullet pierced through my jacket and into the flesh of my

left arm. I felt like it went in slow motion, like I could see

the bullet the whole way but without anyway of dodging it.

I fell to the ground, gasping for air. I was in shock. I never

felt this type of pain before. Even though the rain was

pouring down, I couldn't hear it. I only heard the casing of

the bullets collide with the concrete. I cried out. "Oh God! I

can't feel my arm." I felt a burning sensation on my arm

where the bullet wound was. It burned like hell. There was

no exit wound, the bullet was still inside of me. My arm

was burning. The bullet was stopped by my bone. I was

sure of it. I continued to scream!

Ms. Laurent came down on her knees and put pressure on the wound. "Calvin, I need you to put pressure on the wound while I call 9-1-1!"

"No!" I struggled to blurt out. "I don't have insurance. The police will only make things worse. Please." I begged. I was choking on every word that came out of my mouth.

"Calvin, you're hurt! You need to go to the hospital!" She argued.

"Miss, please," I spoke and grunted at the same time.

She stopped reaching into her bag. She grabbed the gun that was still in my hand and put it into her purse. Blood continued to pour out of my arm. I looked at my arm in shock. A lot of people say they don't feel the pain right after they get shot. But I did, there was no adrenaline going through my body. Straight pain.

Ms. Laurent helped me to my feet. "C'mon. I will patch you up at my apartment." I struggled to get to my feet. I struggled to take deep breaths, I was focused on the pain. I dragged my feet walking out of the alleyway towards Ms. Laurent's place. "My apartment isn't far from here. Like ten minutes. We need to move fast, you're losing blood."

I didn't even remember the walk to Ms. Laurent's house, but we were here and she was above me with a knife in her hand as I sat on her sofa. "I need to get the bullet out before I clean and patch the wound." I was shirtless. I didn't remember my shirt coming off.

"No way! Not with that!" I refused.

She grabbed a cloth from behind her and stuck it in my mouth. "Calvin, this needs to happen." She began to dig the knife into the skin beside my wound in attempt to scoop out the bullet.

The sound of pain-filled whimpers and moans came from my cloth-filled mouth. I spat it out. "Son of a bitch!" I yelled. I followed the yell with screams. The bullet came out of my arm and it sounded like a piece of glass hitting the floor when it fell to the hardwood. I didn't shed a tear. I looked at Ms. Laurent and she quickly leaned in to hug me. She was no longer wearing her leather jacket. Just a grey crop top and the muddy white skirt. I felt lightheaded. We were both soaking wet from the rain.

She walked away and came back with gauze and large Steri-Strips, which were like Band-Aids to cover my wound. After she handled the wound, she brought me water and painkillers. She put them on the coffee table beside me. I began looking around. Her house light was dimmed. Actually she just had candles lit. "Let me ask you something," I said. "What the fuck is wrong with you?"

She gave me a dirty look. "You're telling me, when someone is following you…your brain tells you to run down an alleyway? What kind of idiot does that? For a teacher that was a dumb move. The first thing I told you when I met you was not to go out at night. I meant that. Whatever happened to your 7:00 p.m. curfew?" I wasn't lightening up on her. I could tell that she was still shaken up. But at this point I've heard gun shots so much it didn't even make me flinch anymore. "This ain't your small town in Canada. This is The Bronx! Either you think smart or get killed like an idiot!" She had tears in her eyes. I didn't care. "You probably came here thinking New York was the city of dreams, that you were coming here to find yourself. Well, everything has a lifeline – if it was created, it can be destroyed. That almost happened tonight." I was furious, mostly because I was in so much pain. "Next time…just stay home." I grabbed the pills and put them in my mouth, I grabbed the water and drank it right after. I stood up. Ms.

Laurent was always on her feet since we got to her house. I walked past her towards her door.

"Where you going?" she asked.

I turned around to look at her. "Home, you should go too." I said. "Canada."

"Calvin, stop. You don't even have your clothes," She said. "You think I meant for that to happen?" I didn't reply. "I want to thank you...for saving my life."

"That's for saving me from expulsion," I said. "We're even. Where's my clothes." I rushed through my words.

"Calvin sit down," she begged.

I sighed but I listened. I walked back over to the sofa, she sat beside me. "I wanna know the real reason," I demanded.

"Real reason for what?" She asked confused.

"Why'd you leave your city?" I clarified.

She looked at me and rubbed my bandages. "I have a sling that you can use for your arm." She was focused on the bandages. "I'm guessing because you don't like the police, you're good at keeping secrets." She was still looking at my bandages, tracing the indents from the muscles on my arm.

"I'm not a snitch…if that's what you're asking," I explained.

She nodded her head and finally looked me in the eyes. I looked at her brown eyes. I kept a straight face. "I didn't leave. I was sent away."

"Why?" I asked again. She looked at my lips, slowly approaching my face. I stayed still. In that moment, I wanted to stop it, thinking about Aaliyah. But I pictured Aaliyah. Our lips met and I felt how soft they were. Our tongues touched and I felt the texture of hers, I thought as if

I could feel every taste bud on her tongue. I leaned back and she pulled me in again. Her hands were holding my face. I now know why she was sent away. I pushed her off me. "Stop," I said, calmly.

"What's wrong?" She asked, worried.

"Your secret is safe with me, but I can't do this. I'm seeing someone," I replied.

"Seriously?" She sounded surprised. I was surprised I said that too.

"Yeah...I just can't do that to her," I confirmed. I stood up. "Where's my clothes?" I asked.

"Are you afraid?" She asked, in a cocky tone, while she stood up.

"What?" I got livid right away. "Afraid of what? Are you kidding? You ain't built for this. You couldn't even shoot the gun. You are the reason someone else might get raped tonight." I shook my head. I didn't regret a word I said and I still had more on my mind that I planned to say. "You see a nigga with a tattooed face and you feel uncomfortable. You get scared being in the hood. People don't just die here, they get kille–"

She cut me off right away. "But I'm here aren't I?"

"Why are you here? Anyone can come here. Not everyone can live here. Cause at the end of the day you can just leave!" I yelled. "I can't, none of us can. Those kids you teach, they are their only hope. Them. Themselves. Their parents depend on them. They say don't have kids if you can't provide a good future for them. But the kids are the future the parents hope to have. They're the ones who are gonna nourish the streets. They're the ones that're gonna clean these streets. You thought you were coming here to change lives, you ain't gonna do nothing, no one can. It was built like this, your people built it like this."

"Calvin, you don't think I know you and I were raised differently? I didn't decide where I was born," she explained.

"I know, and either did I. Just be grateful for what you have. You're idea of giving back is ignorance compared to my idea of giving back. You're here to make yourself feel good. I give back to make my people give back; a ripple effect, fix the hood one person, one street, one block at a time."

She turned around. She didn't want me to see her facial expression. She walked across the room. She came back and handed me my shirt, sweater and jacket which were behind her apartment door. "I'm going to get you the sling… for your arm," she was speaking awkwardly. She struggled to give me eye contact. When she returned she sat down on the sofa again. She asked me to sit down too. I could see blood seeping through the bandages. I ignored it. She rewrapped my arm, cleaning up all the blood. She helped put my arm in the sling. I grunted in pain a few times.

"What's your first name?" I asked. I thought we were on a first-name basis after that kiss.

"Serena," she said nervously.

"Serena, I'm gonna need the gun back," I explained.

"Calvin, you shouldn't have a gun. It's not good. Look at what happened to your arm. Guns kill people," she pleaded with me.

"Yeah, look at my arm. This would be your forehead right now if I didn't have this gun. There ain't no makeup that'll covering up a bullet hole. You're dead. Ask my brother." I disarmed her argument right away. "You'd be raped and killed," I said, way too calmly. I stood up. "Please just get me the gun." She stood up too. Her purse was on the ground beside the entrance. She picked it up and put her hand inside to pull out the gun. She slammed it onto my palm. I looked at her while she did it. She was upset. I could see she was holding back tears. All I could ever do was make people sad. "I'm sorry," I said. I didn't want to apologize. I struggled to put my clothes on. She put my jacket on me. "What'd the guy looked like?" I asked.

"Um, I can't remember, it was too dark. I...was scared," she hesitated. I didn't say anything. The left sleeves of my clothing dangled as my arm was strapped up in the sling.

I raised my voice, also trying to cope with the pain. "Are you kidding me?" I shouted. I turned around, I didn't want to look at her. "How didn't you see him? You looked the man who tried to take your life in the eyes. We could have stopped him...right now." I turned back to her. I could only imagine how vicious my face looked.

"You don't understand, I was terrified!" She yelled back.

"I do! That's why I said you're not built for this life. This is The Bronx!" I matched her volume.

"I get it!" She had tears flowing still.

I calmed down. "I guess I don't owe you one no more. We're even," I explained. She was able to get me in one of her classes. "Stay off the streets," I demanded. I walked to the door without saying anything else. When I left the apartment, I wasn't sure where I was. I walked through her hallway looking at the door numbers until I hit the stairs. I was walking down from the third floor. I don't remember getting up these stairs, I was probably in shock after being shot. My arm still felt numb. I could barely move my fingers.

It was late at night. The rain hadn't stopped. I looked over to my shoulder after I heard a loud engine roar down the street. Someone was riding their motorcycle around 12 a.m. It was March so I guess it was okay to ride bikes again. I passed Paulo's again. I thought about how I just came to get a burger, ending up getting shot. I walked up the steps to my apartment, I was drenched.

I got inside to see my mom fell asleep on the couch. I was going to wake her up so she could sleep in her room but I didn't want her to see my arm. I went to her room and grabbed her blanket. I came back to the living room to put it on her. I went to my room. I struggled to take off my jacket and sweater. My phone began to ring and I shut my room door immediately. I pulled it out of my pocket to see that it was soaking wet. I quickly put it in a towel and tried to dry it off. I answered the call, putting the phone to my ear. "Yeah?"

"Calvin, please answer your door." I could hear a very soft voice. They were obviously stressed. I knew who it was but I couldn't believe it. I tried to focus more on the voice then the pain in my arm. I put my jacket back on. I had nothing on underneath it, just the sling and bandages. I walked down the stairs inside the apartment to get to the front door and open it. I looked at her face, her hair was soaked, stuck to her face. It wasn't braided. It was always braided. She wasn't wearing any makeup. Although it was raining, I could tell which streams of water were tears versus the rain. She wasn't wearing a jacket. Her hoodie was bright grey turned dark because of the rain. I could tell she'd been crying for a while. Like coming here was a hard decision for her. I put my head down. In an attempt to look away. "Calvin, look at me," she requested. Her voice cracked but it was more of a choke on her words.

I attempted to hold the emotionless face I had. I was in pain, physically and emotionally. I took a deep breath and gave her the eye contact she deserved. She looked perfect. "Aaliyah, why are you here?" I struggled to ask. I said it in an angered and annoyed tone. I stayed as low voiced as possible as my mom was sleeping. I pulled her inside.

She began to raise her voice. "I can't stop thinking about you, Calvin. And I know you feel the same. So why are you fighting it? What happened the day you left my house?" She demanded to know.

"You need to lower your voice! Don't you hear me whispering?" I said.

"I'm sad, I'm frustrated! You cut me off and didn't give me a fucking reason," she explained with the same loud tone.

"How'd you find out where I live?" I asked.

"Gio," she said. I stayed silent. I closed the door behind her. "Calvin, look at me! I've been crying. You broke my heart." She broke down crying again. I put my right hand over her mouth to muffle the noise. She never broke eye contact with me. The lights weren't on in the house, but I could see the tears in her eyes. Her skin was more pale than usual. I put my only functioning arm around her neck to pull her in to hug me. She buried her face in my chest.

"Aaliyah, you gotta go home." My chin rested on the top of her head. I was happy at this moment. I didn't deserve to be.

She released from the hug. "Why are you doing this? I know you're not talking to anyone else," she said.

I wasn't but Ms. Laurent thought it was okay for her to desire her students. "I'm not." I said. I took my jacket off and helped her put it on. She was obviously cold. I was too but I really cared about her. It was big on her, although it was wet, it would keep her warm.

"What happened to your arm?" She was worried.

"Nothing."

"Calvin, there is blood coming out of the bandages. Did you get shot?" She was beyond concerned.

"I'm fine, Aaliyah. You really need to leave."

"Look me in the eyes and tell me you want me to leave," she spoke with tears continuing down her face.

I looked her in the eyes, I used my right hand to wipe the tears coming down her face. "Go home. Straight home. Nowhere else," I said strictly. She waited, looking at me. She thought I was going to kiss her. I couldn't. Not in the same night Ms. Laurent kissed me. I had respect for Aaliyah. She was everything I wanted. But with people shooting at me, I couldn't have her in the crossfire. I had a price on my head.

"Why does someone have to get hurt for you to heal? You're lying to yourself," she wanted me to reconsider.

"I am. You know I am. But you have to go. You won't understand right now. But you will soon. I promise, I'll explain. All of it." I readjusted my jacket on her, "Please, just go straight home," I pleaded again. I wiped the last of her tears. "Don't cry." I opened the door for her so she could leave. I felt like she didn't know what she was understanding but she understood. She turned to exit through the door. She didn't look back at me. I didn't think she was going to leave without looking back. I closed the door behind her. I put my back to the door and slowly dropped to the floor. I sat there. I couldn't move. I didn't feel good about anything.

Chapter Twenty: Blackout

My eyes shot open. I woke up to a flash of light through my bedroom window, lightning was striking New York. Cracks and pops of thunder boomed through my window. The rain hadn't stopped all night. I laid awake. It must have been the middle of the night. I looked at my phone which was dying. My charger wasn't working. I got up to turn on the lights. The switch wouldn't work. I don't think my mom paid the bill. I looked out my window. The streetlights weren't even on. I laid back in bed, on my back. I think New York was in a power outage. This wasn't good. Everything was free during power outages. Not by choice, by force. Loss of power turns into gain of power. Power outages turned into riots if they lasted long enough. At least in the projects. The young people in the boroughs outside of Manhattan were reckless enough to riot. Only time would tell. My phone began to ring. I looked at the number calling that I didn't recognize. "Who is this?" I asked right away. It was too early for anyone to be calling me.

"Is this Calvin?" The voice was way too calm. It was to the point where it seemed like the person was overstressed.

"Yeah, who is this?" I asked again.

"Aaliyah's mother," she clarified.

"Oh! How are you doing, Ms. Morales?" I fixed my tone.

"I'm fine. I went through Aaliyah's phone last night, you were the last person she spoke to. Could you please come to the Bronx-Lebanon Hospital?" She asked.

"Yeah, I'm leaving now. What happened?" I asked worriedly. She hung up on me. I didn't know if it was on purpose.

I got outside to see a few elementary kids playing in the rain. I didn't know why, it was about five in the morning. The sun wasn't even out yet. Things were feeling unusual. It was warm out and the puddles were large. I ran to the hospital in my Timberlands, it was only a small walk from my house. I ran through the automatic doors, running straight to the secretary. I told her who I was looking for. She pointed me in the direction I needed to go. I noticed that all the lights in the hospital were working. I ran up a few stairs and saw another secretary desk. I walked over while I read the sign above it. *ICU.* I only grew more concerned. I asked for Ms. Morales at the front desk again. A woman came from my left, "Calvin?" She was a little shorter than me in her heels.

"Yes, Ms. Morales? I ran the whole way! Is everything okay?" I looked at her eyes. I knew she knew I was worried. I wiped the rain water that was dripping from my hair onto my face.

"Calvin. You saw Aaliyah last night. How do you know her?" She had tears in her eyes. None of them fell down her face.

I couldn't lie to her. "I met her at the boxing gym. We were talking as more than friends. She came to my house last night, I told her it was better if we stayed as friends. I told her to walk straight home after. Ms. Morales, you're scaring me," I explained. "What happened?"

"Calvin, I need you to be strong," she spoke like I didn't have a choice. "Aaliyah is in a coma," she said, with tears that were heavy enough to fall from her eyes.

"No, I don't believe you! Don't tell me that!" my heart sunk. "Don't tell me that! I don't wanna hear that!" I kept repeating those words. I didn't want it to be true.

Ms. Morales spoke over me. "She was raped and shot twice, Calvin. One bullet in her thigh and one in her chest."

I broke down. I could feel tears coming to my eyes as I constantly shook my head. "No. Stop. You're lying. I just saw her," I explained. "I just saw her she's fine." I turned my head away from her. She grabbed my head and pulled it over her shoulder to hug me. I wasn't expecting it, but I accepted it. When we released from the hug my head was down I was looking at the ground around her feet. A tear fell out of one of my eyes. I watched it fall all the way to the white tiles. She was holding my hands. I didn't put my sling on, I was in a rush to get to the hospital. The pain from the bullet wound seemed minor compared to how I was feeling, hearing about Aaliyah. "Ms. Morales, I'm really sorry about this," I said with a tear rolling down my cheek. "Every time I've seen her I've walked her home. And every time she's gotten home safely. I'm sorry, Ma'am. This is my fault," I said.

She wiped my tears, then went back to holding both my hands like we were praying. "Calvin don't say that. I appreciate your love for my daughter and your eagerness to keep her safe, but no one could have stopped this." I turned my head away because I really thought I could have. "Listen to me, Calvin." She tightened the grip on my hand and it forced me to look at her again. It was hard for me to look her in the eyes. "It could have happened any other way. It was the work of the devil. Now we leave it in God's hands." I nodded my head at her. "If you have a problem, leave it in God's hands and it will be okay." I sniffed up all the mucus in my nose. She hugged me again. "Do you want to see her?" She asked me.

I took a deep breath then nodded my head. "Yes, ma'am." I tried to clean up all my slang and grammar when talking to her but it was hard to focus on my way of speaking in this situation. The only thing on my mind was the thought of losing my girl.

When I entered the room, I first saw Aaliyah's legs.
I was afraid to look at her face. I walked in holding Ms.
Morales' hand. I turned away from Aaliyah to look back at
Ms. Morales. "I'm so sorry, Ma'am. I'm sorry. This
shouldn't have happened." I put my one free hand on my
forehead in disbelief.

"Be strong, Calvin," she squeezed my hand.

I turned back to look at Aaliyah. I finally looked at
her face. She looked so pale, but still so peaceful. Her hair
was down, but messy. It was still wet from the rain. I
looked at her eyes which were shut. I closed my eyes. The
image of Aaliyah when she was at my house popped into
my head. "I'm sorry, Aaliyah," I muttered under my breath.
I opened my eyes. Aaliyah had an oxygen mask over her
mouth and nose. I was in shock. She had on a hospital
gown, but she was covered by sheets from the waist down.
Ms. Morales let go of my hand and I walked to the other
side of the bed. I slowly reached out with my hand to hold

Aaliyah's hand. *So soft.* I thought to myself. She was innocent.

"Calvin, I'm going to leave you here with Aaliyah for a bit. The police will be arriving soon to speak to me."

I nodded my head. "Okay, Ma'am."

"I think it would be a good idea if we got some food in our systems. I'm going to go to the food court afterwards." She opened the door to the room. "Do you want anything?" She asked.

"No Ms. Morales. I'm okay." I couldn't eat at a time like this. My body wouldn't allow me.

"Calvin, you need to eat. I will be back." She was going to force me to eat, I knew her type. She was Latina. I didn't understand why she asked if she was just going to force me. The door shut closed.

I went down on my knees by the bedside. I put my hands on the bed and interlocked my fingers as I began to speak to Aaliyah. "I'm sorry, Aaliyah. I know you'd say it's not my fault if you could hear me, but I wasn't there to protect you. I'm sorry... I wish I was there to protect you. I know I could have protected you... I promise you I'll never let anyone hurt you again... Including me. I know I hurt you. And I'm sorry. It's not just because of where we are now. I promise." I paused for about 20 minutes. I just sat there with my eyes closed. So many thoughts went through my head. "Aaliyah..." I heard the door open again. I could hear paper bags ruffling as the clicking of heels entered the room. I knew it was Ms. Morales. My eyes stayed closed. "My mom used to read me and Jace a poem... when we were younger, before he died. Every day I pray that he's resting in peace." I took a deep breath.

"You are the church that keeps my faith alive.

The passion of a pastor is articulated by your mind,

Your heart is the organ that bleeds music to these ears of mine.

My body, ignited by the powerful lyrics of your choir.

By nightfall, candles are lit, myself aligned with the fire.

Down on my knees, elbows bent high,

Face to the heavens, and palms exposed to the sky.

Believe I'll avoid sin, pay no heed to temptations coming every now and then.

Until next Sunday, keep my faith until we meet again."

I opened my eyes. The room was silent besides the consistent beep of the heart monitor. I looked up at Ms. Morales. She made a subtle smile at me. She put her food on the table beside Aaliyah. "Ms. Morales…I'm not sure what your exact religion is…but I would love to say a prayer with you. I believe everything will be okay, if we trust in Him," I explained.

She nodded her head. "I would love that, Calvin."

I stood up and reached for Ms. Morales' hand, which was on the other side of the bed. I grabbed Aaliyah's hand as well, Ms. Morales did the same. I closed my eyes tightly, I imagined Aaliyah when she was in good health. "Lord, we are here to thank you for watching over us. So many times people call upon your name to ask for something. But I wanna start off by thanking you for everything we have. Thank you God for having mercy on Aaliyah's life. Thank you Lord for keeping Ms. Morales strong in this unfortunate and tragic situation. I understand the situation could have been a lot worse, but we are grateful that you have had mercy on us so many times. Lord, I have lost a lot. And I don't know if Jace is with you now, but I pray you're watching over him. I pray you're protecting him. We've lost one soldier recently, please protect us here, and protect our family, friends, all of our loved ones. Please Lord, give Aaliyah the strength to wake up! Give Ms. Morales good health to be here for Aaliyah. I want to thank you for being a dependable and everlasting Heavenly Father. You've watched over us and I beg you to continue. Keep us in good health and happiness. I humbly say these things in Jesus's name. Amen." I opened my eyes to look at the tears streaming down Ms. Morales' face. "Are you okay?" I asked.

"Thank you, Calvin. You're a good boy. May God bless you," she added.

I nodded my head. "No worries and thank you," I replied. I sat down in one of the two chairs behind me. Ms.

Morales walked over to me with the food in her hand and sat down beside me. She handed me a brown paper bag. "I'm good, thank you," I explained. It was getting to 6 a.m., but I never really ate breakfast. I wasn't in the mood to eat right now.

"I'm not offering, Calvin. I'm forcing you. You're young, you're still growing. You need to eat." I knew she wasn't going to take no for an answer.

I grabbed the bag from her. "Thank you, Miss." I looked at her, she had brown eyes and thick brown hair that was slicked back into a ponytail. She had a little bit of wrinkles around her eyes, but she was still looking really young. She had on black heels, black dress pants and a white collar shirt.

I pulled the sandwich out of the paper bag. As I unwrapped it, Ms. Morales began to speak. "Calvin, may I ask who Jace is?" She asked softly.

I continued to look at my sandwich. I stopped unwrapping it. I slowly turned my head to look at Ms. Morales. "Jace…my brother," I finished. I began unwrapping my sandwich again.

"He passed away?" She investigated.

I spoke looking back down. "Yes." I wrapped my food back up. I wasn't going to eat this morning.

"You don't have to talk about it if you don't want to." I could tell she felt as if she was intruding.

"He was shot in December. They found him in a ditch about a week later." I looked back at her. "I've been in this position before, Miss. But Aaliyah will be okay. I know she will. She's a strong girl." Ms. Morales was smiling. "You did a great job raising her. She has great morals and has respect for herself. God will seek justice for you. I promise…it will be okay." I tried to reassure that everything would work out. Even if I wasn't sure myself.

"I'm sorry about Jace," she said.

"It's okay. He's a good man. Sometimes, things just happen," I explained. "I think there was a reason he left. It may have not been revealed yet. But he didn't just die for nothing."

"Everything happens for a reason. It will be revealed soon enough. My mother used to tell me God works in mysterious ways," she said. She was right. The room went quiet for a few minutes, but the beeping sound of the heart monitor continued to pierce through my eardrums. I felt pain with that noise. I don't know why, it was just the sound of tragedy to me.

I stayed with Ms. Morales and Aaliyah for about six more hours. I was getting to know Aaliyah's mother. She seemed to really like me. I could understand, after speaking to her, why Aaliyah thought she was so strict. I could also hear a small Spanish accent in her voice. "Calvin, you're missing school right now?" She was concerned.

"Yeah," I replied. I didn't care. I wanted to be here with them.

"Calvin, you should collect your work and then you can come back."

"Okay. I'll go and come back." I wasn't going to argue with her. "I'll be back in a few hours." I stood up. I walked towards the door. "I want to let you know that I really appreciate you calling me to see Aaliyah. You're a great mother."

She smiled at me before she spoke. "Thank you, Calvin. You're a good boy." I nodded my head at her. I held my sandwich in my hand. I left the hospital right after. I didn't have my jacket. The rain was still coming down. I quickly ran up a hill to get to Grand Concourse. On this road there was the subway station 174-175. None of the businesses and stores were open. I walked down the stairs to enter the subway tunnel while eating my sandwich. It was cold and a little wet from the rain. I stayed at the station for about twenty minutes waiting for the train. I was sitting on a bench, staring at the train tracks. The train never came, no trains came. The Bronx was still in a power outage. I got out of the tunnel and back onto street level. I began walking to school.

When I arrived to the school it was a quarter past 1 p.m. I walked up to the front doors of the school. Gio's cousin was there again. "Wassup, G?" I asked. The slang and the slurring of words came back to me after leaving Ms. Morales.

"Tryna get a dolla," he said.

"I feel that... Does the school have power?"

"Yeah, they got a power generator over here."

"Oh, for real? You think you could let me in?"

"Damn, Calv." He was shocked.

"What?"

"Last time... you pulled up with an empty backpack... no books." He laughed. "You ain't even bring the bag this time, G." He was laughing as he opened the door.

I shook my head. I couldn't laugh. "Whatever, son." I walked through the door. The door shut behind me. I walked straight to Ms. Laurent's class. I looked into the class through the small glass window there was on the door. The class was full and a student was reading out of a book to the whole class. I opened the door and it made a loud screeching sound. I walked through the door without caring about disturbing the entire class. I walked to the back of the class and sat at the only open desk. As the student continued to read, I leaned back a bit in my chair. I wasn't there because I needed to be, I was here to please

Aaliyah's mother. I was silent. No one cared about what I

had to say so I just kept to myself.

The student continued to read out of the book. I

looked up at Ms. Laurent. She was staring at me. I looked

at her with a dirty look. I blamed her for what happened to

Aaliyah. It wouldn't have happened if she shot him. I rested

my head on my hand and my elbow rested on the desk. I

looked away from Ms. Laurent. I think I dozed off a few

times. I was woken up by a bell. I stayed seated while the

class rose up to leave. Voices scattered as everyone walked

through the door. I was at my desk, I didn't move an inch.

Ms. Laurent was sitting on top of her desk, with her legs

hanging off the edge. She got off the desk, pulling some

papers and a textbook off of it. Ms. Laurent slowly started

walking over to me. "Calvin, where have you been? Your

teachers told me you missed every class today." She was

shaking her head. I continued looking at her as she dropped the papers on my desk. She continued to hold the textbook. "This is all the work you didn't do today. We have until 4:30 p.m. today." She was still going to try and catch me up with all of my school work. "Where have you been?" She demanded to know. I was stubborn. I didn't speak, I wasn't going to speak. "Calvin, you need to start talking. Why are you showing up late to class again? You've changed. You're not like this anymore." She began to raise her voice. But she brought it back down for her next choice of words. "You have guns now! Are you crazy?"

I looked her in her eyes. "There are people who are alive…lucky to be alive. There are people fighting for their lives. There are people dead." I had so much on my mind, but those were the words I opened my mouth to speak.

She shook her head to clear her mind. She had the look of confusion fused with attitude. "What are you saying right now?" She was towering over me as I stayed seated. I didn't say anything after I spoke those words. She sat down in the desk beside me. She stared at the side of my head. I didn't look at her. I continued to stare straight. She opened the math textbook. "Calvin, look at me." I didn't budge. "C-Calvin!" She grunted. "I'm not gonna sit here and let you disrespect me." She stood up. "If you're not ready to learn then you can just go home right now. This is bullshit, Calvin."

I stood up. "Facts." I didn't have anything nice to say to her. I was trying to keep cool. I grabbed the homework off the desk. "Take care," I said. I began walking towards the door.

"You're ridiculous, Calvin." She tried to get her last words in.

I was at the door when I turned around to look at her. "Ridiculous? You wanna know what I find ridiculous?" I dropped the paper onto the ground. "Serena, the girl I'm seeing... she was –" I stopped myself. I took a deep breath, avoiding the emotion that was rushing to my eyes in tear form. "My girl was raped. Raped and shot... twice. The same man who came after you, the same man did that to her. What's ridiculous is... it woulda never happened, y'know? It woulda never happened, if you just pulled that trigger. Pull that trigger, save my girl." I kept my voice at a calm tone. "If you need me I'll be at the fucking hospital," I said. I left without saying anything else or looking at Ms. Laurent's face.

It was past three. The rain was flooding the streets. The power still wasn't on. People were on the streets, more people were on the roads then cars. A lot of people were surrounding stores. I ignored it. I continued walking. I was going to go home and shower before I went back to the hospital. I heard a loud crashing sound. I thought it was a car crash. I turned my head drastically towards the sound.

There were about 20 people jumping through a large shop window. They broke in. I stopped to watch people running out with electronics. Two men helped lift a flat screen TV out of the window. I continued walking. The police would be arriving shortly. I was sure of it. I walked about 10 blocks and heard sirens in the distance. I walked up the stairs of the apartment. I took off all of my clothes, it was hard because they were stuck to my body. I looked at myself in the mirror. I looked like I was stressed. I hopped into the shower. *You're in a shocked state,* I told myself that. I didn't know if that was true. But I diagnosed myself.

Chapter Twenty-One: 8 Days, Unconscious Conscience

Day One: Friday

I got dressed, I didn't think about anything but Aaliyah. I left the gun in my drawer. My mom wasn't home. I left the home without hesitating, it was the evening.

I arrived at the hospital and the nurse that was attending to Aaliyah made me sign in. She needed to monitor who was coming in and how often. Security searched me. "Why wasn't I searched earlier?"

"It was when Aaliyah was first admitted to the hospital. It's just precautions don't worry." I was worried. If a security guard has to search me down that means they're worried. The idea of me bringing in a weapon was on their mind, which means it's happened before. The only thing that tells me is that someone had been sent to the hospital and another person came in to finish the job.

I walked past them and into Aaliyah's room. No one was in there. I sat down in one of the chairs. I could hear her breathing. It was heartbreaking to me. To hear her so alive, but to see her so lifeless.

I spoke, in my head. *Aaliyah, I know I'm not a good guy. I know I probably put you through hell. I just don't see what I could have done. This is exactly what I was afraid of. Harming you. You getting hurt was the last thing I wanted. I have people out there trying to put me in a bed next to you, if not, next to Jace. But to be honest, in this moment, I'd rather me be in that bed instead of you. Cause when I saw you for the first time in the gym, I just loved how alive you were. I saw you doing those drills, you were so alive. But I can't believe this. I hate seeing you like this. You got a breathing mask on. It's hard for me to see you struggling to breathe. It's hard for me to see you barely alive cause you made me feel so alive. I know I've only met you a couple of weeks ago. But I swear spiritually, I've known you my whole life. If you could hear me right now…I think you'd agree with that. Please, Aaliyah… wake up.*

Day Two: Saturday

I walked to the hospital straight from school. It was still raining. It slowed down, but it was still going. It hadn't stopped for three days now. The power was still out. The hospital's generators lasted up to two weeks depending on how many people they were nursing. At least that's what the nurse told me. I walked into Aaliyah's room after signing in again. She hadn't moved at all. She was alone. I sat down. "I miss you, Aaliyah."

Everything I am, everything I will be… I want you to be there for it. I found happiness through you. I'm sorry I took yours away. I promise you when you're back at one hundred percent, I'll make the most of everything with you. You will be back right? You're everything to me. I don't wanna think like this but… if you don't come back at one hundred percent, I want you to live your dreams through me. Aaliyah, I just want to see you happy. I want to see you smile. I miss you calling me crazy all the time. I miss you grabbing my face. You are so aggressive. You were so aggressive. I miss that. Please, Aaliyah… I don't want to rush you. I don't want to rush what God has planned, but please… Aaliyah, please… wake up.

Day Three: Sunday

I miss you. I wish I could have taken the bullets for you. I wish you wouldn't be in pain. I wish you were moving, smiling, loving. I wish you were loving me. They say you never know what you have until you lose it. But I've always known. You're my everything. You have my heart. If you leave me... I will leave too... with you. A part of me would die with you, Aaliyah. I never thought anyone could mean this much to me. But when I saw you, I knew you would. I was just scared, scared of this. I didn't want to open up to anyone. Cause everyone ends up leaving. Whether they want to or not. Here we are, you're on the fence. Please, Aaliyah...stay on this side. Please, wake up.

Day Four: Monday

Everything I am... isn't what I want to be, but what I need to be. At least that's what I thought. I wanna know about all your problems whether they are physical or emotional. I want to hold on to the pain for you, if you don't want me to talk about it then I won't speak about it. Because if someone I love is going through it... I'd rather it be me. I'd shed blood for you. I want to protect you. Aaliyah, I promise to protect you and anyone else in danger. I promise. Whether we're together or not. I swear to keep you safe. Hold me to those words. Cause I mean it. Anything you want I will do my best to give it to you. If you can dream it, you can have it. I want to work so you don't have to.

I want your mother to like me, I want her to know how much I care about you. I care about you. Aaliyah, please...wake up.

"When you're ready, I'll be here," I said as I stood up to go home. Visiting hours were almost done. I held Aaliyah's hand before I left. I slowly let go. I was hoping she would grip my hand. She didn't. I began walking to the door. The door swung open. "Mr. Mike." I stared at him.

"Calvin, what are you doing here?" He was surprised.

"I thought I'd come see a real fighter," I said.

He smiled. "She's gonna be okay. I'm sure of it." He reached out for a handshake.

"I hope so." I shook his hand. "Sir…Mr. Mike. I'm ready to come back. I never stopped training. I've been working out at home," I explained. I wanted to bring Aaliyah happiness and make something of myself. "To the gym. I wanna fight. Real fights." I wanted opponents.

"I can make it happen, Calvin," he replied.

I nodded my head. "It was good seeing you, Mr. Mike."

"Likewise. See you tomorrow. 4:00 p.m. Don't be late." He was demanding. I nodded my head and left the room.

I got home to see Gio waiting outside for me. "My guy, why didn't you go in? It's pouring out here."

"It's not even raining that hard." He followed me up the stairs and into the apartment. "So how is she? Is she looking better?" He was asking about Aaliyah.

"Honestly…I don't know man. I'm worried. I hate seeing her like that." I shook my head.

"She's a fighter, she's gonna make it," he reassured. It was Monday and the lights were still out from the blackout. Gio was looking around the apartment. He was confused. "Why are all your clocks so late?" Gio asked.

"We're in a power outage. What do you expect?"

"No…the clocks running on batteries are late," he explained.

"Who cares, they'll be right twice a day," I justified.

Gio stopped to look at me. "Bruh, that's not at all how it works, my guy." He laughed at me.

"Whatever, man." I shook it off. "I saw Mr. Mike today. I told him I'm coming back."

"Word?" He needed confirmation.

"I wanna fight…for real."

"You can do it. I'm serious. You got that raw talent." He was excited.

"I'm the comeback kid," I said calmly.

Day Five: Tuesday

Gio and I walked into the gym with our gloves around our shoulders. I stopped at the entrance to take in the banners on the walls again. It was tough to be here. I felt like I had to fight for Aaliyah to fight. I couldn't ask her to fight if I couldn't. If that was really the case, then I would fight till death. I went into the change room with Gio. I took off my shirt but struggled. My arm was no longer in the sling but it was still in pain. I wasn't thinking. I wouldn't be able to train hard. I had my arm in bandages still. "You good, Calv?" Gio said looking at the bandages.

"G, you won't believe it. You know the rapist?"

"The rapist? I don't know him. But I've heard about it. It's everywhere," he explained.

"I was walking home from Paulo's and I seen him following Ms. Laurent. I stopped him from raping her, maybe even killing her." I started rubbing my shoulder. "I just wish I could have done the same for Aaliyah."

"Calv, that ain't your fault. No one knew this would happen," he explained.

"But I knew, G. I knew there was a madman out there. I still let her walk home alone." I shook my head. "I can't stop thinking about how lonely she was walking home. How she feared for her life. Now she's fighting for it. I'm pissed. I wanna murder that man, G. If he's taking lives...he doesn't deserve his," I yelled in frustration.

"Calvin. Keep your mind straight. Focus on the better things." He reached in to give me a handshake. "Don't do no crazy shit without talking to me."

"You gonna try and stop me, huh?" I questioned.

"If you really need to kill a killer... I'm not about to let you do it alone." He was still holding onto my hand. He grabbed the back of my head with his free hand and lightly bumped his forehead against mine. "We're brothers. I'll ride with mine, I'll die for mine… and if it has to come down to it… I'll kill for mine." He expressed his loyalty.

"You're really my brother." I never seen such loyalty in my life. I've had my own blood betray me and my family. Gio was more than a friend.

"So what happened to your arm then?" He was still confused.

"The rapist tackled me to the ground. He don't care about life. He ran up on Miss… stole her gun and started shooting at us. I shielded her from the bullet. It could have been worse. I'm mad as fuck that I didn't see his face. He could be walking with us daily. We wouldn't even know it." I clenched my fist.

"He'll pay… don't even worry about that. But how you supposed to train?"

"I know. I wasn't thinking about that. My left arm is so weak right now. I gotta tell him I'm not going all out today."

When we got out, Mr. Mike was waiting for us. "Tape those gloves up! We back baby! We came to stay!" He was getting me hyped up. I didn't think I could get hyped after the recent events.

"We callin' him the comeback kid now!" claimed Gio.

"You ready, Calvin?" Mr. Mike asked, seriously.

I nodded my head. "I'm here now." Right away, Mr. Mike made me spar with him. He showed me several different combinations. I was catching on to them way too easily. I kept my hands up, bouncing back and forth. My left arm felt really sore. Hard jabs and strong uppercuts was what I was throwing, but only with my right hand. I could see Mr. Mike was impressed. I had a lot of strength behind my punches. "Can we slow this down? I want to do some technique training. Defense mechanisms."

I didn't think Mr. Mike would agree with that. But today he had more sympathy. "Alright, technique and cardio for the rest of the practice." For once I wasn't too mad about doing cardio. It was a lesser strain on my barely functioning arm.

After the gym, Gio and I went to visit Aaliyah. Bea came with us. I could see on the walk over that they were a good couple. I noticed that Gio was really happy, I was glad there was someone who could keep him in a positive mindset. At the hospital, we met with Ms. Morales. I gave her a hug, she was happy to see me but I could tell she was still really stressed. I understood why, not just focusing on the health of her daughter, but the aftermath that included medical bills, rehabilitation and therapy. It was just a lot to put on one person. I wish I could have helped. But most of the money I stole from Xavier was already given to my mother. I sat down beside Ms. Morales. We both looked at Aaliyah, with all the tubes and machines connected to her, I feared for her life. I tried to stay hopeful though.

"How do you know Aaliyah?" Ms. Morales was asking Gio.

"Uh, Calvin and I both went to the gym with her," Gio spoke with a soft tone. "This is my girlfriend, Bea."

"Thank you both for coming," said Ms. Morales. She was more tense than usual.

I looked at Aaliyah's mother. She wouldn't look back at me. She could see me from the corner of her eye. "Ms. Morales..." I put my hand on her hand which was rested on her thigh. "It's going to be okay. I promise. You just need to be faithful." She finally looked at me to smile.

We all shared the good times we had with Aaliyah at the gym. I told Ms. Morales about how respectful Aaliyah was. How she never fails to put a smile on my face.

The visiting hours were coming to an end. I didn't talk much besides the words I said to Ms. Morales. She got up and kissed Aaliyah's forehead. "I have to go to work, Calvin." She was working overtime I guessed. I could only imagine what she was going through. "Thank you for coming to see Aaliyah. It was nice meeting you two."

"It was a pleasure meeting you too," Gio responded to Ms. Morales. Bea smiled and said her goodbyes to Ms. Morales as well.

As Ms. Morales began walking to the door I got up to follow her. I felt like I had to say something to her before she left. We got outside of Aaliyah's room. "Wait, Ms.

Morales." She turned to look at me. I closed the room door behind me. "I just wanted to give you a hug."

"Calvin, please… I have to go to work." She was trying to hide her emotions from me.

I still walked up to her with my arms wide open. She let me hug her. She wasn't wearing heels and I now towered over her. I could hear her start to cry. Her body was trembling. I held back my tears. I was good at that. "You don't always gotta be strong," I said. "It's okay to show emotion."

She was still in my arms, crying. "You deserve to be with my daughter. You're good for her."

I wasn't expecting those words but I accepted and appreciated them. "Thank you, ma'am." We released from the hug and she looked at me. Her mascara was running down her cheeks. "My mom used to say to me, the Lord gives the toughest battles to His strongest soldiers. I know

Aaliyah will overcome this battle…and when she does…she's going to need us here. To be strong for her." After speaking these words to Ms. Morales, she forced a smile without teeth. She turned away from me to leave. I watched her walk away.

I entered the room again. Bea and Gio were silent. The sound of the heart monitor continued to beep. "Calv, we gotta go now." Gio said standing up along with Bea. They walked over to the door where I was standing.

"Yeah, it's all good. Get home safely… and let me know when y'all do."

Gio stuck his handout for a handshake and I gave him one. "It'll all be good, bro." I nodded my head at him. They left without saying anything else.

I had told Ms. Morales that it was going to be okay but I didn't know if I believed that myself. I walked over to the other side of Aaliyah's bed, sitting down on one of the chairs. I plugged my phone into the outlet on the wall. I had to charge my phone at the hospital because my apartment and other parts of the borough still didn't have the electricity back. I looked up at Aaliyah. Still so quiet, still peaceful.

I'm sorry this happened to you. I just want to see you happy again. God please. I know I'm not doing as well as I should be. I know I may not be on the right path but I want to be. And if I'm going to ask you to do things for me, then I'm going to need to be on the right path. But I just need a favor from you. I won't ask for nothing else, I don't want nothing else. I just need to know...are you going to take Aaliyah from me, from us? And if you really are going to take her from us...please God, let me take her place. I don't want Ms. Morales to lose her.

My thoughts were interrupted by a call on my phone. I picked up my phone to see who was calling. It was a random number from an area code I wasn't familiar with. I answered the call. Waiting for a voice. "Yo!" yelled the person.

"Who is this?" I asked.

"It's K.C. and Jerem!" Jerem yelled from a distance. They were really excited to talk to me.

"What the hell! Y'all good?" I was shocked to hear their voices after all the news.

"Good, my man. We're good. Just feeling a little crazy from everything. It feels weird being home," said Jerem.

"It's almost like we never left, but like I swear I went crazy over there. For real, people over here are taking their lives for granted. I look at them like they wouldn't have survived one day on the compound. They had kids holding guns, taking lives. Eight years old. They should be holding crayons or playing video games. I swear my mentality right now is a bit psychotic," said K.C. "I feel like life is no big deal to me. Like killing isn't a problem. It's crazy," he clarified.

I didn't know how to reply the right way. "I hear you, bro. It's crazy out there. It's a warzone out here too. We got a serial killer out here... He almost took my girl's life too. I'm with her right now. She's in a coma."

"I'm sorry about that man. But look, be thankful she's still here. Y'all will be okay, let God do His thing," K.C. said. I nodded my head without saying anything. They didn't know I nodded my head. "Be strong," K.C. said.

"Y'all are the strong ones. People go through situations like that and come back with their brains messed up. They can't function," I said. "But y'all sound the same on this side of the phone."

"We were in it together, so it could have been way worse. Like I had Jerem, Jameson and Troy," he explained.

"Who?" I was confused.

"We were all child soldiers. Troy's gone. He was killed tryna protect the group," Jerem said.

"May he rest in peace," K.C. interrupted.

"Jameson was a little wild at the beginning but he's our brother now. He's a real ride or die type of guy. My mom sponsored him. So he's with us now." Jerem finished explaining. They had a small Ghanaian accent on their English.

"That's good, I'm glad y'all made it out," I whispered.

"Sometimes I do think about killing... how easy it is. I almost killed someone my first day back. Jameson had to stop me. I wouldn't have stopped myself. I wasn't going to stop. I just feel like life is nothing and that's why it's so special." K.C. paused for a few seconds. "You could leave, just like that."

"You're right," I said.

The call was silent for a bit. "Calvin, I'm sorry to hear about Jace," K.C. said with sympathy.

"Yeah, we heard. It's never easy," Jerem included.

I looked up from the ground, focusing on Aaliyah. "Never easy. We've lost a lot. But let's focus on the people we have... while we still have them."

"I agree," K.C. said softly.

"I gotta go... but I'll come visit y'all as soon as school is out," I promised.

"Yeah, just let me know," K.C. replied.

I hung up the phone and looked at Aaliyah again. "You'll be okay," I said. I stood up and left the hospital room.

Day Six: Wednesday

I sat in front of Aaliyah for over an hour without saying anything, I wasn't thinking about much either. I was just looking at her. She was so pure to me. I didn't understand why anyone would do this to her. I looked at her lips through the breathing mask. They were really dry. I just remembered her lips always being so perfect, always so irresistible. I shook my head.

Aaliyah, I miss you. Everything about you. I just can't see you like this no more. Because so much blood was shed for nothing. You used to be the one to give me life, you made feel alive. I want that feeling again. You have way too much to live for. I went back to the gym for you. I struggled, but I wanted to remind myself that the gym was my happy place. It's because I met you there. I forgot that for a bit but I'm back now. I won't leave again. I'm going to protect you, I promise. I've lost too much. I don't want to add to the list. I promise to protect you. I'm going to make whoever did this, regret it. That's the only thing that will make me feel better. You wouldn't want me to do that. But I've already made up my mind. I'm going to kill a killer. I was raised eye for an eye. But the killer has a whole crowd watching him now. I want nothing but revenge. I won't settle for less.

The door closed, I looked up. "Hello…Calvin. Visiting hours are about to end. I'm sorry, you have to go now," said the nurse.

"Yeah, it's all good. I understand. I was just leaving." I put both of my hands on each armrest on the chair. I pushed myself up and felt a sharp pain in my left arm. I collapsed and fell back into the chair. "Damn it!" I yelled. I held my left arm. I felt the pain of the bullet wound. I looked up at the nurse who was staring at me.

"What's wrong?" She asked.

"Uh…nah don't worry about it. I'm good," I replied.

"No…you're not. You're in pain. Tell me what the problem is," she demanded.

"I was boxing…It's just a bruise. I'm good, don't worry." I stood up without using the armrests. "Now if you excuse me, I'll be on my way." I started walking to the door.

"Prove it," she said, blocking the door.

I laughed a bit. "You can't be serious right now."

"I can. Show me the bruise," she demanded.

I sighed, slowly pulling off my jacket to reveal the wound, I watched the nurse's face the whole time. "See…just a bruise," I said, smiling without teeth. I looked at my arm. The gauze I put on it was now red. It was originally white. *How is it still bleeding?* I asked myself.

"Calvin! Sit down! Are you crazy?" She left the room and came back within seconds. She carried in a lot of tools with her on some cart.

"I don't know what you think you're about to do…but I don't got insurance and I'm not about to pay for any of this," I reassured.

"Remove the bandages." She ignored everything I said.

"Okay, what's your name, lady?"

She laughed. "It's Jazelle."

"Jazelle, I don't want you touching me. I actually cannot afford any type of medical treatment at the moment," I explained again.

"This one is on the house! Don't worry, just remove your bandages," she clarified.

"Who's house? Because like I said before –"

She cut me off. "Calvin, relax. It's okay...just remove your bandages."

I continued looking at her for a few seconds. She was looking at me too. I nodded my head. "Alright... I hope you're not a screamer," I said.

She laughed again before seeing the opened wound. Her face went blank. She became focused with still eyes. "Oh my God, did you get shot or something?" She began applying pressure around the wound and a little stream of blood began to pour out. "This is terrible."

"It's just a bruise," I explained.

"Calvin, when did this happen? You need stitches." She began playing with her tools on the cart.

"Like a week ago, not that long," I said.

"Not that long? Do we need to check you into the psychiatric ward too?" She didn't even laugh.

"Very funny." I shook my head. "What are you gonna do?"

"I'm going to do my best, stay still." She began disinfecting the wound with some type of rubbing alcohol looking bottle. The wound was hard to look at. It was pale all around the interior part. It was also swollen and looked like it had be sitting in water for a long time. All the skin around it looked soft and fragile. It also smelled horrible. I stared at her attending to my gunshot wound. She seemed kind of young. I was speaking to her as if she was, I assumed she was in her late 20s. Jazelle had the lower half of her face covered with a surgical mask. Her eyes were brown and she was black. Her hair was single braids tied up in a bun.

"Where you from Jazelle?" I asked.

"Nigeria," she answered. She was very focused on the wound. She put a needle into the skin around the wound. She began squeezing while I grunted in pain.

"What are you putting into my skin?" I clenched my fists as she continued.

"I'm freezing the skin so I can stitch it up." Her eyes never broke away from the wound.

I continued to half-grunt, half-speak. "If it's frozen...why does it still hurt?"

"Calvin, you can't be leaving a wound like this. You have to understand that it could have gotten infected, next thing you know you have to cut your arm off."

"What! Chill!" I yelled while in pain. She began stitching up my arm. I looked at Aaliyah to ease my pain. I thought what I was going through right now was bad. Aaliyah had it so much worse. "That's my girlfriend in that bed right there," I said to Jazelle.

She looked up at me. "I'm very sorry about your girlfriend."

"She'll be okay. I know it."

"Not everything is in the hands of the doctors...We even pray for God's assistance when dealing with patients. We can only do what God allows us to do," she said to me.

I looked back over to Jazelle and nodded my head. "I understand. Thank you, Jazelle."

"Okay! All done." She rubbed some type of gel on and around the stitches. She then wrapped it with brand new gauze. "Be careful! Next time, come in! I don't care if you're afraid of the medical bills. I will see what I can do for you."

I was sure she could've lost her job for helping me. "Thank you, Jazelle. I appreciate you…for everything. Thank you for looking after Aaliyah."

"She's a strong girl. Stay hopeful," she said.

"I will." I stood up. My arm felt weird. I put my jacket back on and I looked at Aaliyah one last time. *See you tomorrow.* I walked through the doors to leave the hospital.

It was almost pitch black when I left the hospital. The streetlights were still off. The city hadn't had electricity for as long as Aaliyah had been unconscious. I continued my walk home in the darkness. It matched my emotions. I watched police patrol the Bronx, in cars and on foot. It wasn't raining but I could tell the skies were filled with clouds. I couldn't see the moon. Things weren't looking too bright.

Day Seven: Thursday

I spoke to Ms. Morales outside of Aaliyah's room. She was in her church clothes. She came from a church mass with a few deacons but she was headed home now. I couldn't remember the last time I went to church. I never stopped being faithful though. I always believed in better

times. It was just a matter of when they were coming.
Things weren't normal. I didn't know what I was supposed
to be feeling but I knew what emotions I was experiencing
at this stage. I was angry at the person who caused this pain
for Aaliyah, her mother, and all of her loved ones. I was
frustrated at the fact that she hadn't woken up yet. I was
broken, almost.

"Calvin, how are you feeling today?" Ms. Morales
asked me.

"I'm feeling…faithful," I said, in a soft tone. I
intended to give her hope.

She smiled. "Me too." I think she was telling the
truth. I wasn't. I didn't want to doubt my faith. Doubting
my faith was doubting Aaliyah's strength. I knew she was
strong, I was just scared for once. "I have to run to work
but I'm glad you're here to keep Aaliyah company. She

needs to feel that people are here for her and that they care for her." She *really* had faith.

I nodded my head. "I'll be here for her," I said. She opened her arms up for a hug. I quickly gave her one and she began walking down the hall.

I looked at Aaliyah's door. I opened the door to walk over and sit down on a chair beside her. It was a few minutes past 7:00 p.m. I had school tomorrow and I didn't plan on going. I just knew that everyone would want me to. I stared at Aaliyah who looked so innocent. She was so still she looked so soft and pale. "Aaliyah, I'm here for you," I said. I thought about what she would say back if she wasn't in this situation. *I don't need no protecting. I could probably hurt you.* I shook my head. She was always aggressive but that would probably change now. I put my head down. Looking at the floor. *Lord, I can't do this no more. I need Aaliyah back. She doesn't deserve this. She shouldn't be going through this pain. She's done nothing but good. I want to take her spot. I need to know she is going to be okay. Don't let her get hurt no more. God, please give me the strength to defend Aaliyah at all times. I just can't be sure that she's safe. I don't know if she's going to be okay. Is she going to be okay?* I stood up in frustration. I paced back and forth in the room. I started speaking out loud. "Is she going to be okay? I need to know. I can't do this no more. I'm suffering watching her suffer." I wanted to punch a wall but I was trying to keep my cool. "God! This isn't fair. Why is she going through this? Please! Don't put her through all this pain just to take her away from us." I came to the other side of the bed, looking at Aaliyah and the reflection of the room from the window. It was brighter inside than it was outside, so I could only see myself in the window. I bent down to kneel beside Aaliyah. I closed my eyes. "Lord. Please. Don't put

Aaliyah through all this pain. Don't put us through pain. I can't take the stress. I need to know it's going to be okay, I need a sign, God. If you are going to fix things... If you're going to make everything okay, please just give me a sign! I can't watch this no more." I was crying out loud, I needed answers. "I know... and I understand if I'm not worthy. But I want you to know I believe in you. I believe only good comes from you. Give me a sign. Tell me it'll be alright. If Aaliyah is going to be Alright, please God... show me!" I opened my eyes. I had tears forming in them. I felt a stream trickle down my face, a tear slid down my left cheek. A flash of light caught my attention through the windows. The streetlights came back on. I looked out the window, shocked at the timing. *A sign during the sign of the times.* I thought to myself. *Thank you, God.* I took a deep breath. I got up from my knees. I walked around the bed to the chairs. Sitting down and looked and looking Aaliyah, I spoke. "It'll be okay. When you're ready to come back...I'll be here." I sat patiently waiting for my girl to wake up.

I fell in and out of sleep while holding onto Aaliyah's hand. It was like that for a few hours. I was supposed to go home but Jazelle was kind to me. She asked me if I was staying overnight. I would, I just didn't have my things. She explained to me that it was always good for Aaliyah to have company with her, whether she knows it's there or not. Jazelle said she feels as if people in comas could feel the energy and vibes around them. I believed that too, which is why I've come to see Aaliyah every day since the tragedy. I spent several hours in this room this for the past week. I slept in an awkward position on the chair. It wasn't comfortable but it would do. I felt a squeeze on my hand. I damn near broke my neck looking up at Aaliyah. She was still unconscious. My frustration only grew larger.

I have all these thoughts in my head, these thoughts on how I feel about you. Thoughts that you never got to hear. But they're the thoughts I want to tell you. I need you to wake up. I looked at her face. She still had the breathing mask on. I could see emotion on her face. I rubbed her hand with my thumb as I held onto her hand. I spoke to her for a few minutes. "You know I never really thought anyone could care about me as much as you do. I never thought I would mean something to someone. I just caused too many problems to be loved by someone… well, that's what I told myself. You changed my mind, you've changed my whole mindset on life. You taught me how to care. I'm still learning how to love. I wanna learning to love you more than I already do. It's crazy. No one's ever made me feel like this. I wish I didn't have to tell you all of this under these circumstances… but I want to be with you." I paused. I thought about all the possible things I could do to hurt her in the future. I followed up with all the ways to avoid those situations. I wanted her to have nothing but happiness on her face. "I promise you'll never hear the words, 'sorry I cheated on you.' That's something I will never have to say to you. Not because I'm lying. It's just always gonna be you that I want. I want no one but you." I felt my hand get rubbed back. Softly.

I closed my eyes. Taking a deep breath, I opened them again. I slowly moved my eyes from the floor to her face. I watched her eyes slowly open up with widened eyes that sharply scanned the room for an idea of where she was. The light was really bright for her. "Don't move," I said. "Just breathe, you're gonna to be okay," I said. She forced a smile. I knew she was in pain. I got up to quickly turn off the lights then went right back to holding her hand. "Squeeze my hand if you know who I am." I said full of hope. I wanted to make sure she didn't have any memory loss. Jazelle was the one who told me that amnesia was common for patients recovering from comas.

She lightly squeezed my hand. I could tell her body was really weak at the moment. "Calvin," Her voice was muffled by the breathing mask, it also sounded like an overly raspy morning voice. I smiled, fighting my tears. "I missed you." She really struggled to get those words out.

"Don't speak, just rest," I replied. "But... I missed you too. More than you'll ever know. You had me worried, but I knew you'd be back... you're a fighter," I explained.

"Back?" She was too stubborn to take my advice on getting rest.

"You were in a coma... for about a week. Don't worry about that. You're back now," I explained. "Just focus on getting rest, Aaliyah. I'll be here for you. I'll protect you. I promise."

She gave me a dirty look. Like she didn't believe me. I didn't know how to react. We were still holding hands. "Calvin… I can't," I saw tears coming from her eyes. It broke my heart. "I can't remember what happened. I don't know what happened." I could barely hear her words through the breathing mask.

I put my hand on her forehead, stroking backwards to her hair. "Hey, chill…it's okay. Don't think about that now." I looked her in her eyes. Something that was normally so hard for me to do. I saw fear in her eyes. I never thought I'd see that from a woman who I knew was so strong. "Aaliyah… take your time. You'll be okay. Right now… I just want you to focus on recovering." I looked toward the door. I knew I was supposed to get Jazelle. "Heal now, think later," I clarified. That was code to me for rest now, revenge later. I didn't plan on letting her being the only person in pain. She closed her eyes again. It made me nervous. Seeing her with her eyes closed for so long just triggered discomfort in my mind. I let go of her hand, standing up to go talk to Jazelle.

I got into the hall, and asked the receptionist for Jazelle. I waited for about two minutes before Jazelle showed up. "Hey, Calvin. How is everything?" She was concerned looking at my face. She could probably tell I was emotional. I froze. "Calvin?"

"She's awake," I said.

"That's amazing! Okay, did it just happen?" She went from a friend back to a nurse in a split second.

"Yeah, like five minutes ago."

"Okay, I'm going to set a few things up. We gotta take some tests to checkup on her," she confirmed.

"Do what you gotta do." I turned to walk back to the room.

"Calvin. Do you want to call her mom for me?"

"Yeah, I can do that." I nodded my head.

Jazelle walked into Aaliyah's room, while I walked down the hall to make a call. "Hey Calvin, is everything okay?"

"Um… It's good. I think you should come see Aaliyah…if you can. She just woke up." I paused.

"Thank you, God." I could hear Ms. Morales weeping on the other side of the phone. "I'll be there soon," she struggled to say.

"I'll be here."

I sat on the floor in the hallway waiting for Ms. Morales. It took her about thirty minutes to arrive. "Calvin!" She had a worried look on her face but she was more grateful than anything. I stood up as soon as I heard my name. She gave me a very firm hug. "Is she okay?"

"She's awake," I said with a monotone voice. I was worried too, there was no saying how long her recovery would be. Ms. Morales held my hand as we walked into Aaliyah's room together.

Jazelle was just walking out when we tried to enter. "Hey, how's my baby?" Asked Ms. Morales.

"She's doing well. She just needs to stay calm and rest." Jazelle closed the room door to keep us out in the hall as we spoke. "It's hard for a patient to accept what happened after they wake up from a coma. It's better to wait for them to heal before you ask them anything about what happened prior. Your daughter will be okay. Just give her time," Jazelle confirmed.

"Can I see her?" Asked Ms. Morales. That was odd to me. If that was my child in there, I would just walk in.

"Yes, but just let her rest. Try not to make her talk much. I cannot stress that enough," Jazelle said before walking away.

We entered the room to see Aaliyah laying with her eyes open. "Mami." She began crying. "I'm scared."

"Sh-sh-sh... it's okay. You're okay." Ms. Morales began to comfort her right away. I sat down on one of the chairs. Aaliyah wasn't focused on me but I was focused on them. Her mother spoke in Spanish. I wasn't able to understand but I could understand that she was trying to calm Aaliyah down. The tears stopped and the English returned. I stayed silent, praying in my mind. I knew it was going to be okay. I just didn't know when it was going to be okay. I needed Aaliyah to remember what happened.

Day Eight

The hospital security stopped searching me, I came so frequently that they weren't worried about Aaliyah's security. They knew I wasn't coming to harm anyone. I brought the gun with me. I smiled at security as I walked by. I bumped into Jazelle.

"Hey Jazelle, how you doing?" I asked.

"I'm well… and you?"

"I'm fine."

"How's the arm?" She asked.

"It's healing, it looks healthy."

"Health care," she said smiling and laughing.

I laughed too, walking past her into Aaliyah's room. I had to figure things out.

I sat down, it was about five o'clock in the evening. I looked at Aaliyah who was awake. She no longer had the breathing mask on. She seemed to be more stable.

"When was the last time you slept?" I was worried.

"I can't sleep." Laying on her back, she was looking at the ceiling.

"Why not? What's wrong?"

"Calvin... I was raped. He tried to take my life," she spoke with anger and fear with a bit of an attitude. Which was more than understandable.

"Who... Who was it?" I asked right away.

She paused. "Calvin... who did you tell about this?"

"About you?" I needed her question to be clarified.

"About me in the hospital." Fear was in her voice.

"Just Gio... I didn't even tell my mom." I explained.

"Good. Only talk to Gio," she demanded.

"Why only Gio?"

"Please just listen to me." She started crying.

I got worried, I didn't want any doctors or nurses entering the room thinking that I was causing trouble. "Aaliyah, please don't cry. I just need to know who did this."

She finally looked at me. "Calvin, I don't want you going out there looking for this man thinking you're avenging me," she explained.

"Aaliyah." She didn't say anything. She continued to weep as my heart dropped. I watched her. "Do I know who did this?" She stayed silent. The cries continued. "You said you didn't remember what happened... why didn't you say anything?" She cried, no words came out of her mouth. "Aaliyah, say something!" I raised my voice, then went into a whisper right away. "Aaliyah, if you know who did this… just please tell me. I will deal with it."

"But what does that mean, Calvin? We have to let the police deal with it. Let them do their job."

"The police ain't gonna do shit! My brother been buried for months, ain't a damn word spoken by the police on who did it. I'm not letting it happen again."

"Calvin." She paused. "You're not the answer."

"I'm not the answer," I confirmed. "I'm the problem," I explained.

She was obviously upset with me. "Calvin. Just stay by Gio's side. Only Gio. You're always focused on dangerous situations. You get yourself into too much trouble, Calvin. Gio thinks logically, why don't you?"

I ignored most of what she said. "Are you worried they might come back?" I asked with no shame.

She struggled to speak, "Yes."

"Let's just hope they don't run into the problem… cause I'm trouble."

"What… no. Calvin, this isn't what I want!" She was able to use enough strength to yell at me.

"Do I know the guy who did this?" I asked one last time. She didn't say anything. But she looked into my eyes and I knew the answer to my question. My heart dropped. "What's his name?"

"Calvin, I don't know." She was obviously frustrated with me.

"What's he look like?" I asked each question right after her answer.

"Promise me something," she begged.

"I can't make no promises right now, Aaliyah." I continued looking into her eyes.

She took a deep breath. She was scared. I knew it. I let my emotions get the best of me. I let them, I didn't stop my motive. "I saw him with you… the night you left my house. The night we broke up." She started crying again.

I whispered, "Xavier." I lost all feeling in my body. *He's dead.* I made that decision in my head. I bent over and kissed Aaliyah on her forehead. "I'mma go see Gio. I can't be here right now."

"Calvin, no! Don't lie to me. Stop." She watched me walking over to the door.

"Aaliyah… I'm going to talk to Gio. I need to get this off my mind," I explained.

"Stay here with me. I need you here with me," She continued to beg with tears flowing down her face.

She knew me well enough to know I wasn't planning on seeing Gio. "I promise you I'm gonna go to Gio's place." I took a deep breath. "I promise." I walked back over to her. Standing over her I looked her in the eyes.

She looked back into mine. "I love you, Aaliyah."

"Stay," She said.

"I promise."

Chapter Twenty-Two: Unleashed

I knocked on Gio's door, waiting for him to open it. When it swung open I asked him a question right away. "Is your momma home?"

"Nah, why?" I walked past him.

I slammed my gun on his kitchen table, shaking everything on it. "I'm gonna kill Xavier." My voice wasn't raised. It was calm. I'd already made up my mind.

"What? Why?" Gio didn't seem too shocked.

I sat down. "It was him. He raped Aaliyah. He tried to kill her. So now… eye for an eye."

His eyes widened. "You're serious? I knew that nigga was no good from the get go." He got upset real quick. "But how do you know?" He questioned.

"She just woke up, bro. She's going to be okay," I said.

"That's good to hear, bro." He nodded his head.

"But Gio, I can't believe it man. The night he killed that guy in front of me, he picked me up from Aaliyah's house. He told me she was fine," I spoke shaking my head. "He took that man's life so easily. Just like that. It was over. Blood everywhere. Killing was like... like second nature to him. I can't believe it. That was Jace's best friend. A killer. Murderer." Gio stared at me, I wasn't looking at him but I could see him from the corner of my eye. I was staring at the gun on the table.

"Y'all killed a man? What the fuck, Calvin!" Gio yelled as he scrambled to find the words. "When were you gonna tell me?" he demanded.

"You're not listening," I said. "I didn't kill him, it was Xavier... I couldn't kill that man." I never looked at

Gio once while speaking. "Xavier took me to the man's spot...told me it was Jace's murderer. But I look that guy in the eyes, G. It wasn't him. I could tell. Then bang! Xavier shot him in the head."

"Oh my God, it doesn't matter if you did it or not. You were there!"

I looked at Gio. "No I wasn't – let's not talk about it no more." I looked back at the gun.

He nodded his head. I know he was shocked but he brought his focus back to the original point. He spoke in a calm voice, he wasn't trying to command me, just trying to help me think logically. "Calv, I know you want revenge. But right now, you got too many people riding for you." I didn't say anything. I was too focused on the gun. "Look if you got arrested right now, you'd be leaving your mom. Who else does she have? You're all she's got. Calvin, you're not only risking your life. It's your mother's life too.

You can't be doing this. You know I ain't for the police, but… tell me what other options we got?" He asked.

"I don't want anyone doing my dirty work," I explained, still looking at the gun.

"Calvin! This doesn't have to be up to you! Think about it for a second, please Calvin! Please fucking think! This isn't just about you!" He yelled these words at me.

"If this was about me, G, I wouldn't even speak about it. I'm here right now because Aaliyah woke up this time… what about next time? What about the next girl?" Huh?" I waited for a second. He didn't respond. "Exactly. It stops tonight."

"You already got your mind made up… right?" I didn't speak a word and I didn't move an inch. I had my eyes on the gun. I was studying it. I read the engraved text on the side of the gun. I struggled to breathe as my heart skipped a beat. "I ride for my guy, I die for my guy, and if it comes to it, I'll kill for my brother." Gio sat down. "But if we're really gonna do this… we gotta be smart about it. I got a kid on the way. I promised myself I wouldn't be a deadbeat," he spoke with determination. "Calv, you good?"

I stood up. "It was him G, it was –" I stopped myself. I put my hands on my head. I could barely breathe.

"What happened? What's wrong?" Gio was confused.

"He killed him," I said.

"Killed who?"

"Xavier."

"What?"

I picked up the gun. I ran my thumb over the text on the gun. I mumbled the name of the gun. "CZ 85 Combat." I continued struggling to breathe.

"Calvin, look at me." Gio stood up and grabbed my face. He slapped me lightly until I looked at him. "Calv, man, look at me! What happened? Who killed who?"

There was a long pause as I looked into Giovanni's eyes. I sighed. "Xavier, he killed Jace," I said softly.

Gio let go of my face, staring at me while he frowned. "How do you know?" He asked, putting his hand on his mouth.

"This is the gun." My words were fast and choppy.

He spoke quickly too. "How would you know?" He needed an explanation.

"The officer told me. This is the gun that killed Jace. CZ-USA – CZ 85 Combat." I fell onto one knee, in the middle of Gio's kitchen. "This whole time breaking bread with the enemy," I said. I took a deep breath. "He lied about everything. How could he have my brother's hat? He said he never saw him the night he was killed. An-

and the guy in B.K." Gio helped me stand up. My body was now filled with adrenaline. I was angry, beyond furious. "He killed that man to cover up his tracks. If my brother was really his boy, he would have searched for the Brooklyn boy a long time ago." Millions of thoughts were pouring into my mind before I could even turn them into sentences. Gio didn't say anything. "He killed my brother, the man in BK, killed all those girls. He's the serial killer." My eyes shuddered back and forth like I was watching a film filled with Xavier's deceit. I couldn't imagine what my face looked like but looking at Gio's I must've looked psychotic. "I'm going to take his life." I unloaded the gun to see how many bullets I had left. I had twelve out of the sixteen that were supposed to be in there. "He doesn't deserve it." Gio became distracted when his phone began ringing. I turned around to walk towards the door.

"Ay, ay, ay! Where you going?" Gio ran to block me from the door. "Calv, please chill!" His phone continued to ring. He declined the call. "Calv. We need to think of a way to actually handle this."

"I did," I said, emotionless.

Gio's phone began to ring again. "Calv, please bro. We gotta figure out a way where it'll work out properly. Where we won't get caught!" He said pushing against my chest.

"I don't know what you're thinking... But I'm thinking you got a child on the way. I don't want you involved."

He declined the call again. "But is that really your choice?" He asked. He was pledging his loyalty.

"This doesn't involve you, G." I looked Gio straight in his eyes. He knew how this made me feel. I was protective over my family. "Xavier killed my brother."

"You're my brother, right? And Jace is your brother... so that makes him my brother." He was patting my chest with the back of his hand. Trying to convince me to analyze the situation.

I was too upset to think about Gio's words logically. "Now if you were in my shoes, would you let you go with me?"

"I'm not in your shoes." His phone started to ring for the third time.

"G, just pick it up." He looked at me, then down at his phone. Answering his phone, he looked me in the eyes. "Bea." I couldn't hear what she was saying, but the look on Gio's face wasn't hard to understand. "Yeah, stay there. I'm coming. N-no! Stay there, Bea! I'm coming." Gio looked at me again. "Calv. Please. Don't do nothing without hitting my line first. You can't be alone for this. You know what Xavier's done already. You know he's carrying a lot of heat!"

"If I gotta go, then that's how it goes. But I know you gonna put the pain on the man if I don't come back. So I ain't worried, G."

We left his apartment. We walked down the stairs together. He stopped me and looked me in my eyes. "Calvin. I'm saying this as your brother. You're not in this alone." He stuck his hand out for a handshake. "I can't stop you from doing what's on your mind. So call me so you're not going solo." He lightly bumped his forehead against mine and walked away.

I walked in the opposite direction from Gio. I was walking towards the AJ guy's house. That's the last place Xavier was staying since his apartment was raided. I walked the whole way. It was about fifteen blocks away from Giovanni's apartment. The gun was in my waistband. I pulled it out and continued walking. It was about seven o'clock. I didn't care who was staring. There were people on the streets hanging out, no one said anything to me. I made sure the gun was properly loaded. I didn't want to take a life but my mind wouldn't let my body stop walking towards the house.

He wanted me to think Jace was resting peacefully, he wanted me to stop accusing him. I could smell the fake on him. Right under my nose... the whole time. I got more upset with every thought that entered my mind. *My whole life I've been in the trenches. Feeding off the scraps thrown at me. I'm done.* That's what Mr. Mike told me. *If you need a job done well you gotta take care of it yourself.* I was worried about my mother. I hadn't seen her in a few days. She didn't know what was going on. I thought about Aaliyah, how mad she would be with what I was doing right now. *You're always focused on dangerous situations. You get yourself into too much trouble, Calvin.* Aaliyah was right. I just couldn't rest. Not with my brother's murderer alive and free. *Calvin, come on. You really think I'd do that? Look, there's more to it.* I remembered a dream I had. I was sure it was Jace…warning me about Xavier. I blocked out the thoughts that would stop me from what I was about to do. I had one last thought. *Off with his head.*

I stood in front of the door. I put the gun in the front of my waistband. I pulled out my phone to text Gio. "Tell Aaliyah I'm sorry. Take care of your kid. You'll be a great father." I put the phone in my pocket.

I banged on the door. I heard mumbling behind it. The door slowly opened. The door was only opened enough for me to see a face. It was AJ. "Where's Xavier?" I demanded, raising my voice.

"Um, hold on." He looked back.

I pulled out the gun. "Open this shit up!" I kicked the door, which forced AJ to back up a bit more. I pointed the gun at his head. "Back the fuck up, AJ!" He put his hands up in fear. I was fearless in this moment.

I saw Xavier come from another room, "Hey! Calvin, chill! What the fuck you doing, son?" he spoke in a crescendo.

"Shut the fuck up!" I silenced him real quick, pointing the gun towards his face. "AJ, I'm giving you three seconds to leave this house."

He laughed, putting his hands down he spoke. "I'm not leaving my house...what's wrong wi–"

I shot a bullet into the ceiling of the apartment. Looking at AJ, his eyes widened. "Get out," I said calmly.

He put his hands back up. "Dude! What the fuck!" He slowly started walking towards his door to leave the apartment.

"Calvin, what the fuck is going on. You acting real disrespectful right now." Xavier was too calm. I didn't like that.

I pointed the gun at him. "Shut up! I know what you did!" I started raising my voice again. "You raped Aaliyah."

"I don't know where you got that information from but it's wrong." His voice was steady and his face was straight.

My palms were sweating and I could feel my heart beating out of my chest. "It was you!" I yelled. "I know you did it! She saw your face."

He seemed shocked. He must have thought she was dead. "Calvin, it wasn't me!"

I pulled back the hammer on the gun. "Sit down." The gun in my hand followed his movements. He sat down on a couch a few yards in front of me.

He was facing me. I could feel he was scared, but I couldn't see it. "So what? You're here for what? Payback? You gonna kill me or something?" He laughed.

"Yeah," I replied.

He went silent for a moment. "Okay, Calvin. Put the gun down. I'm serious."

"Shut up! I know you're the serial killer! Why you doing this?" I needed answers.

"If I was supposed to be stopped. I would have been stopped. It's not me," he said with a smirk on his face.

"Fuck you," I replied. I was livid. "I'm gonna kill you."

"Calvin, I didn't do what you think I did." I could hear the fear in his voice now.

I spoke right after he finished his sentence. "I know you killed Jace!" He shook his head. Uncontrollable emotion came into my body. "You put a bullet in my brother's head!" I yelled and frowned at the same time. All of my emotions came out through my voice.

"Calvin, you don't know what you're talking about!" He started to raise his voice too. "Put the fucking gun down!"

"I'm not playing with you!" I jerked the gun backwards than forward in a quick motion. "Do you know what you put my mother through?" I could feel the tears coming to my eyes. I tried my best to shake them off. "You had the nerve, the bravery and...the audacity to come to my brother's funeral!" I put the gun down. Staring at him. "You ruined my family."

He didn't have any words. I looked at him with blurry vision. Tears filled my eyes. I wiped my eyes with my one free hand, looking back at Xavier to see him lunging at me. I quickly the gun and pulled the trigger.

Xavier cried out in pain. I took a step back and saw that I'd shot him in his left forearm. His arm swung back but he still had the momentum to tackle me. I kept hold of the gun in my right hand as we both fell to the ground. He was on top of me, wrestling me for the gun. He put his knee onto my chest. His right arm was pinning my right arm to the ground. I pulled the trigger to scare him. The bullet hit the glass light and a shattering sound pierced my eardrum. Sparks floated down to the ground. He slammed my hand on the ground a number of times in attempt to force the gun out of my hands. The gun slid out of my hand and Xavier began punching me in the face. I was punched about four times before I powered him off of me. I got up and began throwing fists at him. We traded punch for punch. I felt like he was doing more damage than I was. I stumbled backwards. My arm was still sore from him shooting my arm when I saved Ms. Laurent. But I was the boxer. He was freshly wounded. I took a step back.

"You soft!" He yelled with a smile on his face.

I couldn't think much during the fight. With all the emotions running through my mind. All the adrenaline filling my body, I only had one clear thought come to my mind. *I'm in the trenches.* I had to retrieve the mental strength to take him out. I put my hands up. "Let's go!" I yelled. He started throwing punches. I began dodging them with ease. I threw a hard right jab at him. It hit him clean on his nose. His knees buckled. "Come on! Fight me!" I shouted. "You're a killer! You're a killer, right? Show me! Lemme see it! Kill me!" I continued to raise my voice. He tried to come at me again. I bobbed out of the way of his right fist. I lunged forward with all my power put into my right fist. I gave him a right hook to his left eye that forced him to fall back and onto one knee. I bent down to pick up the gun that had slid a few yards away. I pointed it and him. "Now I'm the killer. I'm trouble." His eye was bulging. He was clearly in pain and I enjoyed it. He had blood coming out of his nose and he was breathing very heavily. He was kneeling in front of the couch. "Look at me. I'm your killer." I walked up close to him. Standing over him, I pointed the gun a few inches from his forehead.

"Do it already," he said softly.

"I want you to suffer," I answered. Xavier tried to stand up. I kicked him in the chest, forcing him back onto the couch. "Why'd you kill my brother?" I needed closure. I didn't want to believe my brother died a wicked man.

Xavier looked me in my eyes. "He was weak," he explained, coughing out blood.

"And what does that make you?" I questioned.

He spat out the blood onto the hardwood in front of me. "Loyal," he claimed. "Jace wanted out. There is no out. This gang shit is for life. Once you in… you're in. That's it."

I pointed the gun at his face again. I tried so hard to pull the trigger. I couldn't, I promised myself I'd never come down this pathway in my lifetime. I put the gun down.

"You're weak!" He slurred his words. "Just like your girl. She felt so good." He was trying to smile at me. "She was so helpless."

"Shut up!" I yelled.

"And your brother…" I looked at him. He was coughing blood, his nose was crooked, his eyes were bloodshot and blood was all over his face.

"Shut up!" I repeated with a louder tone.

"I'd do it all over again." He forced a laugh.

"Stop!" I shouted at the top of my lungs. I pointed the gun at his chest and pulled the trigger. Boom. I watched the gun jerk up after the bullet left the barrel, piercing through his shirt and into his flesh. A bit of black smoke went into the air. He gasped for air, struggling to breathe. I could see the life draining out of him. Although, tears were flowing from my eyes, Xavier's screams of pain gave me comfort. All the pain and emotions I'd held in seemed to be coming out now. I had so many words for him. "I saw you at my brother's funeral and I knew you were no good. The pain y-you put my mother through... I wanna put a bullet in you for every girl you killed but I want you to die slowly, I wanna see you suffer," I spoke with a serious but dull tone.

He held his chest where the bullet wound was. I could see the blood pouring between his fingers. I walked up close to him. I looked him in the eyes. As he was gasping for air. Blood was now pouring out of his mouth but he kept eye contact with me. I could see the struggle for life in his eyes. He was falling in and out of consciousness. I spoke with a malicious tone, "Bleed." He didn't have enough life in him to say anything back. I watched him slump over to his side. I walked backwards to the entrance,

opening the door to leave. I put the gun in my waistband

and began walking down the street. I looked down to see

blood sprayed onto my clothes. *Rest easy, Jace.*

It was probably eight o'clock in the evening. I

began walking to see Jace. I saw AJ, he was on a street

corner, beside a deli. He looked at me as I walked past him.

I stared back. "I could kill you too," I said, angrily, I never

stopped walking. I couldn't clear my mind. I was shaking. I

kept looking over my shoulder. I just needed to talk to Jace.

I was stepping on puddles of rainwater. I felt like I was

psychotic. *Could taking a life really fix all the problems?* I

went back and forth on that thought.

I hopped the fence of the cemetery. It was closed at

these hours but I didn't care. I already broke one major law tonight. I walked through the spiritual field. I found Jace's headstone, "Paulo says hey." I looked to the ground to sit down in front of Jace, I began to speak out loud.

"Jace…You've probably already heard. I don't know if it was the right thing to do but I know I had to do something. It was justified. He killed eight girls. It could have been nine if I didn't save Ms. Laurent and ten if Aaliyah wasn't as strong as she is," I explained "I love that girl, Jace. I couldn't watch her go down like that. Blame Xavier for everything that happened. I can't believe I didn't see it any sooner." I shook my head. "I'm sorry I didn't realize it any sooner. Mom was struggling, I needed fast money. I used that for good. The ends justified the means." I looked both ways. I was paranoid in the moment. "Jace look… I just wanted to avenge you and Aaliyah… and all the other girls that lost their lives or could've lost their lives. It's just not fair. You don't know how… what it's like… you were a good man, you had a good heart… people make mistakes."

I looked up to the sky for about ten seconds. I looked back down at the head stone. "I wanted to say sorry before you interrupt me, let me explain. I know why you left the house that night. You wanted out. You were done with that mess. So am I." I pulled the gun out of my waistband. I stood up and threw it as hard as I could in a random direction. I sat back down. "I'm sorry, Jace." I continued to sit for a few minutes. I heard sirens going off in the background. I thought about leaving but I had a feeling I needed to stay with Jace. "Mom's going to be alone now, huh? I messed up. I couldn't have Gio involved though! You heard he's about to be a pops! That boy a father now. It's crazy, son." I smiled and forced a laugh. "Jace…you and I grew apart as we got older. But I want you to know that you were a good brother. There ain't a day that goes by that I don't think about you." I heard the sirens get louder. I could see the lights flashing around the fences of the cemetery. Tears flowed down my face. I could cry for my brother now. I held it all back because I thought it was his fault. He was selfless. He was correcting his wrongs. He just didn't have enough time to finish. I went on one knee. "Rest easy, Jace, my brother. Until we meet again."

I could hear dogs barking and flashlights waving around the pathways of the burial ground. Soon police officers surrounded me. I stood up with my hands in the air. The flashlights were being pointed at my face. I could barely see. A few officers were dressed in body armour, boots and helmets on. Like it was a warzone. They held rifles. *For one guy?* The dogs were on their back legs a few yards away, trying to attack me. They were held back by the officers holding them on leashes. I stayed calm. There was nowhere to go. It was the end. I shielded my eyes from the light.

"Calvin?"

"What?" I replied.

"You're under arrest."

"For?" I looked at the hand full of dogs barking at me. Officers used a lot of strength to hold them back. The officers that weren't holding dogs had guns pointed at me.

About ten officers stood around me. "You're under arrest for the murder of Xavier Henderson."

"Alright." I put my hands behind my back and fell to my knees. I was pushed to the ground from behind. They pushed my face into the dirt. Two officers held each of my arms. Two stood in front of me, and on top of Jace. A fifth officer put me in handcuffs. They forced me to stand up. They began searching me for weapons. They didn't find anything. I stayed focused on Jace's headstone. They tried tugging on me to walk back to the entrance of the cemetery. I stood my ground for a second, looking at Jace, I nodded my head. "Until we meet again, brother." I walked away

with the officers. *Life*.

Chapter Twenty-Three: Convict

I was pulled into a detaining room for the officers to ask me questions I didn't intend on answering. There were three officers in the room with me. The thought of me saving future victims from rape was enough to keep me sane. I didn't know if I truly redeemed Jace and Aaliyah. I didn't know if that was the way.

"Sit here." The officer shoved me onto a bench. I hit my head against the wall. I was still in handcuffs and could feel pressure coming from my bullet wound because of the position my arm was in. "What's your full name?"

I thought to myself about how they would know my first name. It had to be because of AJ. I looked at the officer. "Calvin."

"Last name?" he asked.

I kept a straight face. "Lawyer," I replied.

He looked at me like I wasn't even a second-class citizen. He was disgusted. "Eye colour?"

"Greenish-Lawyer," I responded, still holding onto my emotionless face. I looked down to the spots of blood on me.

"Smart guy, huh?" He shook his head. "Hair colour?"

"Rights, huh?" I was matching his energy.

"Skin colour?" He stared at me.

"You're looking at me." I stared back. I knew all about the policing and prison system in the state of New York. I knew they had to make a quota for every month or so on the amount of people they locked up. The state got tax money and a lot depending on the amount of people put in prison. It was supposed to be used on the inmates and the prisons, but they didn't do that. It was used for whatever selfish cravings they had. They got money and built more prisons and morgues. It was a business. They could be building schools and hospitals.

"Want to tell me what happened tonight?" The officer's eyebrows sunk.

I had no respect for him. I knew he had no respect for me. He didn't care why I did it or how long I would be in prison for. He probably had killed more people than me. *Legal murderers and race soldiers.* "Want to wait for me to get a lawyer?" I was still considered a minor at the age of 17. I stared with a poker face. I wasn't the idiot they thought they arrested. "Can I go to my cell now?"

Two officers reached for each of my arms, pulling me up aggressively out of the room. The third officer took off the handcuffs and pushed me to a wall. I put my back to the wall and faced them. They took mugshots. I gave a dirty look.

"Turn to your left." The officer was demanding. I listened to his instructions. "Turn to the right." I was probably going to spend 25 years minimum in a prison. It was worth it. "Come here. Spread your fingers out." The officer who was in the middle grabbed my index finger and began stamping it in ink, then onto a sheet of paper. They collected all of my fingerprints. I didn't think much of it.

The same officer bent down in front of me. "Ay! Chill! Whatchu doin'?" I asked.

"Hey! Don't move. You don't want to regret it," he spoke with a stern attitude in his voice.

"Is that a threat?" I questioned. The two other officers were still holding onto my arms. He looked me in the eyes. "You're going to cooperate because things aren't looking good for you right now."

"Is that supposed to make me shake? Things never looked good for me. You couldn't relate to struggle. Y'all just some white boys who ain't ever struggled. Everything got handed to you. Y'all just killing my people every day. Fuck you, fuck you, and fuck you. Licensed killers. Fucking pigs," I spoke arrogantly. The officer in front of me reached for my shoe and I moved my foot so he wouldn't be able to touch it. One of the officers holding onto my arms hit me at the back of my head. I stumbled forward but they held me tight so I wouldn't fall. I felt dizzy for a few seconds. They took my shoes off, pulled the strings from my hoodie, and checked me for jewelry. The two officers began pushing me out of the room. I knew they would treat me like shit. I didn't care. I was happy with what I said and what I did. I did what they couldn't. They shoved me into a holding cell. It was just me in there. My heart skipped a beat when the bars slammed shut, followed by an echo. *Alone.*

I heard the bars slide open. The echo rang through the cell. "Let's go." I stood up, looking at two officers. One was the same from last night, the other was a new guy. I didn't sleep all night if this was the morning. I didn't trust the officers. I wanted to keep my eyes open. They handed me a navy blue jump suit and shoes that look like slip-on nursing shoes. I had to change in front of them. They didn't trust me one bit. I didn't care how they felt. "Turn around." I looked at the officer without moving. "Turn! Around!" he raised his voice this time.

"Make me." The officer grabbed me, spun me around and pressed me against a wall. His elbow was in the back of my neck. The second officer came and put me in handcuffs. They pulled me to a door. I could see the sun peeking out. Right away, I thought about my mom. I didn't know if she was back home, or what she was thinking. If she was back home, she was worried about where I was. The cops didn't let me make a phone call, didn't read my rights and they didn't let me speak to a lawyer. We walked outside of the station, the sun wasn't fully out yet. It was still a bit dark outside. They put me in a paddy van.

It was me and two other inmates in there along with four police officers. I was falling in and out of sleep on the drive. I didn't know anyone, I didn't want to risk being off guard. The trip was about four and a half hours upstate. I woke up to see Auburn Correctional Facility. "Welcome to the castle, princesses." One of the officers spoke with a sarcastic tone. One of the inmates kissed his teeth. They opened the doors for us to get out. It was still early, the sun was in the middle of the sky. All three of us were connected, bound together by chains. I could only move if the other two moved. I was the last one in the line. An officer led the line, two stood on each side and one was behind us. I wasn't afraid of the officers. I was only worried about fighting inmates without backup. I didn't know anyone, I didn't have backup. Normally, I had Gio to back me up. But this time, for the first time in a long time, I'd be alone. We walked through sliding gates. There were two towers that stood tall and guards were in each of them. They held rifles. We entered the building and as soon as we passed a few gate doors. I heard inmates yelling at us. The guys I was chained against seemed to be in their early twenties. Maybe a bit older. I was supposed to go to a juvenile correctional facility. When I arrived at this prison, I knew it was an adult facility. They had no remorse. "Fresh Meat!" yelled a few people. A few more did some gang calls. I kept my head up as I walked. I noticed the other guys kept their heads down. I never controlled my facial expression. If I saw something I didn't like, it was going to show on my face.

The guards unchained us, shoving us into our cells along with sheets and mattresses. No one was in my cell yet. The same echoing sound from the holding cell vibrated in my ear as these bars closed. I set up the mattress and sheets on the top bunk because I heard it was always better to have the higher ground. My thoughts were everywhere. I needed to get to a phone. I needed to call my mom. I laid down until I fell asleep.

I woke up to the gates sliding open again. I saw men walking by my cell. I got up to leave my cell. I began walking with the crowd. I walked down a few stairs, it was lunch time by the looks of things. I didn't go to the food right away, a few telephones caught my attention. I walked over to see if I could call my mother. There were three telephones and three lines formed. I waited patiently without speaking to anyone. Several people stared at me but I didn't break from my poker face or pay them any attention. I was next in the middle line and the man in front of me had just finished his call. I picked up the phone.

There was no tone buzzing in my ear. I didn't think the phone worked. I stopped the man who was on the phone before me, "My brother, lemme ask you somethin' right quick. Why'd it work for you and not me?" He walked back two steps and pushed a button on the telephone. He shook his head and looked at me like I was new. I was.

I put the phone to my ear and heard the buzzing. I started dialing my mama's number. The phone rang about four times. My heart was beating fast. *How do I tell my mother that I'm in prison?* I heard a long beep. Then breathing. "It's been a long time since you have called here! What is the problem? You forgot about us? I've been putting money on your account. You can't even call to say thank you? Kwesi! I can't take this no more!" My mom was yelling, she cursed in Twi as well. I never heard her get this upset that fast.

"Chill, ma! It's my first day here. How'd you know I was here?"

"C-Calvin?" The fear on my mother's voice put a strain on my chest. My heart dropped, I knew it broke her heart to hear me on the other side of the call.

"Ma, I'm sorry."

"What did you do?" Her question pierced through my ear.

I struggled to speak. "I… I killed–"

She cut me off before I could finish my sentence. "You did what? A-Are you not thinking? Is your brain broken? What a stupid thing! What a-a-a criminal. You, Calvin! You! I never ever expected this from you!"

"Ma, they got me in here cause I killed Jace's killer. But the thing is… he was also that serial killer on the news all the time." I heard my mom kiss her teeth. "Ma, please listen to me when I say this and listen carefully."

"You want me to listen carefully. Foolish! Look at where you are. You want me to listen to what you're about to say," she was shouting.

"Mom – please. Stay away from anyone who claims to be Jace's old friend. Anyone that you saw Jace and Xavier with."

"Why?" She needed a legitimate reason, Ghanaian parents were too prideful when it came to listening to their children.

A man behind me tapped on my shoulder, trying to get me to hurry up on my call. "Chill! I ain't done." I said looking back at him. I focused on the telephone call again. "Mom, Xavier was the one who killed Jace and murdered all those girls."

"What?" I didn't know if she was shocked, or genuinely didn't hear me.

"It was Xavier. Xavier killed Jace." I didn't hear any response. "Hello? Mom?" I looked at the phone to see a finger holding down a button on the telephone. When he let go I heard the buzzing noise again. "What the fuck, man! I wasn't done."

"You are now," he replied. He and I were the same height but he was a lot wider than me.

I slammed the telephone back onto its holder. "You better back the fuck up." I was furious.

"Make me, little boy." He wasn't scared at all.

A guard a few yards away yelled at us. "Knock it off, you two!"

The man and I were in each other's faces. He was a black man with a lot of face tattoos. There was tattooed tear drop was stationed under his left eye. "This is my penitentiary. Get with it." He said, brushing past my shoulder to pick up the telephone. I watched him as I walked away.

It was lunch time and everyone was in the cafeteria room. I walked up to the serving line to grab a tray. The food didn't look great but I hadn't eaten in a while. I walked through the line as the inmate workers dropped food onto my tray. I had beans, something that looked like pulled pork, stale slices of bread and some mixed vegetables. It didn't look appetizing. I walked over to an empty bench in the back corner and sat alone. I people watched as I ate. I didn't think I would be able to get along with anyone here. I wasn't like any of these people. I noticed that the Latinos stuck together on one side. Majority of the blacks stuck together on another side. The few white people stuck with themselves on their side.

A big black guy walked over to me with two of his boys, I assumed. They stood on the other side of the table. They were all black. He stood in the middle of them. "How you doin' partna?" He sounded southern but we were Upstate in New York. I didn't say nothing. I kept forcing the food down my throat. "I asked you a question, right?" He spoke like he was disciplining me.

I smiled. "You're not about to talk to me like that," I replied. The last thing I would take from anyone is disrespect. I wasn't an adult. My birthday was in the summer but he wasn't my father, or my guardian. I wasn't going to take that.

They walked over to my side of the table. I continued to look straight as the big guy spoke to me. "Nah, you betta understand who you're talking to. I be the big guns up in this bitch. I run this shit." He was slurring all of his words but it wasn't too hard to understand the southern accents.

"Well, that's a little confusing cause ya boy over there just told me that he ran this penitentiary. You should probably handle that." I pointed in the direction of the man who hung the phone up for me a few minutes ago. I spoke calmly the whole time.

"Look here, bitch." I was still looking straight ahead. I saw a man staring in my direction. "This is my shit, you don't look hungry." He grabbed my tray.

I stood up immediately and tried to grab my tray back. He pushed me back. "I'm only gonna say this once. Give me my food back." He flung the tray and the food went all over my jumpsuit. I looked at my clothes soiled by the food. I swung my right fist and hit him in the face. I connected with his cheekbone and he stumbled back holding his face. I knew I hit him real hard but he was probably immune to heavy hitters.

"Get that motha' fucka'!" He yelled. The two other guys came at me. I swung again connecting with one of the guy's noses. He fell to the ground unconscious. I stepped back trying to prepare for the last guy who grabbed me. I saw two other guys from behind him get up and come over. They started to fight me too. I couldn't defend myself so I covered my head and prepped for all the blows I was receiving. I got a few direct punches to the face. I couldn't do nothing to protect myself. No guards were coming from what I could see. One of them grabbed me and threw me onto the ground. The men started stomping on me and I tried to brace myself for all that I could take. I felt most of what they came at me with. I could taste blood in my mouth. I heard a few grunts and I struggled to look up. I noticed a few guys had come over to defend me. I saw that there were more people on the ground than just me and the guy that I knocked out. I saw blood on the ground beside me. I saw a very muscular man exchanging fists with the man who tried to steal my food. They went head to head until an alarm began to go off. All of the inmates fell to the ground immediately. I heard loud hammering noises on the walls near us. The guards were shooting bullets into the walls to ensure the fight was broken up.

Several other guards came over dressed in body armour. "On your stomachs and hands behind your back!" They yelled. I listened. I didn't want to take any chances. I knew rebelling would lead to a very harsh punishment. The guards began putting the inmates involved in the fight into handcuffs. They lifted me off the ground and I felt fluid coming from my face. I watched blood drip from my face and hit the floor. My face was aching. I left the cafeteria with two guards pulling me away. "You want to know what we reward fighters with." They asked, while putting me into a really segregated cell. "The shoe." the guard said. The door slammed shut and it was silent. *Alone.*

Chapter Twenty-Four: Ultra-Light Beam

I figured out that shoe really meant. S.H.U. Which meant Secure Housing Unit. It was small, quiet and lonely. There was a small beam of light coming from a window that was too high up for me to look out of. I laid down on the thin mattress. The paint on the walls was peeling and I could tell people were scratching at them. I wouldn't be surprised if someone died in here. I heard muffled yells through the walls. I felt like they only put psychotic people in here, I wasn't psychotic. Not yet. A few of the guys involved in the fight were dragged down here with me but we all had separate cells. I looked back up at the light coming through the window. It showed all the dust flying through the room. The beam of light reminded me of a Kanye West song. I began to sing quietly to myself. "We on that ultralight beam, we on that ultralight beam...This is a God dream, this is a God dream...This is everything…everything. I'm tryna keep my faith, but I'm looking for more, somewhere I can feel safe and end my holy war." I closed my eyes. "This little of light of mine…glory be to God." I prayed to myself. It didn't know what a prayer would do for me at this moment. But I needed to be closer to God. He was the person keeping me sane. I kept my eyes closed to catch up on the sleep I desperately needed.

I woke up smelling food. There was a plate with prison food on the floor by the door. I picked it up and sat on the bed to eat. It was night, I could tell by the missing ultralight beam. I began eating, the food was cold. There was nothing I could do. I forced it down my throat. *Pause*. I heard squeaking. I looked down to see a rat that squeezed through a crack. It started towards me. I was used to the rats. I kicked it hard enough for it to hit the wall and run back into the hole. I looked at my food and thought for a second. I lost my appetite. I felt like rats could have been all over the food. I put the plate down by the door again. I laid back in the bed. There was nothing to do. I never been this bored in my life. With all the entertainment in the boogie down Bronx, this was the complete opposite. I thought about missing the summer. Loud music coming from the cars, motor bikes in Harlem and girls in sundresses. The thought of a female made me think about Aaliyah. She wasn't going to hear the news. Not for a while. I didn't have her number memorized so I couldn't call her. I had Gio's number memorized. I didn't know how to call him without tearing him apart. The idea of him hearing, *"you're receiving a call from the Auburn Correctional Facility, would you like to accept the charges?"* Gio would go into shock.

The days went on and on in the SHU. I was there for twenty three hours a day. I felt like the time went by slowly. Everything I had contemplated revolved around my

family and my loved ones. I didn't think I was worthy

enough to be in anyone's thoughts. At least not anymore.

Chapter Twenty-Five: Attorney

The guards unchained me. I sat down in the visitor's room after five days of being in the SHU. I sat down staring at the man in front of me. He had white skin and brown hair. He wore a suit and tie with glasses. He was old. I saw several wrinkles on his face. His belly hit the table. "So, Kevin, I need you to know...I'm not a miracle worker. But I'm a hard worker. Now you're first hearing is in less than a month. I need you to understand that you're facing twenty-five to life for the murder of Xavier Henderson. If there's anything I can do to lower this sentence or prove your innocence...I need you to speak up. I know you thugs think it's cool to keep a vow of silence. I'm going to tell you right now that this...front...this cool guy attitude isn't going to do you no good. Right now, they cannot find the murder weapon. They are lacking the evidence to prove you killed him. But this is legal aid. I need you to understand that tax dollars are paying for this. I can only go to certain lengths for you. Now I'm only going to be able to help you if you're willing to help me." He pushed the papers towards me, placing a fancy pen on top of the stack of papers. "Sign these papers please and you will have yourself a lawyer." He interlocked his fingers waiting for me.

I was looking at my wrists. They were sliced from the handcuffs. I looked up at him to speak. "It's Calvin."

"Excuse me?" The lawyer was confused.

"My name...it's Calvin. What's your name?" I asked.

"Edwin Goldwyn." He cleared his throat. His chest was still big. He was prideful.

"Whether they find the weapon or not...I killed Xavier...and I'd do it again. He raped and killed all those girls and he killed my brother. He was the serial rapist and killer, or whatever y'all wanna call it, but he did it. I killed him. Fuck him. I hope he goes to hell. I shot him and watched him bleed, I'm glad he's dead," I calmly clarified.

"You're telling me you killed the serial killer?" He needed me to confirm it.

"Have you found anymore female bodies since?" I asked.

He stood up, "I will be back. One week."

I watched him walk away. "I'll be here," I muttered under my breath. The guards came over to escort me back to the inmates.

Chapter Twenty-Six: Familiar Faces, Part III

I heard three bangs outside of my cell. I still didn't have a cellmate. I had been in here for about three weeks. I sat up and looked from the top bunk to the bars to see a correctional officer. "You got a visitor, Ayew." I laid back down again, I didn't like the attorney. I didn't care how the trial went anymore. I made myself comfortable with staying here for the rest of my life. I didn't want to get my hopes up. Things didn't usually end right for African-Americans in the so-called justice system. "Ay! What I say? Visitor! Get up!" I kissed my teeth and jumped off the top bunk. I put my hands through an open slot in the bars for the officer to cuff me. I pulled them back through and he opened the bars up. We walked to the visitation rooms, this time was different. I normally sat with my attorney at a regular table. This time they put glass in front of me. I would have to speak through a telephone.

I looked at the guard confused as he removed the handcuffs. "My man, why you got me talking to my attorney through glass?"

"I don't make the rules," he said. "Booth six." He pointed to my seat then walked away.

I walked over to see my mother. I froze. She already had tears coming down her face. I sat down without speaking but millions of thoughts ran through my mind. I picked up the phone. She began crying and shaking her head after seeing my face. "Calvin, why am I here right now?" I could see the reflection of my face on the glass between us. I had a black eye still, it wasn't done healing. I had cuts on my face from the fight in the cafeteria. My mom wasn't prepared for this.

"I told you, Ma."

"You're all over the news. Do you know that?" She shook her head. "They're saying you killed the serial killer."

"The news…" I paused to think. "I did. I told you, Ma," I confirmed.

"Calvin! Don't speak like that," She raised her voice.

"Mom. Xavier killed Jace. He raped and killed those women." I didn't break eye contact with her. "You know yourself, the police weren't doing nothing. They didn't with Jace! They were gonna do nothing for those girls neither. So I handled it myself."

"So what? Who said that it was up to you?" She tried to rebuttal.

"No one. Mom, think about all the times Xavier came to eat dinner at our house. All the times he slept over, claimed to be Jace's friend. He even had the nerve to come to Jace's funeral. I'm not sorry I killed him." I felt my face frowning.

"Calvin, what makes you think you were responsible for punishing Xavier? What makes you think that you were responsible for taking away his life?" She looked at me with a very disappointed look in her eyes.

"Do you remember what grandma use to say to me… and Jace?" She looked at me waiting for me to finish. "Trouble troubles those who trouble, trouble." My mom shook her head at me. "Eye for an eye, is the motto we were raised upon. You take mine I'mma get yours," I replied.

My mom was done talking to me. "Be careful, Calvin."

"I will. I'll be home soon. I promise." I stood up with the phone still pressed against my ear.

My mother gave me a dirty look. "Sit your ass down! You think we drove all this time for a five minute talk," she raised her voice.

I sat back down. "What do you mean… we?" I was confused.

My mom waved her hand, signalling people to come over. They were to her left. I closed my eyes. I was preparing for who I was about to see. Knowing my mom she was inviting a pastor to pray over me. I kept the phone to my ear. I could hear my mom instructing the person to grab another chair. I looked down into my lap. I was in a beige jumpsuit. I looked up to see Gio and Aaliyah staring at me. I looked at Gio but quickly changed my focus to Aaliyah. I couldn't stop looking at her. She was glowing. I could see she was stressed, she was still recovering. I was still in awe. "Calv, I told you not to do anything without me man…look where you at."

"Everyone wants to say, 'look where you at! Look where you at!' Y'all don't think I don't know? I'm living this, not you, my guy. I was looking at it like this. That boy killed my brother. What kinda man would I be if I made you do the dirty work with me? Now before you go 'Calv, you my boy' lemme say something. G, you got a kid on the way. Ain't no way I want your kid growing up like we did, man. You supposed to be on that side of the glass, making sure your kid don't end up on this side of the glass. Alright? Hold your chin up. We good, that's that. No more about that. I killed Xavier, I'd do it again."

Gio was at a loss of words. He wasn't the type to stay silent. In this moment there wasn't much to say. "It's just wild."

"I know, prison ain't the place to be," I explained.

"Nah, I'm talking Uptown. You got the streets going wild for you. They be chanting "Free Calvin!" They know you killed the rapist.

"They protesting?"

"Yeah."

"Word? Damn, I thought they ain't care about a brother. Is it like a riot or a peaceful protest?"

"Peaceful…A white girl started it," he said laughing.

"A white girl? What…stop playing, G."

"I ain't playing. Same teacher that broke our fight up! You got a couple hundred people marching for you."

"Ms. Laurent?" I said, shocked.

"Never underestimate a white girl with a sign."

I laughed. "Man – that shit never works. This is America, they don't care about no sit-ins."

"Have a little faith," he begged.

"Faith went out the window, G. They got me in an adult facility at the age of seventeen. They don't care about me or my future. I ain't supposed to be in this joint right now. I bet they'll trial me as an adult too."

Gio looked at me, he knew the situation was a tough one. "I know it's hard and I don't got the answers for you... but you gotta have faith."

I nodded my head. "Alright, I will."

"Calvin, take care of yourself."

I could see Aaliyah staring at me. But I tried to focus on Gio. "You know I will. I'll be home soon." I didn't believe those words but I needed to feed them hope, I was going to be here for a long time. They couldn't hold onto me but they could hold onto hope. "Giovanni."

"Yeah?"

"Take care of your kid for me and treat Beatrice like a princess. Be an example. I know you'll be great, I ain't worried about you, but I gotta remind you. Stay strong, brother."

He nodded his head and put his fist to the glass and I did the same thing. "Later, Calv." He stood up and walked away to leave me alone with Aaliyah.

It was silent for about twenty seconds. "Harlem," I said with a straight face.

"Crazy," she replied with a tear slowly falling down her right cheek. "Calvin, why did you do it? I want to be with you right now. I needed you...you abandoned me."

I felt my heart drop after she spoke those words. I didn't know what I could say. I could only apologize to her. But that would never be enough. "I'm sorry, Aaliyah." I tried to hold my tears back. "How you feeling?"

"How do you think?" She was choking on her words and taking deep breaths. "I wasn't even supposed to come. I'm supposed to be on bed rest."

"You didn't have to come for me. Aaliyah, I'm sorry I'm here. There isn't much I can do but tell you how I feel about you. But you already know how I feel. You're everything to me. Never met someone so special so...strong." I couldn't believe how beautiful she looked. She was a goddess.

"If I was so special, you would have listened to me when I said to stay with Gio."

I went silent. I continued looking at her brown eyes. "I'm sorry."

"Sorry isn't going to bring you on this side of the glass, Calvin."

I raised my voice. "I'm trying, Aaliyah." I lowered my voice before I began speaking again. "I can't go back in time. That's why I changed the future. I can't do anything to change this situation. I just need you to know that I know I ruined things for us." I didn't have anything to say that'd fix the situation.

She refused to match my tone. "I'm here for you," she said. "But I can't protect you, you always get yourself into problems without thinking about the consequences. You don't listen. Look at you! What happened to you?"

I didn't say anything.

"I worry about you."

"Try not to." I stopped her. "There is no up from here...so it'd be better if you'd forget about me."

"I can't just stop caring. I love you, Calvin. Glass and handcuffs ain't gonna change that!" she said wiping her tears away.

A guard tapped me on the shoulder, he was letting me know time was up. I shook my head and I started to get out my last words. "I love you too, Harlem. Be strong for me." I continued looking into her brown eyes. They locked me in. They shined brighter with the tears forming. "Please don't cry. I'll be back soon." I put my free hand up pressing my palm against the glass. She put hers to mine. "I'm crazy about you, Aaliyah." The guard began to pull me up.

"Be careful, Calvin." She continued to mouth words as I was pulled away. I couldn't understand them all. Two guards held me as another put me in handcuffs again.

They began pulling me away, I looked to my right as I walked to see other inmates having conversations with their visitors. I saw the man who helped me when I was getting jumped by the guy in the cafeteria. I looked at the lady he was talking to. "What? Mom…How do you know this guy?" I asked confused and a bit enraged. The guards forced me out of the room while I fought back. "How do you know him?" I yelled again. The three of them overpowered me. They shoved me out of the visitation center. I was furious by the time I got back to my cell. I didn't know how my mom knew him. The way they spoke, the way they looked at each other, they had chemistry. My mother never stopped giving him eye contact. She gazed into his eyes. *Love.*

A few hours later, I found myself sitting down on a bench in the cafeteria. I people watched. I never thought I would cherish this time in the cafeteria but after being in the SHU for so long I felt like this was freedom. I watched a group of men walk over to me again. I didn't look at any of their faces. "I don't want any trouble," I said. I didn't want to do anything that would force me back into the SHU.

"This is a peaceful meeting," said the man in the middle. He chuckled a bit.

That's when I looked up. He was the guy who helped fight off the bully for me, the man talking to my mother. Him and a few of his partners. I stood up right away. "You were talking to my mom today...How do you know her?" I demanded to know.

"I was talking to my wife," he responded calmly, but with confidence. My eyes widened. I stared into his eyes as thousands of thoughts ran into my head. He looked different, I think. I didn't know the last time I saw my father, I forgot how he looked. I shook my head and held back my emotions. He wasn't supposed to be in here. I could see how much he changed.

I stuck my hand out for a handshake. "Father." There was a loud clapping sound as his hand made contact with mine. "Nice to see you again." We shook hands and he stared into my eyes.

He pulled me in for a hug. "Nice to see you too." When he released I saw he had a big smile on his face. It's like he forgot where we were.

I felt like it was just us here, like everyone around us disappeared. I didn't have much emotions in this moment. I was in shock. I felt bad. I felt betrayed. I felt like a traitor. All these years, I never thought to visit him once. I've been here for a few days. I felt insane already, I could only imagine. "I'm sorry."

"For what?" He asked.

"For not coming to see you. I'm sorry I forgot about you," I said.

"You didn't forget about me. You've been busy with all the wrong things." His smile quickly left. "Why are you here?" He looked at me and didn't blink. He was serious.

"You heard about Jace... I'm guessing." He still hadn't blinked. "I killed his killer," I said with a straight face.

"You're a killer?" He asked.

"I wouldn't say that," I replied, I really didn't think I was.

"Would you do it again?"

I looked away. I didn't think I'd be receiving all these questions. "For that reason, yes I would. Eye for an eye," I explained.

I stood in front of my father, like it was judgement day. He pulled my head to the top of his chest by holding onto the back of my neck. "We protect our own, we avenge our blood, and we shall overcome."

I took a step back to look at him. I nodded my head. "Don't speak about that killing again. The day has pased, so you've overcame it. You shouldn't think about it anymore."

"I'll keep it to myself... we shall overcome." I stuck with my father and the group he established. He seemed to be the leader. I was the leader's son. Untouchable. It was race versus race in here. We were the origin, we already had the upper hand.

Chapter Twenty-Seven: Familiar Faces, Part IV

They cuffed my wrists and my ankles. They connected them with chains. You could hear them clank as they dangled off my body. I walked through the cellblock listening to the inmates yell. A few of them threatened me. I ignored. A few of them threatened the officers. The officers spoke back, telling the inmates to watch their words.

They sat me down at a table, I was supposed to be meeting with my attorney. I was at the table before him. I sat down for about three minutes waiting. I looked over to the officer that brought me over. He was watching the door. When I looked back, a man in a suit and tie stood beside my table. I looked up to see a light-skinned man with a short haircut and a clean-shaven beard. He put his briefcase on the metal table. "Chill," I said. He continued to sit down. "Yo! Fam, this isn't your stop. I'm waiting for my attorney," I said.

"I'm your attorney," he said, confidently.

"No you're not. You're confused," I clarified.

"Calvin…you don't recognize me?" He was disappointed.

"No, son! I ain't seen you a day in my life." I was slurring my words.

"Look at me," he pleaded.

"Boy, if you don't stop…I can tell you're worried. We're both having a hard time right now."

"Yeah, how's prison treating you?" He asked. He seemed genuine but I wasn't going to believe that was a genuine question.

"It's prison, what do you think?"

"I think you'll be fine," he said with a smile. The more he spoke the more familiar his voice became.

"Oh yeah? And what makes you so sure?" I asked.

"The Lord gives his toughest battles to his strongest soldiers," he said, staring at me.

I looked at the man and into his eyes for about 30 seconds. "Nah. Stop! Stop, playing. Y'all be playing too much! Cornelius! That's you, now? Wow!" I shook my head in disbelief. "I thought I only gave you three G's, why you out here looking like a million bucks?" I smiled for the first time. "You cut the dreads, son? You look clean though, real fresh, I'll give you that." I continued laughing. "I'd hug you but these fools would probably give me some warning shots!"

"You still got a high spirit despite where you are. I'm going to try my best to get you off with self-defence or just a lesser sentence if I can," said Cornelius. "Right now, with these type of prosecutors you're looking at life in prison. I've seen it before. They push your court date back and back just to trial you as an adult. You're going to have to tell me everything about what happened. What changed between now and the time I last saw you? I'll keep it to myself. That's my law."

I'll keep it to myself. Cornelius told me everything I needed to hear. "I found out who killed my brother. But me, I could never change. I'm one hundred percent Calvin. Forever." I looked at him. "Wait, you never told me you were a lawyer! This is just crazy as hell."

"Alright, let's talk business. They got you on the ropes." Cornelius tried to put the legal terms into analogies I'd understand. "They have no problem ruining your future, Calvin. They live for that. That's how they do black folks out here. They are essentially taking lives. Lives that hold so much potential. I won't let them have yours."

I nodded my head. "How'd you hear about my case, Cornelius?" I was still shocked.

"You're all over the news, Calvin. When I saw that, I knew I had to step in to help. You got my life back on track. You saved lives, Calvin. Many lives. You even have people protesting for you," he looked at me with a serious face. "The people care about you."

"The New Yorkers?" I laughed. "They don't give a fuck about me."

"Never underestimate a white girl with a sign," he said in a serious tone.

"You sound like Gio." I laughed, but then I thought. "Ms. Laurent. Is that her name? Serena Laurent?"

"Uh...yeah, she set up the peaceful protest," he further explained.

"Damn..." It was hard for me to believe it. "Peaceful?"

"Yes."

"Now, I know you lyin'. Real Uptown New Yorkers don't do peaceful. Protest means riot on those streets. If someone needs something, they knocking something down to get it. I know that, I lived by that," I reassured him.

"Well, you're wrong." He stopped me.

"You're gonna argue with me right here, Corny? Right now?" I was testing him.

"Focus, Calvin." He pointed to some papers. "We need you free. People like you…need to be free." I continued to discuss a ton of legal things with Cornelius. He was going to do what he could. I trusted him. I had a trial or a hearing or whatever they called it, coming up in a few weeks. I wasn't sure. I didn't know what any of it meant. I just knew that it was life or death. Because living captive was death in the eyes of freedom.

"Whether this ends horribly or not, I need you to promise me something. Please."

"Talk to me." He was eager to help.

"I'm asking you this with a sincere heart." He nodded his head at me. "My father was wrongly convicted. He doesn't deserve to serve another man's sentence. Could you please look into his case? At least when you and I are done?"

"I can promise you I will help to the best of my ability." Cornelius pledged his loyalty. I nodded my head to thank him. "Calvin, I spoke to your mother before coming here."

"For real?" I asked. "Was she mad?"

"Look where you are," he replied. "She told me to tell you not to do no more stupid stuff…and I agree. You cannot risk getting any additional charges. Be careful in here."

"I give you my word, Cornelius." I spoke with a straight face. "Look out for my mom, Cornelius. She's alone now. You're my eyes and ears."

"Times up!" I heard an officer yell.

"Yeah, yeah." I stood up. Still in the chains.

"Keep your head up, Calvin," said Cornelius as I walked away.

"Always," I muttered under my breath.

I was escorted all the way back to my cell by a guard. I thought about Ms. Laurent. I almost forgot she existed but she never forgot about me. It was hard for me to believe she cared that much. Most people in the Bronx were forgotten after they were locked up.

When I returned to my cell there was someone in it.

"Who are you?" I asked. He stared at me for a few seconds.

But I realized he was a guy from my father's posse.

"What's your name, partna'?"

"Antwan. You're Kwesi-Attah's son right?" He

tried to clarify.

But I didn't know my Pop's middle name. I wasn't

close enough with him. It wasn't like my mom never spoke

about him. It was the fact that I never asked about him.

"Yeah. Calv." I stuck my hand out for a handshake.

"What's good?"

"Ain't a thing. Surviving." I hopped up the bunkbed

to sit on the top bunk. "Don't bother, we got dinner soon." I

didn't even know what time it was. My sense of time was

lost since I came out of the SHU.

I jumped back down. "Say no more."

A buzzer when off and the cell bars opened. The rattling of the bars no longer got to me. I didn't flinch no more. It didn't faze me. I met with Kwesi-Attah and we walked to the cafeteria.

We sat down with our food and he stared at me. While I ate. I laughed. "Why you looking at me like that? Got me nervous eating in this joint."

"You ever just take a step back and admire a creation?" He asked me rhetorically.

"Nah," I responded.

"You don't have passion for anything?" I stayed silent while I continued to eat. "What are you passionate about?" I still didn't respond. The only thing I cared about was family and Aaliyah. Giovanni was family. "What do you do? After school…where did you go? Besides a job." He was confused, or annoyed. I couldn't tell.

"I boxed...in a gym," I shared. The men around the table smiled. A few of them said some remarks about boxers.

"Young Floyd!" Said Antwan.

"No, No, he's bigger than Floyd. He's like Muhammad Ali or Mike Tyson!" said another guy. A few laughed but all of them smiled.

My father continued staring at me. "You gotta stop doing that, G," I said to him.

"G, who?" He was shocked. The table went silent. "Who you calling, G? I'm not one of your friends. I'm your father," he claimed.

"Ight," I said.

"Ight? Ight? No. It's Yes, dad."

"Yes, Kwesi-Attah," I said.

He shook his head at me. "Why aren't you training anymore?" He asked.

I looked around, using my face to highlight how I felt about the surroundings. "We in prison," I said. "I'll probably be here for awhile."

"Don't count the days. Make the days count," he said with a tone of voice that was determined.

I knew that quote. It was on Mr. Mike's gym wall. "Muhammad Ali. The greatest of all time."

"Train. In here," he replied.

"You're not serious," I said.

"What's the problem? We have weights. We have a sandbag. You can train."

"Ight –" I stopped myself. "Okay, I will," I said. I pushed my food to the side.

"Eat up. You'll need the weight," he explained.

"I can't, it tastes like shit." I frowned.

"It was hard for me to adjust after eating your mama's food all the time," he smiled. "You'll get used to it," he said.

I shook my head. "I hope not." I stood up.

"Where you going?" He asked.

"To train," I replied. He nodded his head and I walked away.

The gym was nothing special. The weights were chipped and the sandbag was falling apart. They had to tape it up with duct tape. I observed the place as I stretched. I looked at the walls, the paint was chipped. I could see concrete. It reminded me of my mom's apartment. I thought about whether she'd be able to pay for the bills without me. I got into my own head. I made myself mad. I put my mom in a worse situation then she was after Jace died. I promised myself I'd take care of her. I failed her.

They didn't have boxing gloves, I had to use duct tape on my knuckles. My hands had no blood circulation after the tape job. I put my hands up and began to lightly punch the sandbag. I was focusing on my technique rather than strength. I was dodging imaginary punches, I was returning the punches. I began to think of Aaliyah. Boxing made me feel closer to her. I quickly stopped thinking of her. I was focused. I began throwing stronger jabs. The sandbag began to swing back and forth as no one was holding it. I could hear the chain make noise after every punch. Two right jabs, one left hook, one left jab. I took a step back and used the remaining strength I had to punch the bag with my right fist. The bag fell off the chain and hit the ground, a dust cloud flew up as it made contact with the ground. Sand began pouring out of the side of the bag.

I knew what I was going to do when I got out of this

hellhole.

Chapter Twenty-Eight: The Riot

"Calv! Come with me!" Antwan screamed at me. I didn't need to say anything. I dropped the weights I was using and ran to catch up with him. I got to the cafeteria to see a huge circle around my dad and the man who tried to jump me when I first got here. I immediately shoved through the wall of people. We don't fight fair. There was no such thing as a one-on-one in the Bronx. When I stood beside my dad, the rest of his friends joined us too, including Antwan. The man we were about to fight had about six people with him. We had more than that. "Your call," said Kwesi-Attah.

"You'll lose your life messing with me." Replied the man.

"You soft. Your whole team soft. I'd crush all y'all," I began walking towards them. I didn't care if anyone with me followed. I was going for the boss man.

One of his henchmen stood in front of him. "Lemme handle this, Zion!" He threw a wild punch at me, it was easy to dodge.

I followed my dodge with a right hook. He dropped to the floor. Stunned. His friends didn't move yet. Either did my clique. "Get your boy some napkins," I said.

After the man fell to the floor, a lot of inmates watching grunted like they were the ones who got hit. "Damn!" Yelled another inmate.

"You're going to wish you never did that," said Zion, looking at his unconscious friend.

"It's getting late. You wanna sleep too?" I asked.

"Everyone back to their cells!" Yelled a correctional officer. Nobody moved. "Back to your cells, or we're going on twenty-three-hour lock downs."

"Chill!" Yelled an inmate.

"Move it!" The officers yelled back.

"Come on y'all!" Twenty-three-hour lockdowns weren't worth it. I began walking with the crowd, hoping the officers didn't see me knock the man out.

"Keep your head down," my dad ordered me. I listened. I found my way back to my cell. I watched the officers attend to my victim after all the inmates were back in their cells.

"Damn, Calv! You're a monster." Antwan laughed. "You really got them Mike Tyson hands."

"Only to protect my own." I rubbed my knuckles as they throbbed. "My knuckles hurt. That dude got a hard head."

"You wild for that one." He continued to laugh.

"Nah, Antwan! You seen the way he came at me." I began to laugh too. "You come at me like that, you just asking to get dropped," I explained.

"You right." He gave me a high five. "You're a natural fighter."

I shrugged my shoulders. "Something like that," I replied.

A few weeks later, I sat in a courthouse beside Cornelius. He told me not to speak unless spoken to. Keep the words to a minimum. I was too "street" for the legal system, apparently. *They're too extra for me,* I thought. If they truly cared about what happened, they would just ask me. If I was the judge and someone got into a dispute like mine, I would ask them what they were thinking, why they did it, and the sentence they think they deserved. The American justice system had everything backwards. There shouldn't be two people who did the same crime and received two different sentences. We did the same crime, right? Why do I have to be here longer and in maximum security? I was ready to lose this legal war. My skin colour already had me in last place.

I sat in front of a ton of white people who held the power to ruin my life. By saying a few words and signing a few papers they could keep me locked up until the day of my funeral. They all looked scared or mad. I prayed in my head. Not for me but for my family. I prayed I would get justice but for my mother. She needed me. I promised myself I would take care of her. If I got the chance. I didn't care about my life. It was crazy for me to think that. But I did. I looked at Cornelius, he seemed confident. I wasn't.

At the end of the day, it was me serving the sentence not

him. I was still in my jumpsuit. I had chains all around my

body. Binding me together. I was trapped.

I didn't know if this was a trial or not, Cornelius

spoke to me but I zoned out a lot during all the legal terms.

What's a kid from The Bronx know about the legal system

besides its real crooked. I was called up to some separate

seat where the prosecutor asked me several questions. They

asked me to state my age, height, weight, education and

more. Before answering any of these questions I looked at

Cornelius. He nodded at me and that's when I began

answering the questions. I couldn't let them use any of my

words against me. I looked at the judge. I read her name

that was put just below her microphone. *Nicole Becker.* She

was a white female with brunette hair. She wore that gown

that judges usually wear but I thought she was kind of

young. I use to think all judges were old. She seemed like

she would be nice outside of the courthouse. Her facial expression were very hard to read. I was worried they were going to look at what I did, instead of why I did it. I felt like why I did it didn't stick out as much as the actually incident that took place.

Some prosecutor type of man began to speak. He was old and white with white hair and a receding lineup. He wore a suit that was black and he had a red tie. "Mr. Ayew, we've already gone through the details of that night, we understand your side of the story has already been expressed and acknowledged by the jury and Judge Becker. Is there anything else you would like to say?"

Cornelius had already given me a story to follow. It would make sense in the eyes of the court, hopefully. "I'd like you to understand that what happened that night wasn't me attacking someone. I was attacked. I was defending myself... defending everyone. I was threatened by the man who murdered my brother in cold blood. My brother was trying to better his life prior to this tragic event… He also raped and killed several females and attempted to do the same to my best female friend, Aaliyah Morales, and my teacher, Serena Laurent." I shook my head. I was told by Cornelius to let out real emotions during my testimony of the situation. I didn't think I was capable of feeling anymore, I thought I was numb to all accounts of emotion. I really thought I had ran out of sympathy for myself. When bad things happen I tell myself to prep for the next tragedy. I looked at the judge, I didn't care that the prosecutor was asking me questions. I could feel the emotion coming out, talking about what had happened out loud was bringing back the emotion I thought would be gone forever. "Your honour… with all due respect, I don't want to hide nothing from you. I feel like my total honesty would help you make your decision, regardless of if it sees me in prison for the rest of my natural life." I took all the slang and shortcuts out of my vocabulary. "My brother was gang-affiliated…

he was best friends with Xavier. Xavier introduced him into that lifestyle. The last time I saw my brother he was leaving my mom's apartment at night. I told him not to go, it was really late. You could imagine how The Bronx is at night. He looked at me and told me to stop him if I wanted him to stay home. I let him walk out I regret that to this day. I didn't know why he was leaving. The police asked my mother to come identify a body, she was out of town so I went instead. They pulled the cover back and I saw my brother... a completely different man compared to the man I knew a week before that day. I asked myself why my brother left that night, over and over. I learned from Xavier why he left that night. My brother went to tell Xavier that he was done with the gang life that he chose to live. He wanted out of that terrible lifestyle, your honour. My brother wanted to get his life back on track. We all make mistakes and I feel like people deserve the chance to correct their mistakes. But Xavier denied Jace Ayew's request. Xavier told me on that night…" I stopped. I looked around the courthouse. I could see everyone had their eyes on me. There were tears in the crowd. My mother wasn't here. Either was Gio, or Aaliyah. I looked at the jury section. It was filled with a majority of white people and one black woman.

Nicole Becker spoke into her mic. "Calvin – Mr. Ayew, what did Mr. Xavier Henderson say to you?" I looked back at the judge.

"He told me… he wouldn't hesitate to kill Jace again." I closed my eyes. I thought of my brother. Everything he didn't want me a part of, I was a part of since his funeral. "I felt like if he was willing to kill my brother again, he was willing to rape and kill several females again. Being in that situation, it is very hard to think logically. But in that moment I wasn't thinking about Jace. He couldn't be killed twice. But there are more females out there. It could be someone's daughter, mother, or sister. I just couldn't live with myself knowing he was the one who did that. My family used to cater for him, we showed him great hospitality. We fed and sheltered him for months at a time. Now… Xavier was known for dealing drugs and handling weapons. Everyone on the block knew him for that. Personally, I could never get involved in drugs, my mom told me once never to touch that stuff and I respected her wish from day one. I don't know if drugs were a factor in his behaviour but I told him all of his killing mentality needs to come to an end and he needed to turn himself in." This was the story Cornelius and I had come up with. We needed the sympathy of the court.

"Xavier laughed at my demand. He pulled his gun on me… The CZ 85 or whatever it's called. I ain't – I'm not really sure of the correct name, I just know it is the same gun that was used to kill my brother and the same gun he used to try and take my life. I read in the paper that that same gun was used to take the life of several females that were raped and killed, according to the bullets found in the autopsies. As soon as he pulled the gun on me I lunged at him and he shot at me. I still have the scar from the bullet wound on my arm." I saw the judges eyes light up as I shifted my body to show the scar. The chains danced as I shifted back. The short sleeve jumpsuit helped me display the scar. "Your honor... I wrestled with Xavier until I possessed the gun. He came at me and I pushed him onto the couch in that apartment. With my one good arm I held the gun I fired the gun twice. I admit it may have been excessive...I feared for my life while I was already bleeding out. I just felt like – like I wasn't just defending myself but the city from a ruthless monster." I looked at the prosecutor.

He stared at me with a disrespectful look, at least it was disrespectful to me. "Mr. Ayew, when the police arrested you in front of your brother's burial grounds. The police report claims you did not have any major physical injuries."

I saw Cornelius stand up from the corner of my eye. "Your honour, it should be noted that my client also informed me that he was physically and verbally abused by the police in the holding cell and his rights were never read to him…however, the officers didn't include that in their synopsis either." He spoke those words with passion and intensity before he sat back down.

Damn Corny…he really is a lawyer. I looked at him in shock. I didn't think when I gave him ten dollars the first time meeting him that he would be defending me in the court of law a few months later.

"Thank you, Mr. Clay," said Nicole Becker.

Clay? Cornelius Clay? I was just learning his last name now.

"At this time I would like the court to take a recess. I would ask the juries to relocate to the jury room to see if they can reach a verdict in the case of The State versus

Calvin Ayew, whom is being charged with the Second Degree Murder of Xavier Henderson. I'd ask that the court please report back within two hours. I stayed in my seat until a police officer came and escorted me out of the courtroom and into a separate room, which looked like a room for interrogations. I sat there alone. My wrists chained to the table. I put my head down. I lost hope. I didn't think the jury would have any type of sympathy for me. I killed someone. *I murdered a murderer.*

The door swung open and two police officers stood me up and escorted me out of the interrogation room. I sat down in the courtroom beside Cornelius. I looked back at the mini crowd. I saw my mother, she was with Gio. I nodded my head. It was bad they were late but I was more worried about them hearing bad news. I looked forward at the judge again. After everyone went quiet, she spoke some words and later she looked over at the jury speaking into the mic. "Ladies and gentlemen, it is to my understanding that the jury has reached a verdict. The verdict form has been handed to the bailiff. Please come forward." A clerk walked forward to the front of the court room.

Verdict? Damn, already? I looked at Cornelius, I probably had a worried look on my face. "Verdict?"

"Be strong. It's in God's hands." He had a decent poker face but he wasn't confident. I could tell.

"We shall overcome," I muttered under my breath. *Please God.*

Judge Nicole Becker continued to speak. "The clerk will read and record the verdict."

A blonde lady stood in front of the court with a few pieces of paper stapled together. I took a deep breath and exhaled. I was sweating and my heart was pounding. I always saw these things on CNN, I never thought I'd be in this position. You'll never know how it feels until you're in the seat yourself. I looked at the judge. She looked away from me as soon as I made eye contact with her. I looked at the clerk as she began to read. "The state of New York versus Calvin Ayew, verdict count one. We the jury, impanelled and sworn, taking action upon our oaths, do find the defendant as to count one: Possession of a firearm with intent to discharge that weapon, not guilty." She spoke without emotion.

I heard my mama sigh in the background, along with a few others that seemed happy for me. I didn't move an inch because that wasn't the charge I was worried about. I've had several people on my block get arrested for that and came back home soon enough. I couldn't even blink, I felt like my body shut down. My heart was the only thing functioning and it was pounding as the woman continued to speak.

"Is this the true verdict of the jury, so say you one and all?" asked the clerk.

All the jurors responded at once, "Yes."

She then went on to ask each and everyone one of them if it was their true verdict. They all agreed. She continued to read off of the paper. "On count two, we the jury find the defendant on the second and final count: Second-degree murder of Xavier Henderson," She paused and my heart stopped. You could hear a pin drop in the courtroom. I closed my eyes. Her pause only caused tension. "Not guilty." I heard my mom cry out in joy, I couldn't see her face but I could imagine the tears flowing down her face. I could hear the crowd chatting amongst themselves. The judge quickly silenced them.

The clerk continued to ask each juror if this was their decision. All of them continued to agree.

Cornelius put his hand on my closest shoulder to him and squeezed.

"Calvin, you're seventeen years old right?" asked Judge Becker.

"Yes, your honour." I replied.

"I'm glad the jury got this decision right." She paused to look at the papers in front of her. "You're not a killer. I don't believe you entered that apartment that night with intent to hurt someone. I believe you entered that apartment believing you would be saving future lives. I don't think you ever had a motive of killing someone in the past, yes I think you may have been motivated by revenge but I can't speak about what I think. I'm going to speak about what I know. I know that you are brave. I know you have a good heart. When I first looked at this story I looked at each of your records. Henderson had several charges to his name. You had none. I saw how they claimed that Xavier Henderson, the deceased in the case, had raped and killed at least eight girls... I thought about my daughter. How much I love and care about her and how she is my whole world. I wouldn't want any monster to take her innocence or her life. As a judge, I am a servant to the public and I am not supposed to involve my feelings in this case or any case for that matter. But I'm also a human and in these cases you have to involve your feelings. This is because you involved your feelings, I have to understand where you're coming from to be able to process this trial." She choked on her words in her last sentence. She was emotional. I held a straight face the whole time.

I didn't think I could cry anymore for as long as I lived. I felt like it was just Judge Becker and me in the courtroom. I felt like she had pulled me aside to tell me how she felt about my actions. She took off her glasses and placed them in front of her. She wiped her face and looked back up at me. "Calvin Ayew, you're a strong young man, I looked at your criminal history and you have no criminal background. I looked at your childhood as a factor, and you have lost your father at a young age to the justice system.

Your representative, Mr. Clay, informed me about that. I promise we will look into that for you. No one deserves to live without a parent their whole life. I've seen the justice system in America tear families apart before. It's wrong. That's why I took it upon myself to become a judge. To judge situations accordingly and to make sure the right people are convicted for their crimes. I've been doing this for twenty-seven years. I know the difference between the intent to hurt and the intent to protect. You are a protector. You also lost your brother a few months ago. I see you and I think for you to survive all this, stay away from so-called coping mechanisms like drugs and alcohol, at the age of seventeen… you've already made it in life. You're already so strong." She took a deep breath and continued. "You being tried as an adult is ridiculous. You're seventeen. You have your whole life to live. You're a protector, but you need to understand you have to stay out of trouble as well. Now I grew up in Yonkers, it's not far off from where you reside. I know how it gets, Calvin. Stay away from people that will influence you in a negative way, prepare yourself and set goals to the bright future you have and deserve." She looked around the courthouse. She put her glasses back on. "When you walk out of the prison tomorrow, which you will… I want you to start preparing for your future. Can you promise me that?"

A mountain came off of my shoulders and I struggled to process it. I felt lighter. "Ye – yes, your honor. I promise." I looked into her eyes. That's a promise I was going to keep. I didn't want her to know what I did. But I was going to pursue it, full-time, with all my power and energy.

The judge looked me in the eyes to speak. She spoke from her chest and with great authority for the next few words. "The defendant is not guilty on all counts and I ask for the correctional facility to handle the paperwork in a timely manner… today, leading to his immediate discharge.

Thank you to the jury. Thank you, everyone. Take care,

Calvin." She slammed the gavel. The echo released a surge

of energy that brought life back to my body.

As everyone got up. I stayed seated, Cornelius

hugged me and though I was still in handcuffs I tried to hug

him back. I looked back at my mom and Gio and nodded

my head at them. *I'll be home soon,* I thought to myself.

The police escorted me out of the courthouse.

Chapter Twenty-Nine: The Riot, Part II:

The doors opened to the patty van. I was back at the prison, away from the city. *I'll keep it to myself,* I thought. No one needed to know the news except for Kwesi-Attah. I knew jealousy was a trait almost every inmate carried. It was an inmate characteristic. *If I can't get out, no one can,* type of mentality. I wouldn't make it out alive. I was escorted to a gate. The guards unchained me and pushed me through. There was another gate. They closed the first one before they opened the second one. They normally escorted me all the way to my cell. I was confused. I looked back to the guards. "What's going on?"

"Go to your cell, inmate."

"Whatever," I replied with attitude. I was getting released and I only had to put up with it for a few more hours.

I began to walk and I heard static through the gates coming from one of the guard's walkie-talkies. "Suit up… dispatch and dismantle." The second gate rattled behind me as it closed. "Lockdown!" said a guard in a stern voice.

"Lockdown?" I turned to look at the guards but they were gone. I began walking to my cell. An alarm began to go off. A siren, piercing my ears. As I walked I heard people yelling. People panicking. Right away my guard went up. I watched a few inmates run across my path, one of them had blood on their tan jumpsuit. Right away I thought to myself, *survive*. I walked, constantly looking in all directions. I didn't think anyone was in their cell. I continued to hear screams and cries. I got to the cafeteria to see and officer on the ground. A pool of blood surrounded him. "Oh fuck… what the hell!" I unzipped the top part of my jump suit. I tied the sleeves around my waist. It was easier to run this way. I just had a tank top underneath. I started to run towards my cellblock, I wanted to find

Kwesi-Attah. I didn't know what was going on. I just felt like a civil war had broken out. Pigs versus cats, one thing we had in common was we were all scavengers. As soon as I reached my cellblock, all of the inmates were out of their cells. Fighting. Inmates beating inmates, police beating inmates, inmates beating police. It was chaotic. People continued to scream. Police were dressed in full body armor. They used batons to fight off the inmates. I ran up some stairs leading to the top level. It was an open staircase, I could see the lower level through the metal gated steps. There were no walls just railing. Upstairs is where my crew's cells would be. I saw a man on top of Antwan, throwing constant blows to his face. I grabbed his jumpsuit and pulled him off. The man stood up and we traded fists. There wasn't much distance between the wall and the railing on the second level. There was about five feet. It took a great amount of technique to handle someone in this setting. I threw several punching combinations that left him dazed with a bloody nose. I shoved him over the railing of the second level. I helped up Antwan then continued the search for Kwesi-Attah without looking back. "Calv, thank you."

"Where's my pops?" I asked worriedly.

"I don't know." We spoke as we dodged groups of men fighting. Police officers were being stripped of their body armour, inmates were teaming up on their oppressors.

I saw Zion and his boys circling Kwesi-Attah. I began sprinting as fast as I could. I was pushing through crowds. Throwing people out of my way. About ten officers held up shields in attempt to block me from saving Kwesi-Attah. Two rows of five pigs, each row facing a different way. I pushed against them. I was throwing fists. Punching the shield several times led to the numbing of my right fists knuckles as they began to drip blood. I could see the blood smudged onto their clear shields.

I watched as Zion and his friends began attacking my Kwesi-Attah. He was strong. He took several hits. There was probably eight people surrounding my pops. "No!" The unorganized dispute was hard to follow as I tried to fight through a barricade. I screamed at the top of my lungs as I watched Zion used a jagged edged weapon to pierce through my father's gut. I heard my father scream in pain. The scream was a piece of life leaving him and it found its way to me as a jolt of adrenaline attacked my body. I punched the first officer I saw in the face. I shoved him into the other officers forcing my way through the barricade. My left arm was grabbed by an officer, I turned around swung my right fist in one motion. I made contact with the officer's helmet. It hurt me, but it was hard enough for the officer to lose his grip on my arm. Antwan found his way through the barricade with me.

I sprinted over to Zion, his boys got in the way. I was prepared to lose my life today. I was throwing knockout punches to all of his teammates. I watched a man seize up as he fell to the ground after I threw a fist. My vision became blurry as tears formed in my eyes. I never stopped throwing my fist. I didn't know who I was but the boy I was before was gone. I took out four of his henchmen. I was now facing Zion. He had three more people with him. I didn't think Antwan was behind me. I didn't care. I saw my dad on the ground gasping for air. *It's too late,* I thought. My father was taking his last breaths. I went at Zion and he moved sideways slashing me in the face with his makeshift dagger. I felt my face, around my left cheek. I looked down at my hand to see blood. His friends started coming at me. I was circled, I didn't care. *This is a fight to the death. Nothing less. One of us isn't leaving.* The first one that ran at me I shoved him over the railing. He fell to his death, hopefully. I threw several punches at Zion again. A few hit him as he tried to slash me again, but his crew kept getting in my way. Antwan step in grabbing one of Zion's henchmen by the neck. Pushing him against the wall the henchman was being choked out. The last man came at me grabbing me by my right arm. "Get him!" He yelled. Zion lunged at me with his knife, aiming for my throat. I grabbed the arm of the hand he had the knife in with my free hand. I redirected it towards his friend. It stabbed the man holding me. Zion's eyes widened as the man fell to his knees, losing his grip on me. He was choking and coughing up blood, while the knife stayed in his neck. He fell to his back. Beside my father. I grabbed Zion's neck whose focus was on his friend. I pushed him to the ledge. I was squeezing, cutting off all of his air. "You're dying today," I said, staring into his eyes, I saw that he was scared. I could see someone ready to come at me from the corner of my eye. I couldn't tell who it was but I assumed it was one of his friends ready to jump on me.

"Touch me and he's dead," I explained. I meant every word. They backed up. I began to lean him backwards, he was now clinging onto me. If I threw him over I would fall too. For a moment I didn't care. I started leaning us over the ledge. I was tackled from behind. I fell beside my dad. I looked up to see army-like officers. Full body armour, helmets and automatic rifles. I saw Zion on his knees coughing and gasping for air. He's lucky, I was dying to kill him. They forced every inmate to put their hands up. I stayed on the ground beside my dad. I grabbed him. "Dad. Look at me. Please." I slapped his face lightly a few times. I saw his eyes rolling back and forth. I put my ear to his mouth to see if I could hear him breathing. It was a very light breeze of air flowing in and out of his mouth. I put pressure against his stab wound. I looked at him, he didn't deserve this. He looked peaceful. I could see sweat running down his face. Short hair, combed, always combed. He had a goatee. I could see a gold tooth shining from inside his mouth. His head laid in my lap. "Dad. If you can hear me… if you can hear me. Take care of Jace on that side. I'll take care of mom over here." I shook my head and looked at him. His eyes came back to this side. "I'm getting out. I was forgiven. I will be out soon." Tears flowed down my face.

"Calvin, my son…" He spoke very softly. The alarm continued to buzz but somehow I could hear him perfectly. Like I was supposed to hear this. I could only hear this. "You hold our legacy…Be strong. You shall overcome." He was gone.

I cried looking at my father's lifeless body. "We shall overcome," I replied.

I was grabbed by the officers. I tried to fight them off, I wanted to stay with my father. They finally pulled me up and away. I broke away from them to look at Zion.

"Your blood is valuable. It's all I want." The officers grabbed me again. They were very aggressive. One of them punched me in the ribs. I stumbled to one knee. "I'm going to kill you," I said looking directly at Zion. This riot lasted under an hour. The ground was filled with blood. It was the American way. They'd always have blood on their hands. As they dragged me away, I looked down to the second floor. Police officers infested the whole prison.

I was in the SHU again. It was inhumane but no one cared about me. I wasn't sane. "My condolences, Calvin. Don't lose hope," I told myself. "Could I lose something I never had?" The prison found itself in a twenty-three-hour lockdowns for almost four weeks.

Chapter Thirty: Liberty

One Month Later

I walked out of the station with 50 dollars cash and the clothes I came into prison with. It was crazy to me, I was arrested with about one grand in my pocket. I know the police pocketed my money. Nothing was permanent, it seemed. I was still seventeen. I was in prison for about two months, I wasn't supposed to be in an adult facility. I walked to the nearest subway station. I didn't know if my mother knew I was coming home today. But she knew I was getting out one of these days. I looked at where I was. Manhattan. It was busy. People were bumping into me as I walked. Everyone in New York thought their destination was more important than the next person's. On the train there was a lady who walked on right after me. She had arrows tattooed onto her arms, feathers surrounded each arrow and her hair was wrapped up. She appeared to be native. The real owners of the land of the free, if there really were any owners. She held an empty coffee cup that had a few dollars and change in it. She shook it as she walked from the back of the cart towards the front. Her clothes were old, I could smell her as she walked by. She was obviously homeless. "Could anyone please spare some change? I'm homeless and I have no food to eat… please, I'm hungry." Her voice was raspy and the few teeth she had were yellow.

Immediately, a man sitting down attacked her with words. "Yes! We all have money! But, no! We don't got no money for you! We can't spare no money for you! I'm homeless too! It's called get a fucking job! I can't afford rent, I got a kid! He stay at his mamma's house! I help pay her rent! I got a phone, it's still up! There's no excuse!" He was going on a rant. The homeless lady tried to ignore him and continued shaking her cup. "My kid got video games and a PlayStation! I been paying for his prep school! I pay for his uniform! There is no excuse, it's New York, shit sucks! You have to fight through it! Stop fucking begging! That shit is annoying! Everyone is struggling." Everyone was silent after this. The lady made her way to the other end of the cart and went through the doors into the next train cart. *Ain't a thing changed.* I smiled tryna hold back a laugh.

I rode the B-train all the way uptown to the 174-175 station in the Bronx. I thought it was crazy that you could never tell where anyone was coming from. Everyone on that train had a completely different starting point and destination. I just got out of the penitentiary. I felt at home again. I walked up the stairs of the apartment. I tried to open the door but it was locked. The doors were bolted shut. A red coloured sign was on the door. I looked at it.

Final Notice of Eviction...A Court Order has been issued requiring that all persons and their possessions be removed from this property. Persons remaining on the premise may and will be subjected to arrest and tried for trespassing. I took a step back and sat down on the stairs. I watched a few boys walk by. They stopped in front of me and stared. "You Calvin Ayew, right?"

I studied the group of boys. They weren't gangsters. Just kids, holding a basketball and backpacks. They were thirteen years of age at the most. "How do you know me?"

"It's all love, baby. I appreciate you," said the boy holding the basketball.

"Yeah, my momma marched for you," another boy added. There was four of them.

I stood up and walked down the steps. I shook all their hands. "Y'all be good. Respect your mommas." They nodded at me and walked away. I could hear the ball being dribbled in the distance. Cars rolled past me blasting music. There were lots of people on the streets. I loved it here, I was glad to be back.

I walked down the street to Paulo's. I went inside. I didn't speak a word, he looked at me and a huge smile came to his face as he walked around the counter and gave me a handshake. "Thank you, Calvin. You did us a huge favor."

"I missed your accent, G." I smiled.

He smiled back. "You hungry, my boy?"

"I'm hungry as hell, that prison food is shit!" I was exhausted.

I sat down in the only chair in the shop. Paulo stayed behind the counter. "You want the original?" He asked.

"Yeah, and let me get two Sprites." I missed that drink. I pulled out some money. "Here."

"No, no! It's on the house! As you Americans say!" He smiled.

"Thanks, G." The food came out and I ate quietly. Paulo was nothing less than a good guy. He always looked out for me. I respected him. We continued to talk and I spoke to him about prison, how it was and who I met. He didn't think I was built for prison. No one was.

"People recognize me, Paulo. I was walking the streets and I some boys came up to me saying everyone and their mommas were marching for me."

"Yes! You had an army of people. It was in the paper, in the news. They see you as a hero." He seemed excited.

"An army? You were there?" I was shocked.

"No!" He laughed. "I have a shop to run! Bills to pay."

"Wow…thanks, Paulo." I laughed too.

"Are you ready for the press conference? He asked.

"Press?" I replied.

"Tomorrow," he elaborated.

"What are you talking about?" I was genuinely confused.

He threw a newspaper at me. "Look, your lawyer set it up. The city wants to hear your story," he explained.

"Story? There ain't a lot to it." I shook my head. "I'm not a hero," I clarified.

"The city thinks so." He smiled. "I do too."

I looked at the paper shaking my head. I was the wrong person to idolize. "Do you got a phone I could borrow?"

I spoke with my mom and left the shop a few minutes later.

I met my mom at Cornelius's office. She gave me a big hug. I missed my mom. The first thing I planned on doing for her was finding her a new apartment. I could see the stress on her face. "Is everything okay?" Cornelius asked us.

"We don't have a place to stay but I'm just grateful to be out of prison." I smiled. Cornelius pulled a notebook from out of his drawer. He started writing while I continued to talk. "What's this press conference I'm hearing about? I'm not an athlete. I'm not the president. I'm not a superhero. What do they expect me to say?"

"Be quiet!" My mom had no shame. I hadn't spoken to her since she first visited me. I was in the SHU since the riot ended. I was still getting used to the human interactions.

I looked at my mom in shock. "Wow… that's how you're feeling, son?"

Cornelius slid a small piece of paper to me. "Find a place for your mother."

"Chill…" I looked at the paper. "Cornelius. This is five thousand dollars."

"What?" My mom stood up in shock.

"Are you sure about this?" I asked.

"Calvin, you helped me get back on my feet. I wouldn't be in this position if it wasn't for you. This is my attempt to pay you back."

"You got me out of prison, man!" I spoke with a grateful tone.

"Yes, but there is no price that can be put on life. That's what you did for me… You got me my life back," he said.

My mom ran behind his desk and gave him a hug! "Thank you! Thank you!" She began to cry.

"Tomorrow, Calvin! Meet me here. 9 a.m. sharp. Wear a tie…please," he said with little hope.

My mom finally stopped hugging him and I gave him a handshake. "I'll be here. Thank you, Cornelius. For everything, my guy. You're the most honest man I've ever met. God be with you."

"You deserve the best. I'm glad to have you back," he said.

I left the criminal justice office with my mother. "Ma, I gotta see Gio and Aaliyah. But I can meet you later. Where have you been staying?"

"With Uncle Kofi." She hugged me. "I'll go looking for apartments with him today if we can."

"Okay. I'll be there tonight," I explained. "And mom… I'm sorry about Dad. I did everything I could," I explained.

"It's okay. You go. We'll talk later." She didn't want that on her mind at the moment. I could tell.

I'll keep it to myself.

I got on a subway headed Uptown. I used to take so much for granted. I wanted to be someone who was proud of themselves. I didn't really care what strangers thought of me. I just wanted the people around me to be fine with the person I am.

I swung the doors open. I could hear the sandbag being punched very hard. It was the evening but the sun was still out. I didn't know what the day was, but I knew it was a good day. I could smell the sweat. There was a strong energy coming out of the gym. It was an intense vibe. Hard work is all Mr. Mike wanted. I stood, watching from the front doors. They were about 20 feet from me. He held the sandbag as Aaliyah punched it. I was looking at her back, while I could only see a piece of Mr. Mike's head behind the sandbag. I could hear Aaliyah grunting with every punch she landed. She was not hitting like her usual self. She seemed frustrated. She was not focused. "Come on, baby girl!" Yelled Mr. Mike. "Focus!"

She stopped to take a deep breath. "I can't! It hurts!" She screamed after her words. "I just can't! I thought I could!"

I started walking towards them. Aaliyah stood with her arms by her side. Mr. Mike came from around the sandbag and immediately looked at me. He was surprised. A smile followed his shocked reaction. "Wow."

"What?" Aaliyah said in confusion. She turned around and looked at me. I looked into her eyes. Still shining, they always forced me to lose my train of thought. Tears began to fall down her face. "Calvin," she whispered. I could see how worried she was about me. I knew how much she cared about me. I never wanted to hurt her, but I knew the damage was done. She was still so strong.

I stopped five feet in front of her. She was wearing her hair in two large cornrows as usual. I couldn't imagine her boxing any other way. Black tank top and pink shorts. She still wore the gloves that had the pink rose coming out of the concrete. I felt like I hadn't been here in years. It felt like I hadn't been free in years but I forgot all of that once I saw her. "Coach, I think she got better… But she could use some work on her technique," I said.

She laughed and cried at the same time. "Crazy," she said. Mr. Mike walked over to me first and shook my hand. "Welcome back, Calvin. You're a soldier."

"I'm ready to come back, sir! Put me back on that sign-up list!" I said with a smile.

"You never left the list brother." He let go of my hand.

"Is it possible to sign me up for a fight a few weeks from now?" I asked. I wanted to build a name for myself.

"I'll look for some fighters in the boroughs and see what we can do," he explained.

"Respect. Thank you, Mr. Mike," I replied.

"Glad to have you back, man! I'm going to give you two some space," he said. "I got business to take care of anyway." He patted me on the back and walked away.

Aaliyah didn't move. She was trying to take off her gloves. She didn't know how to react to me being in front of her. "Crazy! Crazy! Crazy!" She said shaking her head. I couldn't help but smile at her. I started to walk over to her with my arms wide open. When I hugged her, I could feel her body tremble as she cried. Her arms wrapped around me. "I'm here to stay. I promise."

"You don't know what you put me through," she said. Those words broke my heart. I knew I caused her pain. I couldn't change the past but I could fix the future. She backed away after the hug. But I was still holding onto her.

"I missed you. Even though I lost you, you were still with me." I never stopped looking into her eyes. "Things will be different now. I have my priorities straight." I leaned in to kiss her, she met me halfway. I felt like we didn't spend any time apart. I couldn't remember life before I met her. It was odd. I missed this. I missed her before I even met her. I missed something I never had. But I have it now, I wanted to do nothing but cherish her. "I have a press conference thing to go to tomorrow, I want you to come with me," I stated, it wasn't much of a question.

"What conference? When were you released?" She asked.

"This afternoon," I replied. "What day is it?"

"Wow, it's Thursday…May 24th."

"Damn. Thursday?"

"Yeah… why what's wrong?" She was confused, wiping away the rest of her tears.

"You woulda thought they'd release me on a Monday." I just felt like Monday would be the day to be released. I stopped to look at the clock. It was a quarter past seven. "How long you here for?" I asked.

"Uh, I'm good to go, whenever. I've been here since four." She explained.

"You're a beast. You're recovering so well…I'm proud of you, Harlem."

"I missed that name." She laughed. "I hate you! You scared the shit out of me. I saw you behind the glass and I didn't want to believe it. Your face was all bruised and I couldn't hold back the tears." She punched my chest! "What is that scar on your face? How'd it happen?" she demanded.

"You still got a hitting problem? And... I don't remember." I got it from Zion. He slashed me with his prison-made knife. I lied to Aaliyah. What happened in prison will stay in prison.

"Right...So why'd you ask me how long I've been here for?" She asked.

"I was gonna go see Gio. You wanna come?" I asked.

"I can't. I promised my mom I'd be home by eight."

"Okay, let's go," I said.

"Where?"

"To see my mother-in-law," I said.

She smiled. "You're crazy. She's gonna be leaving for work."

"Okay, she's gonna see me walking you home." I was never going to let Aaliyah walk home by herself again.

"Alright, let me change." She walked away.

We walked up the steps of her apartment together. I was nervous. I didn't know how Ms. Morales would react. The door opened before Aaliyah could put her key in. Right away, there was shock on Ms. Morales's face. "Calvin." Her tone said it all.

"Hey, Ms. Morales. How are you doing?"

She walked down a few steps to where I was. She looked me in the eyes. She cut straight to the chase. "I'm not at all proud of the way you handled the situation!"

I stared right back into her eyes. I didn't think I was allowed to look away. "Either am I," I said.

"I guess someone had to do it." She shook her head. "I'm glad you're okay, Calvin… and thank you for coming… and for walking Aaliyah home."

"Thank you, Ms. Morales. I'm sorry for the stress I caused. That was never my intention but I lost sight of what was right. I just felt the need to protect my people. He was the same man that killed my brother. I didn't want to lose anyone else," I explained. I looked over at Aaliyah, she looked worried. I looked back at Ms. Morales.

"I understand, Calvin, and I hope you're okay. We'll talk more, I have to get to work." She gave me a hug and continued down the stairs.

I looked at Aaliyah. She was watching her mom walk away. "Are you okay?"

"I'm worried," she said.

I could see the stress in her eyes. "What's wrong?"

"My mom sees you as a killer," she replied.

The look on her face had made me nervous. "Do you?" That's all that mattered to me.

She paused. "No."

"You hesitated," I said without hesitating.

"I don't think you're a killer…I know that's not who you are, but you didn't go to jail for nothing." She shook her head. "I'm just worried. My mom's opinion is important to me. But I really don't wanna lose you again."

"I'm here now. To stay. I don't wanna leave you."

"But you did."

"I didn't ask for that," I quickly responded.

"You knew what you were getting yourself into."

"Yeah, and I knew who I was doing it for, too." She had time to argue and so did I.

"Wow, Calvin. That's not fair. I never asked you to do anything for me." She was offended.

"I'm sorry. I had good intentions but bad actions."

"I feel like we find ourselves here all the time." She was exhausted.

"It doesn't have to be like this," I explained. She shrugged her shoulders, her attitude was coming out. I couldn't blame her, I was provoking her. "You gonna come with me tomorrow?" I asked.

"Sure," she replied.

I gave her a head nod. "See you tomorrow." I turned around and walked down the steps.

"Stay outta trouble!" She yelled at me.

I shook my head and continued walking. I had one more stop to make.

I knocked on the door and walked back down the steps. I looked up at the window. It slid up and a head popped out. "You're lying!" The window slammed shut. I started laughing. The front door swung open within seconds. Giovanni jumped the whole set of stairs and hugged me. "You're back! The kid is back!" He hugged me for about ten seconds. "What it do, brother?"

"It's been a hot minute, huh?" I laughed, we were both smiling. "I've been good. It feels good to be back, G."

"You look like you got beaten up pretty bad, I hope you got them back."

I quickly stopped smiling. I touched my face. I could feel the scar under my eye. *Zion.* "I will get them back," I said.

"How'd you get that?" He asked.

"Riot, my Pops was killed, G."

"Your Pops?" He needed an explanation.

"Yeah, I met him in prison. Wack. He was in for a crime he didn't commit. America…" I shook my head and continued my story. "A man stabbed him. I fought him but I was pulled off by the officers. I was ready to kill him. I would've."

"I'm sorry about that… He's with Jace now. Don't stress." He shook my hand one more time.

I wanted to believe that. I didn't know if I could. "I got a conference to go to tomorrow. For these news channels or something. You down to come with me?" I asked.

Gio nodded his head. "I'll be there." He smiled.

We sat down on his steps and continued talking until after the sunset. He caught me up on everything. I was happy to hear about him and Bea still going strong. Gio was passionate about her. Things didn't change around here. I think I did. I was different, I've been a victim of the system. I saw this coming but I was still so surprised. *Life,* I thought. *No, life in America,* I corrected myself. I didn't belong. None of us did.

Chapter Thirty-One: Spoken Words

The crowd silenced themselves. Cameras flashed in my face. I looked to my mom who was on my right. She nodded at me. She had told me to be careful. She wanted me to be the ideal child. It was too late for that. Cornelius told me to watch my words, no slang, speak with respect and try to clean up my accents. He thought I had a bit of a Ghanaian accent. He was trying to tell me to be whiter. I couldn't do that. I refused. I was respectful until people provoked me. African-Americans have been portrayed as those who have anger, attitude, and people who disregarded authority. Maybe because the authorized individuals were also our oppressors. There was a lot to it. I looked to my left. Aaliyah and Gio stood beside me. I looked back to see Cornelius right behind me. I looked forward again. At least five hundred people were here. A lot of people held up signs, a lot of them had pictures of broken handcuffs. I read one that said *Free Calvin.* They seemed to care about me. We were outside of city hall. We were on top of the highest step, while the reporters and everyone else was on the street level. The streets were blocked off, police cars were on each side of the crowd with their lights on. The sky was clear and the sun shone on my face. It felt like freedom. But my thoughts were prisoners – I wasn't allowed to free them. I looked at the microphones, there were about four, beside them were voice-recording devices. I smiled and shook my head. They didn't care what I had to say when I was locked up.

On the podium, there was a piece of paper. Cornelius wrote it for me. I was supposed to say this to the people. But they came to hear Calvin speak, not Cornelius. I raised my hand, flipping it. "Um… Questions?" I asked.

"Here!" One person yelled.

"Calvin!" said another reporter. There were too many voices asking for my attention.

Cornelius tapped my shoulder. I didn't look back. He whispered into my ear, "Read the paper, Calvin." I nodded my head.

I spoke into the mic. "Chill. I got something to say," I said.

"Oh God," muttered Cornelius.

In my head I read a few sentences off of the paper. It wasn't me. I looked back at the crowd. "I want to start off by saying… Everyone has made mistakes in their lives… I've made plenty. I'm thankful for that. Mistakes help people grow. I could have gone without some of my mistakes but it's too late to think about what could have happened. Just gotta analyze, adapt, and overcome the situation. That's what I'm trying to do. I had a few kids come up to me yesterday. They told me that their mommas marched for me…That they saw me as a hero. I'm not a hero. Far from it. If there are any heroes out there it's the people who marched. The protestors. The person who came up with the idea to protest. So, to that little boy's momma… thank you. You're my hero. To the person who started the protest, you're my hero. Ms. Laurent…is she here?" I looked around the crowd, there was movement around the back. The sun was in my eyes, I couldn't see much. The crowd shuffled as Ms. Laurent moved to the front of the crowd. "Come up here," I said.

She passed the journalists, photographers and security at the front of the crowd. She walked up the steps and stood beside me. "Hello, Calvin. Long time, no talk." she said with a smile.

I believed she would be the person to start this. I gave her a hug. "Thank you. Seriously… I appreciate you." We released from the hug and I looked into her brown eyes as she smiled at me.

"It was nothing, Calvin." She smiled.

I spoke into the mic again. "Thank you to this woman, Ms. Laurent, for doing this for me, my family, my friends, and anyone who's ever believed in a good cause. This woman right here is my teacher or... was. She believed in my potential when no one else did. I don't only appreciate her for protesting but for believing I can do something special with my life. She didn't see me as destruction." I nodded and smiled at her. "A lot of people have questions for me. They wanna know if I would correct my mistakes if I had the chance... I don't think we'd learn our lessons if we could just fix our mistakes." I looked in the distance. The jungle I was in brought out the survival instinct in me. "People want to know, if I could go back in time, would I kill Xavier again? Yes, I would." There was a long pause. The cameras continued to flash. There was a buzz of conversations in the crowd. I shook my head.

"Get back to the script." Cornelius whispered in my ear.

I looked at the paper, then back up at the people. I wasn't intrigued by Cornelius's words. "Eye for an eye. I think that's fair... I think Xavier should have lost several eyes. The amount of girls' innocence he stole and lives he took was wicked. Me taking matters into my own hands... I saw it as protecting my people. That could have been anyone's mother, sister, wife, or daughter that lost their lives. I was close to losing a person very close to me because of Xavier. I didn't want anyone to feel anything even remotely close to that type of pain." I looked at Aaliyah. She had a tear flowing down from her eye. "Eye for an eye. We lost a good man in prison. I'm going to miss him. The warden didn't even let me attend my father's funeral. He didn't deserve what happened to him. He was serving a sentence that wasn't his. So y'all can't blame me when I seek justice for myself. Where is the justice? The system isn't built for Negros. Y'all don't care about us. I know every brother in the hood just somehow fits the description. Ridiculous. I've changed. I'm different. They had me stay in an adult facility at the age of seventeen. They attempted to trial me as an adult and I was beaten by the police. Ridiculous. There is no justice. Y'all wouldn't care if I rotted in that cell. Look at my face. I gotta wake up every morning looking at this scar now. They tried to kill me in there. No one cared. And if I died, y'all would go about your business. Fuck the police. I'll say that with my last breath. There ain't no justice. That's why I did it myself." I introduced more slang as I spoke. "They want me to be that good boy. Well I'mma hood boy. Born and raised. The Bronx is where I lay. Y'all only come to these ends to watch a baseball game. My brother died and I didn't see a word of it in the news. Xavier killed my brother, it went unreported. He was shot in the head. Dead! Just like that. I did, not what the police couldn't but, what the police wouldn't. They refused to. Useless. My brother's case was closed in three weeks. They had the nerve to say they did 'all that they could'. That's a joke. How do you come back to the mother of a boy who was killed and say: 'your son's murderer is still out there. Free.' If you could see the pain my mother went through, what she still goes through… you'd be broken by now. If you could feel the pain she went through… you wouldn't be alive. My momma is strong. She is the woman who told me to stand up for what I believe in. To do what I can to protect my loved ones. Maybe I misinterpreted the point she was trying to get across, my momma never raised me to take a life. But I don't think I made a mistake. Mostly because if I had a badge like these police officers, or as I refer to them… race soldiers, I wouldn't have been sent to a correctional facility. I would have been off the hook. I know how they like to do black folks out here. I seen it coming… don't worry. Y'all made me smarter. Everyone wants to filter me, but fuck that, fuck the NYPD. They beat me up in that holding cell and they got away with it. Even though I speak about it now, none of the people involved will face consequences." I shook my head. "I apologize for my language, I meant it but the kids don't deserve that."

I looked around at the crowd. They were shocked. Flashes continued to attack my eyes. I looked at my mom who was confident with what I was saying. Our people were not treated fairly in this country, never have been. I looked at Gio. He was happy with what I said. I looked at Aaliyah, she was somewhat shocked. I was sorry for what I was about to say. She wanted me to be the old Calvin. He was dead, along with my brother and father. "I'm gonna make it clear. I'm not an idol. I'm not someone to look up to. Thank you to all the protesters and everyone who made my release possible. I appreciate that. I really do." I looked back to Gio. I raised my fist, a signal for unity and strength. Gio raised his up to. *My brother*, I thought. I began to finish my ghetto speech in the eyes of the Americans. "I don't think I'm a murderer… But I believe in protecting my own. So… to the man who killed my father and idol, Kwesi-Attah Ayew." I paused, taking a deep breath. "You're next."

I looked to my right at my mother. She nodded at me, I saw tears coming from her eyes. I walked over to her to hug her. "I'm sorry, mom…you've lifted me up my whole life. I promise to return the favour now. We're all we have." I held back my tears, crying was for the weak. That's what my father told me. I wanted to do what my father would want me to do. I held our legacy and carried it with me with every step. I walked off the podium and down the steps holding my mom while my posse followed. The cameras continued to flash and the sea of reporters began to ask questions that I wasn't going to answer. Ms. Laurent stayed with the crowd as the security at the conference attempted to hold people back as we all got into Cornelius's car.

"Calvin! You don't get it, this wasn't an act of heroism."

"Weren't you listening? He doesn't think he's a hero," said Gio.

Gio sat behind the driver seat, Aaliyah was in the middle and I was behind my mother who sat in the shotgun seat. "Cornelius… sometimes there are things you don't want to hear but it doesn't mean you don't need to hear it. See, if my mom told me that I fucked up, I'd accept that. She's not afraid to backhand me in front of a crowd. But my mom didn't. People needed to hear about this. Freedom of speech… right?"

"Calvin, you cannot be threatening people on national television." He was driving aggressively. "You can be fined or charged. You don't know the legal system."

I spoke calmly. "I know the legal system. Let them come for me. We got two angels looking over us. And I think I've faced worse charges, and if not... the Lord gives his toughest battles to his strongest soldiers." Cornelius looked back to me after I spoke these words. He didn't say nothing. He put his eyes back on the road. We made eye contact through his rear-view mirror. I nodded my head at him. "We're soldiers. All of us."

Chapter Thirty-Two: Amends

We found ourselves back at the gym. I was lightly sparring with Aaliyah. I felt healthy again. My arm had fully healed from the gunshot wound. Aaliyah was near one hundred percent and looked so promising. We were both exhausted, it was near the end of the night. The air conditioner in the gym was broken. It was warmer inside the gym than it was outside. I didn't have a shirt on, we were both sweating like crazy. I had sweat dripping from my chin as we started our cool down workout. As we practiced our technique, I noticed something bothering her. "You were real quiet after the press conference," I said looking at her. She stayed silent and shrugged her shoulders. "What's wrong?" I asked.

"Calvin, I don't think you'll ever know how appealing you are," she claimed.

"What do you mean?" I asked.

She stopped what she was doing. "Your words today... I wanted to be mad but I couldn't be. You're different." She smiled.

"A good different?"

"You've changed for sure. But it was growth. You're a good guy. I know you don't want to hear it but you're a hero. But I think your dad wouldn't want you to continue the cycle of revenge."

"I understand, I'll stay out of the drama. Thank you, Aaliyah." I looked at Gio who was punching the sandbag while Mr. Mike held it. "You're the people I do it for. You're all I care about."

"We need you here with us." She smiled.

"I love you," I said.

She looked at me and smirked before she started laughing. "Yeah, yeah, I love you too." I shook my head and laughed.

Gio walked over while Mr. Mike went to his office. "Y'all ready to get outta here?"

"I'm down."

"What are y'all tryna do?" Aaliyah asked.

"I'm hungry… Y'all down to get food?" I asked.

"Yeah, let's do that," said Gio. Aaliyah agreed. Things seemed to be getting as close to normal as they could, although they never would.

As we walked to the change rooms Mr. Mike called me into his office. "Is everything okay, sir?" I asked.

"You asked me for a fight, right?"

"Yeah!" I said eagerly.

"We got a fight in Brooklyn. Six weeks from now. You need to get your weight up a couple pounds and you'll be good."

"Thank you, Mr. Mike! I appreciate it."

"Calvin, I'll be training with you. I need you to be focused. This isn't to be taken lightly."

"I know, I'm serious. This is all I want." I nodded my head.

"Good, use that hunger because the winner gets five grand to their name. Probably even more with your name all over the media."

"For real? Just like that?" I was shocked. I was imagining the money already.

"Not just like that. You gotta work for it. You need that hunger. That anger. Everything you've been through, all your past experiences… use that in the fight. You need to be a beast. I don't even know half of what you been through… they don't even know a quarter of it. Show them what they'll never see coming."

"They'll see that I've been fighting my whole life! Everything I am, everything I will be… I promise to show. I promise – my strength, intelligence and my heart. Especially my heart. All of it will be unleashed." Mr. Mike grabbed my head and bumped my forehead against his. I walked out of Mr. Mike's office.

That's how I got here. I fought. Any challenge thrown in my direction, I shall overcome. I lost my mind trying to find it, I was focused on the destination and I got caught up in the journey. Somehow I still made it here, there had to be a reason why I was still here.

After changing, I collected all of my things, walking out of the change room with Giovanni. I saw Aaliyah waiting for us beside the exit. I couldn't see the future but I knew who I wanted in it. Things weren't great, but they could be worse. I gave Aaliyah a hug, I walked out of the building with my arm around her shoulder. Anything that would happen to my people, my family, I promised myself to make amends. Whether I lose them or not, they'll always be with me. I'll keep them to myself and I shall overcome.

Chapter Thirty-Three: Ready to Rumble

Six weeks later.

The bell dinged and we both hopped back and forth in our stances. The crowd cheered and lights flashed all around us. The crowd was packed because of my face being in the media so often. The fight was sold out. A Hispanic male with tattoos all over his chest stood in front of me. He had a huge cross in the middle of his chest. His boxing nickname was the Messiah. He was known as the man who could take any hit and rise up again. He was 22. I was 22 days away from 18. We weighed the same. He was an inch shorter than me. It was the ninth round and we had both been sweating buckets. He had a bruise under his left eye. I wasn't sure how I looked but I felt bruised too. I looked at the man, he resembled Xavier for a second. It was like he came back to haunt me.

I stared him in the eyes. "Let's go! You got nothing! You're soft!" He yelled at me.

I kept my hands up, red gloves, American flagged trunks and black shoes. I continued staring into his eyes. I could only see Xavier. I never spoke a word back to him. It wasn't normal for me to stay silent, especially in these circumstances. He lightly jabbed at me, trying to make me bite his bait. I let him continue to lightly tap my fists. He threw two light jabs with his right fist and I blocked them both with my arms. He quickly threw a left hook that made contact with the right side of my face. Immediately, my knees buckled and I fell backwards, I saw a stream of blood-filled saliva leave my mouth as I made contact with the canvas. I was down and I closed my eyes. I kept them closed for three seconds. A sound grenade went off in my ear. I imagined all the things I had been through. How many times had I been knocked down in life?

The referee was counting. "Five! Six!"

Why should I let this time be any different? I picked myself up.

"Eight!" said the referee as he walked up to me, looking directly into my eyes.

"I'm fine!" I said.

"Are you good?" He asked.

"I'm blessed! I'm good! Come on!" I yelled, slamming my fist together. I grunted. I could hear Giovanni and Aaliyah yelling from the crowd. Mr. Mike was coaching me from the corner, I wasn't paying attention as much as I should've been.

The referee moved from between us and the fight began again. The fighter came at me again. I dodged his shots. I had yet to throw a punch in this round. I was playing defense. I needed to sit down. "Come on!" He yelled. "Stop hiding!" He had a malicious look on his face. I wasn't scared, I was being cautious, he was obviously experienced. I continued to block his punches, but most of them made contact. The blows to my body were more damaging because they tired me out in the long run. The bell rang and my vision was blurry. I walked back to the corner and sat with Mr. Mike and the rest of the crew. They were guys who Mr. Mike put together whenever there was a fight. They cleaned up any blood on my body and patched up any cuts. They put icepacks all over my body. One of them put water into my mouth and ordered me to spit it out into a bucket.

"Calvin! Look at me! You have to start throwing punches! You can't win if you don't hit him!" He was furious but it was motivating.

"You told me when I got you this fight that you were determined. You were going to put your heart into this. You're not showing me that! Calvin, you've been in the trenches your whole life! Show them how it is on this side. You've been in the trenches, only you can get yourself out!" The look on his face was pure passion and charisma. "I need you to tease him a bit, tease him a bit and when he tries to dodge to your right avoiding your left jab, use that right hook that you're impatient with. You don't have to beat him at his own game. Cause it's our game! Show him who you are! One, one. One, one. Two! Left, left. Left, left. Right! Okay?" He never broke eye contact with me, and I never spoke during his speech. I needed to listen.

The referee called us back into the ring. I was ready for round ten.

"Trenches baby! Put him in the trenches!" Mr. Mike yelled at me.

"Let's go, boy!" Yelled Gio.

I slammed my fist together. "For the legacy!" I put my fist up as the fight started again. I did everything Mr. Mike instructed me to do. I jabbed at the fighter with my left fist several times but he was throwing back. I couldn't really continue the planned technique. I started to dodge his hits. We were thirty seconds into the tenth round. There were two more after this one. I took two of his punches to my face. I looked at him, he was about to throw a third one with his left fist. I weaved out of the way, making space for myself to throw a punch. It was a body shot. I hit him in the abdomen. He stumbled backwards after I made contact with my right fist. I knew he was left-handed so he could block better when I threw with my right hand. I reversed the combination I was given. I threw a right jab. It broke his block and it made contact square on his nose. I threw another one and he blocked it. He switched up his stance and how his left side was closer to me. This is what I wanted.

"Show him! Show him the trenches!" Yelled Mr. Mike.

I brought back my left arm, I felt a massive amount of energy enter my body and a massive amount of stress being unleashed. I had nothing left to lose, and I had everything to gain. I threw an uppercut with my left fist, breaking through his attempt to block, catching him on the chin. I watched his mouth guard fly out of his mouth and he fell onto the canvas. His body bounced on the floor, lifelessly. The ring shook as he made contact on the flooring.

I grunted, feeling so much strength in my body. Adrenaline and momentum. I was about to get on top of him, to end it, but the ref quickly intervened and pushed me back.

"Yeah! Count it, ref!" I yelled. The crowd rumbled I threw my fist up in the air. I could barely hear myself yell. "Let's go!" I ran over to my corner, hopping onto the ropes and slamming my fist together. "Boom! Boom! Boom!" I yelled at Giovanni.

"Yeah! Let's get this money!" He yelled!

Aaliyah was yelling at me! "Show them, crazy!" She was emotional. I could see it. I beat my chest with my right fist then pointed it at Aaliyah!

I hopped off the ropes and back into the ring. I looked over my opponent who was knocked out. The referee finished counting to ten. I held up both my fist in celebration. The bell rang to end the fight. I saw his crew come into the ring to help him as I stood over him. I knew I had a future, a future that would provide for my people. It was just unleashed.

Aaliyah, Gio, Mr. Mike and the rest of the crew ran into the ring. The crew cut the tape off my gloves and took them off of my hands. I hugged Gio and Aaliyah. Mr. Mike put a hat that read *Bronx* on my head. "You did it, son!"

"We're out of the trenches!" I said back to him. The crowd continued to cheer for me. I was the underdog. The cameras flashed at me.

My opponent came over to shake my hand and I gave him a hug. "You're strong, brother. You'll build a name for yourself. Be patient," he said to me.

"Good lookin' out, bro! I 'preciate it," I responded. He walked out of the ring while photographers came in.

I could hear the crowd chanting, "Ayew, Bomaye!" Over and over. I wasn't at that level yet, I thought.

I went down on my knees in the middle of the ring. I bent my elbows and exposed my palms to the sky. I showed my face to the heavens. I spoke out loud. "Pops,

Jace...This is the beginning of our legacy. Live through me." I stood up, still sweating bruised and beaten, I looked at my people. Tears flowed down my face as I looked out at the crowd. I had held everything in since the day my brother died. I couldn't do it anymore. I was destroyed, inside and out. I wasn't supposed to hold it all in but I did for my people. I wanted them to know that I was good, they could be too.

A reporter came to ask me questions about the fight. I didn't want to talk about it. I just wanted to be with my people. I held onto Aaliyah and Giovanni as the female reporter asked me a question. "Calvin Ayew! This is an amazing scene! You've won the crowd over after this fight... you were released from prison a little over a month ago and now you're fighting on this pretty large platform! Approximately five thousand people fill this stadium. How are you feeling right now?"

I shook my head. She put the microphone to my mouth. I looked at Mr. Mike and he nodded at me. I looked at Gio, then Aaliyah. I looked at the reporter once again to begin answering her question. "Uh, I focus on the people I do it for. That's how I get past every day, week, month and year...I love you, mom. Rest in peace, Jace. Rest in peace, dad. Everyone with me right now is my family. I love my family and they love me. They've accepted me for who I am, and it's about time I do the same." I began to wipe my tears away. Aaliyah wrapped her arms around me and held me tight.

Gio patted my back. "Let it out, big bro."

I took a deep breath, looking directly into the camera to finish one last statement. "I was who I was, and I am who I am... and I'm proud of both those people." I left the ring with my people. It was the beginning of a legacy.

Made in the USA
Columbia, SC
14 August 2018